PRAISE FOR THE

TEXAS ANTHEM series

"[Kerry Newcomb] knows where the West begins . . . In the tradition of Louis L'Amour and John Jakes, he blends fast-paced action, pulse-raising romance and historically accurate settings."   —*Dallas Morning News*

"Adrenaline-pumping!"   —*Booklist*

PRAISE FOR

THE RED RIPPER

"[A] rangy, fast-moving historical novel [with an] action-filled plot . . . broad-brush sagebrush scenes and the romance of the Texas Republic."   —*Publishers Weekly*

"Readers are rewarded with an entertaining tale of high adventure and low villains."   —*Booklist*

"A sizzler . . . Kerry Newcomb brings to life Big Foot Wallace, a larger-than-life frontiersman who strode boldly into legend. One helluva good book by a storyteller working at top form."   —Matt Braun, Golden Spur Award–winning author of *The Kincaids*

"Kerry Newcomb is one of those writers who lets you know from his very first lines that you're in for a ride. And he keeps his promise. *The Red Ripper* bounds along with unrelenting vigor. This is historical fiction crafted by a writer who never loses his sense of pace, drama, adventure, and fun. Kerry Newcomb knows what he is doing, and does it enviably well."
                —Cameron Judd, Golden Spur Award–nominated author of *Texas Freedom*

MORE . . .

"A compelling mix of passion, revenge, and a gallant people's quest for freedom. With the historical accuracy of a L'Amour novel, the characters are well drawn, leaving the reader to feel the openness and harsh challenges of the Texas frontier . . . Don't expect to get any sleep when you start this one."
                                          —John J. Gobbell, bestselling
                                            author of *The Last Lieutenant*

PRAISE FOR
MAD MORGAN

"Colorful, old-fashioned adventure . . . Awash with treachery and romance, this well-spun yarn fairly crackles with danger and suspense. Vigorous historical fiction."   —*Booklist*

"Swashbuckling adventure!"   —*Indianapolis Star*

ST. MARTIN'S PAPERBACKS TITLES
BY KERRY NEWCOMB

THE LEGEND OF MICKEY FREE
MAD MORGAN
THE RED RIPPER

THE TEXAS ANTHEM SERIES
TEXAS ANTHEM
TEXAS BORN
SHADOW WALKER
ROGUE RIVER
CREED'S LAW

MORNING STAR

Kerry Newcomb

St. Martin's Paperbacks

NOTE: If you purchased this book without a cover you should be aware that this book is stolen property. It was reported as "unsold and destroyed" to the publisher, and neither the author nor the publisher has received any payment for this "stripped book."

MORNING STAR

Copyright © 1983 by Kerry Newcomb.

All rights reserved. No part of this book may be used or reproduced in any manner whatsoever without written permission except in the case of brief quotations embodied in critical articles or reviews. For information address St. Martin's Press, 175 Fifth Avenue, New York, NY 10010.

ISBN: 0-312-98617-3

Printed in the United States of America

Bantam trade edition / July 1983
Bantam paperback edition / January 1986
Bantam reissue / June 1992
St. Martin's Paperbacks edition / February 2003

St. Martin's Paperbacks are published by St. Martin's Press, 175 Fifth Avenue, New York, NY 10010.

10 9 8 7 6 5 4 3 2 1

For Patty, Amy Rose, P.J. and Emily.

Acknowledgments

Although *Morning Star* is a work of fiction, much of the background information concerning the Cheyenne is based on fact. My own experiences living among the Morning Star People was a start, but I must also acknowledge that definitive study, *The Cheyenne Indians*, by George Bird Grinnell, an invaluable source of information. I also wish to thank Ken and Pam Kania, resource persons and dear friends with whom I lived, and who live still, among the bones of the rain.

Gallant men, brave deeds,
Women lovely and true,
A ballad and one to sing it,
A voice to tell the tale,
A heart to listen and remember . . .
Of such things are epics made.

—Otter Creek, a poem

"Thirty year have I been knocking
knocking about these mountains from
Missoura's head as far sothe as the
starving Gila. . . .
What has come of it? And whar's the
dollars as ought to be in my possibles?
Whar's the ind of this, I say. . . . This
child's getting old, and feels like
wanting a woman's face about his lodge
for the balance of his days. . . ."

— *George Frederick Ruxton*
Life In The Far West

The winds of time erase all paths.
—from the journal of Nahkohe

Prologue

May 12, 1865

A tongue of orange-red flame stabbed from the shadows and dissolved against an amber backdrop of sheet lightning. Thunder drowned out the revolver's savage bark. A lead ball cut the air an inch from Joel Ryan's ear. He became a statue on horseback in the rain.

"The next one won't miss," a familiar voice shouted from the yawning expanse of the doorway.

"Nate . . . Nate Ryan. It's me. It's your brother," Joel called out.

"I know," came the chilling reply, then a clicking sound, the ominous spinning of a cylinder to a loaded chamber, the hammer of the revolver thumbed back. "There is nothing here for you."

Puzzled by the reception, Joel waited in the rain, waited to a count of five. He had ridden far and ridden hard since the great surrender in Virginia, this farm ever fixed in his mind, spurring him through hungry days and nights and weary hours in the saddle. He had a right to be here, and no matter what the reason for Nathan's surprising animosity, Joel Ryan was not about to turn around and ride away. He tilted his face to the elements. Rain stung his cheeks and nose. *The Gods of War are loose*, he thought, a grim smile playing on his features as a rolling cannonade of thunder echoed down the land.

"I'm coming in," he shouted above the din. The gelding responded to Joel's muttered command, as anxious to be out of the rain as its rider. Joel braced himself, a tightness creeping up between his shoulder blades. He half expected the roar of a gun to split the night. The years of Civil War had seen more than one brother square off at gun or bayonet point against his own kin.

Joel kept the gelding to the center of the barn as best he could.

"Shoot or strike a match," he said; "I've no wish to dent my skull on a beam."

At last a match flared just ahead, and Nathan's features shimmered with surreal imprecision, like the face of a ghost peeking over the stall near the tack room. Joel shuddered. Match touched lantern wick, and the ghost became a flesh-and-blood being, the older brother Joel had not seen for more than two years. Joel climbed down from the saddle, and ducking beneath the harness that dangled from an overhead beam, he led his bone-tired mount to a bait of oats, unsaddled, and rubbed the animal down with a ratty blanket he found in the stall. Behind him, Nathan grudgingly holstered his revolver and waited for his younger brother to finish.

"Glad Pa taught you to handle that hogleg or you might have taken off my head." Joel shucked his sodden campaign hat and dropped it on a hook to dry.

"I knew what I was doing." Nathan's tone was defensive and not a trifle uncertain. He was the handsomer of the two. His slim build, dark lean features, and gentle brown eyes were the legacy of his mother's forebears. When speaking of the Ryan brothers, folks always referred to Nate as the sensitive one. His delicate fingers, more suited to the poet's pen, lingered near the brutish wooden grip of the revolver.

"I saw you coming up the road. I knew . . . it had to be . . . I knew it was you." Nate studied the rain-drenched intruder, his scrutiny more curious than kind.

Slabs of muscle rippled over Joel's broad shoulders as he finished caring for the gelding. The rebel's six-foot-six frame cast a giant shadow. His features were bold and hinted of humor and wry observation. His eyes were blue as the depths of a frozen pond and as impossible to fathom, the eyes of a man accustomed to hiding his inner feelings. His nose had been broken, set, and allowed to mend between battles and now rested slightly off center from the rest of his features. He was only twenty-six, but as Joel stepped toward the center of the barn, light washed across his thick mane of hair now heavily streaked with silver highlights that gleamed in the feeble glare. Older by a year, Nathan gasped at the transfor-

mation wrought by the war. Joel self-consciously retrieved
his hat, covered his head, and braced himself against the tides
of unwanted memories: the stench of red mud after battle,
garish images of men rendered by grapeshot into shapeless
masses of meat, the tired, hungry ride to the rumor of another
skirmish, and another, and another, another. Nathan lowered
his gaze to the worn gray tunic of a Confederate lieutenant,
Joel Ryan's uniform.

"Why did you come back?" Nathan said, his tone more
cutting than the finest blade, honed on the whetstone of anger
and betrayal.

"This is my home," Joel said. "You and Mother . . ."

"I buried Mother five months ago," Nathan snapped.

Joel closed his eyes. He appeared to shrink in stature, his
features bunched in a spasm of grief that lasted but a few
intense seconds before his control resumed.

"How?" he managed to say.

"You haven't noticed the house, dear brother."

Joel walked to the doorway and looked out through the
curtain of rain toward the house. In the lurid glare of a jagged
bolt of lightning he saw that the second story was a burned
and gutted ruin.

"Lucky it was a night like tonight, or we would have lost
the whole place. I'm restoring the upstairs piece by piece."

"What happened?" Joel asked, his throat tight.

"Rebel raiders," Nathan said. His voice was ripe with disgust. "They hit Seven Forks and rode out this way. Ran off
the beef, trampled the garden, fired the house when they
couldn't find the wall safe. I was fighting the flames and
heard Mother cry out. A slug glancing off the window sill
. . . she died in my arms. I buried her next to Father's marker.
They killed her. Soldiers—" he spat on the straw-littered
floor. "Murderers, I call them. Men in gray. Men like you."

Joel swung around. Nathan's eyes burned with grief and
hatred. Joel started to speak but noticed movement at the
house. The front door opened, and a night-shrouded figure
moved across the yard. Joel shoved his brother back and
darted to one side of the doorway as the figure neared the
barn.

"Wait," Nathan stammered, too late. "It's . . ." As the figure stepped into the light, Joel leaped out, revolver drawn, and caught the intruder by the arm and spun her around.

Her? Rain-soaked, brown tresses plastered to her shoulders, full breasts outlined beneath a drenched bodice, lips that lingered in a permanent pout. The startled woman gasped. And though a chill wind blew across the rain-swept countryside, the flesh of her arms was hot to the touch, as hot as her kisses had first tasted in the burning days of youth.

"Veronica—" Joel said, the sight of her loosing tightly checked remembrances of tender exploration and explosive desire.

She paled and only whispered his name in reply. Her glance flickered to Nathan and back to the man who did not let her go, the man who had promised to marry her and instead had ridden away to war.

"My God, Joel, is it you? . . ."

"It's him," Nathan said, standing and hurrying to part them. "I see you haven't forgotten Veronica," he said to Joel. "You might as well know she is engaged to be married."

Joel made no comment.

"To me," Nathan finished. He reached between the two of them and drew the woman from his brother's grasp. Veronica searched Joel's expression but could discern no reaction, though his eyes never left hers.

"There is no one else about," Nathan said. "I thought Abby might calve tonight, and Veronica came by to help."

"And what does a banker's daughter know about birthing calves?" Joel said, more than passing familiar with the ploys he and Veronica had used to arrange discreet rendezvous.

"You'd be surprised." Veronica glanced up at him, as if daring him to challenge the real reason she was out here all alone with Nathan. She looked at Nathan. "I heard a shot; at least I thought it was. I didn't know but that you might have had an accident. I thought I ought to see."

"His gun just sort of went off," Joel said.

"The citizens of Seven Forks learn there's a rebel close by, and you might find quite a lot of guns just 'sort of' going off. If I were you, I'd light out now," Nathan replied.

"I'll do as I please."

"Not on my farm you won't."

"Nathan, really," Veronica said. "Your own brother. Send him off without a suit of dry clothes or a moment's rest?"

"This does not concern you."

"Ease up, Nathan." Joel was dangerously close to losing control. A cow bawled plaintively from the rear of the barn, breaking the uncomfortable silence. Nathan looked over his shoulder uncertain whether to remain or accompany Joel to the house.

"I'll fry some ham. The coffee's hot," Veronica offered.

"You'll stay here with me," Nathan ordered.

"Not when you act like this. Honest-to-goodness, Nathan, you have the disposition of a snapping turtle, sometimes. I think I will do as I please, thank you." Veronica wrapped herself in her shawl and hurried out into the elements, picking her way across the muddy yard.

"Veronica hasn't changed," Joel mused aloud.

"But she has," Nathan corrected. "She is mine now. Remember that."

The cow bawled again, more urgently than before.

"Just be gone in the morning. You and that uniform are not welcome here anymore."

"The war's over, Nathan."

"Not in Seven Forks it isn't. And not here on this farm."

Argument seemed useless. Joel settled his hat down tight, hunkered down inside his slicker, and raced the pounding rain, slipping and sliding into unseen puddles, across the yard to the house; a jagged bolt of electricity skewered a nearby tree and added impetus to his leap to the porch. Underneath the protecting porch roof, he draped the slicker over the back of a chair and hat in hand stepped inside, a stranger suddenly in the home of his childhood.

Veronica Warren stood just inside the door, in the hall that led to the kitchen and off into the study and parlor and dining room. She stood with her hands on her hips, smelling of rain and rosewater, her face beaded with moisture, the silken strands of her hair brushed back, breasts pressing against her rain-spattered blouse. As he approached, she slapped him, her hand lashing out to catch Joel full in the face, a resounding slap that twisted his head and left his ears ringing.

"You bastard," she hissed.

Joel braced himself against the door.

"Shot at and slapped, I'm beginning to doubt the hospitality in these parts."

Veronica's hand swept back, lashed out. He caught her arm and shoved her into the hall, where she knocked over a three-legged table and went sprawling in a flurry of skirts and ivory-colored silk pantalettes. He stepped around her, glanced at the stairs that led to the ruined second story, and entered the room that had once been the parlor, converted now to serve as a bedroom. There was a fire in the hearth and a portrait of his mother above the mantel; for a moment he thought he might break at the sight of her, and he wondered what the hell had happened to him that he could not cry. He hurried from the room and crossed the dining room, skirting the familiar heavy mahogany table, and stepped through the pantry into the kitchen. Veronica had not lied about the coffee. He filled a mug and burned his throat by gulping down the steaming brew; he helped himself to a wedge of cheese and a thick slice of bread. A second cup of coffee took the edge off his hunger. A door from the kitchen led to the servants' quarters, empty now because there was no one to serve. He leaned against the doorjamb. At least the room still had a bed. He could barely remember the last time he had slept in a real bed. . . .

"My father hired Elma until Nathan and I need her back. She comes out often enough,but Nathan is determined to put the place back together on his own," Veronica said behind him. "Some of your things are stored in the chiffonier."

He nodded and continued into the bedroom. She watched him from the kitchen.

"You really are a bastard, you know. Coming back. Thinking nothing has changed. Everything has changed. You shouldn't have expected me to wait. It was your doing. You left me. What was I supposed to do? Nathan was here. Say something, damn you."

"I am happy for both of you. I mean that." He stopped to test the bed. A real bed. How long since he had experienced such a luxury? Too long.

"Is that all? You're *happy*? Oh, I hate you!"

Joel glanced up at her. "You aren't the only one, it seems." He opened the top drawer of a nightstand near the bed. Inside was a recent daguerreotype of Nathan, elegantly attired, looking the man of the world. Joel smiled. Maybe, in time, Nathan's hurt would heal. He could only hope. And pray. Perfume distracted his thoughts. Veronica was close behind him, her body heat provoking a desire he fought to suppress.

"When are you and Nate planning to make this arrangement formal?"

"Within the month," Veronica said, moving past him to sit on the bed. Her mood softened. "I'm sorry about hitting you."

"That's all right. Sorry I shoved you. I deserved the slap."

"It's just . . . seeing you. I mean you did run off to fight. And I was terribly hurt. I felt used. I suppose we used each other, didn't we?" Veronica sighed. She fussed a moment over a wayward curl, then abandoned her efforts. "The funny thing is, I am really in love with him. That's the other reason I wish you hadn't come back. I love Nathan, and I do not want to lose him."

"How could . . ." Joel looked down at her. Her face tilted up to him, the lips, as ever, inviting. He pulled her to him, his question forgotten as he lifted her to his kiss. She yielded, her arms encircling his neck. An ache, building, growing within and striving to be unleashed. Joel gasped and forced himself away. Veronica's chest rose in rapid breaths. Man and woman both knew where the next kiss would lead.

"I didn't mean for that to happen."

"It's all right," Veronica replied, understanding his hunger. "That was for yesterday."

"And tomorrow?"

"Belongs to Nathan." She touched his cheek, let her fingers trace the hard lines of his face, then abruptly turned and walked from the room, pausing in the ambient kitchen light. She glanced around at him, aware of his desire. He nodded in agreement.

"I am afraid," she said, hugging herself for comfort, moving closer to the Franklin stove.

"No need to be. I'll mind my manners."

"I am afraid of what he may do now."

"Nathan? You worry too much. Sure, he's hurt. But he'll deal with it."

"Not as long as you're here. He hates you and blames you for what happened to your mother. Or maybe he blames himself. It's one and the same. I just don't know anymore. He's driven, to make things as they were. To avenge what has happened. But the raiders are gone. What's done is done. And there is no one to strike out at. At least there wasn't until now."

"I can take care of myself."

"I know that, for God's sake! Nathan is no match for you. But he'll try. And you will have to defend yourself. He is good and dear and sensitive, but as long as you're here, the rage will turn him into something different, something ugly and hurt. He lacked the courage to kill you tonight. Tomorrow morning or the next may be different."

"What do you want me to do?" Joel asked, grudgingly believing her.

"Leave," she said. "Leave before you have to kill him."

"Do you know what you're asking?"

"Yes." Thunder rumbled outside the walls. Veronica shuddered and left the room.

Alone in the bedroom, Joel slumped onto the bed. He lay unmoving, a man weary of travel, contemplating more. No, this was his home as much as Nathan's. Eyelids heavy, weighted with sleep, closed at last. And Joel slept, the taste of Veronica's kiss lingering on his lips . . . the kiss for yesterday.

A field quiet in the mist. *This isn't real.* Dreams loosed in sleep. *It can't be real.* See a mist clearing, like curtains pulled aside. Now a field, and in the distance, a house. Nathan is there, asleep, lying on the ground. Someone standing over him. Joel Ryan. *It isn't real.* Blood streamers, like crimson ribbons unraveled on the ground, pinned to Nathan's chest. Lean forward and see his face, features frozen in pain. His chest rises and with each breath pink bubbles form in his wounds. Joel watches, lifts his smoking Colt revolver. He points the gun at Nathan. Thunder cracks.

Joel woke. Sweat beaded his forehead, the pillow damp to the touch beneath him, he gulped air and managed to calm himself enough to think.

Kill his brother, kill Nathan? No. For heaven's sake, just a dream. A nightmare. Or more? Premonition, warning? He swung his legs over the edge of the mattress and stood.

Would the rain never end? He walked to the window and peered through shifting, spattering droplets at the tempest-stricken night, then he padded out into the hall steering clear of the parlor/bedroom. He reached the study and slipped inside, narrowly avoiding a collision with a hat rack. The room was crammed with furniture salvaged from upstairs. He threaded his way to the walnut desk now buried beneath lamps and an overturned ottoman and boxed linens. The matching leather-backed chair was wedged between an armoire and the bay window. Water was dripping in some dark corner. No point in trying to follow the ping-plop-ping to its source. He sat in the chair, watching the storm. The turbulence soothed him. In a way it mirrored his own confusion. His anger and frustration were detached and freed on the wings of night. He leaned his arm upon the desk, and by chance his hand came to rest on a delicate chain of gold and a cameo locket that had belonged to his mother.

It had been a gift from Joel's father. When word reached them that Cortland Ryan had been killed by Indians out on the frontier, the locket had taken on a special significance, as if it were a link somehow to the dead man. Joel dropped the cameo into his shirt pocket, little enough to take with him when he left.

He stiffened in the chair. The word had almost seemed spoken in his mind. He fished out the locket, stared at it, and at last gripped it tight in his fist. They were here, both of them, mother and father reaching out to guide, to calm the turmoil of his indecision. So be it, he said to himself. It was an unexpected answer he had found, but an answer nonetheless.

This time when he fell asleep he did not dream.

> *Evangeline Ryan*
> BORN *March 18, 1821*
> DIED *December 8, 1864*
> *Dust to dust, ashes to ashes*

A sheen of raindrops glistened in relentless cascade over the graying letters of the wooden headstone. Joel wished he hadn't walked up the slope from the house. There was nothing of his mother here. Only a name. His mother was locked in his heart—all her laughter, understanding, and her comforting strength.

The morning had brought a false promise of clearing. The sun had shown itself for no more than half an hour before succumbing to the thunderheads and gunmetal gray clouds. A steady downpour had begun as Joel was halfway up the slope to the family plot. Now it battered the dried remains of flowers and green shoots of grass rising out of the waiting earth.

"Mother," Joel whispered. "I am so sorry."

Maybe somewhere in heaven she noticed him and, deep in her celestial soul, blamed him as Nathan did. Ah, but he knew her better than that.

A wind tugged at him. Joel smiled. Perhaps that was his lot in life, to follow the wind. He walked away from the grave.

In the dark hours of morning when his mind had sorted itself out into a decision, he had wondered if somehow it was his mother's doing. Thinking so made the day less dreary. Joel left his slicker on the front porch, draped over the back of the swing. He hesitated at the door. Veronica was no doubt still asleep, the hour much too early for a banker's daughter. Joel pictured her in his mind, one arm stretched upon the quilt, her hair flowing outward soft and fragrant on the pillow, the enticing fall and rise of her pink breasts beneath the cotton sleeping gown. Desire hadn't left him. And were he to stay around her for much longer, he doubted his ability to control it. "Nathan's been hurt enough," Joel said to himself as he donned his slicker again. He hefted a sack of food plundered from the kitchen. In his shirt pocket he had placed a pouch containing the locket that had belonged to Evangeline and the daguerreotype of Nathan. His treasures protected from the elements beneath his poncho, Joel trotted across the yard.

Nathan was in the barn. He lay on his back in the hay, his legs splayed wide, a snore rasping in his throat. Joel wrinkled his nose and smelled the liquor before he saw the empty bottle. Seven Forks Prime Sipping Lightning.

"Nathan."

Nathan continued to snore. Joel nudged his boot heel. Nathan grumbled. And snored. Joel glanced toward the house where the gutted second story was slowly taking shape, then tossed the bottle onto a bed of straw. A cannon wouldn't wake Nathan now.

"You'll set things to right," Joel muttered to the sleeping man. All the long ride from Virginia, images and dreams had kept Joel going. Kentucky. Seven Forks. The farm. The foolish hope of recapturing the past.

Joel left his brother's side and saddled the gelding once again, muttering his apology to the animal for the inconvenience. A newborn calf bawled for its mother and stuck its knobby head through the slats in the stall to stare in alarm at Joel, who led the gelding up the aisle past other horses and a carriage. Joel paused in the doorway of the barn to look once again upon his brother. A man had to fight his own wars and make his own peace. Joel tucked the packet of mementos into his saddlebag. The notion struck that he had nothing to leave Nathan. Despite his older brother's antagonism, Joel felt a need to leave something behind, something Nathan would know came from Joel. He studied his precious few belongings, then he reached over his saddle and caught his saber by the hilt and dragged it from its saddle scabbard. He shoved the saber, point first, into the packed earth floor. The basket hilt swayed to and fro as Joel stepped around the trembling blade to look down at his brother.

"Maybe you can beat it into a ploughshare," he muttered. And though he knew Nathan was oblivious, Joel felt better for the saying.

Bluffs of the river, a rider in the rain, a farm in a green valley surrounded by freshly furrowed fields. Joel could al-

most hear his mother's voice echoing over the meadowland,
almost see two brothers, running side by side in a happier
time, almost . . . home.

"Just a place to spend the night," he said, and turning his
horse, Joel Ryan rode west, through the spring rain. Rode
west and did not look back.

July, 1865

1

Golden was the land beneath the sun's burning pool; the wind blew free, and eagles ruled the skies. In mid-July, during the Moon When Horses Fatten, Joel Ryan skylined himself on a spiny ridgetop in the Pryor Mountains of Montana. If the war had aged him, the weeks of travel had hidden the ravages beneath a coating of trail dust. Clouds, rambunctious in a western wind, billowed over the farthermost rim of the Pryors, patching the land with drifting shadows. A breeze gushed upward out of the mountain valley, washing the rim in a cooling surge of energy. At 8,000 feet even summer air has a bite, and Joel sucked in his breath and thrust his hands in his armpits for warmth. The air was clear, and his range of vision extended all the way southward to the Wind River Range and north to the Bearpaws. Dead ahead beyond the Pryors, the snowy summits of the Absarokas filled the horizon with their lonely vastness. Closer to hand, the valley floor was a forested tapestry of white pine and Douglas fir and mountain ash stitched by the twinkling waters of a creek glimpsed through wind-stirred branches.

Joel studied the land below. What he could see of it, before the valley doglegged off to the north and disappeared behind another ridge, appeared devoid of life. At least human kind. Not devoid of game he hoped, and his stomach growled in assent. The gelding pawed the earth, causing a plume of red dust to be whipped away by the wind. Joel took one last look around him, the land lying wide and handsome in every direction, beckoning, challenging him to seek and to explore. As a youth he had resented his father's long absences from their Kentucky farm. Now he began to understand Cortland Ryan's need to cross the next hill, to trace the river to its source, to be free.

How could a man be a stranger at home, and at home in a strange land? Joel had no answer. Only a response. To nudge his boot heels against the flanks of his mount and guide the roan gelding onto the trail leading down from the ridge. Worn into the stone by elk and deer, the path offered slow, tedious going. Joel's attention was riveted to the descent, so much so that he failed to notice a diaphanous tendril of smoke rising from an unseen campfire, a wilderness warning for the watchful—to beware.

Reaching the floor of the valley, Joel rode toward the creek. Within sight of water, a covey of quail broke from cover, spooking the gelding. Joel kept a tight grip on the reins but almost lost control as he fought the animal. The horse flayed at the creek and lost its footing in the rock-strewn bed. Joel gave a curse and brought the animal back onto the bank. He dismounted and checked the gelding's fetlocks. A lame horse would never bring him to the gold fields up at Silver Bow, and he did not relish hiking the next two hundred miles. The gelding's legs were scuffed from the stones, but the animal seemed no worse for the wear.

For a quarter of an hour he followed the twisting bank through emerald shadows. Now and then he paused to let the gelding crop at the sweet grass. And he looked on in envy, knowing that unless he managed to surprise a deer or was lucky with a makeshift trap, there would be beans and poor conversation for supper. It had been a week since Joel had burned his tongue on a cup of good strong coffee, the last of his own supply. The recollection was so vivid he could almost smell the fresh pot bubbling over an open fire.

Almost? He sniffed the summer air and discovered the scent of roasting meat and the unmistakable aroma of coffee. Joel stopped and peered through levels of light and shade, of gloom and slanted sunlight, and at last he caught sight of tethered horses against an overhanging bluff, a lean-to shelter, and the distant figure of a man squatting by a fire. Joel was in a mood to be sociable, and hoping the stranger was of a similar bent, he climbed into the saddle and trotted the gelding at a brisk pace straight for the camp. He splashed across the creek making enough noise to announce his ap-

proach. As he drew closer he heard the singing. The man
was singing in French, his voice deep and melodic. As Joel
approached, he made out other peculiarities of the camp.
There was only one man about, although the horses indicated
others. But what a man this was. The singer had stretched
out against a deadfall, using a spiny gray tree trunk for a
backrest. He wore a beaver cap on his head with a feather
protruding from the crown. He looked to be well under six
feet in height, but he had the widest shoulders, the most
massive chest Joel had ever seen on a man. His beard was
carrot red, his face a gnarled map of flesh, the face of a man
who had spent a lifetime brawling. He was dressed in buckskin breeches and wore a shirt cut and sewn from a Hudson's
Bay blanket with the black, red, and yellow stripes ringing
his incredible girth. At his throat hung a crucifix of pounded
bronze. In contrast to this emblem of Christianity, a Hawken
.54 caliber rifle lay propped in the branch stubs. The hilt of
a revolver jutted from the broad leather belt circling the
man's waist. He continued singing as Joel rode up to the
campfire and dismounted. Joel noticed a rope, coiled at
the man's side and leading off into the lean-to. The man
appeared to take no heed of Joel's puzzled expression.

"Bonjour, my friend. I am Henri Larocque. I am Holy
Hell with the ladies and just plain Hell to my enemies. Sit
here on the other side of this log, monsieur, and we will
entertain ourselves while supper cooks." The carcasses of
four rabbits and a squirrel were spattering the cookfire with
their grease. Larocque positioned himself so that the log was
to his right. He rested his elbow on the weathered wood, arm
crooked upward. Joel realized the man was inviting him to
arm wrestle. The Kentuckian shrugged—amusing Larocque
was a small enough price to pay for a meal.

"Where's the rest? You can't ride all of those horses."

"Ahh. A perceptive man. My companions are checking
the other snares."

Joel sat opposite the Frenchman, close enough to smell
grease on Larocque's blanket shirt. He gripped the Frenchman's paw and looked his opponent square in the eyes.

"My name's Joel Ryan."

"A pleasure to meet you, monsieur. And to beat you."

Larocque exerted his strength. Joel's arm muscles bulged. He gritted his teeth. Larocque's jaws clamped shut. With excruciating slowness Joel's arm gave ground until at last it snapped backward over the log. The Frenchman retained just enough pressure to keep Joel prisoner.

"Larch! Mayo!" the Frenchman called. With a sinking feeling Joel realized the man had purposefully trapped him, imprisoning his gunhand.

Two men emerged from the surrounding forest. Both were lean dark men of average height and build. As they approached, Joel noticed one of them wore a blue uniform and cap and his companion was in a faded plaid shirt and overalls. Plaid Shirt appeared to be no more than a boy of sixteen, though his homely features, centered around a beakish nose, radiated an aura of adult danger through vague, wild eyes.

"Hey?" Joel winced, trying to reach across his body for the holstered revolver. Larocque merely increased pressure on the right hand. Joel gasped and quit his struggle. The youth grinned and, leaning over, removed Joel's revolver.

"Check his saddlebag, Mayo," Larocque said to the other man. Blue Cap nodded and crossed to the gelding. He searched through the meager belongings in the saddlebag and, at last satisfied, turned his attention to Joel's Spencer carbine. Mayo slipped it from the saddle scabbard and checked the action.

"He's nobody," Mayo said and walked back to the fire. He squatted, tilted his blue cap back off his forehead and poured himself a cup of coffee. "Just a drifter. Nobody."

"Now I feel better," Larocque said, releasing his hold. Joel rolled free, right arm dangling at his side.

"What the hell is this anyway?"

"An exercise in caution. You will forgive my rudeness, I trust. Mayo . . . give our friend some coffee. And return the rifle, we are not thieves."

"Let him get his own coffee."

"Mayo is a deserter, you see, and unaccustomed to obeying orders," Larocque said. His arm slashed out, and a knife buried itself in the dirt just below the squatting man's crotch. "This is a different army, is it not, Private Mayo?"

The man called Mayo stared at the Frenchman for a mo-

ment and then handed the carbine, barrel first, to Joel, who
snatched it from the man's grasp. Mayo grumbled beneath
his breath but passed a cup of coffee to Joel as well. Joel
grabbed young Larch by the arm as the youth sidled past
toward the campfire.

"My revolver," Joel said.

Larch complied with syrup-slow smoothness, extending
the Colt butt first, almost daring Joel to try and snatch at it.
Joel let the youth have his fun, took the revolver, and returned it to his holster.

"We meant you no harm," Larocque continued. "I have
enemies and unfortunately must exercise discretion when it
comes to strangers."

"Not a very pleasant way to live," Joel said. He appraised
Mayo and the youth in a single glance. He'd seen their kind
during the war. Larch had the swaggering air of a trouble-
maker, a boy trying to prove himself the equal of the men
around him. Mayo had the look of a coward. But cowards
are frequently the most dangerous of men. Larocque was the
enigma with his veneer of civility barely covering a hard,
ferocious-looking shell. Joel decided the coffee wasn't worth
the company.

"Men I can beat are always welcome at the cookfire of
Henri Larocque," the Frenchman said. He waved toward the
fire.

"No thanks. I appreciate the coffee and the offer, but
there's still some daylight left, and I'm trying to make the
best time I can."

"The gold fields, eh, monsieur?"

"I hear there's a strike up at Silver Bow."

"Yes, it is so. But I have no liking for such brutal labor,"
Larocque said.

"It's the only way I know to strike it rich."

"There's other ways." Young Larch grinned around a
mouthful of cooked rabbit meat. Mayo reached over and
thumped him on the shoulder.

"Shut your mouth, dumbass."

Joel stared at them a moment, then back to Larocque who
shrugged.

"What my associates mean is that we are carrying our own

motherlode around with us, in a manner of speaking."

"You've already made your strike?" Joel asked, anxious for any news that might give him an edge over the other prospectors up at Silver Bow.

"In a manner of speaking," Larocque corrected once more. He looked over at the lean-to. *"Hemené!"* The other two men at the campfire began to chuckle, an audience murmuring in anticipation. *"Hemené!"* Larocque frowned and grabbed the rope at his side. He pulled the line taut and began reeling it in. There came a brief commotion from within the lean-to, and then Joel glimpsed a coppery leg followed by the struggling, kicking torso of an Indian girl. The rope was securely fastened around her ankle. Larch and Mayo laughed aloud.

"Hooked ye a big 'un," Mayo shouted.

Larocque methodically drew her closer and closer. Suddenly she ceased resistance and charged the Frenchman who caught her by the arm, pulled her down, and gripped her about the throat. She tried to break free. Her dirt-streaked features and glaring eyes gave her the look of a wild animal. A captive animal. Eventually, as her lungs received less and less air, she grew quiet. And when he released her, the Indian girl crumbled at his side, gasping for breath. She looked up at Joel. The hatred pouring from her forced him back.

"Hemené. Mourning Dove to you and me. Dove, indeed. Wildcat would be more appropriate."

"That's your gold?" Joel asked.

"But of course. Dove here is Cheyenne. The sister of Sacred Killer, a mighty warrior and taker of many scalps. Many white man scalps. We stole Hemené from her camp. She was bringing in a load of firewood with a few other girls. We have kept to a pretty rough pace for a week with Cheyenne breathing down our necks. But we lost them a couple of days ago. Blue Jacket, the Crow war chief, hates all Cheyenne and especially Sacred Killer. The Crow will pay plenty to have the sister of Sacred Killer for a slave. Blue Jacket's waiting for us down on the Tongue."

"Then your journey's almost over," Joel said. Larocque noticed the distaste in the man's voice.

"Oui. And you are in the middle of yours. Perhaps it is

best if you continue. But watch for the Cheyenne. If you
want to keep your hair."

Joel nodded. He looked at the slender, buckskin-clad
shape huddled beside the Frenchman. Her features were hidden behind a curtain of her long tangled black hair. A dirty-
faced Cheyenne girl was no concern of his, Joel said to himself. He left the coffee cup on a stick by the fire and walked
to his horse. He returned the carbine to its scabbard and
mounted.

"You can follow the creek out of the valley," Mayo said,
more by way of invitation than information. The tops of the
rust-red cliffs were already in shadow, and twilight was coming early to the western rim. Joel calculated he had another
hour of light. Time enough to put a good distance between
him and Larocque's camp. Joel walked the gelding away
from the campsite and the three men with their "motherlode."
The hairs prickled at the nape of his neck, and his spine grew
tense and did not relax until he was completely out of range
and obscured by the forest.

Joel breathed a sigh of relief. He was glad to have departed the camp of Monsieur Henri Larocque and his associates. He rode toward the twilight, a man full of wishes and
dreams and slowly souring moods, suddenly wondering how
far, how fast he would have to ride to leave his conscience
behind.

Hemené watched from beneath the cover of her long black hair as Joel Ryan rode from the camp. For a moment she had thought she had seen pity in his eyes. Pity from a *ve-ho-e*? From a white man? She should have known better. She listened to Mayo and Larch as they squatted by the fire, carving chunks of greasy meat from the spit.

"What do you think, Mister Larocque?" the young one said.

"I could track him and bring back his scalp. Ain't no one gonna cause much fuss about a damn Johnny Reb."

"Zeke," Larocque chuckled. "I thought your allegiance to the Union ceased the moment you ran away."

"I didn't run, Larocque," Mayo snapped. "I just quit is all. There weren't no future in followin' some blame fool gen'ral around Arkansas."

"I stand corrected," Henri Larocque said with a wave of his hand in a tone ripe with insincerity. The understatement was lost on the deserter.

"I don't give a damn where you stand. Do you want me to kill the bastard?"

"You might have a problem with that."

"He didn't look like much," Larch interjected. "We could round him up simple."

"We?" Mayo glanced over at him. "I didn't think you were gonna let the little gal there out of sniffin' distance."

Larch blushed and looked away.

"So, our young companion has the itch beneath his belt," Larocque bellowed. "Well, it is an itch you will not scratch, my friend. Blue Jacket will have no use for her if she has been broken in. And if he discovers it was you who robbed

him, you will end your days singing in a high voice, mark
my words."

"Shee-it," the youth muttered.

"And as for Monsieur Ryan," Larocque went on, "I have
seen his kind before. His interest is in gold. Our little prize
is none of his concern. So he will be none of mine."

Larocque nudged Hemené, tilting her face upward, and
examined her throat for telltale marks. Satisfied she displayed
no ill effects, he motioned to the meat cooking over the fire.

"Eat," he said.

Hemené looked at the remains of one of the rabbits, and
unable to dissuade her hunger, she crawled over toward the
fire. Larch cut a portion and held it out to her. He smiled
and licked his lips. She took the food from the knife blade
and passed the sizzling meat from hand to hand until it
cooled enough to tear off a chunk and swallow it.

"Look at her. She knows every word we say, I swear,"
Larch said.

"And everything you're thinking. She'd have to be blind
not to," Mayo added, reaching over to run his hand along
her leg, bunching her dress as he worked the buckskin up to
her thigh. Hemené reached out and, with a stick near the fire,
swept a cloud of crimson coals onto the deserter's trousers.
Mayo yelped and leaped out of the way, batting at the singed
fabric.

"Red nigger squaw," he yelled and lunged at her. Hemené
darted past him and back behind Larocque who rose like a
behemoth from the ground. Mayo ran up against the French
trapper's Hawken rifle.

"Easy, Mayo."

"Stand aside!"

"Sit down, my friend."

"She burned me."

"And she will pay. Blue Jacket will make her pay. And
we will get paid. Think of the gold Blue Jacket promised us.
Is she worth it?"

Mayo looked past the Frenchman at the girl. At last, reason seeped past his anger. He slammed his fist into the palm
of his hand, whirled around, his mood black as his stubbled
jaw. He returned to the fire.

"You don't level no gun at me again," he said, glaring at the flames.

"It was for your own good, my friend. For all our good," Larocque explained. He crossed to his companions and from beneath his shirt withdrew a silver flask. It was embossed with a family crest; Henri Larocque had not always been among men of such low station. He handed the flask to Mayo, who stared at the offering a moment, unscrewed the flask, and took a sip. Brandy warmed his belly and soothed his damaged ego. Larocque walked back to the girl and, taking up the rope tether, led her off to the creek that she might make her nightly ablutions.

Hemené dutifully followed the trapper into the trees. Their footsteps crackled in the underbrush and then became silent as they reached the sandy bank.

"He's wrong about the reb. An extra horse and gun might come in handy," Larch commented, reaching for a share of the brandy.

"The hell with him," Mayo grumbled.

"The reb?"

"And Larocque," Mayo said. He tilted the flask to his lips. "But not his brandy."

Larocque stood much too close. Hemené blushed and kept her eyes lowered while she attended to herself. She knelt by the waters of the creek, a sense of hopelessness and dread weighing down her spirits. She was alone. And there was no one to help her. With each passing day the fears grew. Each passing day saw her brought farther and farther from her people. Henri Larocque had proved more than a match for Sacred Killer and his trackers. Rescue was no more than a faint possibility. Escape was her only hope. But how? The ankle rope tightened as Larocque gave a tug.

"Hurry, little cat," Larocque called out. "The night is short, and tomorrow brings a long journey."

Hemené knew there was little time to spare. She took the cooked rabbit she had barely nibbled on and placed it near the creek. As she did, she prayed for help in a low voice, *"Ma ah ku tsit o miss i,"* which was to say, "Badger, eat." That which was offered to the earth was considered offered to the badger, a powerful spirit and friend to the Cheyenne. She buried the meat in a shallow depression and covered it over with moist sand.

Larocque caught her by the hair and lifted her to her feet.

"Now what are you doing, little one?" he said.

She twisted in his grasp and slipped free. She darted away toward the opposite bank splashing across the creek bed. The dark line of trees, so close. He was big and much too heavy. She was swift of foot. *Freedom, please*, she cried silently, *oh spirit*. But Larocque hauled back on the rope and sent her sprawling. He dragged her back across the bank, through the creek. She clawed at the muddy bottom, her arms flailing, water in her lungs, and struggled out of the creek still fighting him as she choked and gagged.

When she lay at his feet, her buckskin dress gathered almost to her shoulders, Larocque stared down at her slender legs and rounded girlish hips. Only with great effort did he force common sense to override lust. He sighed and grabbed her by her drenched hair and dragged her erect. His redbearded face inches from hers, he spoke in a voice both soft and unmistakably malevolent.

"Do not try that again."

Hemené blinked and tried to force back the tears that glistened on her cheeks and shamed her. The sister of Sacred Killer must be brave.

"C'mon," Larocque said.

Soaked to the skin and thoroughly downcast, the woman called Mourning Dove led the way back to the camp of her captors.

She was no concern of his. Joel dug beneath his bedroll and hounded out a stone that had been punishing his ribs for the better part of the night. He tossed the offending pebble over a blackberry thicket and stretched out on his blanket. He closed his eyes and tried to fool himself.

She was no concern of his. Just a smudged face . . . He sat upright, unable to blame the stone this time. He stood and walked out of his cold camp. The gelding neighed and pawed at the earth. Joel quieted his horse with a pat and ambled out of the trees to a clearing on the slope, a hundred feet above the valley. Down below, like some baleful accusing eye, the flames of a campfire flickered in the recesses of the black valley.

A strike at Silver Bow. A fortune waiting to be fished out of the streams, nuggets to be dug from the mountainsides. Nuggets as big as a man's fist, or so the stories said. The longer he tarried, the longer he allowed the other men to find his strike, the fewer his chances. Sure, it was too bad about the girl. But she was just an Indian being brought to other Indians. Why stick his nose in where it was none of his business? Anyway, given half a chance she'd probably slit his throat. *Anyway,* there were three dangerous men down there, and one in particular, Larocque, was no one to cross.

What can I do? Joel repeated to himself, adding the litany, "She's no concern of mine."

He gazed at the campfire and pictured again the slim, frightened, defeated captive dragged from the lean-to and subdued by Larocque. Joel turned to start back to his bedroll and paused. He glanced over his shoulder and swung around again.

The war had served him enough trouble without the need to look for more. He'd had his fill; he'd gorged himself on violence. But the image of a frightened girl kept haunting him. And try as he might he could not override the instinct that commanded him to act.

"I can't believe I'm going to do this," he muttered, tabulating what he might need and forming a plan of approach. He gathered together his gear, saddled the gelding, and rode the animal out of the trees and down toward the valley, retracing the path he had followed only a few hours before.

The campfire in the distance, no longer baleful, burned bright as courage, guiding Joel Ryan through the dark.

3

Larocque slept. Hemené pretended to. She lay unmoving, her energy spent. The once-keen edge of her spirit was dull and notched with defeat.

She stirred slightly, enough to watch the Frenchman. Indeed, he looked dead to the world with only his deep rumbling snore like the muted growling of a wild beast to indicate he lived. The woman called Mourning Dove had been deceived before by the appearance of sound sleep in Henri Larocque. Twice, she had tried to crawl from his side, only to have him waken and clamp his foul hand around her throat and drag her to his side, pinning her with his full weight, his hot breath fanning her cheek. More humiliating, he would laugh and encourage her futile struggles. She amused him. It pleased Larocque to see her helpless before his terrible strength. Hemené had no wish to amuse him further; she had learned her lesson.

She lay still and quiet.

And Larocque slept.

Young Billy Larch. No. Wild Billy Larch. That sounded better. The youth by the fire squinted his eyes and tried to imagine how it would be. *Wild Billy Larch, King of the Desperadoes.* He shoved aside his blanket, letting it drop from his shoulders. Mayo stirred nearby and twisted about, hunkering down beneath his army blanket and muttering something in his sleep. Larch watched until the deserter no longer moved, then the youth glanced at the makeshift shelter. He yawned and reminded himself that he had another long hour to be on watch before waking Henri Larocque. Satisfied that his companions were asleep and he was unobserved, Larch adjusted his belt and drew the awkward heavy-

barreled Patterson Colt he had stolen from his stepfather
before running away from the pitiful scrap of land the man
had called a farm. He cocked the gun, the hidden trigger
swung down. Wild Billy Larch threatened the shadows, holding the unseen agents of darkness at gunpoint. He eased the
hammer down, dropped the pistol into the holster, counted
to three, and palmed the weapon in a single, lightning-quick
motion. But thumbing off the first shot was the problem. The
Patterson was a relic. He needed one of the newer Colts like
Mayo and Larocque owned. And he'd be able to afford one
once Blue Jacket paid them for the girl. A vague, unsettling
emotion momentarily soured his mood. Only for a second.
It passed without him ever recognizing the faint stirring of
pity. After all, he couldn't be Wild Billy Larch without a
decent gun. A twig snapped behind him, and he whirled,
leveling the pistol. He squeezed the trigger on reflex; his
thumb caught the hammer as the youth just barely managed
to avoid shooting his horse. My God, all the horses! Free!
A mare trotted toward the creek dragging the line that had
secured the animal beneath the overhanging ledge. The other
horses were already disappearing up the creek.

"Mayo! Larocque!"

Mayo rolled out of his bedroll and clambered to his feet,
still groggy, with one hand struggling to pull on his boots
while he drew his revolver with the other. Larocque stumbled
from the shelter. His face, wreathed in flaming beard and
shaggy mane was flush with apprehension as he glanced
about the camp as if expecting a Cheyenne war party to be
riding down their throats. He swung the Hawken as he
turned, ready to blast the first savage fool enough to show
himself. It took the Frenchman a moment to realize they were
not under attack and only another moment to see that the
horses were gone.

Larocque fixed Billy Larch in an iron stare. It had been
Billy's task to see to the remuda, to secure the tethers, and
keep a watch on the horses.

"You fool," Larocque said beneath his breath. Even with
his pistol drawn, Larch quailed, and with frightened bloodless features, he retreated from the Frenchman.

"And a dumbass," Mayo added. "Our lives ain't worth doodly-squat out here without horses."

"I tied 'em," Larch said, desperate for an explanation.

"Like hell. You—" Larocque threw up his hands in frustration. At last he managed to regain some semblance of control. "After them. Hurry. After them, I say. The mare will run to water, to the creek. And the rest will join her. Mon Dieu, move! Must you always wait for orders?"

"Why don't you just quit your jawin' and come along?" Mayo suggested.

"And leave the girl to run away?" Larocque bellowed with a wave of his hand ordering them. "After the horses."

Wild Billy Larch had already glumly trotted off, following the path to the creek. Mayo yanked on his other boot, stomping his foot to get a good fit around his heel.

"One day I'd like to see you do some of the work around here," he growled.

"I am keeping you two alive. And making you rich. Is that not enough? Capturing the girl, saving you from the Cheyenne. It tasks me even now. Were it not for me your scalps would be decorating Sacred Killer's lance. Gratitude, bah. It is the lot of Henri Larocque never to be appreciated for what he has done."

"Forget it," Mayo muttered, taking off after Larch. It was easier to chase horses than listen to one of Larocque's wounded tirades.

Once the men were out of the clearing, Larocque relaxed his hurt expression and pulled at his beard in thought. He had no wish to thrash around in the dark. Surely two men were enough to retrieve the horses. Billy Larch! The incompetence of the young was something to bemoan. The Frenchman looked around at the overhang beneath which their mounts had been tethered for the night. *I must do everything myself. Keep watch over the girl. Set traps for food. Check the horses.*

He started, memory flooding back to him. He had checked the dragline. The knots had been secure. His anger at Larch was indeed misplaced. But if the horses had been unable to break free, then they had been cut free!

Spinning around, he raced toward the shelter. The trapper

ducked through the narrow opening, his shoulders shattering
the entwined branches.

The girl was gone. The severed bonds lay in a pile at his
feet. The escape route cut in the back of the shelter told him
all he needed to know.

He spoke the name, dredging it up from memory, and
drew his revolver to shatter the stillness with a warning shot.

"Ryan . . . Joel Ryan," he roared in a murderous voice.
Joel Ryan.

It had to be.

"Run," Joel said. Hemené stumbled, dazed from the moment
his knife had sliced an opening in the rear of the shelter.

Joel reached out and caught her wrist and yanked the Indian girl to her feet. Suddenly, she came alive, throwing dirt
in his face and blinding her surprised benefactor. She sprang
away as a shot exploded behind them. Joel muttered a curse
and staggered into a tree taking a painful scrape on the forehead. He wiped at his eyes until the vision cleared enough
for him to catch a glimpse of Mourning Dove thrashing in
the thorny underbrush. She had blundered into a patch of
"Wait-a-bit" thorns. The hooked barbs caught at her buckskin
skirt and streaked her legs with tiny cuts. Despite the punishment, she continued to struggle, pulling free, inch by painful inch. Joel lunged after her, his temper wholly out of
control. What the devil did she think she was doing? By God
he was going to rescue her now if it killed her, killed them
both.

Gunshots sounding again, closer still, spurred Joel to renewed effort. Hemené saw him coming and tried to tear free.
She cried out, caught like some wild animal in the brambles.
Joel reached for her and with a single mighty effort yanked
her from the thorns. She turned on him in a second, her fists
pummeling his chest, driving him back. She kicked and
gouged and clawed. Another gunshot, closer, ever closer.
Joel's fist traveled no more than six inches from his chest to
her chin, a solid little clip that tilted her head. Hemené stared
at him with a sort of blank look of surprise before a veil of
unconsciousness dulled her expression and she collapsed in
his arms. Joel lifted her over his shoulder and continued

through the woods. The thrashing behind him could only be
Henri Larocque, like a charging bear in desperate pursuit.
For one sickening moment Joel thought he had lost his way;
at last he recognized a lightning-blasted cottonwood and, altering his course, found the clearing a hundred yards down
from Larocque's camp.

The gelding was where Joel had left it, but unfortunately
the animal wasn't alone. Two other horses had entered the
clearing, and these were led by Mayo who had only just
stumbled upon Joel's mount. Luck alone had turned Mayo's
back to the gelding's owner as he burst from the underbrush,
his long strides consuming the distance between the two
men. Larocque's shots had already alerted Mayo whose gun
was drawn. He whirled, revolver ready. This time Joel Ryan
did not pull his punch. His left fist exploded against the deserter's jaw, lifting him off the ground. The horses reared in
fright and broke from Mayo's grasp. They had raced from
the clearing by the time Mayo hit the dust. The gelding
pulled at his tether in alarm, then he calmed at seeing Joel,
who carried his burden to the animal and slung the unconscious girl across the saddle. Joel gathered the reins, leaped
behind her, and dug his heels into the animal's flanks.

"C'mon," he yelled, and the gelding leaped forward on
command down a deer trail almost imperceptible in the night.

A squat patch of shadow darker than the rest rose to one
side.

"Ryan!" the shadow snarled and uttered a stream of in-
vective in French.

"C'mon," Joel repeated in urgency, using the reins like a
whip on the frightened animal.

Henri Larocque aimed, leading with the gun barrel; the
pistol bucked and spat flame as its intended target vanished
past the pines. Larocque cursed and kicked at the dirt.

"Ryan!" he shouted, then decided the rebel could not hear
him anyway. A groan off to his left told him Mayo was
regaining consciousness.

The deserter climbed to his feet, staggered, trying to keep
his balance.

"Sumbitch . . . brokmmff . . . jaw," he mumbled as Larocque stepped past, already tapping loads into his revolver.

"Get your gun," the Frenchman said.

Mayo picked his gun off the ground, fought a spasm of nausea, then straightened up and knocked the dirt from the barrel.

"Should've let me kill him," he said, his speech less slurred as feeling in his jaw returned. The whole side of his head hurt. "I hope the bastard broke his hand," he added, groaning.

"Hey," Larch shouted from the direction of the creek. "Larocque . . . Hey Mayo, what's happening? Where are you?" Larch was alarmed by all the gunplay. He had no way of knowing whether they were under attack or not.

"Watch for the horses," Larocque called. "Mayo lost his."

"I ain't the only one who lost somethin'," Mayo grumbled. "I saw what he was carrying. Now what are we gonna do? You let him just waltz right into camp and take her. That leaves us with nothin' but a Cheyenne war party on our heels. You got any more bright ideas, well keep them to yourself. We wore our butts to the bone so the likes of that reb . . ." His complaints died, for Larocque was paying him no mind. Rather, he had knelt at the edge of the clearing and was running his hand across the earth.

"I don't figger you, Larocque," Mayo said with a sigh.

"You never will, mon ami," Larocque said, standing. "We will bring in the horses and return to camp. In the morning I will track this Mister Ryan. I will hunt him down and force him to return our little gold mine. Comprenez-vous?"

"He'll be miles away by morning," Mayo said in disgust.

"I do not think so." Henri Larocque grinned. He held out his hand. The fingers were wet with blood.

4

Joel had just decided everything was going to work out when the gelding faltered, stumbled, and leaped forward a few more feet before its strength failed completely. The animal buckled. Joel had no time to think. He slung the girl in the opposite direction of the fall and tumbled after her, kicking free of the stirrups and just managing to save himself a broken leg. Mourning Dove scrambled to her feet. Still groggy from the blow that had ended her protests, she staggered toward the trees. Joel stretched out and with a swipe of his arm tripped her. She began to squirm in his grasp and claw at him. Joel caught her by the wrists and violently shook her.

"Stop it. Just stop it!" he said. The young woman stared at him and glumly obeyed. This was an unexpected result, and he wondered what was going on in her mind. He considered hitting her again to assure her compliance, but he resisted the urge for now. He pulled her over to the gelding. The animal lay on its side. One of its hooves weakly kicked at the water. Joel knelt and felt along the neck and chest until he came to the frothy bullet hole. The gelding shuddered. Shuddered again. And then was still.

"You were a game one," Joel said, stroking the horse's mane. Now severed was Joel's last link with home. The gelding had carried him off to war and with Joel had emerged miraculously unscathed. "You were game." Lost in his own thoughts he loosened his grip on the woman's wrist.

But Hemené did not run. She had another plan. Also, this strange tenderness in a white man intrigued her. There had been no tenderness in her captors. She watched him until, at last, Joel stood, dragged his blanket loose, untied his saddlebags, and draped them over his shoulder; then digging in the sand beneath the horse, he worked the rifle free. The stock had been broken in the fall.

"Damn," he exclaimed and tossed the rifle into the brush. A man without a rifle was at a significant disadvantage. He checked his revolver and was relieved to find it in one piece. He looked back down the creek then up to the steeply forested slopes rising on either side, disconcertingly like the jaws of a trap. It dawned on him that he was no longer holding the girl, but when he looked around, she was close behind him, staring out at the dark forest. A coyote howled balefully in the distance. Its lonely cry carried on the night air, unanswered. Ghostly battlements of clouds drifted before a sky thick with stars. "Well, we can't stay here," Joel muttered. He caught Hemené by the arm and tugged. She drew away.

"Look," Joel said, "I don't mean you any harm! But we can't stay here. They'll be after us come morning. And I left enough tracks for a blind man to follow. We've got to hide. Understand! We've got to find someplace to hide." He spoke louder as if volume would somehow make her understand. Amazingly enough, the woman looked back the way they had come and then nodded to Joel.

They started up the more gradual slope on their left. The going was relatively easy, and Joel might have felt hopeful were it not for Henri Larocque. Joel Ryan had no illusions about his ability to trick his pursuers. Maybe the other two, but not Larocque. Joel had hinged his escape on surprise and speed. He had gambled on putting sufficient distance between himself and Larocque. It was a wager he had lost, and now he needed a place to make his stand.

They climbed, tripping over roots and half-buried rocks. Fallen trees and moss-covered boulders rose to block their course in the dark.

Five hundred feet up from the creek, the fugitives paused to rest. Joel scanned the surrounding forest and noticed a parting in a stand of pines and in the clearing, a stygian patch of shadow, deeper than the night. The shadow became a cave with a mouth that arched some thirty feet overhead. Hemené drew back. Caves held wild animals, not to mention evil spirits.

"Stay here," Joel said. He could not tell if she understood. He hesitated, but when she did not run, he guessed she had begun to trust him. He walked to the lip of the cave. Cold air emanated from the depths. He searched about and gathered together a nearly straight branch and enough dry grass, and soon he had made a torch. The gun drawn, he entered the cave.

Mourning Dove watched with keen interest. The gun, she needed the gun. This was the plan that had come to her. Only then could she escape and hope to find her people. Without the gun, the Frenchman would find her and capture her again. She could not hope to fight him with her fists. He was too powerful. The gun was her only chance. The ve-ho-e, this white man whose hair was like silver, who had stolen her from the Frenchman's camp, must sleep sometime. And then her chance would come. The ground was littered with rocks to club him. She forced herself to think only of escape; she was certain he had rescued her for his own sinister purpose. Why should he be any different?

Yet Mourning Dove's heart was troubled.

For some undefinable reason, she wanted him to be different.

The cave ran more than three hundred feet deep into the hillside and was half as wide. The domed ceiling vaulted upward eighty feet and boasted a spiky canopy of stalactites like monstrous rows of teeth ready to champ shut. Massive columns of ridged limestone connected floor to ceiling. Through this cold primeval vault, Joel carefully made his way in awe and apprehension, wary of bear and mountain lion, and shivering, chilled by the cold air that filled the chamber. Two hundred feet from the entrance, Joel's boots slipped and he almost fell. He lowered the torch and discovered he was standing on a surface of sheer ice. The ground slowly sloped away. To venture further was to court disaster. To be in the wilderness on foot with Larocque and friends after him, and maybe the Cheyenne too, and with a girl who probably wanted to cut his throat was enough disaster for one day.

One day, God in heaven, how had things fallen apart so

swiftly? He lifted the torch. Light spilled down the ice slope. He could see a drop-off and a dark pit, which in the flickering illumination revealed a rocky bottom covered with bones, the remains of animals that had blundered into the cave and fallen prey to the ice slope. Evidently, the ice remained year round. Rib cages and tusks and various appendages jutted from the ice, a graveyard that bore witness to the sudden stark tragedies of prehistory. Shuddering, he imagined the anguished roars, the violent ravings of beasts imprisoned in the pit, doomed to die a slow starving death. His boots slipped and slid for a sickening moment as he retreated to the level part of the cave and made his way back outside. He was frankly surprised to see Hemené waiting for him. He walked to her side, and when he handed the torch to her, her brown eyes sparkled in the light, sparkled and in the same moment were limpid and watchful. It struck him she was not a child but a woman, a lovely young woman with her fawn-like gaze and long black hair framing a copper-tinted face.

"I need to gather wood. The cave is safe for us. But we will need a fire."

He started off into the woods, and she followed, lighting enough of the forest floor for him to gather deadwood for a fire. When his arms were full, they returned to the cave. Mourning Dove entered hesitantly. When they had a campfire crackling at the mouth of the cave, the woman relaxed enough to venture partway inside. To her mind the dark recesses of the chamber continued to house spirits who whispered indignation at the intrusion. She huddled close to the fire. Joel stepped outside and retrieved his saddlebags and blanket. He crouched close-by, intending to hand her the blanket. Hemené bolted from him like a wild creature at bay and kept her back to the wall.

"I thought we had been through all this," Joel sighed. He started to circle the fire. The woman hissed and picked up a stone. Joel continued to advance, his shadow slowly approaching and at last blending with hers until the two were one in silhouette on the wall. Joel drew his revolver. The woman's eyes widened in alarm, at first, then astonishment as Joel took the gun by the barrel and held it out to her.

"I've lived twenty-six years without raping anyone. I don't intend to start now."

Hemené stared at the gun butt. She had devised ways to steal it, and here he was handing it to her. Was he mad? She grabbed the gun from his hand, cocked it, and pointed it at him. He merely turned around and walked back to the fire.

"I'm out of food," he said over his shoulder. "But I don't imagine your former traveling companions will let us go hungry for long."

Mourning Dove sighted along the barrel. Her finger tightened on the trigger.

Kill him. Kill him and run. But common sense failed to overrule what was in her heart. He had brought her from Larocque's camp. And other than a sore chin she had not been harmed. But white men were not to be trusted. He was an enemy of her people. Or was he? Had she not left an offering of meat for *Ma-hahko-e*, the badger, and beseeched this powerful spirit to rescue her? And only a few hours later she had been rescued. She stared with renewed interest at Joel, seeing him for the first time not as a mortal foe but as someone whom the All-Father had sent. If Ma-hahko-e was the special friend of her people, then this man too must be a friend. The gods would not lie. He turned to look at her. The flames cast a shimmering glow that played upon the silver highlights of his hair and his windburned, tanned features. If the gods were determined to surprise her with whom they had sent to her aid, at least they had chosen someone very handsome.

Hemené, the Mourning Dove, lowered the weapon and offered it to him.

"Take your gun, Jo-el Ry-an."

Joel crossed to her, a knowing look in his eyes.

"I thought you understood what I was saying just a little too quickly." He holstered the revolver again. "I don't blame you for hiding the fact. But who in the world taught you?"

"One who lives among my people."

"A white man?"

"The ve-ho-e are our enemies," she said. "No, he is not white. His skin is like the night."

Joel decided not to ask what had convinced her of his

intentions. He was just grateful they were no longer at odds. Watching out for Henri Larocque was going to be hard enough without having to guard what went on behind his back.

Mourning Dove brushed past him and returned to the campfire. She took the blanket he had offered her before and wrapped it about her slim shivering torso.

"I only meant to give you that," Joel remarked, stretching out by the fire.

"Among my people," Hemené said, looking up at him, her long black hair spilling forward to shade her features, "a brave will choose his wife in this way, by offering her his blanket."

When Joel glanced away in embarrassment, Hemené hid her amusement and lay down beside the fire.

"You have found us a cold place in which to hide, Jo-el Ry-an," she said from beneath the blanket.

"It will have to do," Joel muttered. He stretched his long frame out upon the floor across from the woman. Flames danced between them. Her eyes were closed, else he would not have had the courage to study the clean, almost haughty lines of her face, the firm, slim outline of her body beneath the buckskin shift.

He became conscious of a very real desire. Now that he could see her in repose, under different circumstances, it was easy to understand why any man would want to spirit her away.

Next he'd be agreeing with Larocque's motives, Joel chided himself. He folded his hands behind his head and closed his eyes.

Larocque . . . time enough to worry about him in the morning. Joel turned on his side and placed the Colt revolver close at hand. Working the lever underneath the barrel to free the unloaded cylinder, he replaced it with a loaded one from his saddlebag. He had made the switch outside in the dark, figuring that if he offered the gun to Hemené it might convince her of his intentions. He felt somewhat guilty about the ruse, but not overly so. After all, he wanted to be friends, not dead.

"Jo-el," the woman suddenly spoke. "What will happen in the morning?"

"Larocque will probably come after us."

"And if he does not?"

"Then I will take you back to your home."

"My brother hates all white men."

"I'll win him over with my wit," Joel grunted, digging out a pebble from under his hip.

"I do not understand."

"Never mind."

"My brother will kill you."

"Not if Larocque beats him to it," Joel said. It didn't sound any funnier than he thought it would.

"You are a strange man. I do not understand your ways."

Joel inched nearer to the fire, warming his backside against the chill emanating from the depths of the cave.

"Neither do I," he said. "Neither do I."

5

Joel Ryan woke with a face full of sunshine and the song of Henri Larocque ringing in his ears:

> Love is the fairest flower
> that blows on a summer morn
> But beneath the sweetest blossom
> Lies the sorrow of the thorn.

Joel bolted upright, grabbing for his gun. He glanced across the smoldering coals of last night's campfire and saw that Mourning Dove was awake, her deep brown eyes betraying no trace of the alarm she must have felt within. Joel put his fingers to his lips, cautioning her to remain quiet while he crawled to the lip of the cave, hugging the wall in an effort to present less of a target. About fifty yards away sat Henri Larocque, Mayo, and Billy Larch astride their horses. Sunbeams filtered through the intersecting branches of the trees behind them and formed a backdrop of emerald patches and golden bars that might have been startling in its beauty were it not for the menacing trio. Larocque broke rank and trotted forward. Joel saw a white banner tied to the barrel of the Hawken rifle. Larocque kept the flag of truce in plain sight as he rode up to the cave and dismounted some twenty feet from the yawning entrance.

"You can talk from there," Joel said. Larocque slung the Hawken from his saddle and, holding his arms clear of his body to demonstrate that he was unarmed, continued on to the cave.

"Au contraire, mon ami," Larocque softly exclaimed. "Sound carries. A voice travels far in this big country. And we have things to discuss in private."

Joel could not bring himself to shoot the man in cold blood. He retreated deeper into the cave; Hemené moved near the entrance, the better to watch the other two men. For one so short in stature, Larocque seemed to fill the chamber. He ran a hand through his greasy red beard, his feral gaze flitting from Mourning Dove and back to Ryan.

"I must compliment you, my friend. You fooled even me for a few moments. Long enough to spirit away my little treasure, eh? But no one can hide from Henri Larocque, as you can see. Now I think it is time to return the favor you owe me."

"What favor?" Joel said, watching the man's every move.

"The other night, Mayo wanted to follow you, to kill you. I would not let him go."

"I wish you had. There'd be one less out there now," Joel said.

Larocque chuckled. "I feared as much. You are young. But I see in your eyes, things that make a man old. Very well, you do not owe me a favor. Consider then, these men, Mayo and Larch. I chose them because of their availability. Does Henri Larocque belong with their kind? Hardly. But I think you are one to ride the trails with. The two of us might easily dispatch my companions."

"I'll think about it."

"There is no time to think, mon ami. Early this morning I spotted a cloud of dust up by the gap. Maybe wild horses. Maybe Cheyenne. I do not wish to find out."

"You don't give me much room," Joel said, glancing over at Hemené who was studying him with open apprehension. He could read her thoughts. No doubt the woman was reliving the moment when she had handed the revolver to Joel. Now Hemené was wondering whether or not she had made the right decision. "I prefer to ride alone," Joel said.

Larocque's expression clouded.

"Think, monsieur. You are making a mistake. I am blood brother to the Crow. Blue jacket will pay me what I want for the girl. But a stranger like you, he will simply kill and take what he wants. You need me."

"I am not taking her to any Blue Jacket," Joel explained. "I'm bringing her home to her people."

Mourning Dove visibly relaxed, although it still struck her as unbelievable that Joel was making a stand in her behalf. However, the Frenchman laughed outright.

"You are indeed a fool. My estimation of you drops, my friend. If you are determined to die, I will do this thing for you. Your death at least will be quick. Sacred Killer will have you dancing on brimstone. Oh, you'll make a pretty spectacle. It would almost be worth seeing."

"Why don't you come along then?" Joel snapped.

"But you prefer to ride alone," said Larocque. The Frenchman shook his head. "I am not a heartless man, monsieur. Nor a violent one. The shedding of blood is not necessary. But the gold Blue Jacket will pay means very much to me. Give me the girl, and I will leave you a horse to replace the one I found dead by the creek. You may continue on to Silver Bow."

"I can't do that, Larocque." Joel stepped forward and checked to make certain Mayo and Larch were still across the clearing before motioning for Larocque to leave. The Frenchman drew abreast of Ryan. "I suppose honor means as much to me as Blue Jacket's gold to you," Joel said.

"Honor." Larocque seemed stung by the word, as if Joel had prodded a wound that had never completely healed in the man. He rubbed the bronze crucifix at his throat and spoke in a voice strangely gentle. "Honor is what a poor man carries to the grave. It will not even buy you a coffin, monsieur."

"Perhaps what you say is true, Larocque, but at least I'll enter my house justified," Joel said. He nodded toward the sunlit clearing. "We're through talking."

Larocque colored. His features pinched and filled with malice. The gentleness vanished.

"So be it," he said. "Make yourself ready, Monsieur Ryan."

The Frenchman brushed past Joel and headed straight for his horse. Joel found himself counting the man's steps, watching as one foot lifted to catch a stirrup and the hand reached out to catch the rawhide saddle pommel. The compact, solid weight of the man swung up into place. Wheeling the animal with a wild cry, Henri Larocque held the Hawken rifle like a lance and charged the cave.

Joel reacted on instinct, seeing the flame blossom from the rifle barrel and singe the white banner tied at the sights, blowing apart the emblem of truce in fire and lead. An instant's hesitation and the slug that spattered chunks of rock from the cave wall would have done the same to Joel's skull.

But Joel did not hesitate. Reflexes honed by months of battle saved his life. He dodged and fired his revolver from a crouching stance and saw a chunk of rawhide legging erupt in a gusher of blood just below the Frenchman's right knee.

Larocque howled, the rifle flew from his hand as he doubled over to claw at his leg. Joel fired again and missed. Horse and rider swept past, and through their wake rode Mayo and Larch, revolvers blazing. Slugs glanced off stalactites, columns, and limestone outcroppings. Joel felt stone chips cut his cheek. As he turned he realized Hemené was standing in the path of the ricocheting bullets. He leaped toward her and bore her to the ground, managing to break his fall enough to keep from knocking the air out of her lungs. Even so, his weight pinned her to the rocky floor, her small firm breasts flattened against his chest. She looked at him still somewhat startled, as bullets pinged and caromed into the darkness overhead.

Joel kissed her. His lips covering hers. She felt as if the breath were being sucked out of her.

The kiss ended. And drawing away, Joel touched her cheek.

"That's one I owe those boys," he grinned. Then he left her side and scrambled back toward the entrance. Larch and Mayo were across the clearing again. Larocque was with them. Joel did what they were doing. He reloaded his gun.

A bumblebee explored the cave entrance. It hovered over Joel's hand for a moment and darted upwards when he moved. Joel listened to insects droning.

"Funny," he thought aloud, "buzzing bees and lazy summer afternoons sort of go together."

"It is a good time," said Mourning Dove emerging from the blackness with a tin cup of cold water.

"Yeah, a good time," Joel ruefully repeated, peering past the limestone rim at the line of trees where Larocque and his colleagues waited. He looked back at Mourning Dove. She had washed away the dirt from her face, arms, and legs. She offered him the cup.

"There is a pool of living water," she said, pointing toward the bowels of the cave.

Joel drained the cup. The water tasted somewhat bitter, but it was cold and refreshing.

"At least we won't die of thirst," he said, unable to resist watching her. Eyes like umber pools, fathomless, yet inviting, returned his gaze. Joel felt himself drawn into those depths, destined to lose himself forever. He blinked and shook his head. What the hell was happening to him anyway?

"You better crawl back under cover," he said gruffly, wondering how her red-brown face had come so close to his. A look of disappointment flashed across her countenance and her parted lips pursed in a frown. She sat back on her heels. Joel began to feel uncomfortable with her so close. Her displeasure confused him. He wanted to take her in his arms and . . . his baser thoughts shamed him. Yet what was he to expect? After all, he had been without a woman's comfort for many a month. And here was someone ripe and desirable and lovely. How could he ever have thought her merely a frightened animal? And what made his indecision even worse, Hemené seemed—*Am I utterly mad?* thought Joel— to be inviting him. The proximity of violence and death had become the catalysts of passion.

Joel did not try to understand the source of this overwhelming feeling. He only knew he wanted her. And he began to suspect Mourning Dove shared his feelings. The only problem now was he might not live to find out.

"We should've just gone on in when he ducked out of sight," Mayo said.

"I thought we were just giving Larocque cover," Billy Larch retorted. "I wasn't about to run in on my own."

"You are both idiots," Larocque groaned. He had wrapped a bandana around his leg, just above the right knee. He had taken a tomahawk from his gear and thrust the shaft through a knot, twisting to tighten the tourniquet and close off the ravaged arteries. The lower half of his wounded leg was soaked with blood.

"Merde," he gasped. "Did you never stop to think you might accidentally kill the girl? Maybe you have done so already."

"I like that. Some thanks I get for saving your life," Mayo said.

"I save my life, monsieur. Not you. And I will continue to save it." Larocque glanced toward the cave. "Another day, Monsieur Ryan. There will come another day," he said, through clenched teeth.

"What do you mean?" Mayo asked.

"I am leaving."

"Leaving? Now?" Larch blurted. "Mister Larocque, we got him cornered."

"I have kept my scalp in this howling wilderness because I have learned one very important thing in my life. It would do well if you learn it too, Billy. Know when to quit."

"Bullshit," Mayo snorted. He finished loading his revolver. "You want out of this deal, fine. But I'm gonna get me that girl."

"I reckon I'm with Mayo," Larch added, lifting the Patterson Colt. Mayo squeezed off a shot toward the cave. "We'll pepper him awhile and then make our play." They both began to fire.

Larocque shrugged and trotted his horse beneath the shading pines. Alone with his frustration and his pain, he took some comfort in the fact that it was just as well his companions remained behind. They ought to cause enough commotion to cover his escape.

And escape was uppermost in his thoughts, because he hadn't gone but a couple of hundred yards when he cut sign.

Unshod ponies.

And that meant Indians. He yanked a Navy Colt from beneath his blanket shirt. The pain in his knee was almost unbearable. Sweat beaded his brow. He fought back the nausea. Each step of his horse sent a shock wave of agony coursing through his body. And each tremor punctuated his need for revenge.

Revenge against Joel Ryan.

Despite his torment, a grim smile played across Larocque's face. It had just occurred to him that he might have his vengeance sooner than expected, courtesy of Sacred Killer, war chief of the Cheyenne.

Joel spied the men moving among the trees and quickly related his plan to the woman at his side.

"It cannot be this way," Hemené exclaimed in protest.

"You do as I say," Joel replied. "When they charge, I'll meet them in the open and, if I can, lead them up the slope."

"I do not want to stay here. I go with you. You have helped me. I will help you. I am a Cheyenne woman. I can fight."

"You wait until we're out of sight, and you light out in the other direction. Hide in the woods."

"I will fight," Hemené repeated.

"With what? Look, we don't have time to argue," Joel said. He watched as the two men mounted their horses again, readying themselves for a final assault.

"Jo-el." The woman touched his arm. "Why did you do . . . what you . . . did . . . here?" She touched her lips.

"Damn if I can figure," Joel said. "Seemed like the natural thing to do at the time. I'm not sorry if that's what you're getting at." He looked toward the clearing. "Here they come." He darted out into the sunlight.

"I am not sorry either," Hemené shouted too late. He had not heard.

Joel hit at a dead run toward the line of trees north of the cave. He paid no attention to the two men on horseback. Geysers of dust erupted at his feet as Mayo and Larch tried to run him down, emptying their pistols at the fleeing man.

Joel heard the drum of hoofbeats, the creak of saddle leather as his pursuers closed the gap.

Come on, a voice screamed in his mind. *Make the trees. Give her a chance, for Christ's sake. Run!*

Closer now. Just ahead. A stand of sunlit timber. He could almost hear the breeze among the spring branches, almost smell the clean pungent fragrance of the pines standing so erect, their quaking branches lifting to the sky in emerald symmetry.

Suddenly another cry filled the air. From the forest directly ahead of Joel more than a dozen half-naked savages burst from the underbrush. Their flesh was dyed crimson, and each howling warrior carried a thirteen-foot lance, the shaft adorned with raven feathers up to its six-inch iron point. The warriors rode garishly painted horses that seemed to attack with a frenzy of their own. Every one of the warriors carried a red shield, and each wore horned headgear fashioned from a buffalo head. The horns looked to have been dipped in blood. Joel stopped in his tracks. Behind him, Larch and Mayo were wheeling their horses about, but escape was impossible. Joel faced the braves, determined only to make a good account of himself. The warriors were on him in a second. He raised his Colt and snapped off a shot. But there wasn't time to plan, to aim. Nothing. A brave leaned forward and lowered his war lance. Joel danced out of the angle of attack, ducking beneath the iron tip. But the attackers were in too tight a formation. He collided with another warrior's mount. The revolver flew one way and Joel another. The collision rattled every bone in his body and knocked him into the air where his tumbling form glanced off another mount, driving him hard into the ground. Seconds later, he crawled to his hands and knees. Through blurred vision he saw Mayo trying to surrender. Larch, still screaming, was wriggling like an insect on the point of a lance.

Joel stood. His whole body was numb. His mouth was full of dirt and his vision blurry as he stood. And swimming into definition, a warrior was walking his horse toward Joel. The Kentuckian searched the ground, but his weapon was gone, so he spat out a mouthful of grit and curled his fists. The warrior lowered his spear point toward Joel's chest. He seemed more heavily adorned with raven feathers than the rest of the braves. A fringe of black feathers was sewn down the sides of his leggings. His powerful chest rippled with muscles beneath ridges of scar tissue.

Joel was blood-spattered and dirty. His clothes were ragged, his silver hair in wild disarray. His body, gradually realizing the punishment it had just taken, moved in dull

spasmodic steps. "Try me, you bastard." His voice emerged
a hoarse whisper. He shut his eyes and tried to clear his
senses. He stared at the warrior and waited for something to
happen. It did. But not what he expected. Past the brave, a
black spot slowly expanded, growing wider and wider. Why
didn't the warrior on horseback notice? Wider still, engulfing
the hills, the trees, the clearing, the brave, and at last Joel
himself. As he tilted over into the abyss, he heard a scream
and wondered if it were his own.

6

It made sense. Crawl up out of a black hole and see a black face. The Negro sat back on his heels. His seamed features deepened in what might have been a grimace or a smile. "Well now," the old man said. "Well now." And nothing more.

Next to the colored man, a lance and a red rawhide shield were propped against a tree. The shield was decorated with a curious emblem, a square, angle up, with a line at right angles to each side.

"The Morning Star," the black man explained. "You'll find it on most of their gear."

"Where am I?" Joel asked. He thought he had spoken aloud, but the Negro only looked at him in a puzzled way.

"Where ... am ... I?" Joel repeated, dragging the words across his swollen tongue.

"Among the Morning Star People. The fighting Cheyenne. You took quite a knock. I got 'em to carry you down here by the creek. You missed supper." The Negro wrapped his teeth around a plug of tobacco and tore off a chaw.

"Sacred Killer," Joel said, closing his eyes.

"You got that right, younker. Of course, we ain't to the main camp yet. Ol' Crazy Bear is probably four days away. This here's a bunch of Red Shields."

"What?" Joel said, studying the man again.

"Red Shields," the Negro said, pointing at the shield. "Sacred Killer's chief of the clan. It's a warrior society. Dye everything red before riding into battle. Look like bloody hell. Fight like it too. Your two friends can vouch for that. Well, could have." The Negro gestured to the hours-old scalps dangling from the lance. The night sky was awash with stars.

"They weren't friends of mine, old man," Joel said. It dawned on him what had happened. And why he had been fighting in the first place. "Mourning Dove?" Joel sat upright. The world teetered and he grabbed at the Negro's arm to steady the carousel. At last, the trees quit their spinning, the camp glided into place. There were three campfires. One for Joel and another for the warriors who were not guarding the horses. At the third and farthest, sat the warrior Joel had confronted before collapsing. And by that warrior's side, He-mené.

"She's fine now. And lucky for you. She ran up and kept her brother there from adding that hair of yours to his belt."

"That's Sacred Killer?"

"Yup. And white folks don't take to being introduced to him 'cause he's usually the last thing they'll ever see. About a year back, Colonel Chivington's militia massacred a whole camp of peaceful Cheyenne along Sand Creek, down Colorado way. Sacred Killer lost many a friend. And ever since he's had as much use for white folks as a coon hound has for wood ticks. I'm the exception. 'Course I ain't exactly white."

Joel leaned back and appraised the Negro for the first time. The man would not see sixty again. He was a man of average height, with long bony arms, a gaunt face and narrow jaw. His head was shaved, a shiny ebony pate with a slight peak in the middle of the cranium. The buckskin clothes hung loosely on his spare frame.

"Who exactly are you?" Joel asked.

"Priam. That's all. Just Priam. And you're Joel Ryan. No need to look so funny. I didn't know but I'd have to bury ya. So I checked your saddlebags for a name." Priam glanced past Joel. "Uh-oh."

Joel followed his gaze and saw Sacred Killer crossing the camp toward them. Authority emanated from the Indian with every stride. Joel could sense a palpable rise in anticipation flow among the other braves. Sacred Killer nodded to Priam and then looked long and hard at the white man. Priam rose from his squatting stance, and though physically he looked a poor shadow to Sacred Killer's raw power, Joel guessed the old man could be as tough as whipcord when he needed to be.

"*Nahkohe* is awake," Sacred Killer shouted to the other braves in the camp who laughed at the joke.

"Silvertip grizzly," Priam explained. "That's what you looked like running out of that cave. Ol' Silvertip brought to bay."

Sacred Killer allowed Priam to finish, then stepped between the black man and Joel. He squatted by Joel's side. With the red paint washed away, the warrior appeared somewhat friendlier, though not by much. He was dressed in leggings and moccasins and a beaded buckskin shirt decorated with porcupine quills and raven feathers and tiny glass beads sewn into the fringes. His hair was long and black and hung past his shoulders; an eagle feather had been braided into its thick fall. His eyes were almost as coppery as his skin and Joel felt as if the brave were staring right through him. Here was a man whose very presence demanded honesty. The price of deception might be too high to pay.

"Now we talk, ve-ho-e."

"I am called Joel Ryan."

"Joel Ryan." The war chief nodded. "My sister tells me many things. Things I do not understand. I would hear them from you. Then I may judge. My sister is young. A young woman is blind to things a man is not."

"It is a good thing to know what another feels in his heart," said Joel.

Sacred Killer gave a look toward Priam and then back to the white man.

"Why did you bring my sister from the camp of the Frenchman?" he asked, handling the English surprisingly well.

"I am new to these hills. There is much I do not know. But there are some things a man cannot ride around. Your sister needed help. That seemed reason enough. It still does."

Sacred Killer studied Joel's face. "And then what were you going to do with her?"

"Bring her to her people."

"I am at war with the white-eyes. You knew this. Still you would come."

"I had heard Sacred Killer was a great leader. To me this meant a man of wisdom as well as a mighty warrior. Would a wise man take the life of one who had saved the life of his sister? Should I fear you, Sacred Killer?"

"Only my enemies fear me."

"I am not your enemy."

"We will see. For now, you ride with us. As you are new to our land, so am I new to the path of friendship with a white man. I have spoken." Sacred Killer stood. Joel noticed the war chief had the attention of all the braves as if they were waiting for him to make a decision. He realized then that the warriors were ready to pounce on him in a second. Sacred Killer took up the lance with the fresh scalps dangling near the blade. The war chief of the Red Shield clan broke the lance across his knee and dropped both lengths at the white man's feet. The camp visibly relaxed, Hemené more so than all the rest.

"You sure said all the right things, younker," Priam remarked, squatting by Joel's fire again. The two men watched Sacred Killer return to his sister's side.

"I wonder," Joel said.

"How so?"

"He said I was to come along with him. As a guest or a prisoner?"

"Well now," Priam began. He spewed a long stream of tobacco and extinguished a nearby coal. "Guest and prisoner is one and the same in Cheyenne, if it's any comfort to you."

Henri Larocque seemed to have made good his escape. As for Mayo and Billy Larch, Joel had entertained thoughts of traveling back up the slope to give them a Christian burial, but an inner sense cautioned him that he did not want to see their remains, not after the warriors had spent their fury on the corpses. To steal Hemené for Blue Jacket, the Crow war chief, had been a most heinous crime, and the perpetrators had paid with death and dismemberment.

That morning while the warriors broke camp, Joel had tried to catch Hemené's eye, but she seemed determined not to make contact. Joel had been given Mayo's rather worn-out old pack animal, and when he mounted, it was much to the amusement of the others. Even Mourning Dove hid a smile. Joel's long legs dangled almost to the ground. The stirrups were much too short for him to use, and Joel had to be content with gripping the horse with his knees to steady himself in the saddle.

"Larocque's a wily fellow," Priam exclaimed, allowing his own mount to take one last drink from the creek before they began their journey out of the Pryors. "It galls Sacred Killer no end to let him slip away."

"He's wounded."

"That only makes him more dangerous," Priam said.

"You act like you know him."

"I do. Known him ever since he wore his black robes."

"He was a priest?" Joel asked.

"Yup. A Jes-oo-ite. Seems he sort of fell from grace with a woman up Canada way. He done throwed away his Holy Book and took to the mountains. I figger she left him or maybe she had a husband. Funny thing how a good man can make the baddest man you ever saw." Priam yanked on the reins and backed the animal from the creek. "You say your pa trapped out here?"

"Here and about or so I was told. Cortland Ryan was his name."

"You're Cortland Ryan's boy?!" Priam's milky eyes widened with astonishment.

"Yes. You hear of him?" Joel beamed, proud of the association.

"Nope. Can't say that I have." Priam chuckled and then trotted his horse into line with the others.

Joel blushed with embarrassment; the old bastard had really led him into that one. He noticed the warriors were waiting for him to join them. They were fighters and looked the part even without their red paint.

He did not keep them waiting long.

7

Two days out of the Pryors the land became a rolling plain verdant with buffalo grass that reached to the bellies of the horses. And when the wind came rushing down across the prairie, the grasses danced as if all the world were a single fluid sea stretching ever onward to dash against the Absarokas beyond. Here the western peaks stood stark and forboding, pushing snowcapped purple and gunmetal gray summits to the heavens.

At midday, the Red Shields paused to water their horses at a buffalo wallow. Half the band stood watch, circling the ones who were the first to drink. Joel and Priam were waiting their turn in silence, watching those before them. Here was an oasis in an endless stretch of undulating grasses beneath a sky that seemed to fit the earth like an inverted lid of purest sapphire. Joel took in the vista, exhilarated at the sight. Priam noted the younger man's awed interest. He had once reacted the same way. Not anymore. At least not so one might notice.

"You might say I'm alkalied to this here country," he sighed.

After two days of travel and sleep, Joel was anxious for a conversation. Priam had ridden off with a couple of the braves and only rejoined the war party an hour ago. The reason for his departure was as obvious as the deer carcass draped behind the black man's saddle when he returned. Throughout those two days Hemené had stayed close to her brother. And none of the other warriors had offered more than perfunctory acceptance at their campfire.

"When I first saw you, I figured you came out here after the war, like me," Joel began.

"What war?"

"Between the States," Joel explained, unsure whether or

not the man was putting him on. "The Confederacy . . . and the Federals . . ."

"Oh. Seems I heard tell of it. Are folks still a'carryin' on?"

"No . . ." Joel replied, amazed because he realized the black man was serious.

"Who won?"

"Old-timer, where have you been?"

"Out here," Priam said with a wave of his hand that included the timeless reaches of the prairie and the distant mountains jagged against a shredded line of clouds in a sky limitless as dreams.

"Never mind," Joel sighed. "What I meant was I figured you for a freed man."

Priam swung around and leaned his wrinkled war map of a face close to Joel's.

"I am free, younker. I freed myself, long, long ago."

Just an old colored man in baggy buckskins. A runaway nigger slave with tobacco on his breath and a mouth full of cracked and yellowed teeth. *Scrawny as a scratch-farm bantam*, thought Joel, *but as dangerous as a rattler in tall grass*.

"I see," Joel said.

"No, you don't," Priam replied. "You will, though. Mark me now, you will. If you don't get yourself killed. And I'll help you to see. 'Cause I taken a liking to you, younker. And me a-sitting on back in the trees when you come a-charging out of that cave. Yessir, like ol' Silvertip his almighty self. And the way you stood up to Sacred Killer, you all busted over but ready for more. I said to myself, Priam, if they don't stretch his scalp, why there's a lad just aching to have the space between his ears a-filled with some real mountain savvy." Priam nudged his heels against the flanks of his mount, and the Indian pony started toward the water hole. "Stick with me, younker, and you'll wind up wiser than a whole tree full of owls."

"Looks like I don't have much choice," Joel called after him. He looked down at the blown-out mare beneath him. "You better drink while you can, old lady."

The mare sloughed off down the muddy slope to water and worked its way between Priam and one of the warriors,

a bandy-legged man with the curious name of Rides The
Horse.

"Be gentle with the *moehe-noha*," the brave said as Joel
drew alongside him again. He had indicated the nag. "She
must last you till we reach our people."

"I take it any easier and she'll be riding me," Joel
snapped.

"You can't be no Southern gentleman," Priam chuckled
off to one side. "If'n you refused her."

"You let me worry about my horse. She'll last. I know
animals. And she'll last. Where are we bound for anyway?"

Rides The Horse pointed toward the peaks, wreathed in
their bitter winds, lonely as the moon.

"She'll last," Joel repeated. And beneath his breath
gulped, "I think."

Rides The Horse had exaggerated. They rode not to the peaks
themselves but to the lesser forest-covered mountains that
were the apronlike boundaries of the Absarokas. In the dying
light of the fourth day of their journey, the war party entered
the broad green valley of the Stillwater. Ahead, more than a
hundred and fifty tepees were gathered in a great circle by
the river bank. Several of the Red Shield warriors galloped
on ahead, charging into camp and shouting *e-naho-me-a*.
"She is found."

As excitement swept through the sprawling camp, men,
women, and children thronged toward the center of the site.
The lodges of the Cheyenne were gathered in a circle like a
great wheel at the hub of which was Crazy Bear's tepee. It
was to the hub the people came, waving blankets, firing rifles
into the air, the smaller children leaping and laughing, excited at being spared their usual bedtime.

Sacred Killer watched from the trees. Three of his braves
remained at his side. Behind them sat Mourning Dove astride
her horse and next to her Joel and Priam. Joel had given up
trying to elicit a response from the Cheyenne woman. No
longer did he attempt to attract her attention; rather, the white
man waited close at hand, lost in a cool detachment all his
own.

So he was caught off guard as Sacred Killer motioned

them forward, and Hemené, the Mourning Dove, when her brother wasn't looking, reached over and touched Joel on the arm. He stared at her, his resolve melting before her fawnlike gaze. She hurried then to join her brother lest he notice her unusual behavior.

"Know now what my first lesson is gonna be," Priam wryly observed, watching the silent interchange between the white man and Sacred Killer's sister. "How to stay out of trouble."

Joel ignored him.

Down into the happy commotion they rode and through the encampment from the rim of the "wheel" to the center. Joel was more than aware of the attention he received from warriors who in the midst of their cheering, paused to glare at him, uncertain as to the role he had played in Mourning Dove's abduction.

"Hey," he shouted back to Priam. "What if they get the idea I took the girl?"

"Be ready to duck," the Negro trapper called back. Joel muttered a curse and began to scrutinize the crowd with an eye toward self-protection.

The air was redolent with the smell of cooking meat. The aroma blended with the clean fresh fragrance of the valley and set Joel's stomach growling with hunger. Night had flung its tapestry of stars across the sky when the war party came to a large tepee decorated with scenes of battle and hunting as well as the Morning Star. The Morning Star symbol was evident everywhere, not only on the lodges but worked into the buckskin costumes of the people themselves. A venerable gray-haired man stood before the tepee and waited while the noisy and exuberant welcome slowly subsided. "Crazy Bear," Priam whispered to Joel.

"*Haa-he*," Crazy Bear said, lifting his palm upward to Sacred Killer who dismounted. Hemené followed suit. Only Priam and Joel remained on horseback.

"*Haa-he*, Old Father," Sacred Killer said. "It has been a good hunt."

"I see you have brought much game," Crazy Bear chuckled. "She is safe?"

Sacred Killer nodded.

"It is good," Crazy Bear said. And louder, so that all might hear, he cried out in a voice that in his youth had rung with energy and now betrayed his frail state. Yet the people reacted as if he had bellowed like a God.

"The All-Father has returned Mourning Dove to her people."

The outpouring of sentiment rose to a deafening clamor. Crazy Bear walked up to Hemené and put his arms around her. Then his eyes stopped on Joel. He looked questioningly at Sacred Killer who shook his head no—this was not the one who had taken Hemené.

"He is my guest," Sacred Killer said. "There is much to tell."

"There is much to tell," Crazy Bear conceded.

Priam, who had been translating in a whisper, now motioned for Joel to dismount with him. Joel watched as the chief and the black man embraced. They appeared to be the same age, and Joel could not help but picture them in their youth, two rough and tumble companions looking for trouble.

"Pri-am," the chief said in Cheyenne, "did you teach my braves that an old dog may still catch a young rabbit?"

"I tried," Priam grinned. "Our ears grow deaf, but it is the young who lose their hearing."

"It is the way. There were times we did not listen as well, my friend."

"Wish they were still here," Priam said.

"They are," Crazy Bear said and pointed to his heart and then his head. Priam smiled in agreement.

"This ve-ho-e," Crazy Bear said. Although Joel could understand little of the Cheyenne, he did recognize the term for white man and knew the chief was discussing him. "I do not understand," said Crazy Bear.

"Sacred Killer will explain. He is a friend. He saved the life of Hemené."

"More and more I learn and am confused. I must hear this tale from Sacred Killer. If the ve-ho-e is indeed a friend, it would be best if you took him to your lodge for the night. Until all learn he is not an enemy."

"*E-peva-e.* It is good," Priam agreed.

Priam turned to Joel who was obviously uneasy amidst such a great host of hostile-looking braves.

"Come with me."

"Where?"

"We're going to have our own celebration," Priam explained. "The less you're seen, the less chance there is of you getting your skull split by some buck with a tomahawk."

"I thought I was a friend," Joel said, keeping in step with Priam as the gathering of Cheyenne parted to let them pass.

"You are. But it's gonna take some getting used to on their part."

Joel looked around at the braves. They were making no effort to hide their intentions toward him. One particularly sour individual gestured toward him with his scalping knife.

"Mine too," Joel added.

Near the outer edge of the circle they stopped before a tepee that Priam indicated was his. Joel noticed a separate cluster of lodges off to one side of the main camp.

"What's that?" Joel asked.

"Red Shields. Their society lives apart from the rest of the camp. Don't ask me why. Just the way things are done. The Red Shield warriors are sort of the elite. But there's other soldier clans—the Dog Soldiers, the Fox Soldiers— and each has got their own set of rules."

"The women live there too?" Joel tried to make it sound like an innocent question. He could feel Priam studying him sharply.

"Men, women, children . . . brothers and sisters," Priam replied pointedly.

Back toward the center of the camp, the drums had begun to beat out hypnotic rhythms, and a chorus of chanting voices filled the night.

The festivities were still going strong hours later when the bottle of rye whiskey Priam had fished from his gear sat empty between the two men's bedrolls and the rawhide walls of the tepee's interior grew blurred to their vision. Joel listened to the celebration, amazed it should have continued so long into the night. He kicked off the remainder of his ragged clothes and crawled beneath his blanket.

"They must really think of her as someone special," he said, folding his hands behind his head, every muscle in his body relaxed as he drifted off to sleep.

Priam, across from him, snorted a moment, then cleared his throat.

"Woulda been the same hoopla over any of 'em," he said. "They're all special to each other. It's the way of the Morning Star People."

He rolled over on his side and began to snore. Joel stared at his arm. Funny . . . he could still feel the warm pressure of her hand.

"The Morning Star People," he softly said.

And slept.

8

Joel watched her from hiding, watched as she crept to the river and slipped the buckskin smock from her shoulders. Her hips were smooth and golden, and when she turned, her long black hair covered small rounded breasts. Hemené turned and looked directly at Joel, and Joel blushed, knowing he had been discovered. But she seemed not to care; instead, she raised a hand and motioned for him to join her. And unable to resist his own desire he walked from his hiding place . . .

Joel blinked his eyes. An inch-long tear in the tepee wall admitted a single beam of light that angled as the sun rose and centered for a brief moment over his left eye. He blinked awake and moved his head, angry that he had lost the dream. It took a moment, then Joel gradually became aware that he was no longer beneath his blanket but lying naked and very aroused, which would not have mattered were it not for the roly-poly squaw kneeling next to him. Her round face split in a wide smile revealing a crescent of stained teeth. She obviously approved of his physique and gave him a rather lascivious wink while she clucked good-naturedly in Cheyenne.

With a shout, Joel grabbed for his blanket, and the squaw beat a hasty retreat toward Priam, who sat up and reached for a nearby tomahawk at the sound of Joel's outcry. When the smoke of his own dreams cleared, the Negro glared at the white man.

"Is that the way you folks wake up back in civilized-ashun?"

"Sorry," Joel said. "She was—uh—I mean—what the devil is she doing in here?"

"This is Shell Woman," Priam explained. "She lives here.

With me. She sort of . . . takes care of things." Priam decided
against elaboration. Shell Woman whispered in his ear and
giggled softly. Priam looked over at Joel and chuckled. Joel
refused to meet his gaze and went to work trying to pull on
his trousers while remaining beneath the blanket.

"Ain't much call for modesty, younker. Shell Woman's
old enough to have seen it all."

"I can imagine."

Shell Woman spoke again, and Joel recognized another
word, Nahkohe, which he remembered Sacred Killer had
taken to calling him. "What now?"

"Oh, Shell Woman's just saying she has seen for herself
why you are called Nahkohe, the silvertip grizzly bear. And
I don't think she's meaning your hair."

"Oh Lord," Joel groaned, blushing. He pulled on his
threadbare gray tunic and squirmed into his boots. Shell
Woman was speaking again, and having no desire to learn
what she was saying, he crawled out through the front flap
of the tepee. Joel walked out a few paces and stretched.
Slowly turning on his heels he took his first look at the village in daylight. Priam's horse and the nag were gone, but
ground-tethered to one side was a powerfully built
Appaloosa stallion that appeared to ignore the white man for
the outcropping of sweet grass close by. Joel wondered who
owned such a magnificent animal. No one else was about as
far as he could tell, and he decided the camp was sleeping
late after the night's festivities. Even the mongrel dogs that
migrated with the tribe were curled up like brown bundles
of fur someone had scattered throughout the camp. Irish-
green meadow, twinkling ice-blue ribbon of water dividing
the quiet hills, riverbanks crowded with cattails and pink-
tipped sagittaria. Beyond the river, the sentinel pines grew
in thick profusion, as if marching from the gentle slopes to
the humpbacked ridges a thousand feet above. Minutes
passed and Joel listened and looked and drank it all in. He
breathed deeply and smelled the sweet grass and decaying
pine needles, the cool fragrance of the Stillwater lapping at
its boundaries, woodsmoke and now, as the camp came
awake, cooking meat—all the subtle scents of life, all blend-

ing into one rich tapestry of man and animal and world made one, an odor of sanctity.

Smoke drifted in lazy streamers from the lodge poles; embers were stirred, and live coals were gathered to carry outside, as more women emerged to tend to their cookfires. Every second or third dwelling appeared to have its own cooking site consisting of a circle of stones and a black smudge that indicated where the meals were prepared. Joel recognized racks for tanning, several of which were draped with elk, antelope, and buffalo hides. From other racks dangled strips of meat drying for jerky or for making pemmican, a mixture of pounded meat and berries that Joel had tasted and appreciated during the ride to the valley of the Stillwater. There were posts on which porcupine quills soaked in a yellow dye held an abundance of war shields adorned with the Morning Star. Bows and quivers of arrows and lances were stacked outside each tepee. It appeared rifles were too valuable to leave out for the elements and had been carried inside. As the camp came awake, Joel heard singing, a kind of keening wail that lingered on the wind and set the hairs on his neck prickling. The voice grew soft, then forceful again. It came from the forested slope, and after a moment of searching, Joel made out a figure hidden in the shade of the pines, an old man standing before a hut of pine boughs and young saplings cut and woven into a dwelling place.

Priam stumped out of the tepee, rubbed his eyes with the back of his hand, and spat a mouthful of phlegm off to one side.

"Damn whiskey always leaves a taste in my mouth like I been drinking rattlesnake venom."

"I think we were," Joel replied. He nodded toward the singer in the woods. "Who's that?"

"*Maomé.* Ice, in our lingo. He's a priest. He is big magic."

"He puts on a good show. I thought someone was dying out there."

"Don't take him lightly."

"You really believe such mumbo-jumbo?"

"I believe what I see," Priam replied, cutting him off.

Joel understood and dropped the subject. By now the camp was bustling with activity. The squaws were tending to cookfires or grinding meal for fry bread. The braves had begun to show themselves. Several young men ran in a group down to the riverbank and plunged themselves into the chill waters. Some even went so far as to purge their stomachs before cleansing their bodies. Joel noticed a number of other warriors had gathered in enclaves, and he had the distinct impression that his presence was the topic of conversation. He looked over at the separate encampment of the Red Shields and was rewarded with a glimpse of Hemené who appeared outside her brother's tepee and, in the midst of gathering branches for a fire, paused to look up and meet Joel's gaze. Sacred Killer emerged from the front flap, and Mourning Dove quickly lowered her eyes.

"Shell Woman told me he left the Appaloose for you."

"What?"

"The stallion. Sacred Killer left it last night as a gift for you."

Joel turned to look at the Appaloosa again with renewed appreciation.

"One thing to know about an Injun pony—" Priam began.

"My father raised horses," Joel interrupted. "I know horses, old man." Joel brushed past the Negro and freed the animal's horsehair reins. Another loop of braided rope circled the stallion's belly, providing something for a man to grip his fingers around.

"And *this* is a fine animal," Joel proclaimed, crossing in front of the Appaloosa who had begun to eye the white man with suspicion. The stallion tried backing away, but Joel kept a firm grip on the reins and moving to the left leaped astride the horse.

"Easy as falling off a lo—" Joel never got to complete the sentence. There came an earthquake that began and ended in the Appaloosa. The horse whinnied in terror, bolted forward, lurched to a sickening stop, then bowed its back and leaped into the air, landed with a jolt, bucking and bowing its back, kicking first with the front legs then with the back. As the hooves glanced off the ground, clods of dirt and stone shot away in every direction. Joel grabbed for the belly rope as his feet flew up and out. His grip was loosening, the fingers one by one slipping free. His torso twisted in the saddle, and he experienced the sickening sensation of being airborne as the frightened stallion shot past tepees and squalling children and braves that dived out of harm's way.

"Oh no," Joel shouted. Where were the reins? Reins hell, where was the bellyrope? Rope hell, where was the horse! Head over heels overhead, tumbling and tumbling . . .

He smashed through a stretched deer hide, demolished the frame, and landed spread-eagle, flat on his back in the middle of the camp. The horse continued to buck until a few of the braves caught the reins and dragged the stallion to a standstill by holding the animal's head down.

Joel groaned, gulped air, and watched the pinprick of light before his eyes inflate to become the daylit world. A circle of children's faces looked down at him, laughing. Among the young, a grizzled visage appeared. Joel blinked, and as his vision returned, he saw it was Priam. The Negro was doubled over with laughter. He clutched his sides and laughed as hard as the children.

Joel tried to stand, slipped, and sat once more in the dirt to the delight of the onlookers. The black man held out a hand, and Joel grasped it. The old man hoisted Joel to his feet in an exhibition of steely strength. Joel glanced about and grimaced as a glob of dirt worked its way down the inside of his shirt. Not only were the children laughing but the women and men as well. Everyone, it seemed, was having a good time at his expense.

"What I was trying to tell you is that an Injun pony sort of has to get worked up to lettin' a white man ride him. I reckon he just can't stand the smell," Priam explained.

"Thanks," Joel growled. He noticed Sacred Killer approaching. The war chief of the Red Shields was leading the stallion through the delighted gathering.

"Perhaps I should have brought Silvertip an offering of honey or a nest of fat grubs to eat, instead of this fine horse."

"Or fish from the river," Rides The Horse called out. Everyone enjoyed the remark. And Priam went out of his way to translate for Joel.

Sacred Killer held out the reins to the Kentuckian.

"But no, this is my gift to you, Nahkohe. Wait many

moons until this Appaloosa grows old and tired, and then you will be able to ride it where you wish."

Joel accepted the reins. He looked long and hard at Sacred Killer whose eyes never wavered, whose chiseled features betrayed only haughty amusement.

"Tell your people to stand back," Joel said.

The crowd sensed what was about to happen. They needed no command to disperse as Joel stood alongside the Appaloosa and prepared to mount. He searched the audience of warriors and their women and lighted upon Mourning Dove who watched from the edge of the crowd, her delicate beauty dark with concern.

He reached out to stroke the stallion's charcoal-colored mane. "I'm expecting the worst out of you, boy. Don't let me down."

The Appaloosa didn't. The moment Joel's weight hit his back, the animal shot upward and hit, running. As screams of excitement filled the air, Joel swung his weight to the right and yanked out the reins. The horse swung in that direction on reflex and charged full tilt into the river. Water showered upwards, concealing horse and rider as the gallant animal plunged and kicked, fighting both the rider and the dragging depths of the river. Joel gripped with his legs, holding on for dear life. He rode the animal's frenzy and let him wear himself out in the river. At last the Appaloosa fought its way onto dry land and, in an outburst of renewed energy, raced back into camp. Joel caught a glimpse of faces streaming past, thought he heard Priam cheer him on. "Stay with him, younker, stay with him."

The stallion was airborne again, and Joel almost lost his purchase. His head whipped forward and back, and his spine popped, sending a spasm of pain shooting up his shoulder blades, but he stayed aboard, and when the Appaloosa touched earth and rocketed off at a full gallop, it was with the white man still astride and exhorting the stallion to greater efforts.

As they rushed past, Hemené, breathless with excitement, called out to Joel and then looked about in horror that anyone should have noticed her. She saw her brother with a curious expression on his face. Had he heard? Hemené blushed beneath his scrutiny. She turned and followed the men and women around her who were watching horse and rider disappear in the distance. Then with sinking heart she wondered if such had been Sacred Killer's intention, to provide the white man with the means to escape. Hemené could tell an uneasiness was creeping through the Cheyenne; warriors began heading for their tepees to gather weapons and give pursuit while others looked to Sacred Killer or Crazy Bear who had watched from a safe distance, for a sign that either a guest had left and that was the end of it or a prisoner had escaped and they should take up the chase.

Minute after agonizing minute sloughed past. Then Tall Wolf, a warrior who had run to the edge of camp, gave a startled cry, and Hemené strained to hear and see, not daring to hope, as the cry was repeated and washed over the Cheyenne camp like a summer wind. Silvertip was returning. *Is this not a man of courage? And look, there, how the stallion walks, now trots to his command. Is not such a ride worthy of a song? Worthy of our own warriors?* The children began to laugh and play and mimic the ride. The warriors who had claimed that this Nahkohe was an enemy who had escaped and would surely bring an army of white soldiers to the valley now slunk back to join ranks with the other bucks.

The Cheyenne stepped aside to form an aisle down which Joel walked the Appaloosa until he reached the end where Sacred Killer stood with folded arms. Joel jumped down from horseback and patted the stallion's neck.

"It is indeed a fine gift, Sacred Killer. I am shamed though, for I have nothing to give you in return."

Crazy Bear worked his way forward to join the two men, the crowd parted to let him through.

"Silvertip," he called out. "Why did you come back? The stallion is swift of foot. I think none here could have caught you." Priam translated the chief's words. Joel looked from him to Priam and then to the brother of Mourning Dove.

"Tell the chief I could not leave without having breakfast with Sacred Killer, my friend." Priam groaned but did as Joel asked. Crazy Bear chuckled, and shook his head.

"It is well," he said and turned to leave. His departure served as an unspoken command to the others. The crowd broke apart as families returned to their lodges, still talking of the ride.

Sacred Killer waited until they were alone before speaking. Mourning Dove had drawn close, and she stood dutifully to one side stealing looks at Joel, taking care lest the white man or Sacred Killer notice her interest.

"Nahkohe is worthy of the horse," Sacred Killer conceded. He fixed his attention on Hemené. "My sister has been gone so long she has forgotten how to make a fire and fry the morning bread. But then she is only a little sister and cannot be expected to prepare a meal for a guest or invite her own brother to her cooking pot."

Mourning Dove sucked in her breath and glared in playful anger at her brother.

"Saaa!" she hissed. *"He-mesehe!"* She darted off to the camp of the Red Shields.

Joel glanced quizzically toward Priam.

"Come eat," the Negro translated. "I assume you were talking straight about staying for breakfast?"

"I'd like to stay," Joel said, watching the woman's lithe form bound across the trampled grass. He was oblivious to Sacred Killer's worried expression. His attention was fixed on Mourning Dove and the remnants of a dream that lingered in the mind.

Deep in the woods, the keening wail of the medicine man echoed in the stillness.

9

A day became two days, a week's procrastination led to another. Joel found excuses to remain. Priam's tutelage, a desire to become better acquainted with the Cheyenne language—he never admitted the true reason to Priam or himself because it struck him as hopelessly incredible. And then just incredible but perhaps not hopeless. He planned "accidental" encounters in the village. He watched from afar while she washed her hair at the river. Often he would spy her standing apart from the other women, gathering roots and medicinal herbs, seeming lost in her own thoughts.

Hemené was aware of his presence. And once riding past, he paused astride the Appaloosa, and she looked up from her work, the tall grass matted beneath her bare knees, a smudge of dirt upon her cheek. She smiled in the demure manner of a flirtatious maiden. For a maddeningly brief second their eyes met. How little to hang a dream on, yet Joel was certain he had read in the copper oval of her face the same unsettling desire that haunted him.

From Priam, Joel Ryan had learned that the Cheyenne, though talking of war with the whites, wanted most of all to be left alone, to live their lives without the interference of the United States Army or the hordes of fortune seekers whose greedy paths led north—north to the mountains, north to the hunting grounds of the Cheyenne.

Joel's handling of the Appaloosa had won the grudging admiration of the braves in camp and, more important, a general acceptance. Priam had told Sacred Killer of the great war in the east. The Negro mountain man explained how Joel also had been the enemy of the bluecoats, how his people had lost their war, and how Joel had been left without a homeland. The Cheyenne saw the resemblance between their own state of affairs and Joel's fate. This along with Nah-kohe's prowess with the Appaloosa sealed his welcome. Priam took great enjoyment in telling Joel he was free to come and go as he pleased. The old man, eyes a-twinkle, had emphasized "go," as if knowing Joel had more on his mind than goldfields.

The eastern horizon blushed pink above the hills when Rides The Horse knelt before Priam's tepee.

"Nahkohe," the bandy-legged Cheyenne softly called. Joel poked his head out from the tepee, disappeared inside, then emerged with his knife, revolver, and the Hawken which had once belonged to Larocque. Sacred Killer had declared the weapon spoils of war and instructed it to be sent to Silvertip who had wounded the Frenchman.

"Hurry, Silvertip. The honey trees will all be robbed and the choice grubs eaten," Rides The Horse grinned.

"I hope your rifle shoots as straight as your cleverness," Joel replied, reaching for the reins of his stallion. Joel tow-ered over Rides The Horse as they walked through the camp. Near the bank of the Stillwater two other braves awaited them, Tall Bull and White Frog. Tall Bull was not tall, but he looked as strong as a bull. His features shrouded by his black hair betrayed neither animosity nor affection. White Frog was a much more jovial fellow. He was ill propor-tioned, with an elongated upper torso, but his arms were thickly muscled, and astride his horse, he was more than a match for most men. He was the prankster of the camp and always took the role of the mischievous spirit during the ceremonial dances.

Tall Bull nodded as Joel and Rides The Horse approached and walked his horse into the river.

"We will visit Maomé. He will make magic for us that the antelope will be slow of foot and the buffalo willing to give us his life," said Rides The Horse.

"I have all the magic I need in this Hawken," Joel said.

Rides The Horse stared at him as if the white man were utterly devoid of sense.

"I suppose you can't have too much magic," Joel stut-tered. He had no business treading on their religion, even if it meant hogwash to him. He motioned for Rides The Horse to lead the way, and with Joel last in line, the four crossed the river. Joel gasped as the icy current billowed around his waist. Keeping his rifle above water and with a firm grip on the stallion's mane he made the crossing and stumbled onto the opposite bank seconds after Rides The Horse and the others. They walked their mounts to the edge of the forest. Tall Bull skirted around a stand of aspen, his high-stepping sorrel fighting the reins.

The medicine man's lodge was constructed of hide and interwoven branches, unlike the conical-shaped tepees that made up the Cheyenne village, and loomed out of the dark woods as the braves approached in silence. Joel sensed an otherworldliness to the place, a feeling he immediately attributed to the early morning stillness.

The braves dismounted. Joel followed suit and stood with his Indian companions before the entrance to the hut.

Joel wrinkled his nose and sniffed an odor of burning pine bark and a subtler perfume of alpine flowers. An eerie silence clung to the place as if the sounds of the world, the rustling of branches or the music of the river, could not penetrate the area around the hut of Maomé.

"Grandfather," Tall Bull called. "We have come that you might make your magic and assure us of a good hunt."

"I know why you are here." A high-pitched voice issued from the hut. "You have come to disturb an old man's sleep."

"Grandfather, forgive us. But the antelope drink at first light, and we must hurry," Rides The Horse said.

"The magic I make will bring the antelope to you whether it is first light or brightest noon. Must I be shamed as well as awakened?" The voice croaked, drifting out from the hut in a flow of brittle phrases. The braves glanced at one another.

Just as I thought, Joel said to himself. He understood enough of the speech to gather the old man was being cantankerous.

"Grandfather, the children will go hungry if our hunt is unsuccessful," Rides The Horse said.

"And will you not feel shame then, because you did not help us?" White Frog added.

"I never said I would not help you," the voice cackled behind them. Joel spun around in time to see a humpbacked wizened shape step from the shadows into the gray light. His features were as wrinkled and knobby as the badlands, a tableau of folds and furrows surrounding eyes, pocked nose, and crooked mouth. Maomé thrust his homely visage toward Joel, studying the white man for a moment.

"So this is Nahkohe."

Joel shuddered inwardly. There was no possible way in which the medicine man could have crept from the hut and circled behind them. Why the old man could barely hobble about.

Then how had he managed this feat?

Joel's mind recoiled in disbelief. There was a sensation in his skull as if his brain were being probed by something . . . cold. Chilling. In that moment he remembered what Priam had told him. "Maomé" was the Cheyenne word for ice. The medicine man drew a pouch from his loose-fitting buckskin shirt. He smiled, revealing mottled pink gums in a toothless mouth.

"Hand me your rifle, Silvertip," the medicine man said. He held out his hand. Joel understood the gesture and hefted the heavy rifle by the stock. He gave it to Maomé who rested it butt first on the ground. From the pouch he took a pinch of sweet-smelling gray powder and dusted the sights and the muzzle of the barrel, then Joel himself, smearing the gray dust on the Kentuckian's shoulders, face, and legs. Joel glanced over at Rides The Horse who stood to one side, reverent and calmly waiting his turn.

"I know you," Maomé said in English to Joel. "Now your gun will shoot straight. Your limbs will have strength. And you will see with clear eyes. You are Silvertip. And you think you have found peace. You have. And you have not."

Then Maomé hobbled over to the Appaloosa. To Joel's surprise, the stallion dutifully allowed the old man to approach and dust each of the animal's hooves with the gray powder.

Maomé spoke, and the animal lowered his head for the medicine man to blow a faint cloud of the gray powder into the stallion's ears.

Maomé continued on to the other warriors and repeated the process, anointing them and then their horses with the dust. Joel waited in uneasy silence. He had never spoken to the old man before nor had he confided to Priam or anyone else his desire to remain in the camp, much less the turbulent emotions that coursed through him whenever he caught sight of Mourning Dove.

Had Maomé read his mind? Or worse, his heart?

Impossible!

Joel tried to take comfort in his own reasoning. But there was small refuge to be found there.

Reason failed to explain how the medicine man could have been in the thatch-roofed lodge and seconds later standing in the woods behind them.

"Thank you, Grandfather. We will bring you the choicest cuts from our kill," Tall Bull said.

Maomé waved them away and hobbled toward his dwelling. The braves mounted and rode from the clearing. As Joel swung up astride the Appaloosa, Maomé turned and looked directly at him. Joel walked his horse toward the medicine man. The horizon had changed from pink to molten gold, casting the eastern ridge in stark, jagged relief. The dawn played havoc with the shadows, fabricating shapes out of thin air, obscuring what was real. Joel rubbed his eyes. The medicine man seemed to be standing in a haze that flowed and coiled and covered the aged one from his gray hair to his moccasins. Maomé reached up to stroke the single amulet about his throat, a patch of leather adorned with a black Morning Star against a background of white beads. Other than this and the pouch of gray dust, the hunchback offered a wholly unremarkable sight. Just a ragged old man in a lonely place. Maomé grinned as if reading Joel's evaluation of him. Joel turned his horse toward the trail the others had taken. When he glanced back over his shoulder, the medicine man was gone. Nothing moved except a lizard scurrying through the leaves, and it paused to lift its brown-speckled, scaly head to study Joel. The Kentuckian decided against returning to the lodge. He did not want to discover if it was empty.

He did not want to know.

· · ·

Tall Bull had ridden on ahead, maintaining an aloof distance
from the others. He seemed particularly to bristle at Joel's
presence throughout the morning. As the sun blazed its fiery
path toward noon, Joel, Rides The Horse, and White Frog
paused atop the rocky silence of a granite ridge overlooking
a broad expanse of buffalo grass that covered the park below.
The Absarokas reigned in purple and windswept majesty,
blotting out the western horizon.

Cloud shadows skimmed over the rippling grass, crept up
the timbered slope toward the men on the ridge. So far the
hunt had been unsuccessful. Joel found the view impressive
but beauty never filled a stomach. "Hadn't we . . ." he began,
but Rides The Horse motioned him to silence. He and White
Frog continued to watch the meadow. Joel waited, chafing
to be on with the hunt. Minutes crawled past. Mourning
Dove came to mind, her features as easy to recall as his own
name. He wrestled with the problem of how to catch her
alone, realizing in the same instant that finding her alone was
not the problem. The opportunity had presented itself more
than once, but he had lacked the courage to follow through.
Was he afraid he had misinterpreted her affections? It was a
far easier task to face bullets than rejection. And of the two,
he wondered which offered the cruelest wound.

"Now," White Frog suddenly whispered, pointing toward
a wisp of dust in the distance. Joel glanced southward, curious as to the source of the dust. His questions were answered a quarter of an hour later as a herd of wild mustangs
emerged out of the sun-washed reaches to race the wind
across the glimmering landscape. Joel lost count of the mares
and colts making up the herd. But they were led by a powerfully built black stallion that thundered past the hunting
party's vantage point. Obscured in a sudden swirl of dust,
the herd continued on up the valley, running for the sheer
exhilaration of it. Manes streaming behind like banners, their
pounding hooves echoed like a cannonade long after the herd
had vanished from sight.

"Tall Bull will be watching," White Frog chuckled.

"That is all he will be doing," Rides The Horse grinned. He looked at Joel and explained.

"Tall Bull is a great hunter. His *amesto-ee-seo*"—Rides The Horse mimed the word, and Joel recognized a travois—"is always heavy with meat from the kill. But he has no luck with horses. I have seen him follow such a herd many times, but only once has the All-Father allowed him to capture a single mare."

"And without horses he can never approach the lodge of Sacred Killer," White Frog interjected.

"Why should he go to Sacred Killer?" Joel asked, an unsettling sensation ripping at his thoughts.

"Why, to take Mourning Dove as his woman. Everyone knows this is in his mind," Rides The Horse said.

"Everyone but Mourning Dove," White Frog added. "Poor Tall Bull, it will take many horses to gain the approval of Sacred Killer. Come, let us find our brother. Perhaps he has found a nice fat buffalo cow."

Joel walked with his companions back to their horses. He looked over his shoulder at the plume of dust dissipating above the northern reaches of the plain.

A smart man would track that herd and figure out the right spot to intercept them and cull the black stallion's harem.

A man, Joel confidently reflected, like me.

He leaped astride the Appaloosa, a buoyancy in his motions that had not been there before. When he laughed out loud, Rides The Horse cast a sidelong look in his direction.

"Silvertip. What mood has come upon you?"

"Horses for a bride. Sounds like a good way of doing things," he replied.

"Yes. If a man has horses," said Rides The Horse.

"If, brother . . ." said Joel. "If."

Sacred Killer was in a foul mood. As was the custom of the Red Shield society, a warrior could not partake of food unless it were offered to him. And for the third morning in a row Hemené had left before inviting him to the cookfire. Had her ordeal addled her sense of responsibility? Stomach growling, Sacred Killer walked through the main camp, searching for his sister, his temperament worsening with each

step. Unable to find her, Sacred Killer headed for the lodge
of his friend, Lame Deer, a war chief of the Dog Soldier
clan. Lame Deer's wife, Red Bead Woman, had long been a
friend to Hemené.

Red Bead Woman was the same age as Hemené, but she
had been married almost a year, a fact Sacred Killer had
often pointed out to his sister. Though Red Bead Woman's
belly was swollen with child, pregnancy in no way kept her
from her chores. She was sitting on a log stool outside her
tepee, busily scraping a buffalo hide to be used for bedding.
Now and then she would pause in her work to gather the
hide shavings and drop them into a pot of boiling water.
Lame Deer was a man several years older than Sacred Killer.
He had lost his first wife to the same "spotted sickness" that
had once decimated the tribe. Sacred Killer's parents had also
died during the smallpox epidemic. Lame Deer glanced up
from his work. The father-to-be was laboring over a bow.
With the ease of many years of practice, he fastened together
strips of elk horn, binding them with sinew, next he rubbed
the bound strips of horn with glue that Red Bead Woman
had made by boiling the shavings of buffalo hide. Lame Deer
set aside his work as Sacred Killer approached. The Dog
Soldier knew anger when he saw it, and he wondered what
had put his friend in such a dark mood.

"*Pave-eseeva,* my brother," Lame Deer said, wishing Sacred Killer a good day.

"I have come to speak with your wife," Sacred Killer
explained. "Perhaps she will tell me where to look for my
sister."

"Ah. Those two. Their thoughts are often the same, your
good sister and my wife. They know when one is about to
visit the other. If one is ill, the other brews medicine in the
same moment. The older I grow the less I understand how
this can be. It is worse for you." Lame Deer tried to hide his
grin. The urge to bait his friend was simply too great. "I may
one day grow in understanding because I take a wife and, in
living with her, learn the cause of her moods and the matter
of her thinking. You wifeless men of the Red Shields must
remain in ignorance. So it is said that the Dog Soldiers are
first in wisdom among the warriors of the Cheyenne." Lame

Deer leaned against his backrest and crossed his arms in an attitude of smug defiance.

"And the Red Shields first in battle," Sacred Killer replied, "which is the proper place for a warrior."

Lame Deer chuckled. "You have counted coup upon me. Yet I am glad I was not given the vision of the Red Shield. A wife is great comfort, and the prospect of a son, even more. Talk to Red Bead Woman, then, for I have more important things to attend to, like a bow for my young warrior."

"Better turn your efforts to a doll and cradle," Sacred Killer chided. "One so wise in the ways of women will surely father a daughter to comfort him in his old age."

Lame Deer scowled and continued his bow making.

Red Bead Woman had listened to their conversation but, of course, did not display her feelings in the matter. Rather she pretended surprise when Sacred Killer stood before her, as if he had just arrived.

"You honor our lodge," she said.

"Red Bead Woman, you and my sister played together as children, as maidens were seldom seen one without the other. When she was stolen, you grieved more than anyone, and when she returned to us, your voice led all others in singing your happiness. My sister leaves my lodge early in the morning, today before I was even awake. There is much mystery here. I question Hemené when she returns, and she says she has been root gathering, but her basket is empty, or she has been bathing, but her hair is dry. Where does she go?"

"Perhaps it is as she says," Red Bead Woman replied, unable to meet his gaze. She bit at her lower lip and seemed to shrink from Sacred Killer toward her husband.

"Wife . . ." Lame Deer cautioned in a gentle but firm voice.

"And perhaps it is not," Red Bead Woman stammered. "And if that were so, then she might be back in the forest at the place of sidehill water where the young girls play."

Red Bead Woman resumed her work with a vengeance. The bone scraper sent curls of hide shavings to flutter into the pile at her feet. Sacred Killer, thoroughly puzzled by Red Bead Woman's reticence to speak further, not to mention Hemené's behavior, resolved to find an explanation. Hunger aside, he was determined to discover the meaning behind her actions. He did not wish to be wise in the ways of all women, just one. Just his sister. That would be enough.

Mourning Dove looked up from her handiwork to stare almost longingly at the young girls playing around the spring. The icy water sprang from the earth in a hillside glade and cut a narrow furrow that undulated out of the forest and down to the Stillwater. Leaning against a fallen tree trunk, Hemené daydreamed of such innocent days when she too had followed her friends to this spot and drunk of the clear cold water, and played games, or talked, or pretended to be wives and mothers or animals or mystical figures from legend. Above the glade and safely out of sight, she watched the children and smiled with the notion that some things never changed—games and laughter and pretending. She marveled at how a child's thoughts ran clear and smooth as the Stillwater itself, unworried and reflecting all that it sees. But she was no longer a child; now her thoughts were like the river during a storm when the waters are churned by the wind and rain, left unsettled and unsure of their course, and plunge over the bank to crash against the hills. She returned her attention to the rawhide shirt she held, the product of her skill with quill and sinew. She threaded another bead and stitched it into the sign of the Morning Star taking shape on the chest. The laughter of children faded before a different excitement, for as she worked, she reached into memory for the moment in the cave when Joel had put his lips to hers and his strong body had crushed her to the earth. What she had felt in that instant she had kept to herself and confided in no one, which in itself was characteristic of awakened desire and more—the devilish uncertainty of first love.

"Sister."

Sacred Killer's voice jolted her into reality. She gasped, clutching the shirt to her bosom as he squatted beside her. She started to ask how he had found her, but she could find no words to speak. His angry expression softened, becoming inquisitive as he reached out to touch the fringed buckskin shirt she held.

"Twice have warriors brought horses to my lodge. Twice

I have accepted the tribute only to have you refuse to take these warriors to husband."

"Spotted Wolf is bad tempered. High Walker was too old."

"They are good men. And my heart was heavy to see you choose to remain a maiden. You are all the family I have, Hemené. It is through you I will see sons and daughters and know the pride of a father though I may never take a wife. The way of the Red Shield is harsh. And lonely, Hemené. I came here angry. But I find you doing a strange thing. Leaving the morning cookfire to come here and make a fine shirt. These are the actions of a woman who has seen a man to her liking. My heart is happy. Tell me who he is, and I will send a little bird to whisper in his ear that he might bring horses to my lodge."

Sacred Killer reached out and took the brushed buckskin garment. How reluctantly her fingers let the material slip free. Sacred Killer held it up and sighed loudly noting the beauty of the workmanship and the intricately beaded Morning Star high upon the right breast. She had used the last of her blue beads, and there would be no others, unless they came across a trader willing to chance bargaining with the Cheyenne. Here indeed was a shirt to last a man many moons and one to be worn with pride. It took a moment for the size of the shirt to sink in. Perhaps she was addled after all. For the shirt was much too large for any of the braves in the camp.

"This shirt is worthy of a great warrior, but I fear you have allowed your happiness to cloud your judgment. It is too big. Why, there is no one among our people it would fit," Sacred Killer said good-humoredly. No one so large as to comfortably wear such a shirt, he thought. Except . . .

His mood darkened, and he looked at Mourning Dove who stood facing him.

"I have made the shirt correctly. There is one who could wear it," she said.

Sacred Killer's face grew bloodless, his flesh cold as ice. There was one man in camp the buckskin shirt would fit, Nahkohe. Silvertip. The white man.

"No!"

"I have made it for him."

"No!" Sacred Killer repeated and threw the shirt down between them where it lay like a barrier. Sacred Killer turned from her and walked up the hill, deeper into the forest. He paused beside a stately pine that had weathered storm and snow and fire.

"He is brave," said Mourning Dove, following her brother.

"He is not of the People."

"He is not our enemy."

"He is not of the People!" Sacred Killer repeated. "No more of such talk. Destroy the shirt."

"I will not," Hemené said, backing away from her brother.

"You are young. You cannot mean these words. Destroy the shirt. We will never speak of this again." Sacred Killer took a step toward her and saw her retreat once more. She was frightened of him. He frowned and sadly shook his head.

"Sister . . . it must not be." He reached for her but Hemené spun away. She gathered up the shirt and darted down the slope, scattering the girls who were playing by the spring in her headlong flight back to the village by the Stillwater.

Sacred Killer, with heavy heart, watched her run from his outstretched hand.

The hunters returned at sunset, Tall Bull leading the way, announcing their success. As the women gathered for the distribution of the meat, stories circulated of how Tall Bull, White Frog, Rides The Horse, and Silvertip had tracked a herd of antelope to the upper end of the valley, to the south where the ridge swept up to bar the animal's escape. In this place the hunters struck, making kill after kill until enough game was taken to provide food for all. The hunters had built two travois to haul the dressed carcasses home. The valley was aglow with the merry light of cookfires and the aroma of sizzling steaks permeated the air. And no one mentioned that one of the hunters had been a white man.

Across the Stillwater and into the trees, Joel walked the Appaloosa. He fought his way through an eerie conflagration of fireflies that whirred and buzzed and collided against him. He rode on to the lodge of Maomé. Summoning his courage, the white man approached. A dim glow emanated from within, filtering past the entrance flap. Joel leaned forward and keeping a firm grip on the reins, lowered a packet of choice cuts of meat to the ground in front of the hut. The task accomplished, he turned the stallion about and rode back toward the Cheyenne village. Though he had not looked back, he had the distinct impression the packet had already disappeared inside the hut because this time the swarm of fireflies parted to let him pass.

Joel relaxed against the backrest and watched the coals, like molten rubies, crackle and crack asunder scattering jewels of fire against the stones. He gnawed the last pink morsel of meat from a rib and dropped it on the pile between him and Priam.

"You reckon to try for number six?" Priam asked.

"I'm full as a tick." Joel sighed and folded his hands behind his head. It was a calm and quiet summer's night. Clouds like ghostly barquentines drifted on the sky's dark sea. The stillness of the village below was the happy aftermath of a successful hunt. Proud of his part in the hunt, Joel loosened his belt to give himself some breathing room.

"Appears you got a right powerful case of self-esteem," Priam groaned, rubbing his rounded belly. He called for Shell Woman to bring him his pipe.

"I suppose so, old-timer. Between what white man's lingo White Frog and Rides The Horse have picked up and what I'm able to handle of Cheyenne, we got along pretty well." Joel spoke as Shell Woman crawled out of the lodge and bending low whispered in Priam's ear. She glanced over at Joel and then crawled back inside.

"You ain't plannin' on goin' inside any time soon?" Priam asked, downing the last of the elk mint tea Shell Woman had brewed for them. He wiped a wrinkled wrist across his mouth, winked at Joel, and looked toward the lodge. "Not that Shell Woman would mind, but she and I might keep you awake for a time."

"I haven't finished watching the stars yet," Joel said. And as Priam turned to crawl into the tent, Joel added, "Slow and easy, old-timer. Slow and easy."

"Younker," Priam retorted, looking over his shoulder, "at my age that's all there is."

Though he wanted to rest by the fire, Joel decided to allow Priam and Shell Woman an extra margin of privacy. Restless despite being tired from the day's hunt, he stood and stretched and sauntered away from the fire. He walked through the village, and without thinking, followed an aimless course that brought him to the camp of the Red Shields. He stared at the lodge of Sacred Killer. Joel knew in his heart what had led him to the lodge. His steps had brought him here on more than one occasion. A mongrel pup growled as Joel approached, and he paused in the darkness, aware he had perhaps overstepped the bounds of Sacred Killer's gratitude. The dog continued to growl, hackles rising to a ruff around its shoulders. The flap of the tent was pulled open, and Mourning Dove crawled out to toss a branch at the pup and chase it away from the tepee wall.

As she started back inside, Joel stepped into the firelight, startling the young woman. Her eyes, wide with alarm, darted to the neighboring lodges, relaxing only when she saw that no one was about. Joel waited, and sensing his unspoken invitation, Mourning Dove left her lodge and came to him.

"Bears sleep at night, Nahkohe. They find nice dry caves and curl up in their fur. Do you not know this?"

"I am a bear of a different sort," said Joel.

"You should not be here. I should not speak to you in this way," Hemené said.

"What way?"

"Someone might see us and think . . ."

"What?"

"That you have called me from my lodge, to stand with you in your blanket. It is how a young man courts the one he wishes to take to wife."

Joel was grateful for the night. She could not see him redden.

"But then you cannot know our ways. You are not Cheyenne," Hemené continued, more to herself than to him. And Joel wondered at the strange bitterness in her tone.

"Perhaps we should go where no one can see us. And then there will be no tales to tell."

"Saaaaa . . ." Mourning Dove exclaimed. "Such foolish talk. I must return to my lodge. You had better leave before my brother discovers you are here. He will return soon from council."

Joel noted she made no move of her own. Her face was tilted to him, and her hair hung in long thick braids that covered her breasts. She smelled of wood smoke and mint and an earthier fragrance he found exhilarating.

"I have thought of going," he said, studying her expression. "Not back to Priam's lodge, but west, to the mountains, to Silverbow where men dig the yellow metal from the earth."

"These white men," she scoffed. "Food from the hunt, roots to make our healing medicine, water to drink. The All-Father has given such things to us, freely. Yet the ve-ho-e dig in the earth for the yellow metal. They never have enough. And what does it bring them that my people do not already have?" Suddenly she cut short her outburst and darted behind the lodge, as a head poked out from another tepee. She grabbed Joel's arm and dragged him out of sight.

"See what you have done?" she snapped. "Leave then. Why do you even come to tell me? Do you think I would care? It does not matter to me."

"I said I had thought of going," Joel replied, aware of her hand on his arm. She drew it away as if it had touched a live coal. "But every time I get the notion, something more important keeps me from riding out." He drew close. Moonlight caught the silver of his hair and set it aglow like a tangle of gossamer threads. The young woman's heart was pounding as he towered over her and his strong hands reached out to hers. "You," he finished.

He tilted her chin, and defying every rule of her upbringing, Mourning Dove allowed him to kiss her. His arms folded around her waist and pressed her into him. They melted to each other and became a single patch of shadow among the shadows of the camp.

She heard footsteps and broke from his grasp. Joel looked up in alarm. A couple wrapped in a single blanket walked past. They were blind to everything but themselves, but the interruption allowed Mourning Dove to regain her composure.

"You can't imagine how long I've wanted to do that," Joel said.

"It must not happen again," she said in a hoarse whisper.

"I will talk to your brother."

"No. He would drive you from our village. Or worse."

"We have to tell him."

"Go, Nahkohe! I was wrong. Go to the place where the yellow metal is dug from the ground. Do not stay in this village."

"We need to talk, Hemené."

She pulled from his grasp and entered the glow of the campfires. Joel started after her, but when he rounded the lodge, he spied Sacred Killer walking with swift soundless strides toward the tepee. Joel retreated out of sight. He considered a direct confrontation, but now was not the time or place. He hurried off in the opposite direction from the lodge, keeping it between him and the war chief. He skirted the encampment and entered the village from a different direction, taking no care to hide his movements. He didn't give a damn who noticed him now.

She wants me, he thought, *as much as I want her. And nothing will keep us apart. I'll find a way. There has to be a way.*

Late that night Priam stirred, cocked an eye open, and saw that Joel's bedding had not been slept in. The Negro freed himself from Shell Woman's round meaty thighs and crawled naked to the entrance. He spied Joel sitting by the campfire, wholly absorbed in the dancing flames.

"Younker," he croaked in a sleepy voice. "You can come on in. I weren't intending you to have to sit up the whole bloomin' night. Younker . . ."

Joel continued to stare at the flames. Priam's words went unanswered, and the old man wisely returned to the warmth of his woman.

10

Morning came. With sunrise, wisps of fog like ghostly ser-pents slithered up from the Stillwater to cover the valley in forgetful mist. Through unreal beauty Joel moved with slow, measured steps, guiding the Appaloosa into the river.

Impervious to the current tugging them downstream, horse and rider crossed in the quiet morn to emerge soaked and dripping on the opposite bank. Joel dismounted and, tether-ing the Appaloosa to a pine sapling, proceeded the rest of the way on foot. Mist uncoiled and curled again, circling trees and hiding shrubs and billowed about the Kentuckian's gunbelt obscuring the white man's lower torso. The hut of Maomé loomed before him, a sentient, faintly ominous shape shrouded by the vapors. Undaunted, Joel approached the lodge and, stooping, passed through the crawl space into the dwelling place of Ice, the medicine man.

It took a moment for his eyes to adjust, and he sat still, blinking in the feeble light and listening to Maomé's chant, a softly keening song that Joel found unsettling.

Sight returned.

Joel saw walls and roof of woven branches. Gourd rattles and strips of buckskin and hide pouches hung from the low ceiling. A sharply acrid odor stung his nostrils. But all else paled before the sight of the wizened form of Maomé, sitting cross-legged against a sheep-horn backrest, eagle feathers and animal bones scattered on the earth floor near his ankles, his hands palm upward in his lap. Floating three inches above his open hands was a small round ball of wood, black with pitch and painted in zigzagging strokes of ocher and blood red.

It was all Joel could do to keep from turning tail and

running as far and as fast from the lodge as his long legs could carry him.

The voice cracked.

The song of the medicine man died in his throat. Joel gulped and rubbed his stinging eyes, and when he looked again, Maomé gripped the wood ball in his bony fingers. For a moment, he studied Joel, who was lost in his own private debate whether or not what he had seen had been an illusion. The medicine man startled him with a high-pitched cackle. He dropped the ball into the soot of the previous night's fire.

"Silvertip," he said. He leaned forward, his gray braids swinging forward. He tugged at Joel's silvering hair.

"Young face. Old hair. This is a strange sight."

"I have seen stranger things," Joel said, finding his voice. He gingerly touched the wooden ball. "Whether truth or illusion I cannot tell."

"Sometimes there is no difference. Sometimes"—and Maomé cocked an eye to stare at the white man—"it does not matter. Sometimes we must pretend to know."

Joel held the ball above the dust, dropped it. A cloud of gray ash mushroomed up from where it landed.

"Words to think on, but this is not why I have come."

"No," Maomé agreed. "My tricks are of no use to you."

"But you are wise," Joel said.

"Wisdom is an old man's trinket, unable to enjoy it he waits in hope of a robber."

"Or a needy fool," Joel said. "All night I sat by my fire, my thoughts burning like coals in my head."

"And here," Maomé added, pointing to his chest.

"Yes. In the heart. Then you do know."

"I have a long memory, Silvertip. These gums were not always toothless, these eyes not always dim. You wish me to tell you if a dove may share the lodge of a bear."

Joel's heart began pounding. He was no longer amazed at the medicine man's powers. In a single day, he had learned to accept them, as did everyone else in the Cheyenne village.

"I must know," he replied hoarsely.

Maomé reached down and picked up a gray- and charcoal-colored feather.

"Is this a feather from one eagle or from every eagle that has ever ridden the wind?"

Joel glanced uncomprehendingly from the feather to the man.

"Anything is possible," Maomé said.

Joel decided the old man meant yes. He nodded, encouraged.

"Like all young men you do not ask 'Is it for the best?' " the medicine man observed, as if reading Joel's thoughts.

"Very well then, is it?" Joel asked, his mood souring at the old man's obscurities. Maomé placed the eagle feather in the white man's fist.

"The answer is in your hands," Maomé said.

By noon the sun had burned the mist away and settled its warmth upon the meadows where wild flowers nestled in the parched breeze and grasshoppers arched above the tall grass, their wings rattling; hungry sparrows and buntings and blue jays swept down to intercept the insects in midair. Joel sat back among the trees and watched the meadow below. Half a mile away the village of the Morning Star people shimmered in a hot yellow haze. The lazy minutes ticked past. Joel was content to watch the shifting patterns of the clouds, lost in introspection, his fingers stroking the thin-ribbed structure of the eagle feather. And thinking. Thinking.

The Appaloosa stallion pulled free of its tether and wandered out from the shade of the forest to crop a patch of buffalo grass the other horses of the village had missed. Mourning Dove spied the animal while bringing water up from the river, and though Red Bead Woman was expecting her within the hour, Mourning Dove had decided to change her plans. She set the jug of water on the floor inside her lodge. Sacred Killer was hunting; he would not return before nightfall. Hurrying, she dug beneath her bedding and brought forth the fine shirt she had made and, wrapping it in a blanket, tucked it under her arm. Then she darted from the tepee and started up a well-worn trail into the forest. Once out of sight of the village, she veered from her course and headed up valley.

What if it had not been the Appaloosa? *No, it was.* But

what could come of such shameful conduct? *Saaa! I am only going to give him this fine shirt I have made. He saved my life. I will stay only long enough for him to take the shirt and no longer.*

She almost managed to convince herself as the pace of her steps quickened. What if he were leaving, even as she neared? Hemené paused, moved downslope to get her bearings, and chancing discovery crept out from the shading pines. The Appaloosa was busily grazing less than a hundred yards away, but Joel was nowhere to be seen. Hemené frowned and scrutinized the scattered pine trees here at the edge of the forest. Perturbed that he had slipped away (worse, he might never have been here; the horse might have simply wandered from the village), Hemené returned to the safety of the forest. She dabbed at her perspiring face with the loose corner of the blanket.

She began to run, soundless as a doe among the foliage, seeking to escape the hunter's arrow, seeking safety in the depths of the forest.

She passed trees and tiny hillside flowers bathed in errant beams of brilliance and moss-covered stones humpbacked in the rich brown loam and more trees skimming by like bark-covered columns or the massive bars of a cage.

Running. Away or to? One and the same. No difference.

A dark bronze hand lashed out and caught her arm, spinning her off balance, holding her upright and at arm's length.

The blanket-wrapped shirt went skidding off among the pine needles. "Hemené," he said, startled at the way she had burst out of the forest. The woman called Mourning Dove gasped in lungfuls of air. She wrested free of his grasp. Her face bunched in momentary anger at the way he had frightened her. She took a step back. Then anger faded, and her eyes clouded with tears.

"Hemené?" Joel asked, still worried. He had sought the peace of the forest in hopes of calming the turmoil in his spirit. And now, here before him was the object of that turmoil. How could one so slight and delicate cause so much distress?

She raised her hand to her mouth, biting her knuckles, poised on the brink of a decision. All night long he had been

with her in her thoughts, the warmth of his arms, the taste
of him on her lips; he had been with her until daylight dispelled the dream leaving her empty and unfulfilled.

Hemené had no words for the feeling; she was not a creature of rhyme and cadence and flowery discourse. Nature was
the raw and elemental poetry that fueled her. A woman's
heart had blossomed in her girlish frame. A woman's desires.
A woman's need.

The tears were for the girl forever in the past and the
woman who had suddenly realized there was no turning
back. The shirt had been an excuse.

Hemené was done with excuses.

She had made her choice.

She rushed to Joel's waiting arms.

Pleasure covered them like water, swept over their naked
forms while they rippled and explored with passionate interest the curves and hollows of each other's flesh. Hemené
shuddered as his fingers lightly traced paths of glorious en-
ticement, as his lips rained kisses of fire over throat, breasts,
stomach, knees, thighs until centering at last on the wondrous
flower of her sex, as she lay in supine splendor upon a bed
of boughs, her hips tense as the delightful palpitations, in
increasing intensity, coursed through her body. She arched
toward him, bucking and twisting and crying out for Joel to
stop, for the turmoil was impossible to bear, and he must
free her. But his hands cupped her buttocks; he ignored her
pleas as the spasms grew more violent, her outstretched
hands ripping at the earth, her mouth open in a silent scream
of ecstasy. He held her until the tremors subsided and, in the
false calm that followed, raised on his knees to stroke her
legs and soothe her with gentle murmurings of love. She
could not bear the parting and knelt on her own somewhat
shaky legs to enfold him in her arms, crushing his swollen
staff against her belly.

"Nahkohe," she purred, nuzzling his neck, her fingertips
exploring the musculature of his powerful hips. "Make me
your woman, Nahkohe." She stroked the small of his back,
then his legs like great trunks of muscle and bone, and at

last the twin fruits beneath his manhood, the sac taut to the touch.

"Make me your woman," she repeated, and she turned from him to press the small smooth spheres of her buttocks against his phallus, her ankles now to either side of his. She fell forward on her hands while he kissed the length of her spine. His hand slid over her rounded hips and crept up to her breasts as she tilted upward. Joel, lost to desire, lunged forward to impale her, and Hemené cried out, first at the sudden swift pain, and again at the stormy surrender of herself to fulfillment, and a third time as the bonds of restraint were swept away before the savage onrush of his seed . . .

The aftermath of every storm is tranquillity. And so it was for these two. Their sun-dappled marriage bed was all the earth; their blanket, the verdant branches overhead, shading the lovers asleep in one another's arms, a sweet happiness permeating the still and almost innocent tableau.

11

One month ended and another crept in, dramatically altering the life of the Cheyenne village. Game was hunted closer to home in an effort to gather in as many provisions as possible before the long winter months set in. Soon the tribe would begin their trek to the lower ranges to escape the savage snowstorms that would bury the passes beneath an impenetrable mantle of white. Joel had dutifully inserted himself into the activities of the village. It made sense that if he were to approach Sacred Killer for his sister's hand, the war chief must think of Joel as more Cheyenne than white. Out of sheer necessity, Joel had gained a stumbling command of the language. And the more time spent with Rides The Horse and White Frog, the more proficient he became in the customs of the Morning Star People.

The stolen hours with Mourning Dove kept him from going utterly mad for want of her. Their time together was brief but passionate. They were moments to be harbored in the heart.

The Moon When Cherries Ripen had come to the mountains in all its unabashed fury, bringing a hot heavy wind from the desert lands to parch the lonesome parks and valleys. Driven from their dry havens in the hills, the wild game sought relief at the springs and upland creeks nourishing the Stillwater where the Cheyenne hunters awaited their exodus. The warriors were much too absorbed in the success or failure of each day's hunt to notice the increasingly strange behavior of the man called Silvertip. Only Shell Woman took note how the white man would ride away from the village with the rest of the hunters and yet never returned with game although his clothes would be dusty and worn from hard travel. How could this be so, especially for one who had

proved himself so able a marksman and tracker? Shell
Woman mentioned this to Priam who ordered her to keep
such knowledge to herself. She promised to comply.

She lied.

Late in the month, Shell Woman found an excuse to visit
Lame Deer's lodge and whisper in Red Bead Woman's ear
of Silvertip's unusual disappearances. Red Bead Woman listened to the gossip, promised to keep it to herself, and then
repeated what she had learned to her husband. That night,
Lame Deer presented the information at council in Crazy
Bear's lodge. All eyes turned to Sacred Killer. He had
brought the white man into camp. The war chief of the Red
Shields could offer no explanation for Joel's behavior, but
Sacred Killer, fearing the worst, volunteered to discover Silvertip's motives. And if there was mischief afoot, Hemené's
brother vowed to correct the matter, personally.

August ended in a downpour that lasted the night. The first
day of September dawned clear and bright, promising to be
another in a string of unusually warm days. The moisture
rising from the damp earth increased the humidity and left
the morning to drag cloyingly on toward noon. Sacred Killer
sweated in the shade, his limbs cramped from the tedium of
his vigil. His patience was rewarded when Joel exited from
Priam's tepee and walked toward the meadow just below the
war chief's vantage point.

Joel climbed the close-cropped slope to the Appaloosa.
The stallion grazed alone, some distance apart from a pair
of bay mares.

Joel spoke to the Appaloosa in soft soothing tones as he
approached. Slowly, methodically he fitted the rope bridle
over the stallion's head and strapped the makeshift saddle he
had made on the animal's back. When he mounted, the stallion bucked for a few minutes in a half-hearted effort to
dislodge Joel, to let the Kentuckian know he might be boss
but never master. Sacred Killer stepped deeper into the shade
of the forest as Joel rode out of the meadow, heading north.
Sacred Killer, on his pinto war pony, followed at a safe in-
terval, keeping under cover. Perhaps Silvertip was hunting
after all. Or perhaps—and this was the troublesome notion—

Sacred Killer had made a mistake allowing the white man the freedom of the village. He hoped not. He had taken a liking to the young white man and would not enjoy killing him.

At least Mourning Dove appeared to have taken his words to heart concerning Silvertip Ryan. Here was something to be thankful for. And yet, Sacred Killer took scarce comfort in this unexpected victory over his strong-willed sister. He was, by nature, a cautious man.

After a two-hour ride from the village across winding gulleys, through stands of pine and cedar, Joel Ryan headed up a narrow gorge Priam had shown him a month before. The stallion knew the way by now and followed the twists and turns of the gorge until the cliffs drew back and horse and rider came to the box canyon at the end of the trail. The canyon had proved ideally suited for Joel's purposes. The gorge provided the only access, and he kept it blocked with a makeshift barricade constructed of hand-split rails and fallen timbers. Now, he opened a passage for the Appaloosa and brought the stallion inside, where an unclimbable barrier of cliffs surrounded a grassy area roughly a hundred yards in diameter. The Appaloosa whinnied and tossed its mane. Seven mares grazing by a stand of box elders at the rear of the canyon answered his call. Joel patted the stallion's neck.

"Go on, boy, have your romp with the ladies," Joel said, standing in the yellow grass. He slapped his hat down across the animal's rump, and the Appaloosa bolted off after the harem.

Joel started back toward his barricade, took three steps and froze. Carrying his war shield and rifle, Sacred Killer sat astride his pinto in the middle of the entrance Joel had made. Scolding himself for allowing any man to catch him by surprise, Joel continued on to the war chief and climbed the barricade to take a seat almost directly opposite the brave. There was nothing to be done but play the hand fate had dealt.

"I figured it was only a matter of time before somebody got curious."

"Your horses?" Sacred Killer said, pointing to the mares.

"It took me a while, but I cut them out of a wild herd and chased them into this canyon. I had the timber ready to seal it off. There's water at the back and decent grazing through-out. I've been taking my time breaking them in."

"You have done well, Silvertip," Sacred Killer exclaimed, more relieved than the white man would ever guess.

"It's been quite a job," Joel admitted, his mind scanning days of bone-jarring rides and the countless times he'd been thrown in the dust, near trampled. Always, he had climbed back for more, challenging one after another, until all seven of the horses would accept a rider with only a minimum of protest. He had never meant to break their spirits, only gentle them to a bridle. Every muscle, every bone in his body ached, but he was proud of his accomplishment.

"Such fine animals will make you a wealthy man among my people."

"I have not done this for myself," Joel said. His courage wavered. He doubted whether he should continue. Sacred Killer watched him for a moment with interest. The war chief walked his pinto past Joel and once clear of the barricade trotted at a brisk pace into the valley. Dust rose in the wake of his sturdy pony and billowed back toward Joel in a gritty cloud. The sun beat down, its dry heavy heat already purging the land of any moisture that had lingered from the evening rain. Joel shielded his eyes and watched as the war chief of the Red Shields neared the mares. The Appaloosa neighed a warning for the pinto to remain at a respectful distance. A few minutes later, Sacred Killer wheeled his mount and gal-loped back to the barricade. And Joel marveled how the Red Shield without his skin dye and garish face paint still looked the part of a fierce warrior. His motions were fluid, econom-ical, wholly in tune with the movement of his war pony.

"Fine horses indeed, Silvertip. They will breed well," said Sacred Killer. "But your words are strange to my ears. If the horses are not for you, then for whom?"

Joel swung his legs over the topmost rail and let them dangle as he spoke. He decided there was nothing to be gained in stalling.

"They are for you."

Sacred Killer betrayed no emotion. He simply glanced

over his shoulder at the mares and then back to Joel.

"My sister," he said quietly.

"Priam told me it is the custom, soon after the Harvest Moon, for a warrior to think of taking a wife. The winters are long and lonely, and it is good to have a woman to share a lodge with. Mourning Dove is in my heart, Sacred Killer. She has been since the moment I first set eyes on her. I would honor her above my life. She would want for nothing. I—"

"You are not Cheyenne," the war chief snapped in reply.

"I have lived these many weeks in peace with the Cheyenne. I have learned your tongue. Your customs will be my customs."

The pinto pawed at the ground, mirroring its rider's discomfort. Thistles rattled in the wind. A hawk circled overhead searching for something to kill. The war chief calmed his restless mount, then fixed Joel in an unwavering stare.

"And suppose it is my custom to make war against the white-eyes once again. For it will surely come. Like a storm that is many hills away, yet we hear the thunder and know it will darken our skies as well, so it is with the men who come to dig the gold, the settlers who come to claim Cheyenne land as their own. Tell me, Silvertip Ryan, will you fight with us against your own kind? Or will you choose to spill the blood of your woman's people?"

"Neither," Joel said. "I wish only to live in peace with Mourning Dove as my wife. I know what you are saying, Sacred Killer, but these are paths yet to be traveled. The storm may come, but then again it may not." Joel glanced upward. "For now," he continued, "the sky is clear, and tomorrow I will bring my horses to your lodge and claim Hemené for my wife."

Sacred Killer scowled, and his face drew taut over his sharp cheekbones. For a moment Joel feared the brave might attack him, but the war chief of the Red Shields turned away in disdain. He slapped the barrel of his rifle across the pinto's rump. The animal darted through the barricade and out of sight beyond the gravel-strewn walls of the gorge.

Joel watched the serpentine plume of dust mar the brilliant blue of the sky. Sacred Killer would see the light. He'd have to. Joel considered rounding up the mares and bringing them into camp this afternoon. But tomorrow was a celebration of thanksgiving. Drying racks hung thick with meat for the winter. And an abundance of chokecherries had been gathered along the creek banks. Such a celebration always began with the various suitors bringing in their horses and other wealth to the tepees of the young maidens each had set his hopes on. In the evening if the gifts had been accepted, the brave brought his wife-to-be to the center of the village. Once the couples had received the blessing of Crazy Bear, pounding drums and shrill flutes would signal the marriage dance to begin.

Joel, in his effort to ensure the tribe's acceptance, was loath to break such a tradition. Tomorrow wasn't all that long to wait. He stared at the settling dust. What could happen?

Tall Bull worked his knife blade through the back tendons of the antelope he had brought down. He fitted a length of rawhide through the holes and tied the carcass to a pole he had managed to lift all alone and set between the forked branches of a post oak. It was late in the afternoon, and he intended to let the carcass bleed overnight before bringing it to the village. He heard the rider's approach before he saw and recognized Sacred Killer astride his lathered pinto. Sacred Killer held one hand palm outward to show he carried no weapons and, dismounting, left his horse grazing alongside Tall Bull's.

"Another good kill," Sacred Killer said in praise.

"The All-Father guides my arrows," Tall Bull replied proudly.

"There will be much feasting in your mother's lodge."

"My brothers and sisters will share in my good fortune."

Sacred Killer circled the carcass, his nostrils accustomed to the stench of death. The antelope's eyes appeared to be studying the blood-flecked dirt inches from its black nose. Sacred Killer pretended to scrutinize the carcass, though his gaze, in truth, flicked from time to time over to the hunter, as if he were debating his next course of action.

"You should have a woman to tend your lodge," Sacred Killer said, watching the man closely now. Tall Bull began

to gut the animal. Soon his flesh glistened to the elbow with
blood.

"One day, perhaps I will," the Dog Soldier said.

"One day? Why not now? You have counted coup in battle. The scalps of your enemies adorn your shield."

"I have no wealth to offer what she is worth. Three ponies
I have captured from the Crow. But she is worth much
more."

"And who is this maiden whose marriage offering must
be so great?"

"You know who," Tall Bull said, yanking the entrails free
with a savage jerk of his hand. "We are not children, you
and I, yet you have ridden all this way from the valley of
the Stillwater to play a game with me. It is Mourning Dove
of whom I speak. You know this as well as I."

"No game, my brother. When *eshe-he*, the sun, next
climbs the sky, the men of our village who have proved
themselves worthy will seek out the women of their choice.
It is only fitting that one such as you would do the same."

"But Mourning Dove is worth far more than three horses.
My gift would be an insult to your family."

"It is true." Sacred Killer looked back down the valley,
toward the trail he had taken from the gorge, miles away.
"She is worth at least ten fine ponies."

"Then it is settled," Tall Bull replied bitterly. "Why did
you come here? Your sister's beauty is like the sun dancing
on the water. It is like the bow of many colors after a rain.
The more it is seen the more it is desired. But I have not the
horses to offer for her. I have no time to find them. My
family would go hungry while I searched the hills. And
where would I look?"

Tall Bull resumed his butchering, angry that he had been
made sport of by the brother of the woman he coveted above
all others.

"I know a place," Sacred Killer answered. A hot wind
rushed up the slope, and the bloody carcass swung to and
fro, to and fro between the two men.

With the western horizon glazed in the russet and purples of
sunset, Joel Ryan paused in the meadowlands rolling down

to the Stillwater. He watched, awhile, the flurry of activity as women exchanged one chore for another, as the children were rounded up from play, and old men stalking the aromatic trails of an evening meal traced supper to its source. In the encampment of the Red Shields, a roughly circular patch of crimson coals like an open wound upon the night-blackened earth painted in tones of orange-red heat the faces of the women tending the firing. In the morning, once the soot and unburned woodchips were cleared away, the newly bisqued pots would be distributed. It dawned on him that Mourning Dove was probably in that circle of women and his heart ached for want of her. Joel forced himself to look away, and he wondered what his brother Nate, or the neighbors and citizens of Seven Forks, Kentucky, would say if he showed up with a Cheyenne bride. They'd be appalled more than likely, but then, such worries were useless. It didn't matter what they thought. He was never going back.

He rode toward the village receiving only perfunctory attention from the inhabitants, and headed straight for Priam's lodge.

Shell Woman waved as he approached. She was squatting by the cookfire; several rainbow trout were impaled on sticks dangling above the flames. Remembering the old Negro had mentioned something about trying his luck upriver, Joel had the distinct impression luck had nothing to do with Priam's accomplishments. Men like him just knew what they were about. Or as Priam himself had put it, he was "alkalied to the wilderness." Joel Ryan wondered if one day he would say the same thing about himself. Well, he had made a good start; he had an Indian name, Silvertip, and soon a Cheyenne wife.

Priam was inside the tepee, his back propped against his willow-wood backrest, his frail-looking legs outstretched and crossed at the ankles, eyes closed, his chest rising and falling in even, easy breaths. Joel sat on the rolled bedding Shell Woman had made for him.

"You asleep?" he said.

"Not now," Priam replied.

"I'll be needing your help tomorrow."

"You're really going through with it?" Priam asked, cocking an eye in Joel's direction.

"I figure the two of us ought to be able to bring the mares in."

"You caught them on your lonesome," Priam observed, sitting up and wincing as his lower vertebrae ground together.

"I just want to be sure nothing happens," Joel said. "This is important to me."

Priam nodded and leaned forward on his elbows.

"Sacred Killer ain't gonna be too thrilled when you ride up with them horses."

"He has nothing to say in the matter."

"The hell he doesn't; he's her brother."

"But I am asking Mourning Dove. Not him. And she'll accept."

"She will, huh?"

"We have an understanding."

"Maybe too much of an understanding."

Joel glanced over at the Negro. The old man's face gleamed like a slab of obsidian in the dying light.

"Don't think I can't see what's plain in front of my eyes, younker. I watched your comings and goings. Seem to always coincide with Sacred Killer's comings and goings. You just lucky it's me knows and no one else. Cheyenne women ain't ever s'posed to know a man until they're married. Husband find his wife ain't a virgin, she gets run out of camp in disgrace. Minus a piece of her nose, I might add."

"I haven't the faintest notion what you are referring to, old man," Joel snapped. "But even if I did, what you say doesn't matter. Because Mourning Dove will be marrying me."

"Have it your way," Priam sighed. "Figured I ought to tell you is all."

"I am tired of people telling me. This is between me and Mourning Dove. Now can I count on your help?"

"Why not?" Priam shrugged. "I was young once." He crawled to the entrance. Shell Woman pointed to the trout, and motioned to him. "Was young . . . and as poor a liar as you," Priam added, ducking out the entrance.

The flap fluttered into place.

Tomorrow, Joel said to himself. He waited for the flush of embarrassment to leave his features and thought about tomorrow.

12

The center of the barricade had been stripped away. Split rails littered the mouth of the canyon, the solid timber rolled to either side of the passage. Joel slipped his Colt revolver from its holster as he walked the Appaloosa through the gap and into the meadow. Priam held back, his rifle ready, his gaze swept over the rimrock walls. Reassured they weren't riding into a trap, he let his horse break a path through the brittle underbrush that fringed the meadow. A covey of quail exploded directly to his left. Startled, he swung the rifle barrel in their direction but managed to hold his fire.

"Damn birds," he muttered and spat, then wiped a forearm over his mouth.

Joel paused, offering himself as a target as he turned slowly in the saddle, checking first the grove of box elders and the spring at the rear of the canyon and then the irregular patterns of the gray canyon walls, studying every cranny in the stone, every clump of thistle, his mind refusing to believe what his heart knew had happened.

"Gone," he said weakly as Priam broke cover and trotted up alongside the younger man.

"I could've told you the minute I seen them timbers. Either you civilized them horses so much they took smart and freed themselves which would be a first, or they had help. Someone who figured he had a use for them. Maybe same as you. I didn't see no Crow sign riding in. But that don't mean much, 'cause these lights of mine ain't as bright as they used to be. And I reckon you ain't the onliest white man to come along; there's folks on the way up to Silverbow all the time. Some prospector might have spied the barricade and figured to take a look-see. Or it could have . . ."

"Sacred Killer."

"Huh?"

"It was Sacred Killer," Joel said in a murderous tone.

"Younker, such talk ain't the quickest way to lose that scalp of yours, but it will do, till somethin' better comes along."

"He tracked me here. He knew what I intended."

"That's the first I heard."

"I thought it wasn't important. You told me Sacred Killer was an honorable man."

"There's no such thing where family's concerned."

"He won't get away with it," Joel said.

The Appaloosa reared on its heels and pawed at the air. "C'mon," Joel yelled. The stallion touched earth at a gallop, leaped the broken remnants of the barricade. Horse and rider rushed pell mell through the gorge. Priam brought his spooked gelding under control and followed the Appaloosa's trail up the twisting passage. Aware he had no chance of winning the race to the Cheyenne village, Priam only hoped he could arrive in time to avert disaster.

All morning Hemené watched as young braves came into the village bringing their caches of pelts and strings of war ponies to the tepees of the maidens they wished to wed. Her heart was heavy, for Sacred Killer had confronted her with his knowledge of Joel's intentions. He spoke of how Silvertip Ryan had listened and heard the wisdom in the war chief's words and decided against bringing his marriage offer to camp. Sacred Killer went even further to announce that Tall Bull intended to ask for her hand, presenting ten fine horses as a wedding gift! Mourning Dove had the distinct impression her brother was at the bottom of this scheme. Joel would never give her up. And so she waited.

An hour passed. Then two. The sun angled high overhead and burned its fiery path toward noon. And still the woman called Mourning Dove kept her anxious vigil. Sacred Killer, returning to his lodge from that of his friend's, Lame Deer, noticed how absorbed his sister had become, her intense expression as she searched the hills.

"Do not worry, my sister. Tall Bull will come for you. But

it is not fitting for a young maiden to appear too eager. Wait within the lodge, Mourning Dove. You will know when he comes, for our people will surely gather around our lodge at the sight of one who brings a gift greater than any brave has yet to offer."

"Let Tall Bull come. And then go, quickly."

Sacred Killer scowled and caught her by the arm and jerked her into the privacy of their tepee. The air was redolent with the fragrance of pine cones and smoked meat and the biting sweetness of crushed chokecherries. Dust motes danced in the shaft of sunlight beaming down through the smoke hole.

"What is this, disobedient one?" The war chief of the Red Shields stood between Mourning Dove and the entrance.

"I will not have Tall Bull for my husband," she said.

"He will come, and you will accept his offer. I have spoken."

"If he is your choice, then you take him."

"Do not mock me." Sacred Killer advanced upon her, his finely honed features were flecked with sweat, a storm brewed in his eyes. "Tall Bull is a man of honor. He is strong in battle. He will be a good provider and give you fine sons." Sacred Killer looked away, managed to bring his temper under control. When he turned back to her his expression had softened. "To see your children, to be their second father would make my life complete." When he saw that she was unmoved, his tone grew hard once more. Such disobedience could only be the result of Silvertip Ryan's influence. "Remain within this lodge," he ordered, "until I give you permission to leave. I will accept Tall Bull's offer in your name. A brother may speak for his sister."

"I will not stand with him in the Two-Called-Together ceremony."

"A sister does not obey her brother. Is this more white man's thinking? I have let Silvertip Ryan live too long among the People. He has confused your thoughts. I had hoped he would learn our ways; instead he tries to destroy them. I swear this shall not happen."

The sound of celebration and welcome filtered through the hide walls of the tepee. Amid cries of enthusiasm and good-natured encouragements, several horsemen approached the camp of the Red Shields. The rumble of the hooves drowned out every other sound as they approached and circled the lodge of Sacred Killer. Mourning Dove waited, scarcely daring to breathe, praying that it was Joel. Before the gathering of her people she would agree to be wife to him. Then let her brother try to stop them! The horses rumbled to a ragged stop.

"Sacred Killer."

Mourning Dove, to her horror, recognized the voice of Knows His Gun, father of Tall Bull.

"Such a young man, Tall Bull, wishes your sister, Mourning Dove, for his wife!"

The proper announcement delivered, Knows His Gun backed his skittish stallion into the throng, leaving his son to await Sacred Killer's decision. Tall Bull beamed with confidence. He already knew what the war chief's reply would be. They had worked it out yesterday.

Within the lodge, Mourning Dove confronted her brother in a last desperate attempt.

"My brother . . ." she said, her eyes brimming with tears. "Do not force me to shame you."

"There is no shame in seeing my sister take Tall Bull for her husband. Sit here upon your blankets. We must not seem too eager."

Mourning Dove did as he requested, and drawing her legs up beneath her, lowered her head and prayed to all the protective spirits that Joel might arrive with his own gifts of equal or greater worth than Tall Bull's.

"Ten mares," White Frog's voice called out, for he had been appointed by Sacred Killer as one whose task it was to inspect the gifts and announce what was brought. "Fleet of foot, strong animals, they will breed well. Two buffalo robes. A rifle with powder and shot."

Ten horses!

Hemené glanced up in alarm. How had Tall Bull ever come by such wealth?

"Do you hear how Tall Bull honors you?" Sacred Killer said.

"He is a man of generosity and courage as you say. But

Silvertip Ryan is also a man of courage. Have you forgotten so soon what he did for me?"

"I have not forgotten . . . that he is a white man."

"He is in my heart. Not Tall Bull."

"You will learn. These are feelings of a foolish girl. They will change once you become his wife."

"I will never be his wife. Saaa! You do not know what you are doing. Silvertip will also come bringing gifts, and you will see how much he honors our lodge."

"He has nothing to bring." Sacred Killer smiled. His sister's expression clouded.

"What do you mean? My brother, what have you done?"

"Tall Bull has waited long enough," Sacred Killer replied, unable to meet her accusing stare. "I will announce that a Two-Called-Together ceremony may take place. This night you will sleep within the lodge of your husband."

Sacred Killer started toward the entrance, his hand reached out to pull the elk hide flap aside.

"My brother, wait. You must listen to me." Mourning Dove had tried to avoid telling him the secret no one knew, not even Joel. Now she could find no other way.

"I have listened too much," Sacred Killer said with a disdainful wave of his hand. He walked out into the sunlight, and all eyes were upon him. Tall Bull stood before the horses, the buffalo hides and rifle were spread out at his feet. He stood with arms folded, legs apart, a knowing look on his face.

Sacred Killer milked the moment for all it was worth. He held out his arms, raising his hands as if to take in the entire audience of men and women who had gathered to learn Hemené's decision.

"Let the marriage lodge be built," Sacred Killer shouted.

An enthusiastic cheer erupted from the crowd and Tall Bull loosed his own wild cry and leaped astride his horse.

"Aaaiiieeee!" he roared. "E-peva-e!" It is good! "Father, do you hear? Aaaiiieee!" The brave fired his rifle, and his friends responded in kind, emptying their guns into the air. The wild mares rolled their eyes in terror and fought against the ropes looping their necks. It was all Tall Bull's friends could do to control them. Tall Bull danced his own pony in a tight circle so that everyone might appreciate the manner in which he had trained his stallion. As he put the animal through its motions, the warrior continued to cry out his happiness. And Sacred Killer folded his arms and smiled and looked about him at the people of his village. There would be five marriage lodges built. And five couples brought forth in the Two-Called-Together ceremony. This time next year he might even be an uncle.

It was good, he told himself. Mourning Dove would one day thank him.

Too late.

Joel saw the horses—*his* horses—and the celebration and knew in the pit of his soul what had happened.

He slowly descended the slope to the village allowing time for the gathering before Sacred Killer's lodge to disperse. As he passed among the excited Cheyenne, he heard the name Tall Bull. Tall Bull had been accepted to wed the sister of Sacred Killer. Tall Bull had brought many horses! Such an honor! Had the All-Father aided him? How had he come by such wealth?

Joel knew. His fingers tightened on the rifle stock.

"Steady, younker," Priam said behind him.

"Leave me alone, old man."

"Just like to see a body exercise as much sense as I give him credit for."

Joel looked around at the village, the knowledge striking home that he was a stranger here. Lifting a hand against Sacred Killer would only invite disaster.

"Ease off, lad. I got me some home brew hid beneath my blankets. Ease off. Let it rest for now."

Joel saw Sacred Killer turn, and their eyes met and locked. Noise, dust, celebration, barking dogs and squealing children, voices, leaden heat of day—nothing existed between them. Only two men, standing as if alone in all the world.

"For now," Joel muttered.

Only these two, red man and white, watching one another. Watching.

13

Drums brought on the darkness, their throbbing, incessant rhythm announced the cutting of the lodge poles and the ritualistic construction of the marriage lodges down near the Stillwater. The sun was no more than a burnished smear above the hilltops when Priam knelt before the water pot and, using a gourd dipper, took a taste. He spat to one side.

"Bah! What is this? Dead water at my lodge?"

Shell Woman, taken by surprise, left the kettle of stew she had been attending and waddled over to the Negro.

"I carried it up from the river only an hour ago," she said.

"*E-haveseve-eno-e!* It tastes bad! I will have living water in my lodge," Priam complained, dumping it out. A muddy stain darkened the dirt, spreading to the Appaloosa tethered nearby.

"I will bring living water up from the river," Shell Woman replied, exasperated at his outburst. She lifted the clay water pot under one arm, balanced the bottom rim on her hip, and trundled off through camp toward the river.

Priam watched her leave and then, with a sigh of satisfaction, entered the tepee once more. Joel looked up from rummaging among the Negro's gear.

"What the devil you doin'?" the black man said.

"I saw a Dragoon Colt in here once. I need it."

"I killed a man named Strang nary two years ago. Caught him searchin' my war bag. Like you, he had no business in it."

"I need that gun," Joel said, ignoring the implied threat. "Ah . . ." He dragged a heavy-barreled, cap and ball revolver out from under Priam's backrest. The huge old .44 carried enough steel in its frame to make a decent club after all the chambers had been fired. The revolver was loaded, Joel noted, checking the cylinder. "I'm going after Mourning Dove."

"You're loco," Priam said.

Joel could not see arguing the point; the black man was undoubtedly correct. He slipped the revolver in his gunbelt and tried a cross draw with moderate success. He removed his own Confederate issue Navy Colt and spun the cylinder to make sure none of the loads had come dislodged, then he returned it to its holster.

"I ought to stop you," Priam said.

"You mean 'try,' " Joel retorted. "Oh hell. I thought we were friends, old man."

"Reckon that's what I mean. I ought to save you from getting yourself killed. Lord in heaven, you saw what happened to Larocque's friends."

"I'm not Larocque or Mayo or what's his name. No one is going to catch us," Joel replied, dropping the revolver back into its holster. "Or bring us back."

"The boneyards are full of knobheads who said them very same words." Priam scowled. He kicked at the dirt floor. "Tarnation, you don't know things have turned out just the way Mourning Dove hoped they would."

"Tall Bull was Sacred Killer's choice, not hers."

"You can't be certain." Priam studied the younger man's expression and saw that Ryan was indeed certain. Joel stripped off his gray cavalry blouse and donned the buckskin shirt Mourning Dove had made for him. Until now he had only worn it out of sight of the village. He no longer cared who saw him in it. After tonight, none of that would matter.

"Have it your way," Priam muttered, and slipping a knife from the top of his calf-high moccasin, he tossed it on the ground between them. "She's got good balance. For throwin'. You might need an ace up your sleeve. Or in your boot tops one day."

"Thanks," Joel said. "I'd rather have you for me than against me, old man."

The Negro shrugged. "Ain't no call I should stand in the way of true love."

As Joel bent down to retrieve the knife, Priam snatched a grinding stone from his pocket and raised it high in his dark fist, calculating in a single second how much force he would need to knock Joel unconscious without causing any permanent damage. Suddenly a coppery hand ensnared his wrist. Joel straightened and retreated in alarm from Priam's stone bludgeon, tensing as he saw Sacred Killer looming in the entranceway. The war chief of the Red Shields had braided his hair with raven feathers and dabbed a smear of crimson across his eyes. The effect was as if he were wearing a narrow mask that glistened bloodlike in the feeble light. Priam dropped the rock and lowered his arm. He looked at Joel.

"I was trying to save your hide, younker."

Joel waited, his fingers touching the wood grip of his gun.

"Come with me," Sacred Killer said. He ducked out of the lodge.

"My oh my oh my," Priam muttered beneath his breath as he stooped to pass through the opening. Joel tucked the knife in his boot top. So much for one pat hand, he thought. From here on out it's play the cards as they come. Filled with misgivings and expecting to be set upon the minute he showed himself, Joel followed Priam out of the tepee. Sacred Killer was already walking his horse up the slope toward the forest.

"What does he want?" Joel asked, watching him.

"Your guess is as good as mine. But if he wanted war, you two would already be at it. Better bring the Appaloosa."

"Yeah. And thanks for the knife," Joel said.

"I was—"

"I know. Only trying to save my hide." With Joel's stallion dutifully in tow, the two men followed the well-worn path the war chief had taken. Five minutes later and two hundred feet higher, Joel paused to peer over his shoulder at the conical marriage lodges rising out of the landscape near the river. As his gaze drifted to the camp of the Red Shields, his thoughts focused once more on the problem at hand. Sacred Killer had caught him off guard, but it wasn't going to change anything.

Priam had pulled ahead, and as Joel entered the woods, he spied the black man standing stock-still alongside three horses, tethered in the darkness. Sacred Killer was there too, and he wasn't alone. Mourning Dove stood beside him. Hardly daring to believe what his eyes told him to be true, Joel drew near. Mourning Dove lifted her tear-reddened eyes to him. She started forward, hesitated.

"*Ta-naestse!*" snapped her brother. "Go to him. It is what you wanted." She faltered. Joel Ryan held out his arms. She left her brother's side and hurried to Joel's waiting embrace. His arms enfolded her, and his heart beat wilder than the drums. She was his again, and he would never let her go.

"There is food." Sacred Killer gestured to the packets strapped to the horses. "You will not need to hunt for several days, but you will have to find what shelter you can. Far from these hunting grounds." He turned to Priam. "You know better than I the trails that lead over the divide. It will not be easy at night. But it will give these two an extra day. Maybe more. You can show them and return before morning, Priam."

"I don't understand what in thunder is happening, but I will do as you ask," Priam said. "I'll point 'em east toward the Yellowstone." He pulled at his chin and sighed in disbelief.

"I will say I have had a vision and cannot give chase," Sacred Killer continued, staring down at the village. "That does not mean Tall Bull will not follow. Perhaps other braves with him. If that happens, then, Silvertip, you will have to fight."

"Sacred Killer . . . why are you doing this for us?" Joel asked.

"Not for you. Only my sister, to save her from being cast out and cut with the knife. Know, Silvertip, I have streaked my eyes with the war color of the Red Shields, and I look upon you now for the last time in peace. You have stolen my sister. I will never be second father to a son. I am the last of my line, and my blood is buried with me. Do not let me see you again, Silvertip, or my war lance will surely find your heart. I swear this before the All-Father."

Without another word Sacred Killer brushed past them and vanished in the darkness. Joel tightened his embrace as if some unseen force might try to wrest his beloved away.

"He's right. I can bring you over the divide by a trail nary a one of them bucks knows of, 'ceptin' maybe old Crazy Bear," Priam said, mounting up. "Afterwards, I'll cut around and make tracks like you headed west, to Silverbow. It might fool 'em, and it might not."

"I still don't understand," Joel said, lowering his gaze to the village.

"I told him I was no longer a maiden," Mourning Dove explained. "And that I am carrying the child of Silvertip Ryan."

Priam whistled low and long beneath his breath. Joel tilted her chin. A beam of moonlight illuminated her features, tender with passion, yet resolute and determined. A gentle breeze had dried away her tears. And Joel saw she spoke the truth.

"My God . . . when . . . are you . . . will you . . ."

"During the spring moon," Mourning Dove said. "I am sorry . . ." Words of helplessness failed.

"Don't ever say that again," Joel replied, kissing her forehead and cheek, then her lips. "I love you."

"This is what you wanted," Priam said behind them, in a grave voice. "Let's go."

"Silvertip . . . my husband . . ." Mourning Dove whispered. Joel put his fingers to her lips. Tomorrow come what may, he had never felt so alive and so happy.

"You heard Priam," he gently said. "Let's go."

14

Otter Creek was a year-round trickle of water. Now, in April, it ran lead gray beneath a layer of ice. Joel Ryan's boot cracked through the creek's frozen surface as he leaped across to the snow-covered bank opposite him. His right leg slipped, and ice water splashed his calf as he stumbled and slipped in the mud.

Might as well be hunting with a whole marching band for all the quiet I'm keeping, he fumed. *Keep your mind on the hunt, Ryan.* Sound advice, but hard to follow with Hemené due any time now. Only an empty larder had pried him from her side into the forest in search of food. He paused in the shadow of the riverbank to catch his breath in the icy air. Here along the creek, the oak trees lifted barren spiny limbs as if in supplication to the god of spring to rescue them from their mantle of white. Beneath a gunmetal gray sky, Joel's breath was a billowing mist soon lost against the muted colors of the hoary countryside. As he rested, his mind retraced the tedious journey that had ended here at Otter Creek, more than three hundred miles from the Stillwater. Near exhaustion, Joel and Mourning Dove had followed the creek to an abandoned homestead. A one-room cabin, a half-built corral, and a ramshackle barn with its roof near collapse weren't much. But they were a start. Someone had dreamed and lost.

"But we won't lose," Joel had promised. "We'll make it work."

A late norther allowed them enough time to chase the coyotes out of the cabin, start a woodpile, and make some necessary repairs on the chimney.

The first blizzard struck in late November, ending their improvements, sealing them in with their plans for spring.

Christmas passed unnoticed by Joel.

The new year dawned, dropping temperatures to forty below at times. Hard days to be sure, but days of peace that soothed Joel's apprehensions. Gradually the two lovers came to accept the fact that they had indeed eluded pursuit. And though alone in the "howling wilderness," they were at last free to make a life for themselves.

"Ne-a-ese ma-heono," Joel gently intoned, a simple Cheyenne prayer of thanksgiving to the All-Father. A fluttering snowflake landed on his bearded cheek, another in his eye. Then quiet as a creeping cat, the snowfall began in earnest to conceal the surrounding woods behind a veil of shimmering ivory, covering the tracks of the antelope buck Joel had been following.

He had to have a kill. He had to have it today.

Dejectedly, the hunter started up the bank, slipped, jammed his knee on a log, and using the Hawken for support lunged forward. His head poked above the edge of the bank and ducked under just as quickly. About twenty-five yards from the creek, the antelope had stopped to nibble at the trunk of a willow tree. Sound and sight were muffled by the falling snow, hiding the hunter from the hunted. Joel Ryan peered over the lip of the creekbank. A gust of wind stirred the flakes into a whirling, rippling barrier that in another minute would completely obscure his quarry.

No time for finesse, he had to take his shot. In his mind Joel muttered the prayer Rides The Horse had taught him, *"Vokaa-e,* antelope brother, give me your life."

He whipped the Hawken to his shoulder and fired.

She was frightened and tried not to admit it to herself. But all morning she had felt a change at work within her body. Her time was at hand. Mourning Dove fed the last of the logs to the fire. Wood chips spiraled up the stone flue as the weight of new wood splintered the charred remains of branches. The hearth cast a merry glow, painting the interior of the one-room cabin with flickering shades of orange light. She padded across the pelt-covered floor to the opposite wall of the cabin where she and Joel made their bed. She gingerly lowered her swollen form to the backrest. A moment to catch her breath, a moment more to feel the life force within her stir as her belly spasmed.

"You have been restless all day, little one," she said aloud. She tried to drive the worry from her mind. She wished Joel had not picked this day to hunt. But they needed food, and he had yet to make a kill in three days. Shadows danced upon the log walls. Her thoughts turned from apprehension to expectation. The child would be a son. He would grow to be a fine strong man, one to make his father proud. A man— ah, but he must be a baby first. With that she reached for the nearly completed cradle, and using a thorn for a needle, she began stitching the last of the rawhide patches into place upon the wood frame. A fat fleecy snowflake blew in through a hole in the mud chinking. It lingered in iridescent splendor upon a buffalo robe, then succumbed to the warmth, its crystalline architecture turning opaque and dissolving into the hide's shaggy surface.

Mourning Dove shivered and sighed, glaring at the hole. A fine sprinkling of icy precipitation driven by a piercing draft sliced through the warmth cast by the fire in the hearth. Mourning Dove set her work aside and, struggling against her own ungainly shape, stood and walked over to the wall. She picked a handful of loose dry clods of clay from the floor and moistened it with her spittle. She had to kneel to pack the opening. Her belly cramped from the effort. She uttered a small gasp, waited for the pain to subside, and continued working the mud into the wall until the aperture was sealed. A sheen of perspiration coated her forehead and cheeks. Placing the palm of her hand flat to the wall, she braced herself and stood. She looked down and noticed the front of her dress was damp and clung to her thighs. She doubled forward and stumbled toward the bedding, each step agony. By gulping in great draughts of air, she found the pain lessened. She sank to the floor and crawled the remaining feet to the backrest. Panic clutched her heart in a grip of iron. She began to whimper and bite at her knuckles. Not now, she prayed, not here, alone. *I am still Cheyenne. I am Silvertip's woman. Not a little girl to weep in fear.* What woman was not afraid when her time came? a voice seemed to whisper. And yet, children were born. It was the way.

But now? Alone?

Silly woman. Foolish one. Alone if need be. I am of the Morning Star People and will do what must be done.

The panic lessened although the fear remained. But now her mind had something to work with. Preparations. She reached behind the backrest for a packet of herbs and roots and powders gathered months ago in the valley of the Stillwater, before the hectic escape from her people. A sadness plagued the once happy memories of life with the Morning Star People, but she never regretted the decision to leave, not during the grueling month-long ride from the village and not now. Only she wished that maybe Red Bead Woman were here at her side.

She took a small flint knife from the packet. With such as this, she had seen mothers sever the umbilical cords of their newborns. She unfolded a swatch of brushed buckskin to keep the infant from any chill. She placed beside the cloth a pouch containing a fine powder derived from the prairie puffball to dust the infant before bundling in the soft wrappings. There was bark medicine to ensure an easy delivery, but Mourning Dove had the feeling it was too late for medicinal tea.

She almost lost consciousness so severe was the next cramp.

"Help me, my mother," she gasped. "My mother . . ."

Again the pain eased. With trembling fingers she took the last item from the packet, a short thick length of twisted rawhide. No Cheyenne maternity kit would be without it. Hemené placed it between her teeth and bit down in time to keep from screaming as the next series of contractions struck. She closed her eyes and listened to her own rasping breath. How long she remained like this she could not tell. Was it the pain? She heard something. Was she going mad? She listened, concentrated . . . yes . . . a chant . . . only in her mind . . . it must be in her mind . . . only because she was frightened . . . but heard still . . . the voice of Maomé seemed to fill the room. She trembled and kept her eyes tightly closed. Maomé's voice was strength. His words told of a people renewed. The Birthing Song. It told of the last days. It told of dying ways. It told of how the strength of a people is in the children. It told of tragic courage. And salvation in the land. It told of the love of man and woman and the son who would mirror such a love.

Mourning Dove listened.

And endured, until the chant faded, becoming one with the groaning chorus of the wind. Joel, she prayed. My husband, I need you. Then something, she heard something, footsteps? He had returned. At last, had returned. She lifted her sweat-beaded face as the door frame rattled, the latch lifted, the door swung open. A flurry of snowflakes gusted into the room.

And a stranger entered.

The antelope kicked at the red snow, not realizing what had happened, that it was dying. The muffled explosion of the rifle had reached out through the drifting flakes as in the same instant the lead slug knocked the animal to the ground. The antelope tried to stand and thought it succeeded, thought it was running, escaping into the same forest that had shielded its executioner. Across the snowy landscape, the hunter's voice began to sing in Cheyenne. The low, repetitious tones soothed the antelope. The animal was no longer afraid. The sleek brown head lay back upon the earth. Snow settled on the sad round eyes that saw no longer.

Joel finished the chant. Certain customs were becoming a way of life to him. He did not dwell on the change. He was too busy struggling to stay alive. Joel knelt by the antelope, worked a length of rope through the prong horns. The snow was falling too thickly now to attempt dragging the carcass to where the Appaloosa was tethered. Joel tossed the end of the rope over a limb of the willow and hoisted all two hundred and fifty pounds of the animal into the air where it dangled out of reach of predators. He butchered enough meat to last a couple of days, taking care to bury a portion as an offering to the earth, and packed the remaining cuts in a leather pouch inside his shirt. The wind pelted his cheeks with ice. Snowflakes lost themselves in his silvery beard. He slung the Hawken over his shoulder and retraced his already obliterated tracks toward Otter Creek, calculating that an hour would bring him in sight of the cabin. The prospect of a hot meal quickened his steps. The packet of freshly butchered meat warmed against his stomach. After days of his fruitless efforts, Hemené would be pleasantly surprised.

15

Joel reached the homesite by midafternoon. The Appaloosa needed no prompting to head for the stable. The animal lowered its head and, with breath steaming from its nostrils, ploughed a furrow through the remaining yard of drifting snow.

"Spring is a merry season," Joel muttered grimly as he swung down to open the barn door. He had started to enter when the stallion whinnied and pulled back on the rein. Joel wiped the frozen perspiration from his face and saw what had startled his horse. A freight wagon piled high with barrels and boxes beneath a water-stained tarpaulin blocked the center aisle. Joel stared in disbelief at the wagon as a brace of braying mules, still in harness, bawled in alarm at his intrusion. Joel lifted the cover of the tarp and read "Nails" on one barrel and "dried apples" on the next. Wire fencing, coffee tins, salt, metal pans—a small fortune in supplies.

He coaxed the wary Appaloosa to an unoccupied stall and hastily latched the gate before edging past the wagon to the doorway. He looked out at the cabin's squat, vague silhouette crouched behind a curtain of snow. Things looked peaceful enough, but that meant nothing, absolutely nothing. The windows were shuttered against the storm. He had no way of finding out who was inside, at least not by stealth. But he knew his wife was in there and, in her present condition, helpless. Joel stepped into the yard and struggled toward the cabin; his stiffened fingers dug into the pocket of his gray woolen cavalry coat, working through the hole in the lining to close around the wood grip of his holstered revolver. He unbuttoned the lower half of his coat to allow a speedier draw. The storm seemed to be abating; perhaps they were faced with something less than a blizzard. However, he didn't intend to start feeling grateful until he discovered who owned the wagon and mules in his barn. He slogged the remaining few feet and worked the door handle to release the inside latch. The panel refused to budge. Alarmed now, and casting caution aside, Joel pommeled the door with his left hand and shouted to his wife. He heard the latch within rasp along its track. The door opened, seconds later.

A smooth-skinned, square-jawed, thoroughly homely face peered at him from under a floppy-brimmed hat. It took a moment for Joel to realize he was looking at a woman and a moment more for the gut-tightening stench of raw whiskey and fresh blood to assail his senses. The big, raw-boned woman in flannel workshirt dodged out of his path as he lunged into the room.

"Who are you?" Joel snapped. "What the hell is going on here?"

The woman tucked a strand of drab brown hair behind her ear, and placing her hands on her hips, she fixed Joel in a steely stare.

"You watch your tongue and lower your tone, Mister Ryan. Ain't fittin' a babe come all new and fresh into this world and hear the likes of cussin'!"

A squalling protest issued from beneath a pile of blankets.

"There you've gone and waked him. For shame. And the mother, too."

Joel turned ashen.

"Him . . . baby . . ." he spun around in time for Mourning Dove to poke her delicate features over the edge of the blankets. Something stirred beside her in the bedding, and a tiny copper fist poked upward as if in defiance.

"Hemené," Joel gasped, making his way to the bed. He leaned forward, winced, and removed the packet of meat from his shirt, then leaned forward again to behold his son.

"Now see you warm them paws of yours, Mister Silvertip Ryan, before you go maulin' that young'un," the woman said.

Hemené smiled weakly. "Nahkohe has a son." Joel blew on his fingers and then reached out to touch the bunched and wrinkled features, to stroke the coal black hair of his son.

"He's such a Little Bear," Joel said in awe. The infant's wrinkled hand closed around his father's finger. His cries had

subsided; the baby was content to snuggle in the loving hollow of his mother's arms. Joel sat back on his haunches, the
fact they weren't alone in the room returning to mind. He
slowly turned and noticed their uninvited visitor was busily
stirring a kettle of soup she had hung on hooks over the
flames. The woman lifted the wooden spoon to her lips,
sniffed, blew the steam away, took a sip, and shrugged her
shoulders.

"Needs salt," she said, "but I'll settle for what I have,
'cause the salt's in my wagon, and I cannot see that it's worth
freezing to death just to show how particular I am. Now the
Romans had a saying that 'hunger is the best seasoning' and
I warrant they had a point there. Who am I to argue with
them Romans?"

"Her name is Sweeney. She helped us both," Hemené
said, hugging the infant at her side.

"And I know your handle," Sweeney added. "Your
woman told me, Silvertip Joel Ryan. A name folks might
remember."

"Where did you come from? I mean, what are you doing
here?" Joel looked back toward his family, then to the
woman. He was still confused.

"I could ask the same question of you. In fact, I will. Your
papoose there was on the way, and I didn't have much time
to chitchat with the missus. As for me, I brought my wagon
up from Denver. Took me two tries. I had a run-in with the
Crow down in Wyoming, and they done cleaned me out. So
I headed right on back to Denver and sweet-talked a storekeeper into trusting me on consignment. Them consarned
Crows . . . Ol' Blue Jacket makes peace one day and war the
next. I had to travel at night part of the way just to sneak
past them." Sweeney took a tin cup from another hook by
the hearth and filled it with broth, holding it out for Joel who
walked across the room and took the cup in his hands, grimaced, and looked for the nearest place to set it down. He
settled for the stone lip of the fireplace.

"Careful, it's hot," Sweeney added as an afterthought. The
cabin's sparse furnishings consisted of a hand-hewn table
with more splinters than a prickly pear has thorns and four
three-legged stools. Sweeney nudged one of the stools closer

to the fire and squatted down. She filled a cup of her own
from the kettle. Joel studied the woman as she helped herself
to the meal she had prepared. Her broad shoulders strained
the seams of her workshirt, and her neck was thick with
muscles where the smooth flesh joined to her torso. An extra
panel of cloth had been sewn into her dungarees, and the
blue denim was stretched tight across the impressive proportions of her stomach.

"I saw your wagon in the barn," Joel said. "You must
have used some mighty 'sweet' words. I have found mer-
chants, for the most part, to be a heartless race."

"Well . . ." Sweeney pursed her lips and tucked the same
strand of hair behind her ear. "If the truth be known . . . I
held him upside down in one of his pickle barrels until he
seen that I could be trusted." She chuckled at the memory,
and Joel smiled, taking a liking to the woman.

"Funny thing," Sweeney said, staring at the flames in the
hearth, "snow was getting so thick I couldn't see where I
was heading, and then all of a sudden it was like I heard
singing."

"Singing?"

"Well . . . kind of. I called out but never got no answer,
but I started headin' for the sound. And you'll think I been
drinkin' that whiskey instead of using it for the birthin', but
I swear it was like being pulled. Pulled right to here. 'Cause
it stopped when I seen the barn, and I have never been so
happy to set eyes on anything so pretty. These spring snows
up here are killers if a body ain't ready for them. Oh, I
reckon it was the wind playin' tricks. Anyway, I come on
in, saw your woman there, and could tell what she was about.
Didn't have much time but to pour some of that cheap forty
rod of mine over my knife blade and cut the cord when the
baby showed himself. That gal's gritty as fish eggs in sand,
mark my word." Sweeney glanced over at mother and child
and winked at them. Joel tilted the cup of soup to his lips.
The broth thawed the chill in his bones, and he emptied the
contents down his gullet, smacking his lips in gratitude.

"Ain't much. Just some boiled jerky," Sweeney said, leaning forward as the firelight danced on her stoic, solid expression. "Where's Gilchrist?"

"Who?" Joel asked, caught off guard. Sweeney saw he was honestly puzzled.

"Bob Gilchrist. You're sitting 'neath his roof. Now that the war back east is over, there'll be a flood of folks headin' out for these parts. And they'll be needin' supplies and such on the way. Ol' Bob and I had it figured to open a store up on the Yellowstone. Sell wood to the riverboats and build a landing for them to dock at. And when folks climb off, there be my store offerin' just what they need in the way of supplies. I picked out the right spot and everything, but I was countin' on Bob's help. He said he'd be waitin' for me. 'Course it took me longer than I planned."

"The only ones living here were owls and coyotes, and I chased them out," Joel said. "The barn was half finished. We finished it. The cabin needed repairs. We fixed it up. The place had been abandoned for months."

"Just like Bob," Sweeney said with a wag of her head. "My pappy always used to say, 'If'n you're gonna lean on a tree, pick a stout one.' I knew Bob's middle name was 'break,' but I just didn't want to see it. A man would have to be plumb daft to take a fancy to the likes . . ." She glanced over at Joel, her voice fading. "I 'spect I'd find him up at Silverbow. With the rest of the hopeful fools. If I cared to look."

A single tear gleamed in the corner of her eye. She wiped it away with the back of her calloused hand. "I'll make do without him."

Joel cleared his throat, uncertain what to say, elated at the birth of his son, yet struck with sympathy for the woman who had helped them. He noticed Hemené and the baby were fast asleep, and he smiled at them both, snug beneath the blankets and buffalo robe. Then he held his hand out to the woman across from him.

"Sweeney . . . I am honored to meet you. Truly honored. I won't forget your help."

Sweeney lifted her gaze from the fire to Joel and reached out to clasp his hand in anything but a dainty grip.

"I'm in your debt," Joel said. The wind moaned and rattled the door like some monstrous animal wanting to enter, refusing to leave.

"If that's the case," Sweeney said, with a grin that suddenly dispelled the self-pity she had been feeling, "then you can bring in the firewood. And string up a blanket or two across the room here so I can bed down in private. I'm a lady, you know."

The storm blew itself out by afternoon. A Chinook wind arrived two days later to scour the snow drifts from all but the deepest shaded combs and hollows. Sweeney stayed on, much to Hemené and Joel's delight. She was a personable gal, an avid storyteller, and an able, willing worker. With her help, Joel finished the corral and repaired a plough; the former owner had damaged it on a hidden rock while trying to begin a garden. There was time, with the temperature moderating as spring unfolded upon the land, for picnics with a blanket spread in the sun, and Little Bear—or "Cub" as Joel had taken to calling him—was the center of attraction while proud papa and loving mama sat nearby and beamed in pride and happiness at their first offspring. By May, Sweeney had gone from stranger to member of the family, which suited the mulewacker just fine. However, the affection Sweeney felt for these two with their baby could not dissuade her own ambition. On the other hand, it did give her an idea.

The double-bladed ax bit deep into the end of the log. Joel lifted the chunk of wood and slammed it down. The blade sank further into the wood, splitting it in half. Joel tossed the halves into a pile and started on another. He wanted to have the woodpile topped off by evening, which wasn't too far away. His stomach growled as the aroma of frying steaks and grease bread wafted out into the yard. He paused to listen to his son exercise his lungs. The bawling subsided as mother evidently took him to breast.

"Got me a notion," Sweeney said, startling him. "Sorry," she muttered.

"Didn't hear you come up," Joel said. "I guess I was talking to myself."

"I been thinking."

"Sounds serious. Stay in bed, I'll bring you a toddy," he

replied, good-naturedly. He split another log and added the halves to his growing pile.

"I'm leaving come sunup," the raw-boned woman replied.

The ax paused in midair, then slowly lowered to the earth as Joel turned to her. He wiped his arm across his face and squinted through the sheen of perspiration stinging his eyes. Sweeney's broad, flat features were unable to conceal her subterfuge. She had simply lived too direct a life. "We'll miss you," Joel said, uncertainly.

"No you won't," Sweeney blurted out, excited now. "Because you and Mourning Dove are coming with me."

"This is our home."

"Sure it is, but that don't mean you can't take advantage of my offer."

"What offer?"

"Well now," and Sweeney plopped her ample behind down on the log Joel had been about to split. "You tell me you got plans to lay claim to this whole valley and build you a ranch. You figure to build you a herd from the wild horses you can round up. Well and good, but why not add some cattle? Them gold miners up in places like Silverbow got to eat."

"I know that," Joel said. He leaned on the ax handle and in his own mind the dream formed, the dream that had haunted him since the moment he had first beheld the cabin at Otter Creek. A splendid ranch house, cool valleys, and sunlit meadows alive with cattle, colts and mares, and children in the yard. Lots of children. The dream, like all dreams, had its limits in reality.

"Good breeding stock costs money."

"My point exactly," Sweeney said. Tucking her brown hair back under her hat, she leaned forward on her elbows. "I'll need help on the Yellowstone. What say we be partners?"

"What can I buy in with?"

"Sweat. That's as good a commodity out here as any. Put your marker in the yard so folks know who the cabin belongs to, and come with me up on the Yellowstone. Help me build my place, set the store to right, chop wood for the steamboats, and I'll cut you in on the profits, fifty-fifty, after expenses. You won't be more than two days' ride on a fast horse, so you can always check on things. The baby will slow us down, but we can make do if we leave tomorrow."

The offer was attractive, even generous. Joel looked about him. Here was home, and the thought of leaving even for only a couple of months was almost more than he could bear. But if leaving meant that they were closer to realizing his vision of a Ryan ranch, then it was wholly worthwhile.

"You think on it. Chew it over with your meat and biscuits, and let me know come morning." Sweeney stood and started across the yard.

"Aren't you going to have supper with us?"

"I ate. I'll be gettin' my wagon ready. Reckon I'll sleep in the barn tonight."

"Sweeney, I can help you later. You don't need to spend the night in the barn."

The heavyset woman put her hands on her hips and wagged her head in dismay. "For posin' as a right smart fellow sometimes, Mister Silvertip Ryan, you got the sense of a jughead."

Night wind.

A sound of distant baying. The wilderness is restless, tonight of all nights. But within the cabin lingers a stillness, the quiet aftermath of fulfillment. Yet the dark wind whispers and passion holds the night.

The glow from the hearth bathed their bodies in its warmth; their naked flesh glistened like molten gold, and Joel's hair, held away from his face by a beaded leather headband, hung in thick cords of silver to his shoulders.

"So this is what she meant by sleeping in the barn," he grinned. Mourning Dove brushed her hands over his thighs and curled down to nibble at his knee. He started to laugh. She hushed him and pointed at the infant sleeping soundly in his bundled bedding across the room from them.

"Little Cub has ears that can hear the flight of the bee."

"He listens to his dreams, for now," Joel said. "Not us." He leaned over and kissed her hip and side. She rolled atop him, raising up on her hands, her arms extended. A single pearly drop of milk formed on her nipple, and she lowered herself to his lips, shuddering as he kissed her. She tilted her head and let him kiss her throat. She felt him stirring, his manhood aroused and brushing the inside of her thigh with the coursing of his blood.

"Perhaps Little Bear would like a brother," she said, easing backward to settle on his hard, velvet length.

"Or sister." Joel gasped as she tightened and began her brief sweet ride toward a climax of silent pleading, of muscles taut and eyes closed, her head thrown back and black hair whipping in wild disarray as she drove herself against him. His fingers dug into her hips as passion tore her being and one tumult was conquered only to plunge raging into another.

Again and again and again . . .

"Ne-mehotatse," she said in a sleepy voice.

"I love you too," Joel said, nuzzling her smooth back and hugging her close.

"Then we will leave?"

"For a time."

"I am sorry to leave. I am glad we will be able to help Sweeney. She has done much for us. It is good we do this for her. But there is sadness in leaving."

"Yes. Now go to sleep." He stroked her hair.

"Husband. I have two wishes. To share our life always, in this, our valley. That is one. But I have another."

Joel nodded forward, his head settling upon her shoulder. "Husband . . ."

"I . . . I'm listening," he said in a muffled voice.

"I wish our son to know his people. Someday."

The suggestion roused Joel into wakefulness. Sacred Killer had promised to take Joel's life should they ever meet, and though he wasn't afraid, Joel wanted no part of such a confrontation.

"We are Little Bear's people," Joel said. He stared past her coppery shoulder at the crackling blaze burning in the hearth. "Do you know what you are saying? Have you forgotten your brother's words to me?" he added.

"No," Hemené said. "But I know my brother in this way better than he knows himself. He could not hate our little one. As long as the Stillwater flows, the Morning Star People will build their summer lodges along its bank. Perhaps we could . . ."

"Mourning Dove . . . we can never go back. To do such a thing would be not to care whether we lived or died. Do you understand what I am saying?"

"It was only a wish," she sighed. "You are right, my husband. I will speak no more of it."

She pulled the blanket to her shoulders and turned toward the fire, her head pillowed on Joel's arm.

In the silence, Joel's thoughts assailed him. *Why hadn't she lost her temper? Anger always made it easier to refuse someone what she wanted. Roll over and go to sleep leaving him to feel like a heel instead of a man exercising good common sense. He was right, blast it all. God in heaven, what did she want from him?* Of course, he knew. For all the love and the happiness and satisfaction of building a life together, part of her would always regret the way they had left, part of her would ache to be reconciled with her brother. Was that so difficult to understand? Joel had felt that way himself, many a time, many a wakeful night with the memory of his Kentucky farm a "might have been" forever nipping at his solitary thoughts.

"Mourning Dove . . ." He knew she was awake. "Someday. We will try, someday. And Cub will know all his people."

She turned in his embrace and nestled close to his chest, her arms entwined in his. Joel needed no words to tell he had made his wife happy. She showed him. And later, after the last dear act of joyous consummation, drifting gentle and becalmed, borne on the tides of sleep, Joel in a last conscious moment of utter happiness made the mistake of thinking it would last forever.

16

The Moon When Horses Fatten . . . the sun a burning pool. . . . It was July when they returned to Otter Creek. Beneath Joel's steady guidance, the freight wagon crested the ridge trail leading down the valley floor, all ablush with bitterroots. Joel allowed the mules a momentary breather. His wife, babe in arms, repositioned herself on the wagon seat.

Behind them lay better than eight hard weeks of labor. Together, with Sweeney, they had built a single-room store, felling timber and hoisting the hastily trimmed logs into place. They had notched the corners for a snug fit and left Hemené to chink the gaps in the walls with mud from the Yellowstone. Then as Sweeney worked on the interior, Joel spent his time stockpiling wood. He was working on his second cord when the first stern-wheeler blasted the air with its shrill whistle and set Cub to crying. Word that there was a new stop up on the Yellowstone, closer to the gold fields by better than a hundred and fifty miles, had spread throughout St. Louis, thanks to Sweeney's foresight in sending a letter to Captain Bixby, a friend who always wintered at the St. Louis docks. It was Bixby's mountain boat, a crude triple decker, that first rounded the bend and hailed the landing. Sweeney sold just about everything in stock. Luckily, she had arranged for Bixby to bring in more merchandise as well as three milk cows that arrived none the worse for wear. Shovels, shirts, boots, rifles, and gunpowder were in much demand, along with coffee, fresh milk, salt pork, and beans. Apples were at a premium. Sweeney put a couple of the more destitute newcomers to work on a real dock, which freed Joel to head his family for home. Joel took one of the three milk cows as payment for his labors, telling Sweeney to reinvest any other money in the store. He considered the wagon and mule team only as a loan.

At last the time had come for departure. Sweeney had insisted on loading their wagon with enough supplies to last into the fall. While Joel tethered the Appaloosa, the two mares, and the cow to the wagon gate, Sweeney hugged Mourning Dove, and then she grudgingly handed over Little Bear to his father.

"You be careful," Sweeney said, her square jaw trembling. She pursed her lips and wiped at her eyes.

"Be seeing you, partner," Joel said, and leaning over, he kissed her on the cheek. Sweeney turned beet red. And remained that way long after the wagon had rolled out of sight.

"Oh look," Mourning Dove said beside him. Half-a-dozen wild geese lifted from the twinkling surface of the creek to trace a lazy spiral in the sky, the music of their call drifted on the listless afternoon. Joel lifted his son from Hemené's grasp and held the gurgling infant up as if the baby could actually focus on the wild geese, now mere pinpricks of ivory lost against the hazy horizon.

"From where we stand, my son," he whispered in the little one's ear, "this valley, and the meadows beyond, is our land. Ryan land."

A place needed a name.

Their home needed . . . a name. The valley had endured the terrible ravages of winter, raging winds, burial beneath solemn silent layers of snow, only to rise again in unconquerable and glorious display. Pink and ivory petals trembled in the warm breath of summer, symbols of something permanent and timeless. Like the valley. Like the Cheyenne themselves, the children of the Morning Star.

"This is Ryan land," Joel said in hushed tones. "This is Morning Star."

"It's good to be home," Mourning Dove said, hugging her husband, thankful the three days of travel were at an end. Joel passed the infant back to her waiting arms.

"C'mon, mules, you heard what the lady said. We're home." Joel began making plans. He intended to finish the corral and then start on a new house, larger, much larger

than the cabin and farther back from the creek to ease the
mosquito problem during the warm months. And he needed
a smokehouse. With the money he would eventually earn
from his share of Sweeney's profits, a small herd of cattle
was a distinct possibility now. As they angled down into the
yard, he was relieved to see the stone cairn he had erected
in the front yard was still intact. The paper he had left with
his name on it was still pinned beneath the topmost rock.

"I'll put the wagon in the barn and turn the horses out to
graze. Why don't you get out of the sun?" he suggested.

"And I can chase the spiders out before you come to the
cabin," Mourning Dove replied knowingly.

Joel started to protest, but she laughed. And he figured
protesting would just prolong his embarrassment. He did not
like spiders.

"Just see you start the coffee," he said as she stepped
down. Mourning Dove nodded in mock seriousness and
walked up the steps to the pinewood porch. She worked the
latch and disappeared into the cabin.

Joel brought the wagon to a halt before the barn. He
jumped down from the wagon seat and crossed around to the
Appaloosa, freeing the stallion's reins, then untying the cow
and then the mares. The stallion tossed his head and whinnied.

"Show the ladies a good time," Joel said, swatting his hat
at the Appaloosa as the mares trotted off toward the creek,
tracking the scent of water. Joel started back around to the
mules. The stallion whinnied again and pawed at the earth.
Weary from three days of travel and preoccupied with his
plans for the future, Joel was oblivious to the animal's warning.

He entered the barn.

The Crow warrior lunged out of the shadows. Joel heard
the rustle of straw and glimpsed movement on the periphery
of his vision. Sunlight glinted along a length of steel. The
Crow loosed a wild war cry and closed for the kill. Joel
twisted as the knife blade slashed his upper arm, and continuing his spin, he crashed through the slats of the nearest stall
and landed on his back on the hard-packed earth. Dazed and
struggling for breath, Joel watched a pool of blackness ex-

pand to swallow the world. A gunshot exploded nearby. From the cabin? The cabin! Hemené! He fought the dark and won; his vision cleared. He dragged the Colt Dragoon from his belt as the brave with the knife regained his momentum. Assuming the white man was mortally wounded, the brave leaped across the shaft of sunlight beaming through the doorway. Joel glimpsed eagle feathers, black braids, and a face streaked with yellow war paint, all in the second before the Dragoon thundered in his fist. The brave flew backward and collapsed in the dust of his own charge.

The cabin!

Joel struggled to his feet. His hat was gone, and when he staggered out into the yard, his hair bristled in silver disarray like the coat of a wild beast. He saw a peg-legged man emerge from the cabin, and Joel sensed recognition, although he could not see the features. But the man raised a revolver and fired. A bullet cut the air inches from Joel's head and plunked into the barn door. The Dragoon roared, and the man ducked around behind the cabin.

"Hemené," Joel shouted.

He heard the horrid whisper of an arrow as it arced through the air and buried its iron point in the wood panel of the freight wagon. Another arrow tugged at his pants leg as two warriors on horseback charged from the edge of the forest, galloping full tilt down between the barn and the cabin.

Joel dropped to the ground and rolled beneath the wagon. An arrow glanced off the wheel hub as Joel balanced his gun barrel on a wood spoke and squeezed off the four shots left in his cylinder. Black powder momentarily obscured his targets. He heard a horse rush past. And through the acrid cloud of gunsmoke, he spied the other pony as it swerved aside, leaving its rider to continue straight ahead. The Crow brave landed atop the wagon, knocked over a barrel of nails and yelped in pain as he jabbed his shin against the rung of a rocking chair. A side of salt pork hit the earth, and then the warrior landed with a grunt on top of it. Joel dropped the Dragoon pistol and drew his Navy Colt from its holster. The brave reached for the worn grip of flintlock pistol protruding above his waistband. Yellow flame spat from the muzzle of the Navy Colt, and the warrior doubled over and fell on his side. Joel crawled out from beneath the wagon. The other warrior had wheeled his horse at the edge of the creek, surprised to find himself all alone. Joel drew his knife from his boot top and brandishing the blade in his left hand, the gun in his right, advanced down the slope. His eyes were wide and flashing the fire of battle, blood dripped the length of his wounded arm, and when he wiped his face on the sleeve, his face smeared with crimson. His hair gleamed silver and shimmered in the dying breeze. His lips curled back as he snarled, "C'mon. C'mon, you son of a bitch!"

The remaining Crow brave chose discretion over valor. He leaped his pony across the creek and vanished among the sentinel pines.

It was over as quickly as it had begun. Slowly his muscles relaxed as Joel turned back to his homesite. He could hear the cow bawling in terror from the depths of the barn. The mules in their traces strained against the wagon brakes and brayed in frustration and fear. A low guttural sigh issued from the mortally wounded brave by the wagon. His legs stiffened and then relaxed in death.

Over. And two men had died in a matter of seconds. Two men and who else? The peg-leg man was nowhere to be seen. But the shot from the cabin . . .

"Hemené," Joel rasped, his voice barely audible. He began to run, his long legs eating the distance in strides that pounded in unison with the panic tearing at his heart. Now he heard what he had not heard before, the faint, hungry cry of an infant.

"Hemené."

The peg-leg man . . . Had his beard been red, wreathing his face in fire? Oh God, not him. Not him.

"Hemené."

A baby is crying. A name goes unanswered. Thunder splits the mind, horror rises to the throat. Joel runs, and a name on his lips is repeated over and over like an echo that never stops. Hemené. Mourning Dove. Never stops.

Never.

He flings the door open. And steps inside, searching the shadows, and finding her at last. She is sprawled upon the floor in a garish semblance of sleep. But who will wake her from the sleep of blood? And there in her hand, see how it clutches the bronze crucifix of Henri Larocque.

If she is dead . . . She can't be. Not true. Not true.

A cry starts deep in the soul, deep where the hurt lies longest. Unleashed now, it claws the throat in an anguished wail, in an outpouring of betrayal and fury and insufferable torment.

Raging.

Raging.

17

The moon cast its silver sheen upon the world, draping the valley of the Stillwater in its magic glow, bathing the world with its false promise of peace.

Sacred Killer knew better than to trust the moon. She was a notorious trickster who clouded the judgment of men. Tonight, as they had every night for the past month, the walls of his lodge closed round to smother him. He resisted as best he could, but the demons of solitude were too many. He stepped across the untouched meal Red Bead Woman had left for him and ducked through the opening out into the night. The village slept in silence, in a night dotted by ruby campfires. No one stirred. The dogs were still. It was as if a spell had been placed upon all the world save himself, thought Sacred Killer. Was this another of Maomé's enchantments? Wait, something moved. Was someone out there? Just beyond the encampment of the Red Shields. Watching. Why keep such a suspicious vigil? Was it a ghost or flesh and blood?

Sacred Killer took up his rifle and walked from the encampment toward the figure in the dark. He strode boldly across the buffalo grass as if daring the watcher to declare himself. The moon swept aside its gown of gossamer clouds, casting the war chief and the mysterious visitor in stark relief.

Sacred Killer halted, scarcely able to believe his own eyes. The tall, broad-shouldered figure astride the stallion could only be one man.

As horse and rider started forward, Sacred Killer thumbed back the hammer on his rifle. The stallion came to a stop a few short feet from where the warrior stood.

"I have had a dream," Sacred Killer said, still unable to

discern if this were a vision. He stared at Joel, studying the hollow cheeks, the eyes blasted by grief. "I saw my sister, dead. Is this true?"

Joel nodded. Sacred Killer looked past the horseman toward the black horizon, black as the sorrow in his heart.

No vision. No ghost. But a man. A man who could die.

"I vowed to kill you, Silvertip, if our paths should ever cross. You stole my sister in life, now follow her in death."

He raised the rifle, sighted on Joel's chest.

A voice carried to him, the voice of an infant roused from sleep. Sacred Killer held his fire as Joel reached beneath his coat and brought forth the babe he had lifted from Mourning Dove's dying embrace. The child began to cry in a loud and indignant voice.

"It was her wish that Little Bear, our son, should know his second father," said Silvertip Joel Ryan. "My journey is complete. Do what you will."

The rifle wavered. Sacred Killer had made a vow. A blood oath. This could not be denied. The vow must be honored. The vow . . . He eased the hammer forward.

The vow . . .

The war chief of the Red Shields lowered the rifle and dropped it in the buffalo grass. Sacred Killer could blame the white man no longer, unless he himself shared the blame. The burden of anger he had carried for almost a year suddenly left him. The warrior hesitated, took a few steps closer. He stretched out his arms. Joel dismounted and placed the infant in Sacred Killer's hands. The crying stopped.

"Nahkohe-ese," Sacred Killer repeated. Little Bear. And though his eyes were moist with sorrow for his sister, he could not help smiling as the child reached for a raven feather from his hair.

"For too long have we walked down separate trails," the Cheyenne warrior said, looking up at Joel. "Come, my brother."

"No," Joel said. "I must find Henri Larocque, the man who killed her. After I have avenged Hemené, maybe then if the All-Father wills it, I will return."

Sacred Killer studied him a moment more and then, as if reading the white man's thoughts, nodded.

"There are paths you must walk where a Cub may not follow. So be it, Nahkohe." Sacred Killer cradled the infant in his arms, holding the child close. "Red Bead Woman bore Lame Deer a son. But the child died. She weeps for the son who never nursed at her breasts. Little Bear will dry her tears I am thinking." The war chief heard the horse and looked around to see the man he had called Silvertip disappearing into the dark and lonely vastness of the night.

"Ride with the wind, Joel Ryan," said Sacred Killer and he held up the struggling infant that he might see his father.

A coyote howled in the distance.

Then Sacred Killer turned toward the village. His heart was both happy and heavy with sorrow, cradling the joy of his dreams in his arms and sensing the ghostly presence of his sister at his side. The war chief of the Red Shields started down the path, carrying the son of Mourning Dove back to her people.

October, 1874

October, 1874.

18

Joel Ryan knelt by the waters of the Gallatin River and, taking a drink, paused to stare at his reflection in the clear sweet surface. Eight years had turned his face a leathery brown, had seamed the flesh and breathed the raw power of the howling wilderness into the man called Silvertip.

"Like a worn leather belt," Joel muttered to himself, evaluating his appearance. He heard the cry of the geese and glanced upward to stare at the formations spreading over the deep blue of the sky. The music of their passing lingered on the wind. Joel watched awhile, held in place by the beauty of the world, awed by the unwinding of the autumn season. He looked to the snowcapped summits of the Madison range, he looked to the Absarokas over which he had crossed, following the trail of the Cheyenne from their usual camp along the Stillwater to the valley of the Gallatin. The mountains had not aged, they were old and craggy gods lording over this landscape of men. Joel looked down at his watery self again, the cry of the wild geese dying in the distance, and wondered if anyone would believe that beneath the pelt of his silver mane and beard that shimmered indeed like the fur of a grizzly, he was but a man in his mid-thirties. Eight lonely years had robbed the ready gentleness from his features and left him lean. Power rippled beneath the greasy buckskins, raw power in muscles hard as granite, supple as whipcord. His face was masked with introspection, a permanent and haunting set to his features. After the torment, the tortured nights that had dogged every step of his wanderings in that first year after Hemené's death, he had come to terms with suffering and dulled its sting and at last had learned to laugh again and dream of a future. Joel Ryan was too proud a man to go mad. He had remembered what

Mourning Dove had taught him, the power of the circle. All life moved in such a path. The future is born where the past has died.

For Joel this meant a place at Otter Creek, the land that was his destiny . . . Morning Star.

The roan stallion nickered softly behind him. "I hear them," Joel gently answered without looking back over his shoulder. Instead, he continued to drink from his cupped hands, allowing the braves he had heard to creep closer. They must be young for him to have heard them approach. A twig popped, a meadow hawk spiraled upward from the brush, scolding the intruders. Joel grinned. He could envision the young bucks crouching in the tall grass, their coppery muscles tightening as they prepared to attack. How many? Listen. *The juneberry bush just shivered. At least one there. And the twig, that makes two. Three, maybe four to disturb the hawk. Surrounded and outnumbered,* Joel thought. *They're confident. It's made them clumsy. Three or four to one . . . heh heh . . . trying to bring this old silvertip to bay. I must be careful not to kill them. If they're Cheyenne . . .*

A reed snapped.

Mud sucked at the soles of a moccasin.

A grunt, a quick breath, a high-pitched war cry.

Joel straightened, whirled, caught the leaping brave in midair, and glimpsed the youth's Morning Star beadwork. Joel tossed the boy headfirst into the icy Gallatin as a second figure charged toward him out of the underbrush and a third, the oldest of the lot, rose and leveled a rifle. The charging warrior brandished a tomahawk that Joel batted aside, then he clubbed the brave across the back of his neck, dropping him like a stone. He picked the brave up and, using him for a shield, charged the rifleman who hesitated long enough for Joel to knock him down. The rifleman stared in horror as Joel's bowie knife flashed in the air and slashed down, twisting at the last second to tap the flat of the blade against the rifleman's scalp and the buttocks of his barely conscious companion.

"*Hena-haanehe!*" Joel shouted in Cheyenne, the triumphant cry of a warrior who has counted coup on his enemies. He rose to his full height then and stepped back from his would-be attackers.

"What? I ride in search of the village of the Morning Star People. And am attacked by boys. Are there no Red Shields to ride against Nahkohe? What dishonor is this?" He growled then with all the menace of his namesake, growled and shook his silvertipped mane and the blade of his knife glinted before the youths' wide-eyed, frightened faces. The two warriors scrambled over one another in their efforts to escape what must surely be some demon they had mistaken for a man. Joel laughed as they scurried to safety. He heard the splash of water and saw the other brave stagger from the river. My God, this was but a boy whose hastily applied war paint had smeared in garish red swirls disguising features that piqued Joel's interest. But before the man called Silvertip could speak, the youth darted away, disappearing after his cowardly cohorts, making an aisle of crushed reeds as he ran to safety.

"Come here," Joel shouted in English, cursed and spoke in Cheyenne. *"Ne-Naestse!"* But the boy had had his fill of the warrior's life for the time being and scampered out of sight. Joel heard him find his horse and other horses as well. The other two braves no doubt.

Drumming hoofbeats receded in the distance, became a faint tattoo that Joel listened for, lost in his own thoughts, locked in the present and the past, as if time itself had converged on him.

The boy . . . his face beneath the mask of war had been the face of Mourning Dove.

19

Joel spied the smoke from the cookfires long before he saw the village, here in the high solitude of the Gallatin River. Peaks rose from either side, jagged, windswept, boasting cruel-looking snowcapped summits like enormous arrow heads and war clubs. Angry gods had broken this land, angry gods that still quarreled in the earth and tumbled whole mountainsides into valleys, emptied lakes, created new ones and new valleys. The haze that rose above the spires of pine trees guided Joel around the last of the river's turns and revealed two hundred yards ahead, the village of the Cheyenne. Joel gasped at the size and reined the roan to a standstill. He had heard that the tribes were massing for a concerted effort to drive the gold seekers from the mountain ranges west of the headwaters of the Yellowstone. He doffed his hat and tucked it inside his beaded shirt. The wind tugged at his mane, and he thought with grim humor that his scalp would be prime decoration for a war lance.

He slapped the dust from his shirt. The Morning Star emblem Hemené had worked into the cloth was minus a few beads but, he hoped, recognizable at a distance. Even as he started forward, the village seemed to erupt in a flurry of activity. By the time Joel had ridden fifty yards he spotted a dozen Cheyenne braves gallop from camp. Suppressing his urge to head for cover Joel urged the roan into a brisk trot. The air was filled with a chorus of bloodcurdling war whoops as the warriors quickly closed the gap. He recognized the painted lances, the blood red shields, the red war markings on their ponies, and now closer still, the garish streaks of crimson transforming faces into visions of death.

The roan faltered, then responded to the pressure of Joel's knees, the hours of training overriding panic. Joel braced himself for the onslaught. The wind gusted and he tasted grit from the riverbed and kept a firm grip on the reins as the warriors swarmed past him. He closed his eyes as dirt spattered his face. The roan sidestepped skittishly, but Joel kept him pointed toward the camp. The braves wheeled their mounts and charged again, catching the white man about fifty yards from the camp. This time instead of yelling at him, they began to fire their rifles, pointing the weapons toward the sky. The fusillade failed to produce the desired results, for the roan, inured to gunshots, trotted steadfastly ahead. Joel fixed his gaze toward the center of the camp now. He saw that his entrance was causing quite a stir, for it seemed every man, woman, and child were peering at this new arrival. Many were strangers to him and bore the markings of the Gray Bull Cheyenne, a village that had chosen to settle along the Gray Bull River in Wyoming; others were of the Greasy Grass Village, Cheyenne who made their homes upon the grasslands of the Dakotas. Joel recalled old Priam's teachings, how the Cheyenne were really two tribes, from Cheyenne or Tsistsistas and the Suhtai. They had merged and become a great nation ranging from the Great Lakes to the Dakotas. As time passed, smaller groups of this Cheyenne nation began splintering away, drawn ever westward by the fertile hunting grounds ringed by mountains. Where the groups settled often gave the villages their names. As the Cheyenne roamed westward it was inevitable they would encroach on hunting grounds claimed by other tribes, the Pawnee, the Blackfeet, and especially the Crow. Strangely enough, Priam had remarked, the origin of the Morning Star symbol seemed buried in the legends of the tribe. Had a phenomenon seen in the sky given this village its name or a vision received in a sun dance ceremony long ago? Myths alluded to each theory but the truth remained hidden in the mysterious past. Which, Priam said, suited him just fine. He liked being part of a mystery.

A brave rode in front of Joel and fired his rifle into the dirt at the stallion's feet. Joel recognized the warrior as the prankster White Frog. The brave barely managed to conceal a grin as the other Red Shields followed suit, blasting the earth about the roan stallion's hooves as Joel rode proud and

erect through the village toward the separate enclave of the
Red Shield encampment. He found Sacred Killer's tepee and
changed his course toward the lodge of the war chief. The
flap of the tepee was thrown back and Sacred Killer emerged
to stand in his finery of beaded buckskins and raven feathers
and flowing black hair, impassive as ever.

The gunfire ceased at the merest of his gestures. Joel continued in peace although much of the village converged on
the camp of the Red Shields. Many remembered the man
they called Nahkohe, the silvertip grizzly. Others were curious why this ve-ho-e had not been killed outright much less
allowed to enter the village unscathed. Joel reined the stallion
to a halt. The sight and smell of the village overwhelmed
him with memories, the rich aroma of ground chokecherries,
the fragrance of the pines and the strong scent of slaughtered
antelope, wood smoke and brewing cherry bark tea; the faces
too, dark and coppery and handsome. And beyond the people, the tepees with the painted illustrations of battle, of
honor won, pictures recounting the history of a clan or in-
voking the protection of a guardian spirit. And always the
Morning Star, because the Morning Star would last forever,
and the People would last.

The roan snorted and pawed at the ground, and Joel returned to the present to look down at Sacred Killer, aware
that with a single word the Red Shield could have Joel
dragged down and executed.

"I see you have learned to ride a horse since last you lived
among us, Nahkohe." Sacred Killer's eyes twinkled with
amusement.

"I see your braves still have not learned to shoot," Joel
retorted. "Every one of them missed me. Better they should
hand their rifles to the women and learn to give suck." Sacred
Killer stared at him a moment, then tilted his head back and
laughed wholeheartedly at the insult. Tension vanished from
the crowd of onlookers like a flame blown out by a sudden
gust of wind. Joel breathed a sigh of relief and as he dismounted, spied a familiar visage, an old Negro with a face
like a wrinkled sheet of coal black parchment. Priam worked
free of the crowd and, wiping his hands on his baggy buckskin breeches, sized Joel from head to toe.

"Well, younker, you always knew how to make an entrance." The old man seemed as wiry and irascible as ever, but his grin was painful to look at with rows of yellow, broken teeth. One eye appeared to be going blind.

Sacred Killer looked at Joel. "Come," he said and ducked past the flap of his tepee. Joel looked around as the Red Shield warriors disbanded, riding off toward their own lodges. Joel spotted Rides The Horse who lifted his rifle in salute. White Frog waved. Joel returned their greeting and scanned the curiosity-filled faces circling him; more than a few seemed disappointed there had been no fight. Where was the boy he had seen? Could it possibly have been Cub by the river?

"He's inside," Priam chuckled. Joel glanced at him, his questioning expression all a pretense, easily seen through. "Your son," Priam added. He lifted the flap and Joel, blushing at having been caught in an unspoken lie, nodded, breathed deep, and entered.

The boy who had attacked Joel by the river waited at the rear of the tepee, his face washed clean of war paint, although his cheeks still wore a reddish stain. Tall for his age, he came up to about Joel's stomach. Free of his warlike disguise, the boy clearly showed his mother's attributes, the same narrow, sensitive face, the same pride. God in heaven, he was his mother's son, even the eyes. The eyes like his mother's, brown as the earth.

Sacred Killer crouched by the smoldering embers in the center of the lodge. He filled the bowl of his pipe with cherry bark, and taking a coal from the embers, he blew on it till it glowed gold and crimson at the tip, then lit his pipe. He blew a cloud of bluish smoke that billowed between Joel and his son.

"Little Bear," Sacred Killer said. "This is your father. This is Silvertip." He moved past Joel and added as he stepped through the opening, "I will spread the word that the lance has been broken between us. You will not be harmed."

The rawhide flap fluttered into place. Cub crossed his legs and sat, leaning against his uncle's backrest. Joel reached down and took a knife from the sheath inside his boot top, an extra knife he kept handy for emergencies. He held the bone-handle grip toward the boy, who hesitated and then reached out and took it, looking enviously at the blue steel blade.

"Now you have a knife again," Joel said. "And that blade will not break. I forged it myself."

Cub slipped the knife into his beaded belt and then looked over at Joel. This white man seemed terribly fierce, and yet he felt no threat from him. But white men were the enemies of his people. Yet if this ve-ho-e is my father, Cub thought, who are my people?

Joel resisted the urge to reach over and embrace his son. He understood how confused the boy must be at this moment. Cub shifted uncomfortably and at last stood.

"It is getting late and I must bring my uncles' horses down from pasture."

"It is good," Joel said. "We can talk later."

Cub did not say yes or no, he merely headed for the exit, paused, and looked back at Joel who stood now, towering over him.

"Are you truly my father?" Cub asked, in surprisingly good English that gave Joel a start.

"Yes," Joel answered.

"I do not know you," Cub said. He ducked through the opening. Joel followed and watched the boy scamper off toward a few companions his own age. He immediately showed them his knife. Sacred Killer, standing close by, looked up as Joel approached.

"These are not good days, Nahkohe. Why do you come now, when we are gathering for a war council?"

Joel glanced from Priam to the war chief.

"Would any other time have been better? I am thinking not. The boy is like a son to you. Better the father had not returned."

"You have said it. Not I," Sacred Killer frowned. "I told Little Bear all I knew of his father. If the son does not run to the father's arms, whose fault is it? The son's or the father's? I did not drive you from the camp. Even with my sister dead, I offered you a place in my lodge. It was you who rode away."

Joel lowered his gaze, humbled by the warrior's admonition. He looked around at the sprawling encampment.

"I should present myself to Chief Crazy Bear," he said.

"He got himself killed a couple of years ago," Priam told him. "He was on his way to Fort Lincoln to protest all the gold hunters digging up the Madison and Absarokas. The government wasn't supposed to allow anyone in by virtue of the Seventy-two treaty. Only he and a couple of braves got set upon by some likkered up hide hunters. They killed the braves and hung Crazy Bear."

Joel closed his eyes, sighed deeply, and shook his head. Hanging was the worst fate that could befall a Cheyenne brave, who believed the spirit left the body through the mouth at the moment of death. Hanging imprisoned the spirit within and prevented the victim from enjoying an afterlife. A man or woman who had been hanged was never spoken of again. Had Priam not been in camp, Joel knew his queries about the chief would simply have been ignored.

"Broken Bow has called Bear Claw and me to council. You may stay here if you wish or with Priam."

"What about Little Bear?" Joel said.

"Sometimes he sleeps in my lodge," Sacred Killer explained. "Sometimes with Priam, sometimes with Red Bead Woman who nursed him. Lame Deer teaches him the ways of the Dog Soldiers, but he will carry a red shield into battle. Despite Lame Deer's instructions." Sacred Killer glanced warily at Joel as if expecting the white man to offer an objection. Joel cautiously refrained.

Only when he and Priam were out of earshot and walking toward Priam's lodge did Priam look aside at Joel and snort his satisfaction.

"I see you learned some sense," the old man muttered.

"How's that?" Joel asked.

"It takes some folks a whole lifetime to learn when to keep their mouths shut."

Joel made no reply.

"That's what I mean," Priam said.

Cub Ryan. He knew the name. It was his name. As was Nahkohe-ese—Little Bear. Priam had told him, just as Priam had taught him the white man's language. Cub stood among the horses in the meadow and listened to the wind. He removed the knife from his belt. Sunlight from the western peaks made the blade shimmer and glow like gold. Like gold this steel, this gift from his father.

His father . . .

Cub's eight-year-old mind struggled to form an opinion. The boys he played with all had fathers, all knew their fathers, but Cub had only words. And the knowledge that his father was a white man. That had set him apart, not cruelly so, for his mother had been loved by the People, and his uncle was a mighty warrior, a great chief who had assumed the leadership of all the village on the death of Crazy Bear. Yet he knew he was different. Priam had told him to take pride, that his father was also a warrior.

Silvertip.

A man good with horses.

As brave as the grizzly. It was said he killed two Crow braves in battle. Cub was ashamed, because he had been afraid. He had not expected Black Wolf and Spotted Elk, who were six years older than he to run. When he returned to the village and told Sacred Killer what had happened and described the demon they had come upon at the river, the look that came to his uncle's face was never to be forgotten—a distant, almost resigned expression, as if something foretold by the spirits had come to pass.

He stared at the blade.

His father . . .

Who was his father? He returned the knife to his belt and reached inside his medicine pouch and emptied the carved talisman into his hand. The talisman was a smooth bit of intricately carved bone about two inches in length. He spat on the talisman and tossed it onto the ground. At his feet was a large round stone. A foot or so from the stone was a single bitterroot quaking under the weight of a bee. Maomé had given Cub the talisman and instructed him to trust it. He would do so now. He knelt to inspect the carved bone. If the spittle pointed toward the bee, then Cub would leave the village and hide in the mountains until the man called Silvertip departed.

He doubled over and rested his hands upon the earth. The

moist end of the bone talisman pointed toward the stone. Stones did not move. Bees fly away and hide among the thistle. Bees hide. Stones remain. Cub looked toward the village. Already the other boys were driving the horses of their families into the safety of the village, for night came fast to the mountains.

Stones remain.

He returned the talisman to his pouch, then circled around behind the grazing horses. He had started them back when suddenly the mares scattered before the braves who had galloped into their midst. Cub recognized Spotted Elk and Black Wolf. Their fathers had reprimanded them for their actions upon the Gallatin.

"Haa-he, white man's son," Black Wolf called. There was anger in his voice. Cub started to retreat, but Spotted Elk cut him off. The two fourteen-year-olds glared down at Cub.

"It was your fault," Spotted Elk said.

"We told you to wait with the horses. You wanted the first coup. Saaa! You had no right to join warriors."

"Some warriors," Cub said. "He took your own rifle from you, Black Wolf. And you, Spotted Elk, he tossed aside like a baby. He counted coup on you both."

"If you had not alerted him by blundering out of the bushes," Black Wolf retorted. "You spoiled everything."

"And you were the first to run," Cub said.

Black Wolf, a brawny, handsome youth, leaped from horseback and slammed the half-breed boy to the ground. Cub struggled in vain as Black Wolf settled on his chest, pinning him. Black Wolf yelled triumphantly and proceeded to take his frustration and humiliation out on the boy beneath him. He pummeled Cub about the face and neck until Spotted Elk dragged him away.

"No more, my brother. You have taught Nahkohe-ese his lesson," Spotted Elk said, leaning over to pull the older boy away.

"White man's son," Black Wolf scoffed. Little had been made of Cub's father, because the father had never been present. Suddenly, things were different. Cub staggered to his feet and spat blood and wiped the cut above his eye on the sleeve of his buckskin shirt. He stood with fists clenched and watched Black Wolf turn his back contemptuously and mount his horse. Then the two boys rode off into the forest. Cub gingerly probed his bruised face and neck.

All these years he had known he was different yet had managed to fit in, becoming one with his full-blood companions. But these were days of unrest. Even an eight-year-old could see that the Morning Star People were preparing for war, steeling themselves to the task of driving out the pale-skinned intruders. This was Indian land. The People had no use for the incursions of prospectors and settlers. The time was rapidly approaching when the Cheyenne must once more wage war against the white man or forever lose their land. And Cub was a "white man's son."

Priam placed the jug of corn liquor before Joel and ordered Shell Woman from the tepee. Shell Woman had not ceased fussing over Joel. She brought him venison stew and "fry bread" and cool "living water" fresh from the river. Joel finally ate his fill, topping his hearty appetite with the last of the chokecherry pudding. Priam looked on in displeasure. He had anticipated finishing the last of the pudding himself. Joel wiped the gravy from his bowl with a morsel of bread and plopped the biscuit in his mouth.

"You eat these past years?" Priam snorted.

"Barely enough."

"You ain't shrunk a'tall."

"Only inside," Joel said.

"Yeah. A terrible thing. It busted me up when I heard about the girl."

"It's in the past," Joel said, with forced indifference.

"Everything's in the past," Priam reflected.

"Not my son," Joel said.

"Maybe," the Negro said. "Shell Woman, leave us now." He reached for the jug. Shell Woman gave his ear a tug, and for all her rounded girth, she managed to avoid Priam's outstretched hand and the slap aimed at her ample behind. Joel had to grin, and Priam noticed.

"You look about as tickled as the snake that ate the mouse," Priam remarked. A spasm of coughing shook his bony frame. He reached for the jug.

"The way you look, old man, and the way you carry on, there must be a life after death."

Priam shrugged aside what to him sounded a might disparaging. He patted the jug.

"Lame Deer brought this in with a set a' scalps. I told him to keep the hair of the men and give me the hair of the dog." He thumped the jug and sloshed its contents. "C'mon snowflake, here's the blizzard. C'mon bug juice, here's my gizzard."

He tilted the jug to his lips and swallowed deep and wiped the lip and passed the jug to Joel who cut the dust from his throat with several fiery gulps.

"Now let's talk," Priam said.

Eight years.

The trail led north for a spell. Until he lost Larocque's track. Then came a time of restless wandering, days and nights of anger and hurt and hatred for the world that had robbed Joel Ryan of what he treasured most.

Eight years.

There were fights and solitude and mistakes made, tempers lost and blood let. Knives and guns and fists of fury that spent themselves as did the anger.

Joel returned to Otter Creek and, weary of heart, began building a house because the labor healed his wounds. He left then and headed south, retracing the cattle trails, gathering strays and mavericks and driving them north to Montana. The range was choice: The cattle bred. The gold camps were a prime market for beef if a man had grit enough to bring them over the passes.

Joel Ryan had grit. And then some. He finished his house and, not bothering to rest, headed for Wyoming and the Wind River Range; he returned two months later with a string of fine mares to breed and the roan stallion that had taken Joel months to break to saddle. But Joel didn't care how hard the task. He wanted to work. He kept busy. And his wounds healed. Mourning Dove was never far from his thoughts, but the pain of remembrance had lessened. It was something he could live with. The past became bearable.

"And then I knew it was time," Joel said, staring at the

fire Priam leisurely stoked. Joel set down the jug, nearly empty now, in front of the Negro. "I needed my son. And I had a place to bring him to. So I left things in charge of my hired hands and rode out."

"Hope they're good men. You might find yourself robbed blind."

"They're good men," Joel said, slurring his speech. He propped himself against a backrest and closed his eyes.

"Oh God, I feel rotten."

"Yeah, nothin' like a jug of belly-love to straighten things out."

"Will he go with me?"

"Huh?"

"My son, you black heathen, my son," Joel said. Eight years could work up a thirst in a man. Damn if even Shell Woman wasn't beginning to look good. Just what he needed, Joel thought. The throbbing in his skull, the dancing flames, impressions, colors.

"Will he go with me?" Joel sighed, overcome by weariness and liquor.

"I don't know," said Priam, his features set in a worry frown. "Younker, I don't know."

Joel opened his eyes and stared at the darkness and listened to Priam snore and wondered what had lifted him from sleep. He craned his neck around and saw crouched in the entrance to the tepee a small, shadowy figure.

Little Bear!

The figure vanished, and Joel rolled out of his blankets and followed the boy. The village sprawled silent and dark. Joel could sense the unrest, as if in the shadows violence waited to be unleashed. Where was Cub? Had the ground swallowed him up? Nothing stirred. Only the wind, the distant barking of a mongrel pup, and silent banners of smoke wafting from the tops of the lodges. Sweat beaded his forehead. The breeze from the river chilled him. He looked toward the camp of the Red Shields, and finding Sacred Killer's tepee, he headed for it.

Sacred Killer's campfire illuminated the interior with a baleful orange glow. Joel poked his head past the entrance flap and to his surprise found the war chief awake and sitting by the fire. He glanced at Joel and motioned him to enter.

"I hoped to find Cub," Joel explained.

"He often will spend the night with Lame Deer and Red Bead Woman, for she is like a mother to him."

"He came to Priam's lodge. When he realized I was awake, he ran."

"The boy wonders about his father. He must be given time," Sacred Killer said. He stared at the flames. "Broken Bow and Bear Claw thought it strange I did not kill you. Their villages have suffered much at the hands of the white man. Before the Dust-in-the-Face Moon comes, they will decide whether or not to unite our tribes. It troubles them that I treat a ve-ho-e as a friend. It is my wish our people will join together to drive the white man from these mountains. Now they question my leadership. But if you were to live among us again, as a brother to us, and ride with us . . ."

"I have a place, one Mourning Dove and I built, at Otter Creek in the shadow of Moon Woman Mountain. It has good water and grass. I will bring Cub there to live."

A brief flash of displeasure crossed Sacred Killer's features. "If he chooses to go, I will not stop him," he said. "But if he does not wish to leave, then I *will* stop you, Nahkohe, from taking him."

"You'll try," Joel said, uncowed by the war chief's implied threat. "That's fair enough." Joel turned to leave. Sacred Killer smiled ruefully, a thought coming to mind.

"There is another who may interfere with your plans when he returns from his hunt. He has placed a great value on your hair, Nahkohe."

"What is the hunter's name?" Joel asked, pausing in the light that danced.

"Tall Bull, who loved my sister," Sacred Killer replied. "Once, he searched for you. But that was many moons ago. And now, you are here. He will kill you, Nahkohe, if he can."

"Let him try," Joel said.

"You have become a warrior since last we met," Sacred Killer observed. "Did you find the Frenchman, did you kill Larocque?"

Joel shook his head no. He pursed his lips, thought a moment, then met the war chief's patient stare. "It took me many moons to realize that Mourning Dove's spirit did not cry out for blood, but for life. I have heard her in my heart, a whisper, unseen like the wind, yet as present, calling me to bring my son home."

"Maybe you only heard what you wished to. Maybe the voice was your own," Sacred Killer remarked.

"I have come for my son," Joel repeated. "And I shall not leave without him." He turned and stalked off through the opening in the tepee. Sacred Killer leaned back upon his buffalo hide and searched the shifting shadows, the blood red embers, dancing flames, for an answer he did not find.

20

"**S**hell Woman spent the night with her sister," Priam said, opening the tin of Arbuckle's Coffee Joel had brought as a gift for the Negro trapper. Soon the wonderful aroma filled the tepee. The two men rested in these early hours and listened to the water bubble and churn the grounds into a smooth, strong brew.

"When it's as black as me, it's ready," Priam grinned. He peeked beneath the blue enamel lid. "Ready."

He poured a cup for Joel and one for himself.

"Seen you sneak out," he said.

"Cub was here. He ran off when he saw me crack an eye. I wish I knew what to try next. Maybe Maomé would have an answer."

"Some say he's dead," Priam replied.

"I don't understand."

"He's not here," Priam explained. "A few years back, Sacred Killer and some other braves went to his lodge and found it empty. He was plumb gone. Ain't been seen since. At least not so you'd recognize."

"He went off to die?" Joel asked.

"Cheyenne have a different word for it. They say he's changed. Just changed. Knowing old Ice, ha, I believe it. I seen him in a dream, couple a' days ago, just sittin' and watchin' me. Like he knew somethin' I was only about to find out."

"I guess I'm on my own then." Joel sighed and gulped the steaming coffee. The rich flavor rousted the sleep from his stiff muscles.

"That's the way every father feels," Priam said. If he knew from experience, he did not elaborate. "But if I were you, I'd hurry things up a mite. Bear Claw's people were sold blankets infected with smallpox last year. Better than half the tribe went under. Bear Claw ain't got no use for whites. And Broken Bow's people just been shoved out of Wyoming with all the infernal forts being built, so he's on the prod as well."

"Sacred Killer is still my brother," Joel said.

"True, but it means a lot to him for the others to regard him as chief. He wants all three tribes to be one family. He figures it's the only way to stop the white man and hold on to what's left of the People's ancestral hunting grounds."

Priam finished his coffee, poured a second cup, and offered more to Joel who declined. The Negro had started him thinking. He needed to win Cub's trust. And if time was precious, then he'd better start now.

"Can you point Red Bead Woman's lodge out to me?"

"Sure. What for?"

"My son and I are going fishing," Joel said, crawling through the opening.

"Let me finish my—"

"Now, you old bastard. Time's wasting. You said so yourself."

"Okay, okay." Priam followed him outside, grumbling and complaining beneath his breath. "If you hadn't been such a blame fool years ago, you wouldn't be in this fix."

"If I hadn't a been such a blamed fool, I might never have come West, old man. And neither would you," Joel retorted, amused at Priam's cantankerous carrying on. It was nice to know some things didn't change.

Red Bead Woman paused at her scraping rack and watched as Nahkohe-ese returned from his morning bath in the icy waters of the Gallatin. The cuts of the day before had become bruises that the boy gamely disregarded. He wiped long wet strands of black hair out of his face.

"You have worn a hole in the hide with your handiwork," Cub said, pointing at the skin. Red Bead Woman glanced around in alarm before realizing he meant the bullet hole in the antelope skin.

"Oh!" Red Bead Woman exclaimed in mock anger and grabbed a handful of the antelope hair she had scraped clean.

Cub laughed and dodged her attack. She scooped a second handful and darted after the boy. Cub leaped away, and while looking over his shoulder at his foster mother, he collided with Joel's stallion and stumbled back in surprise. As Joel's shadow fell across the boy, Cub remained still.

"Gonna do a little hunting and fishing. Care to ride along?" Joel's craggy features gentled. His voice boomed deep and resonant and carried the tone of command tempered in this instant with invitation.

"Lame Deer is making a bow for me. But it is not finished. I have only a knife."

"Why not use this?" Joel said and passed his Winchester '66 to the boy. Cub looked up in amazement and took the weapon in his hands, gingerly cradling its heavy weight. The long-barreled rifle was almost too big for him. He sighted along its length. He had trouble holding it steady, but he didn't care. The boy glanced toward Red Bead Woman who slowly nodded.

"I'll get my horse," he exclaimed and ran off behind the tepee. Red Bead Woman walked alongside the roan and looked up at Joel.

"For Little Bear's sake I prayed to the All-Father you would someday return for him. For my sake I prayed you would not," she said. Time had filled her figure and rounded her face to a coppery red oval, but her brown eyes were soft and clear and totally beyond subterfuge. Joel read the love in those eyes, love for her people and her husband, love for Cub whom she had nursed and cared for as she would have her own child.

"He will not be gone forever," Joel heard himself saying, and wondered if he lied. "You are as much his mother as the one who bore him, Red Bead Woman. I do not wish to take him from your world; I only wish to show him another. He is of the Morning Star People. But he is also of my people. You will always have his love. And mine."

Red Bead Woman wiped a tear from the corner of her eye.

"I do not know if we are still his people. There has been much fighting. Many wives and mothers have mourned the death of husbands and sons. And all because the white man will not honor his promises. Now that you have come, Little Bear can no longer pass unnoticed among his friends. Now his white father is here for all to see. Already his friends begin to whisper, 'Is Little Bear not also a white man, is he not our enemy, too?' "

"I noticed the bruises," Joel said, glowering at the awakening village as if focusing collective blame on the inhabitants.

"Two of the boys fought with him," the Cheyenne woman said. "Little Bear told me he chased them away." She tried to smile. "There are those who know you for a friend, Nahkohe. Others know only hatred, for all white men."

A horse whinnied and snorted at the dusty earth, alerting Joel to his son's presence. The boy appeared from behind the tepee. He rode a sturdy little pinto pony and carried the Winchester repeater in his right hand.

"I will bring you another no-kaa-e to butcher and clean."

"Be careful it is not your own horse, little hunter," Red Bead Woman laughed.

"We can ride through the village. I want others to see my rifle," Cub said in a proud voice. Joel noticed Red Bead Woman's warning glance, but how could he explain to his own son the shifting attitude toward him by those he considered his own kind? They were together. And Joel was proud of his son, and blast it all if he'd slink through camp like a kicked dog.

"Lead the way, *na-e-ha*," Joel said in Cheyenne. The boy looked at him for a moment, noting the word "na-e-ha," which meant "my son." If he took exception or if it pleased him, he did not show. Only he gave a loud cry as his horse leaped away.

Father and son rode pell mell through the village of the Morning Star People, the Greasy Grass, and Grey Bull, scattering pups and children and leaving in their settling dust looks of astonishment, appreciation, or grumbling disapproval. One brave in particular who had only just ridden in with a travois laden with the carcasses of two mule deers stood unnoticed among the onlookers. His horse was tired from the morning's journey. He would find another. Tall Bull had thought his hunt was over. Spying the man called Silvertip, the Dog Soldier knew it had only just begun.

21

A day's ride from the Cheyenne village, Joel and Cub spotted a small herd of antelope that had eluded the hunters in the lower valley. Cub wanted to try a shot, but in his haste, he allowed the animals to catch his scent, and they scattered up the forested slope and vanished into a forbidding-looking gorge. Joel noted with approval that the boy shrugged aside this setback.

"We will track them in the morning," Cub said, turning to his father.

"We better build a fire," Joel said. "The temperature will be dropping soon." Here in the mighty Gallatins, the warmth of day was a temporary luxury. Joel and the boy rode a short distance and found a perfect site by a clear running stream. The icy water had formed a broad, glossy-surfaced pool no more than two feet deep and fifty feet across before spilling over a granite lip and cutting a swath downslope to join the Gallatin River.

Joel unsaddled the roan and ground-tethered the stallion so the animal could feast on the sweet grass growing near the pool. A trout shattered the pristine surface of the pond. In the waning light, Cub waded out into the water, his steps slow and measured as he carefully placed one foot after the other on the slick riverbed. With each step he sang in a soft voice,

> "Come river dweller,
> old Grandfather fish,
> you are tired, you are tired,
> come be food for my body.
> Let your strength live again within me."

Joel, his breath clouding the air, watched from shore. He held a fairly straight branch and was about to whittle it into a fishing spear but waited for his son to try first. God, but the boy had Hemené's face. He was already strong and tall just as Mourning Dove would have wished. The heart of the man called Silvertip filled with a pride and a love he did not know how to express.

Joel watched and was content. Cub suddenly doubled over; his hands knifed through the dappled surface. He straightened, and in a single fluid motion, he scooped his wriggling catch out of the water and tossed it to the bank almost at Joel's feet. The boy repeated the process twice more in a matter of minutes, and after the third catch, decided he had enough for supper and sloshed his way back to the bank. He glanced at his father, scrutinizing the knife in one hand, the branch to be whittled into a spear in the other.

"What's that for?" Cub asked, picking up the fish. Joel cast a sheepish look at the branch.

"It's, uh, for . . . the fire," he said, salvaging a modicum of pride. He sheathed his knife and broke the branch across his knee.

Cub had cleaned and gutted the trout by the time Joel had built a cheerful blaze. Father and son arranged a rack and skewering the fish placed the albescent meat above the flames. Joel caught Cub watching him, and when he looked questioningly at the boy, Cub leaned forward a little.

"You wear the sign of the People," Cub said, pointing to the beaded Morning Star that adorned the buckskin shirt.

Joel looked down at the smooth, worn buckskin and memories flooded back of the woman who had given him the shirt, the woman he had loved and lost.

"Your mother made this shirt for me," he replied gently.

Cub's eyes widened with interest; he studied the handiwork of the mother he had never known. The fire crackled and popped, calling his attention back to the fish. When it was cooked father and son ate in silence.

Later, Joel lay by the fire and let the night sounds flow around him. Here at the mouth of the gorge, the walls rose steep on either side, thrusting their jagged cliffs in defiant splendor against the black velvet sky. A shooting star trailed a tail of flickering fire, sparkled silver-green, its transcendent beauty lasting but a brief span of seconds, winking out like an ember of a campfire or the final flickering spasm of life—I am . . . I was.

Supper finished. Settled beneath his blankets for the night, Joel switched the train of his drowsy thoughts away from such sobering reflections of mortality. He lived now, and he was reunited with his son. He listened as the eight-year-old stirred, set the Winchester repeater aside, crept slowly over to his father's inert form. Cub reached out, hesitated, continued, his fingers trembling. He stretched and placed his hand upon the Morning Star on Joel's shirt. He did not speak but rested his hand upon the beadwork, as if reaching out to the mother who had been stolen from him long ago.

Joel pretended to sleep, allowing the boy his moment of contact. Cub was not fooled. But he was grateful the man did not interrupt him. He stared at the silver hair, the strong hard face that softened when it looked at him. *My father,* Cub thought, *and I am afraid. I always wanted him to return to me, and now that he has I am afraid. Saaa! I shame my blood.* Suddenly a great feeling of comfort flowed over him. The boy crawled back to his blankets and lay quietly contemplating what had happened. But of course, his mother had spoken to him. *Little Bear, there is your father. Love him as you love the ghost of my memory. You never knew me. Know your father. Know your father. Know . . .*

An owl called in the forest depths, a coyote howled mournfully, a sense of loss in its lingering cry, and Cub surrendered to sleep, his last thoughts of his mother who was forever gone and his father who had returned.

22

A canopy of mist covered the gorge, obscuring the upper reaches of the forest and the top third of the granite cliffs.

Dew drops formed on the spiny limbs of pine trees, on charcoal-colored branches, and outcroppings of black-speckled stone, on face and hands and blue metal rifle barrel. The hunters had only just begun their vigil.

"How do you know the herd will return?" the boy asked.

"Antelope can't fly," said Joel, raising up beside his son to peer over the edge of the blind he had just finished putting together from scavenged dead wood and nature's own tangle of bramble bushes. "This gorge ends in a box canyon. Eventually the herd will have to come right past us."

"And we'll be waiting," Cub said, sighting along the Winchester. He imagined a scrub sapling to be a big buck and pretended to squeeze the trigger.

"Boom. One shot. I bring him down," he said excitedly. Beyond the sapling in the somber reaches of the forest, something moved. Cub's heart pounded in his breast. An antelope, so soon? Or something else. But what?

Joel sensed the boy's tension and followed the youth's line of sight.

"Over there," Cub whispered eagerly, pointing. His fingers tightened on the trigger. He waited. And waited.

"I see nothing," Joel finally answered as softly. Cub's grip loosened on the rifle.

"Nothing," Cub repeated, his spirits plummeting. He desperately wanted to prove himself. To make his kill. And here he was ready to fire at shadows. At the wind in the trees. At nothing.

A cold but gentle rain started to fall. It stopped after a few minutes. And a few minutes later, started again.

"We must be patient," Joel told his son.

"I am not 'patient,' " Cub said, unfamiliar with the word.
"I am a hunter."

"One and the same, boy," Joel said.

They waited, Cub with his mind on the hunt, and Joel,
troubled and watchful. He had seen . . . something . . . for the
merest fraction of a second. The wariness eight years on the
frontier had bred into his character warned him that his eyes
weren't playing tricks. His right hand slipped inside his coat
to pat the grip of the Colt revolver holstered on his right
thigh.

Something had been watching them. The hairs prickled at
the nape of his neck.

Or someone . . .

Morning hours crawl like the turtle, Cub thought to himself.
A stiffness had worked its way up his spine and had lodged
in his right shoulder. The rifle barrel rested in the crook of
a dead branch, and he lay prone upon his stomach, braced
on his elbows. He knew he must be still. Any movement
might spook an animal standing hidden in the shadows. He
had to be careful. Ah, but his leg muscles were beginning to
cramp, and his left ear began to itch unmercifully. A good
hunter did not notice such things.

Crawl, turtle, he silently complained. Foolish morning.
Turtle morning.

Noon.

Joel cast a proud glance at his son, remembering the times
his own father had led him into the forest behind their Kentucky farm. He had stood proud, if a little frightened, in
Cortland Ryan's shadow, hoping to measure up to the one
who had sired him. Joel well knew how important a moment
this was for Cub, and he felt butterflies in his gut, apprehensive that the boy not be disappointed.

He waited alongside his son, sensing the completeness of
the moment, unwilling to trade it for all the gold in the black
mountains.

The sun crept past noon.

• • •

"Hi-ta-in-i-o-mon-i," Joel sang in a low keening voice, *"na-niss-an-i."* The antelope song. Cub stared at his father, startled that a white man should know the sacred chant:

> All will be gone, my children.
> All will be gone.

Beauty and sorrow in those words, the joy of the hunt, the call to death.

The herd emerged from the forest shadows drawn by their thirst or, perhaps, the song that lulled the spirit and beckoned. Beckoned still closer.

We are one in the spirit. We are one in the earth. We have the same mother. Cub tightened his finger on the trigger of the Winchester. An antelope buck turned its large black eyes toward the boy. Silence joined them. The distance held them. Joined in life, in death. The hunt was not sport; the hunt was sacred.

The chant continued. *All will be gone, my children.*

The rifle spat flame and jolted Cub; the report shattered the bond of stillness. The herd of antelope scattered in every direction, vanishing as quickly as a thought, leaving one of their number behind.

"Haa-he!" Joel shouted as Cub sprang from cover and raced toward the dead buck. Joel followed, pausing only to pick up the rifle that Cub in his haste had dropped. The boy knelt by the still-warm carcass and touched his hand to the rib cage no longer swollen with breath, to the sightless eyes, to the bullet hole where the .45 caliber slug had punctured gristle and bone and shattered the great heart. Joel's shadow fell across the boy as the man reached out to place his fingertips into the wound. He raised his red fingertips to his son's face, streaking the boy's cheeks with crimson.

"Haa-he!" Joel shouted again in Cheyenne. "My son has been blooded. My son is a hunter." And the words returned, reverberating from the nearby cliffs. "My son . . . blooded. . . . My son."

• • •

Rather than rig a travois, Joel spent the afternoon butchering the carcass, taking care to spit two choice steaks over the campfire blaze. Here was an extra day to be spent in the company of his son, free from the social activity and pressures of the village. The boy proudly reenacted the kill, kneeling to aim, mimicking the rifle shot and the dying leap of the antelope. And always the questions.

Had Joel ever brought down an animal this big? Cub had certainly joined the ranks of the Cheyenne men; he was a boy no longer. Did he not own a fine rifle and knife? He would return to the village with his horse loaded down with meat and with a skin for Red Bead Woman to scrape, tan, and make into a shirt for him.

Joel listened and nodded and agreed when he was meant to agree. And when the shadows of the late afternoon fell across them, Joel added deadwood to the campfire and from the limb of a nearby tree hung the antelope hide. They wrapped the cuts of meat in leather and placed them in the chill waters of the creek, then returned to the rib steaks roasting over the fire. Hunger was their only seasoning, but Cub was quick to proclaim that never had he eaten a better meal. He grinned at his father. Joel smiled back. The big man had another surprise.

Dessert.

Joel patted out a skillet full of biscuits that he baked, and while they were still steaming hot, he emptied a can of peaches over the top. Cub had never tasted peaches in syrup, but he quickly proclaimed them his favorite food, and displaying an appetite that defied the eight-year-old's frame, the boy consumed all the makeshift peach cobbler but the single serving his amused father had managed to take.

By the time the cold night winds crept down from the mountains, father and son were snug in their bedrolls. Cub drifted off, recounting once more his part in the hunt, the single shot that had dropped the antelope buck in its tracks. Joel kept his revolver close at hand. Dozing, he let his hearing reach into the darkness.

He was uneasy and didn't know why. Only that the years

had taught him to trust his senses. He cocked an eye toward his son and tried to relax in the warm love and pride he felt for the boy. Whatever tomorrow would bring, for now he was happy. He was at peace and prayed it might last.

Joel buried the ashes of the morning campfire while Cub gathered the meat from the creek. Smoke spiraled up from the ashes. Joel watched it dissipate among the cone-laden pine branches. He sipped the last of his coffee, stretching the moment with his son as best he could. The boy was busily loading their horses with the packets of meat. Cub took special care to drape the antelope hide across the back of his pony. As Joel finished the last of the bitter brew, he noticed a cluster of doves explode from a nearby thicket and rise, complaining into the air. His flesh went cold, though he gave no open display of alarm. He walked to Cub as if intent on nothing more than checking the rawhide straps holding Cub's share of the meat in place.

"The rifle . . . get it," Joel said as he tugged on the knots the boy had tied. The load was adequately secured. Cub stared at his father and then did as he was told, frowning, for he thought the rifle had been a gift. Cub retrieved the Winchester from where it leaned against the roots of a fallen tree and brought the weapon to his father.

"Now lead the horses back into the woods," Joel said, taking the Winchester repeater.

Cub stared at him as if the man were mad. "Do as I say!" Joel snapped, the urgency in his voice alerting the boy. Cub took the reins of his pinto and the strawberry roan and led them up from the creek. Joel faced downstream, studying the foliage where the doves had nested. Something had frightened them from cover. He worked the rifle's lever action, ejecting yesterday's spent shell, and as if on signal, Tall Bull rode out of the trees. The warrior was a sobering apparition, his long hair braided with raven feathers, a streak of black like a mask across his eyes contrasting with the sulphurous yellow painted face. He carried a war shield painted the same yellow as his features, and he brandished a Spencer carbine whose .50 caliber slugs could tear a man in two.

"I had hoped the boy might leave us alone," Tall Bull said, his voice as emotionless as an echo in the clearing.

"Now you return to the village, and I can wait no longer." The brave glanced at the boy among the trees. "Leave us, Little Bear."

Cub looked from Tall Bull to Joel, uncertain what to do. Why had Tall Bull come to kill his father?

"Little Bear," Tall Bull said.

"No," shouted the boy.

"Then you will see him killed. As he killed your mother," Tall Bull replied.

"Damn you, Tall Bull," Joel roared. "I loved her. More than you ever could have. And she loved me. Larocque killed her. Henri Larocque."

"Larocque?" Tall Bull held his arms open wide and looked about.

"I have no Henri Larocque, ve-ho-e, I only have you. And I have waited many moons. Too many."

"Then I will talk no more with you, Tall Bull. You hear only the words of hate in your heart. So be it. Come," Joel said, stretching to his full height. He cast a giant shadow, his weathered face grew merciless and deadly to behold. His thick hair rustled in the wind, shimmering like a grizzly's pelt.

"Silvertip," muttered Cub. He jumped, startled by Tall Bull's shriek of defiance and rage. The warrior's rifle boomed, and part of the dead tree trunk behind Joel exploded in a shower of dry, gray bark. The Cheyenne's horse leaped forward and charged. Tall Bull raised his shield and fired over the willow-wood rim. The Spencer boomed again. Joel brought the Winchester up and snapped off a shot. Dust puffed from the yellow shield as the slug ripped through hide and willow wood to shatter Tall Bull's wrist. The brave twisted. His weight threw the horse off balance. One hoof slipped in the mud, and the animal went down, tossing the wounded brave into the creek. The Spencer skidded underneath the horse and broke in half with an audible crack. Tall Bull staggered from the creek. He drew an army issue Patterson Colt revolver from beneath his quill breastplate. The antiquated weapon spat flame from its muzzle as the brave thumbed off a shot. Joel staggered as a slug cut a streak of fire across his arm. Cub held his hands; he could not tear his eyes from the savage struggle as Joel fired, levered a shell, fired again. Tall Bull spun, stumbled, turned and continued his attack. The Winchester once more roared, leaping in Joel's hands. Tall Bull suddenly straightened, staggered backwards, and collapsed in the creek. The indomitable Cheyenne brave slowly raised to a sitting position and lifted his right arm as if to fire the revolver he no longer even held. The brave tried to sing his death chant; his voice faded as he settled on his side, leaving a crimson trail in the bubbling shallows that flowed around the warrior's lifeless form. Cub watched, transfixed, as the echoes of gunfire faded in the purple distance. Joel lowered the rifle, his shoulders bunched wearily forward. He seemed to sigh. The acrid smell of gun-smoke clung to the clearing. Then Cub heard a sound that at first filled the boy with dread, for it was the death chant Tall Bull had tried to sing. But the warrior was dead. Dead!

Suddenly Cub recognized his father's voice, borne on the cool autumn breeze.

> "I return to the wind.
> All-Father,
> I return to the earth.
> All-Father,
> Your child returns."

Joel was singing for the man he had been forced to kill.

> "I return to the wind.
> I return to the earth.
> All-Father, your child returns."

Singing still, Joel gathered Tall Bull's body from the creek and carried him to his horse, which waited nervous and watchful a few yards away.

"What will happen now?" Cub said as Joel strapped the dead man to the warrior's horse. Joel straightened and glanced up at the sky, then over at his son. He couldn't bring himself to express his apprehensions. There were many strangers in the village now, many warriors who disapproved of his pres-ence. He was a ve-ho-e. And he had killed a Cheyenne brave.

23

There was crying in the village. And outrage. A call for blood, for vengeance. Some said Tall Bull died in fair combat, that he had attacked the white man. Others said all that mattered was that one of the People had been killed, yet Joel sat unharmed, unpunished in the lodge of Sacred Killer.

The war chief of the Red Shields was weak. Or mad. Certainly unfit to lead the tribes. Wait and see, counseled the elders. Wait and see. There was wailing and moaning in the lodge of Tall Bull's father. The women keened and shuddered with pity and mourning.

The next day Tall Bull was carried to a burial ground back in the hills. The warrior was placed atop a scaffold and draped with his lances and war shield. His horse was tethered close at hand and then killed so that Tall Bull would have a mount to ride the spirit-land of his ancestors. Sacred Killer was present and left before the others so that he would not have to answer their questions. He had no answers. Or maybe he was afraid he did. That day Broken Bow and Bear Claw called a council. Night came, moonless and somber. Joel wisely remained in the camp of the Red Shields. Sacred Killer did not return until morning. He brought Cub and gestured for the boy to sit next to his father. Sacred Killer looked from Joel to the boy, dreading what he was about to say.

"You must leave us . . ." he began.

Sacred Killer had no choice. From the moment Joel had ridden into the camp with Tall Bull's body, the die had been cast. The war chief's visit with the tribal elders of the Greasy Grass and Gray Bull Cheyenne could have produced only this most painful result. Now he tried to explain it to Cub. The boy looked on, uncomprehending at first. Joel sat within

the lodge and waited with heavy heart for Sacred Killer to
finish. At last the war chief looked up at him.

"You understand why you must go. The other tribes will
not join with the Morning Star People if you remain among
us." Joel nodded and moved closer to his son who was desperately trying to fight back his tears. This was all the life
Cub had ever known, the village, the People.

Sacred Killer continued. "And others, at least for a time,
will look at you, Little Bear, and see not a brother, but another white man, only another enemy. It will pass perhaps.
Still, harm might come to you before it does."

"But you had no choice," Cub said, turning to his father.
"Tall Bull tried to kill you."

"His friends, and those who respected him, will only say
that he was Cheyenne. And I am the white man who took
his life," Joel said.

"Come on, Cub." Priam spoke from the shadows near the
entrance. "I'll take you to Red Bead Woman. She has a
packet of food for you to take with you on the trail." The
old black man held out his hand, and Cub slowly crawled to
his side.

"It isn't fair," the boy said, and then he continued through
the opening.

"Seems kind of early in life to be discovering that fact,"
Priam muttered. He cocked a rheumy eye toward Joel, an
unspoken farewell in his expression. At last he sighed, shook
his head, muttered, "It ain't fair," and left.

Joel turned back to Sacred Killer.

"For a time, an evil little bird whispered in my ear, Nahkohe. I wanted Tall Bull to find you, to kill you even though
we are brothers," said the war chief. "I think this little bird
came because I did not want you to take the boy away. He
has brightened the way for me these many moons. Afterwards, I was shamed for such thoughts, and I asked the All-
Father to keep Tall Bull from camp as long as you were
here." Sacred Killer closed his eyes a moment. "Now I must
choose between my people and the two of you. Twice the
sun has crossed the sky since you brought Tall Bull back to
the village. Our sister the moon has wakened and slept, and
still I kept from making this choice. In a vision during the

dance of sorrow did I see myself leading our people in these our last days. The vision must be fulfilled. The gods must be obeyed." He chuckled mirthlessly. "Now I see the choice was made for me. Long ago." He held out his hand, and Joel clasped it in both of his, reading the wealth of emotions in that noble face. "I am glad you do not say that perhaps it would have been better if you had never returned. Your silence at my grief is an honorable truth."

"I have my son," Joel replied. Whatever problems lay ahead in no way altered the joy and sense of completeness he felt. He did not like the circumstances, but the result was what he had come for. He would ride away with Cub.

"Good-bye, Nahkohe," Sacred Killer said. "My Red Shields will accompany you until you are safely away from the village."

"Perhaps we will meet again," Joel said. "There will always be cattle for the Morning Star People. When hunting is poor, come and take what you will. Gentle lies the land at Otter Creek."

"I know," Sacred Killer said, his eyes distant, as if watching the past. Joel realized that the area had probably been tribal hunting grounds long before the ranchers and homesteaders had come to claim it with their toil and sweat. Joel turned his back on Sacred Killer, stooped, and walked from the lodge.

The crispness of the night had lingered into morning. Winter was fast coming to the mountains. Rides The Horse led the roan up to the white man, who noticed the brave had draped a packet of jerked meat across the saddle. At least there were some who bore him no grudge for Tall Bull's death. Other Red Shield braves were gathering to form a cordon about Joel while warriors and women and children gathered to watch the strange procession that led first to Red Bead Woman's lodge where Cub stood, waiting. Lame Deer held the reins of Cub's pony while the youth mounted. The Dog Soldier displayed none of the distress raging within him. Joel could tell Cub was like a son to this man as well. Lame Deer glanced at Joel, and his eyes narrowed with bitterness as he disappeared inside his lodge. Joel heard someone sobbing within and knew it could only be Red Bead Woman.

Cub did not speak, but stared around him at the faces watching their departure. Suddenly he began to realize he had become a stranger to these people. It was more than he could understand. He focused on the mountain pass deep in the bright distance and rode with Joel Ryan toward it.

They followed the serpentine course of the Gallatin. Cub's senses released one by one the sight, the sounds, and smells of the village. At last the circle of lodges was lost, the barking dogs and children's laughter faded in the soughing wind, the scent of herbs and woodsmoke gave way to the fragrance of longleaf pine.

Rides The Horse and White Frog were the last to leave. They lifted their arms in salute and rode off into the lengthening afternoon shadows. Cub sat motionless in the saddle, staring after their settling dust. His features bunched, but he refused to cry.

Joel, watching his son, had no answers. Men had to learn to live each day at a time. And so did boys.

August, 1878

August, 1878

24

The door to the apartment opened onto near disaster. A five-year-old girl with auburn hair paraded through the starkly furnished living room. She wore a confection of emerald silk and pale yellow ribbons and flowers of silver-stitched satin offsetting the silken theme. The hem and much of the dress dragged across the wood floor.

"Fiona!" Sarah McClinton hadn't meant to shout. The little girl jumped and took off for the bedroom, crying for her older brother. Sarah heard the fabric tear and felt her own heart sink in dismay.

Sean, a red-haired boy of ten, with eyes as green as his mother's, stepped from the bedroom, rubbing sleep from his somewhat dazed appearance. He was a pale youth with studied, serious features and an aura of disapproval, directed for the most part toward his sister.

"Stupid. It's just Ma," he said to the girl crying in the room behind him.

"Hi, Ma."

"You were supposed to watch her," Sarah scolded, charging past him.

"I was," the boy said defensively. "It put me to sleep. I'm not getting any younger, you know." He followed his mother back into the room. Fiona was crouched by the bed. The dress had tangled about her legs and tripped her. She was struggling to stand. Sarah caught her.

"I'm sorry, honey."

"You scared me, Mommy."

"It's just—" Sarah wiped the little girl's wide brown eyes. "Mommy told you . . . what did Mommy tell you?"

"To mind Sean."

"And what else?"

"I don't know," the girl protested, her eyes wide with criminal innocence.

"Fiona!"

"I didn't touch the dress, Mommy. I didn't. I was just wearing it."

"Stupid," Sean said with big brotherly disregard for his sister's feelings.

"And you, young man, were lax in your duties. Why, Fiona could have wandered out the door, and you would never have known the difference."

"I would too," Sean protested. " 'Cause sooner or later she would have gotten herself into trouble by doing something stupid."

"That will be enough!" Sarah managed to extricate her daughter from Olive Barksdale's dress. She took note that the hem was only a little torn.

She sighed in relief, gathered the dress in her arms, and brought it into the living room, her children following her. She sat on the battered sofa that doubled as her bed, and taking needle and thread from her basket, she began to repair the damage.

"Can I go out now?" Sean said, cocking a hip to one side and thrusting his hands into his back pockets. One of the knees was torn; his shirt was dirty, his shoes scuffed.

"You didn't stay inside, did you?"

"You just said to watch her. Anyway, I wasn't out for long."

"Just like your father," Sarah said, threading the needle. "Constantly finding a way to get out of doing what someone asks you to do."

"I went out for just a little bit, Mama. Honest."

"Just long enough to shoot holes in the front door downstairs? They weren't there this morning."

"But that's what I'm trying to tell you. I went out to get my slingshot back from Randy Ellis." Sean produced the weapon from his pocket. "He stole it. It was him that did all the shooting. I fought him for it and chased him off."

"Randy Ellis." Sarah shook her head, her long auburn curls brushing her shoulders. The Ellis boy was the bully of the block. "Well, I would avoid him if I were you, until he has a chance to cool down."

"His kind never cools down," Sean said. "I hate him."

"Young man, have you forgotten the teachings of the Good Book?" Sarah scolded. "Jesus taught us it is wrong to hate." She mended the tear and bit the thread off.

"Jesus never lived in New York . . ."

"Sean!"

"And Randy Ellis never stole His slingshot and shot holes in the front door so's Jesus'd get the blame."

"That will be quite enough!" Sarah said, cutting him off. Sean folded his arms and slumped in a chair by the kitchen table. An alcove served as dining room and kitchen. A set of faded brown-velvet drapes could be drawn across the opening, creating a partition between the two spaces. Sean tugged at the drapes, but they wouldn't budge on the rod. He made a face, stretched his legs, and crossed them at the ankles, slouching down into the straight-backed chair. Just like his father, Sarah thought. She could see Jaimie McClinton in the boy's set-upon expression and attitude of passive defiance. Like his father. But not too much, she prayed. With maternal scrutiny Sarah noticed the boy's cuffs needed letting out. Sean was growing. She wanted him to be a good man, a strong man, able to assume the consequences of his actions.

"I sorry for hurting the dress, Mama," Fiona said.

Sarah reached out and touched her daughter's cheek. "You didn't hurt it," she said, mentally adding a *thank God*. "Next time you must do as Mama says." She fixed the bow in Fiona's auburn hair, carefully arranging the curl and then leaning down to kiss her daughter on the cheek. Fiona had been a premature child, and even after five years, she was still slender and petite with none of the normal tubbiness of little girls.

"I promise," Fiona said. She hugged her mother about the legs and then loosed the embrace to run off into the bedroom. Sean snorted in disgust. Sarah glared at him.

"Okay, okay," he said, holding up his hands in surrender. "But I would cash that promise early if I were you, 'cause it's probably good for about five minutes." He looked away to avoid his mother's accusatory stare, felt it burn into the back of his neck.

"I will," Sarah told him. "And I expect the promise to be kept until I return. I am sure I can count on your cooperation in this."

"In other words, I'm stuck in this sweat box."

"In other words, that is precisely correct," Sarah said. Carefully folding the dress, she fit it into a box on the table, securing the lid with string. Sean retrieved a stack of tabloids from one of the kitchen cabinets. He had contrived a lock out of a bent nail to keep his personal treasures safe from the rapacious hands of his five-year-old sister.

"How long will you be gone?"

"Oh . . . the rest of the morning, and all afternoon I suppose. It's a long walk across town, and I may have to do some last minute fitting."

Sean fished in his pants pocket a moment and produced two quarters. He dropped them on the table. The coins spun and shimmered, settling on the stained wood top.

"Take a trolley," he said. "Buy yourself lunch."

"Where in the world . . ." Sarah began, gingerly touching the coins as if fearful of discovering they could not possibly be real.

"I helped Mister Weimer deliver coal yesterday."

"But I can't take your money," Sarah protested.

"Consider it an advance," Sean said. "Miss Barksdale will pay you today?"

"Yes. And Mrs. Resalli over at the grocery store told me she wanted me to make some dresses for her daughters. And coats for her boys. That's who I saw this morning. Now if only Olive Barksdale will refer me to her friends . . ." Sarah radiated great expectations.

"I can wait till tonight," Sean interjected in his most businesslike tone. "There will only be a slight interest charge."

"Oh!" Sarah exclaimed, mussing his hair. "I think I had better suspend your schooling. You're becoming more like a banker and less like a boy. Next you'll probably be billing me for the privilege of having you for my son."

"I had been considering it." Finally, he could no longer suppress his grin. Sarah scooped up the quarters and plopped them into her cloth purse as Fiona entered from the bedroom, doll in hand. She carried her rag-stuffed playmate over to the table. Sarah had made the scrap doll for Fiona's birthday and, out of more scraps, sewn a dress similar to the one for Olive Barksdale. Just last Sunday, the apartment had rung with Fiona's squeals of delight at finding the doll by her bed when she woke up. They had spent the day together as a family. Sean too had been on his best behavior. Too bad every day couldn't be as happy as that Sunday. At least good times came along every once in a while. There had been only one sour moment, when Fiona wished aloud that her daddy were with them.

Sarah watched Fiona clear a space for herself on the couch. She propped Dolly up against a pillow and began patiently to instruct her make-believe charge to leave Mama's dress alone.

Sarah stared around at the room. Bleak furnishings, sallow wallpaper. And stifling in the summer heat. The bedroom was a trifle cooler because it had a corner window that provided at least some cross-ventilation. Someone yelled in the apartment above them. The last three tenants had been quarrelers. She wondered if contentiousness was a prerequisite to renting a fourth-floor dwelling.

"I had better leave," Sarah sighed. "The sooner departed the sooner returned."

She went into the bedroom to stand before the mirror on the dresser. This single item of furniture looked out of place amidst meager surroundings. Sarah had brought it from Ireland, from her mother's house. The dresser was a precious link to the past. At one time, long ago, there had been an aristocratic ancestor. Yes, long ago, and far away. Sarah patted the walnut grain for a moment and then began readjusting her auburn ringlets. She added a touch of rouge to her cheeks, then hesitating to be sure no small child stood in the doorway, she opened the top drawer to the dresser and found the catalogue where she had hidden it, beneath her undergarments.

COLE'S CATALOGUE

She opened to page fifty-one and stared at a familiar likeness in the upper left hand column. Her likeness. And beneath it, written in a stylized script:

> *Sarah Joy McClinton*
> BORN: *March 27, 1851*
> *Widowed. Two children: boy, ten—girl, five.*
> *Auburn hair. Trim figure. Clean.*
> *Approximately five feet six. Green eyes.*
> *Home educated. Also seamstress. She is a warm,*
> *good-natured woman of obvious physical merit.*
> *An excellent cook.*
> *She is modest. Unassuming . . .*

"Oh God." Sarah brought her hand to her blushing cheek. How could she have been so foolish? To parade herself like a slab of beef at the butcher's. Well, she intended to correct the situation today.

She set the magazine aside and concluded her preparations, entwining her hair into a single thick braid and tucking it beneath a pink felt bonnet. The hat was a perfect compliment to the high-necked dress she wore. In less than a week she had completed this creation of brushed pink cotton meticulously hemmed and trimmed with a choker of white lace. Close scrutiny revealed the dress to be a trifle threadbare, but proper nonetheless. Sarah turned in profile to the mirror and placed her hands at her waist. Trim, the catalogue had said, obvious physical merit; Jaimie had certainly thought so. Eyes like emeralds, he used to say. Emerald eyes . . . poor Jaimie. Ten months now he lay in Pauper's Field, the worms picnicking on his pretty meat. *Oh Jaimie, you took the easy way and left me to carry on.* For Sarah McClinton, hope was an island gradually succumbing to the tides of reality. *What am I to do?* The answer was, of course, what needed to be done. Which did not include continuing to make a fool of herself with this mail-order bride business. She returned *Cole's Catalogue* to its hiding place, resolving to visit Mister Allan Cole and put an end to this nonsense today.

In the kitchen, Sean had arranged various lengths of wood on the tabletop. Fiona and Dolly were watching with intense interest. Fiona's fingers crept toward an ill-used edition of *Harper's Weekly*. As soon as the tabloid began to inch away, Sean's hand would snap out and snatch it from the young girl's grasp. His movements were blindingly quick, totally unconscious, the common legacy of every older brother when confronted by a little sister's interference.

"I found these in the alley," he said, indicating the stack as Sarah emerged from the bedroom. "They're pretty old, but anything will help this place." His pudgy face turned serious, frowning with thought. "Which do you think will look best? I can only frame one. 'The Siege of Chattanooga' or 'Pickett's Charge.' "

He held up two lithographs clipped from *Harper's*, circa 1864. Either one was large enough to hide the waterspots staining the wall with bile-colored blotches. They depicted the clash of arms, the roiling clouds of gunsmoke, flash of artillery, and men gathered in various attitudes of butchery.

"You decide. But don't you think the Civil War motif is a bit morbid?"

"It's what I found," Sean said with a shrug.

"I like this one," Fiona said, pointing to "Chattanooga." Sean rolled his eyes to the heavens.

"You don't know what you like," he said. "You're not old enough."

"I am too," she protested. "I like this one." Now she pointed to "Pickett's Charge." Sean looked beseechingly at his mother. "Please try to hurry," he said.

Sarah gathered up the box and her purse.

"You two try to behave. And keep the door locked." She kissed Fiona and Dolly and forced Sean to turn so she could lightly buss his cheek.

"Mama," Sean said, catching her just as she reached the door. Suddenly he looked his age, a ten-year-old boy with adult worries. "You don't think Mister Pierce will find us here, do you?"

"If he hasn't found us in all this time, I doubt he will," Sarah said, hoping she sounded more convincing than she felt.

"I hope he falls under an ice wagon," Sean muttered.

"Sean! That is a horrible thing to say. I never want to hear such talk again."

"I'm sorry," he said, eyes downcast.

"I wish he would too," Sarah added. Sean glanced up just as the front door swung shut. A smile lit his face once more. He walked to the door and locked it. When he returned to the table, Fiona proudly displayed some unknown artist's caricature of Lincoln, his homely head bloated into macabre proportions and sprouting from a withered, buglike body. Sean grimaced.

"I like this one," she said.

"You would," he replied.

25

A blazing midafternoon sun baked the streets of Manhattan, blistering flesh, scorching brick façades and macadam streets, quickening tempers, driving stray dogs mad with thirst. For much of the summer, the city had endured a purgatory of rainless days and suffocating nights. Through man-made valleys of masonry and stone, the people of Manhattan moved with stoic pride.

It was on brutally hot days like this that Sarah thought most often of Jaimie. The temperature helped leach the anger from her heart. Had fate taken him from her—an accident or a sudden swift illness come to steal away her provider—then anguish would still torment her. But Jaimie, sweet, handsome, clever-with-his-schemes-and-dreams Jaimie had hanged himself. The new world had offered hope only to the hardworking. Jaimie's hands were smooth. She had thrilled to their touch once. Oh yes, a headstrong girl loves smooth hands and tender whispers of endearment in the dark.

But endearments last only the moment. And pain is their legacy when time proves the lover, not false, but weak. Unable to stand in the sun, forever blaming the black luck for one's own failure.

Do you hear that, Jaimie? It was your doing and yours alone. I came with you to America. I bore your children and followed your dreams. But you chose a gambler's life. And you threw in with the likes of Elrod Pierce. The Jaimie I married was dead long before you slipped the noose about your neck...

"Thirty-fifth," the driver called out. Sarah gasped and returned to reality as the trolley angled toward the crowded sidewalk. She looked gratefully out the window and recognized the intersection ahead. She stood and worked her way through a sea of sweat-ripened bodies to the rear exit. The moment she reached the sidewalk, her mood brightened. After all, Olive Barksdale had loved the dress, and she not only paid a dollar bonus but had assured the widow of future work. She intended to recommend Sarah to all her friends. Flush with the prospect of success, Sarah quickened her steps.

Five minutes later she paused, breathless but determined, before a gray stone office building with the number 150 emblazoned in chipped marble over the entrance. Like the other buildings fronting Thirty-fifth Street, this too was bordered by a low wrought-iron fence. A wide series of steps led up to the front door. Others just beyond the iron fence led down to a basement dwelling that Sarah assumed belonged to the superintendent. Lifting her skirt above her ankles, Sarah climbed to the oak front doors, pushed them open, and entered the stifling interior of the hall. She fumbled in her handbag for a moment, while standing just inside the building. She found a cotton handkerchief and dabbed the perspiration from her face, allowing her eyes to adjust to the dimmer light, then she moved silently through the subdued quiet of the hall, feeling out of place and uncomfortable.

A man excused himself as he brushed past and vanished into a law office. Ahead, a door opened just as she drew abreast of the stairway. A bewhiskered gentleman in his early fifties emerged from an office. A frantic energy seemed to fill the hallway. His frock coat hung open and a length of gleaming gold watch chain stretched like a Midas smile across his ample stomach. He turned his back to Sarah and spoke to an unseen party in the office.

"See that Edgewood receives a copy of the statement. And make certain Billy remembers to have someone sign for it. I want to see a name written in on the receipt, or Billy can by God find employment elsewhere."

"Yes, Mister Ryder," another man's voice meekly replied.

Satisfied he had made his point, Mister Ryder covered his thinning hair with a short-brimmed felt hat and closed the office door with the crook of his walking stick.

"Ryder Enterprises" shone with appropriate munificence from the front of the door. He stared at the name in open

respect for its significance, as if beholding the summation of
his life's achievements, then he turned away from the door
almost with a sense of regret, a king leaving his empire for
unknown shores.

His stride slowed as he noticed the auburn-haired young
woman and a bullish swagger befitting a much younger rake
insinuated itself into his steps. As he approached, the busi-
nessman touched the brim of his hat with the grip of his
walking stick. Sweat had already begun to irrigate his double
chin. Sarah started up the stairs before he could introduce
himself. She had no intention of becoming one of Mister
Ryder's enterprises.

The fourth-floor hall was identical to the first. Sarah followed a swath of green carpet toward the rear of the building
where a massive double door, checkered in mahogany relief,
overpowered the offices of lesser men. Running the length
of the top sill in exquisitely carved script almost a foot high,
"Cole's Catalogue" commanded immediate attention. Sarah
took a deep breath, exhaled slowly to calm her nerves. She
twisted the brass doorknob and entered the sumptuous waiting room of Allan Cole's office suite.

Murals, intending to re-create some faraway pastoral
splendor, peeked from behind carefully arranged velvet
drapes, royal blue in color, and stitched with silver thread.
Gaslights fluttered in the corners. Above a false hearth
beamed the portrait of a plump, pretty young woman whose
scantily covered shoulders and bosom shone with health and
desirability. Her powdered wig piled high atop her head and
the artfully applied beauty marks lent her an aura of refined
gentility, a woman whose only task in life was to decide how
deeply to rouge her cheeks.

"Why if it isn't Mrs. McClinton," a voice said behind her.
Allan Cole emerged from his private office and crossed the
room to Sarah. He bowed and brushed a kiss against her
hand.

"I thought I heard the door."

Allan Cole was a man of medium height, sporting a moustache and goatee and close-cropped blond hair. Pince-nez
perched below the bridge of his nose. His hands were in
constant animation as he spoke. His dapper brown tweed coat

appeared much too heavy for the hot weather, yet he seemed not to be bothered. His face was free of sweat. However, he carried a broadleaf fan, gripping its wooden handle in one small fist and stirring the air with unconscious effort.

"I have an engagement at four, but this shouldn't take long." He took Sarah by the arm and escorted her into his private office, a chamber puritan in spirit compared to the waiting room. A massive desk, three comfortably cushioned chairs. A place for business, not designed to impress. Allan Cole held the chair for her, and when she was seated, he took his place behind the desk. Sarah noticed an issue of *Cole's Catalogue* on the desktop near her—the same issue she had purchased a week ago and hidden at home.

"You know, Mrs. McClinton," Cole began without letting her explain the nature of her visit, "I insist the ladies whom I accept within these pages keep me informed if they change their addresses. I was informed by your previous landlord that you had moved some two months ago. More than two months. I cannot tell you how upsetting such news was to me."

"He informed you?"

"When I sent my runner by to see you. Yes. Quite so. And your former employer at City Hospital told me he had not seen you for three weeks. In short, Mrs. McClinton, hardly exemplary behavior. And I have gone to considerable trouble on your behalf."

"Mister Cole, I came here—"

"And fortunately for us both," he interrupted. "You might at least have shown some interest in how we represented you." He opened the catalogue, flipping through various advertisements and product claims and tastefully sketched portraits of would-be brides. He held the catalogue, covers spread wide to the page where Sarah McClinton saw herself once more, profiled, looking toward the edge of the page.

"Mister Cole—" she tried to interrupt.

"Water under the bridge, my dear." Cole waved his hand, took a file from a stack of folders, removed a packet from the folder, and handed it to her.

"This arrived better than a week ago." Cole eased back

in his chair. He began to fan himself. A smile spread in a slow arc between moustache and goatee.

"A Mr. Ryan of Montana wishes to pay you and your family's way out to his ranch for the purpose of matrimony."

"What?" Sarah stared at the packet as if it might leap off the desk at her.

"Marriage, Mrs. McClinton. For heaven's sake. Marriage. Perhaps you had preferred someone from the East? But to be honest, opportunity lies West. Mister Ryan is obviously quite well off. He has a ranch. Go ahead. Pick it up. Look at his picture. Mrs. McClinton . . ."

"Yes?"

"His picture."

She fumbled with the packet. Out slid a series of rail tickets, enough to take her and the children as far as St. Louis.

"Mister Ryan included a draught from a bank in San Francisco. And instructions to purchase your tickets. You are to make connections with a steamboat in St. Louis. I forget the name of the captain, but it is among the information, somewhere. Peruse the material at your leisure. However, I would suggest you consider departing as soon as possible. I have already taken my fee out of what was sent you. And, of course, there will be a small sum for expenses due you at departure. I've made note of every transaction."

Sarah did not answer. She stared down at the daguerreotype that had fallen out of the packet with the rest of the notes and accounting slips Allan Cole provided for his would-be brides.

Joel Ryan looked to be a few inches taller than Sarah. His face was noble, even striking. Dark eyes, sensitive mouth. Clean shaven. Groomed and tailored, dark hair combed away from his face in a single sweep. Rather than posing in the stilted discomfort most subjects displayed, he looked a trifle bemused at the photographer.

"He writes the daguerreotype was made in Kentucky," Cole said. "He is a widower. I admit he looks a trifle young to be a widower . . ." Sarah glanced up at him. Cole cleared his throat. "Of course, such tragedies do happen."

Montana. The word was musical. It rolled off the tongue

inciting a restlessness within. She caught herself. *My God, Sarah Joy McClinton, have you lost your mind?* She stared at the face. His eyes seemed to bore right through her. Why would a man choose a bride from a catalogue? A man so obviously well off. So—admit it, Sarah—handsome.

Her trembling hand placed the picture and packet back on the desk.

"When can you be ready to leave?" Cole said, carefully studying her.

"I am afraid I won't be, Mister Cole."

The smile drooped into a frown. The blond brows knotted in distrust. He ceased fanning himself, his arm frozen.

"How's that? I assure you, Mrs. McClinton, if you are thinking something better may come along, please reconsider. A woman in your position, with two children. In this day and age there aren't many men willing to accept such a responsibility. It is not only a matter of preference but finance as well. These are trying times. Money is scarce."

"I don't want my name in the catalogue. A woman has no business marketing herself in such a way. Trouble and nothing else will come of it."

"In the name of heaven, no one dragged you through the door," Cole said, slamming his fist down on the desk as he stood. He leaned toward her. "I didn't haul you off the street. You came to me. I have a reputation to uphold. I have spent money paying the artist for your likeness, preparing a description."

"I will pay you back." Sarah reached inside her purse and placed three dollars on his desk. "That's only the first installment. Whatever I owe you, I'll make good."

"Oh, fine. And what price shall I put on my reputation? A gentleman sends me a draught in confidence. Why? Because of me. And what I stand for. *Cole's Catalogue* is the finest mail-order bride service in the world."

"Can't you inform Mister Ryan that I have already made other arrangements?" Sarah asked.

"I've spent his money as well," Cole explained. "Besides, if word ever circulated that I had practiced a deception, it would ruin me."

"Mister Cole, this is still a free country, is it not? I am not a slave."

"Of course you aren't."

"Then I can refuse Mister Ryan's generous offer."

"But no one ever refuses. No one!"

"Then perhaps I had better set the precedent."

Allan Cole shrank back into his chair. He placed a hand over his mouth. He studied the packet as if it held other options for him, though he couldn't think of one.

"Believe me, I am sorry for any inconvenience. When I came to you, I was frightened and desperate. My husband was dead. And I did not know what else to do. It was a rash and silly mistake I made in coming here. I saw an old copy of the catalogue, and it seemed like the answer at the time. It wasn't until after the numbness wore off that I realized my mistake. I could never go off with some stranger. Anyway, I need to make my life work for me on my own. I thought about telling you earlier, but I just didn't think anything would come of it. Then I found the issue with my picture in it. I can repay you if it makes things easier. Believe me, I truly regret any inconvenience I have caused you."

"How thoughtful," Cole said, his thumb rubbing the corner of the packet. Sarah tried to think of something, anything that might ameliorate the situation.

"You are making a very bad mistake," Cole finally said. "Not a threat, my dear. Just a fact."

"I've had a lot of practice," Sarah sighed.

"And nothing I say will change your mind?" Cole formed a steeple with his fingers and pressed his fingertips against his lips.

"I am sorry," she said.

"I see." Cole took the packet, shoved it into the folder, and dropped it on top of the stack to his right.

"Then I suppose there isn't anything left to say but goodbye," he said without standing.

"No," Sarah replied haltingly. "I guess not." She stood and left the room, grateful even in her discomfort that the matter was ended. "I will pay you back."

"I am not worried," Cole said, stroking his goatee. "A

woman of your obvious means." He shook his head in a
mixture of derision and disbelief.

Sarah blushed and made her way into the waiting room.
She paused in the silence, pride returning. The matter was
settled, and she was free to pursue her life, determined to
succeed. Nothing was going to stop Sarah McClinton now.

Nothing.

26

The first person Sarah saw in her apartment was Eddie Paris. He was also the only person she saw. She recognized him instantly, and her pulse quickened with a premonition of disaster. Her heart throbbed against her ribs. Sarah licked the inside of her dry mouth. She had seen him before, with her husband and sometimes running errands for Elrod Pierce. She hurried into the bedroom. Empty. God in heaven, empty. Bile rose to her throat. She managed not to vomit, but gathered in the remnants of her courage and walked into the living room. Eddie sat at the kitchen table. He held a crudely framed lithograph of "The Siege of Chattanooga." Sarah recognized her son's handiwork.

"Where are they?" she said, her voice barely rising above a whisper.

"The boy and girl are fine. Believe me, Mrs. McClinton."

"I did not ask that."

"No. Forgive me. I only wished to allay your fears." He worked his finger around the inside of his collar. "Awfully hot in here. You might have done better for yourself and your children. Mister Pierce is a generous man."

"Damn you to hell," she spat. "Where are my children?"

"At the Royale," Eddie said.

Sarah whirled around and started toward the door.

"There's a carriage waiting," Eddie said. "Mister Pierce wanted to offer you every convenience." Sarah stood in the doorway, her fingers bloodless where they gripped the sill.

"If they have been harmed . . ."

"Mrs. McClinton. You have a sensible boy. We told him you were hurt out in the street. Naturally, he opened the door to us. We gathered the two of them up and told him not to make a peep or the girl would suffer. He did not make a peep." Eddie dropped the picture and stood. "Now if you were to cause a scene, perhaps run to the authorities, then Mister Pierce would be left with no other choice than to remove the children . . . but why pursue what will not come about?"

Sarah closed her eyes. She sagged against the sill a moment. All her plans came crashing down, wrecked by one man. Elrod Pierce.

Eddie Paris drew close to her, an odor of whiskey on his breath. She recoiled from his touch. Pierce's lackey shrugged, mildly bemused at her reaction.

"After you," he said.

Together they walked down the stairs and out into the waning sunlight. True to Elrod Pierce's word, a carriage waited.

Night came to Manhattan, bringing a faint promise of relief from the heat. Sarah watched the city slide past as the carriage threaded its way through the crowded streets to the Royale. She knew the name but had never visited the place. Jaimie had gone there to meet Pierce. Tall, gaunt-looking, his eyes ringed with folds of flesh as if he never got enough sleep, Elrod Pierce was a man nature had never intended to be pretty. He had come to the McClinton apartment and spoken of Jaimie's talents, promising them both wealth and position. She had never understood but had been willing to accept on faith. Until Jaimie began to change, to grumble and complain, to drink more than he could handle. Until Pierce came alone and uninvited to their apartment with Jaimie gone. Pierce proposed a liaison between Sarah and himself. What was the price on her honor? She had rebuked his advances. Unleashing her Irish temper. Sarah had driven him off. Yet here she was. She had been wrong to think the city large enough to hide in. Now Sean and Fiona were paying for her mistake.

Though the Royale rose three stories above the pavement, the first floor was actually an immense high-ceilinged room boasting gambling tables and roulette wheels, enough space to satisfy up to five hundred wagering patrons, and a bar capable of handling the thirst of a hundred more. At the far end of the gambling hall was a brightly lit stage for the entertainment-minded. Before backdrops of the Barbary Coast, a bevy of scantily clad young ladies sang and danced to the favorite tunes of the day performed by a ten-piece ensemble housed in an orchestra pit in front of the stage. Music, singing, shouted conversation, bets, and counter wagers all blended into a cacophony that rose through a sea of smoky vapors to massive oil lamp chandeliers creaking overhead. Lengths of heavy chain connected the wheels of illumination to two foot-thick oak beams running the width of the ceiling.

Eddie Paris led Sarah across the main room to the stairway. They passed several couples on the stairs. One man, arm in arm with a heavily painted lady of the night, greeted Eddie and feasted his eyes on Sarah.

"Somebody new, Eddie?" the man said.

"For Elrod," came the reply.

"Greedy bastard always keeps the best for himself."

Sarah reddened at the implication and hurried up the remaining steps to a shadowy L-shaped hallway. The doors on either side were all alike. More than a dozen smoke-shaded oil lamps lined the hall. Wicks burned in perfumed oil, blending with the headier scent of musk.

"This way," Eddie said. Sarah followed. She paused once, hearing a moan of passion issue from one of the rooms. Eddie chuckled and continued on to the corner, disappearing around the angle. His steps quickened as he neared the door at the far end. There in the eerie amber silence, Eddie knocked on the door. He turned to the woman.

"Go in," he said and started back the way they had come.

"Where are my children?"

"Ask him." Eddie nodded toward the apartment. Sarah stared at the door, reached for it with a trembling hand. She took a deep breath, exhaled slowly. The door swung open at her touch.

"Come in, Sarah," a voice said from the center of the room.

She stepped inside and closed the door behind her. Elrod Pierce was seated in a high-backed easy chair, his feet crossed and resting on an ottoman. He held a wineglass and

took tentative sips, as if he were undecided about the quality
of the wine. He wore a brown smoking jacket, stitched with
gold thread, and black trousers to match his hair and brooding brows. He smiled. The look of affection on his face sent
shivers up and down Sarah's spine. But she would not make
a public display of her fear.

"Where are my children?"

Pierce smiled and motioned for her to come closer.
"Hardly a way to begin a romantic evening," he said.

"Where are they?!"

"In the stable out in back. Locked in the tackle room, I
believe." Sarah spun around and started toward the door.

"Under guard, of course, for their protection," Pierce
added. She slowed, closed her eyes a moment. Menace filled
the room.

"What is it you'll be wanting from me, Mister Pierce?"

"Better," Elrod said, sipping from his glass. He liked the
defeat in her voice. "Now then," he leaned forward and filled
a glass for her. "You know, unkindness is a meager virtue
and ill befits one so beautiful."

"Unkind?"

"Yes, my dear. I remember once, approaching with an
offer of true magnitude, exchanging your life of dissatisfac-
tion for one of sumptuous reward. You refused in rather rude
fashion. I am a man of sensitivity, my dear. It is a slight I
haven't forgotten."

"I was a married woman, sir, and you were supposed to
be my husband's friend. Your suggestions then were, as now,
befitting the gutter."

"Jaimie's friend? Don't be absurd." Elrod crossed the
room, opened a gold-inlaid walnut box, and took out a cigar.
He sniffed the tobacco, snipped off the end. "I was his benefactor. I provided him with knowledge and had him tutored,
and how did he repay me? How did both of you repay me?
He hanged himself. And you spurned me for the likes of a
common thief."

"Jaimie . . . No!"

"Yes. It was how he paid his debts. Ask Eddie Paris. He
was your husband's partner. I expected great things from
Jaimie. He had all the right qualities—daring, skill . . . and

moral ineptitude. Yes, all the qualities. I suppose he thought his death would set me back. It did for a little while. But the world is full of thieves. And men who want to be thieves."

"It is full of weak men," Sarah said, understanding more than she cared to admit the sickness of Jaimie's battered spirit. "And you are worse than all of them put together. You feed on their weakness and misfortune. A parasite of human misery."

"A harsh judgment, my dear, and one you may regret. I've been told I have considerable charm. I also have considerable power. People fear me, my dear. And fear has its own attraction, you know. As does beauty. I am a great lover of beauty. Look about you. Fine paintings. A fortune in sculpture. Even these wineglasses are from a village in France where the workmanship is worthy of the art. It is my desire for beauty that led me to you."

"How did you find me?"

"Friends in low places." Elrod chuckled. "Come here and light my cigar." Sarah stayed on her side of the easy chair.

"A single pull on that cord by the door to the bedroom," he indicated a velvet sash, "and my man in the livery stable will be very unkind to your little girl."

Sarah studied him a moment, weighing the wages of resistance, then walked around to the table, took the glass flue off one of the oil lamps, and held the flame to the cigar. Elrod puffed a cloud of bluish white smoke. His hand touched her shoulder and lightly traced a path across her breast.

"I am a man who collects his debts. In my business I cannot afford to be lenient. Lose respect and you lose fear. And fear is the crux of power. Jaimie owed me. But he left it for you to pay his debt. I'm happy he did. You will be, too. I am not without a certain prowess." He smiled. "We will pass the night together, you and I. And in the morning you and your children will be taken to an apartment I have arranged for you. There will be money as well. More than you can possibly hope to make sewing other women's clothes. When I want you, I will send word. From time to time I may require you to share your favors with certain guests. You'll find the work befits one of your obvious appeal. You and your children will want for nothing."

Elrod dropped the cigar into his wineglass; the glowing tip fizzled out. He leaned forward; his bony fingers held her by the arms and drew her to his kiss. She started to resist, but beyond Elrod's shoulder glimpsed the sash he had threatened to pull. The prospect of harm coming to her children burned in her mind. She responded to the kiss, transforming her repulsion into ardor. Elrod's powerful embrace all but crushed the breath from her.

The nightmare seemed eternity.

Mere seconds ticked away. And something lost, irrevocably lost in the clicking of the clock. He cupped her face in his hands and traced her lips with his thumb, studying the depths of her eyes for some hint of desire. Finding none, he resolved to teach her.

"Go into the bedroom. I have left a gown for you to wear." The gambler gave her a gentle shove toward the bedroom door. Sarah numbly complied. She closed the door behind her, and as if through a haze, she saw velvet curtains and a canopied bed and shimmering silken finery arranged upon the sheets.

Soon, now, she would be receiving his lust, hear him grunt and gasp, feel his weight bearing down upon her. She steadied herself against the bedpost, a sense of violation overwhelming her. She glanced over at the mirror and in it saw a young, frightened woman. And in the shadows there, in the corner, the light's odd design, like a hanged man.

Elrod Pierce had destroyed Jaimie.

And now he intended the same fate for her.

The woman in the mirror straightened and wiped the taste of Elrod Pierce from her mouth.

She looked around for a weapon. Nothing but useless clothes and furniture too bulky to move. If not a weapon . . . what? She stared at the door, expecting him at any moment to enter, to stand gloating at her, the amber glare of the lamps playing on his drawn, threatening features . . .

Lamps!

She spun around and hurried to the dresser. If not a weapon, then a diversion, she thought, extinguishing the flame and carrying the oil-filled base over to the velvet drapes. She unscrewed the wick and, struggling to breathe around the tightness in her chest, emptied the lamp onto the velvet, soaking the olive-colored material with coal oil. She tossed the empty lamp into a chair, took another from the dresser and looked wildly for a suitable pyre.

Closet . . . chairs . . . walls . . . nightstand . . . bed.

A smile stole across Sarah's face. She removed the wick and soaked the sheets with the liquid. Quilt, sheet, and canopy glistened in the dim glare of the single remaining lamp on the nightstand. She imagined Elrod noticing the darkening room and assuming that she was turning the lights low for the sake of romance, imagined his quickening pulse, the staccato beat of his heart.

Come then, Mister Elrod Pierce, you'll be wanting to claim your prize. In heat, are you? If not, I'll make you hot. She increased the wick until the reddish yellow tongue of fire danced several inches above the base, oily black smoke spiraling from its tip. She removed the flue and allowed the wick to lap greedily at the hem of the drapery. In an instant, a billowing sheet of fire consumed the curtains and started on the ceiling. Sarah tossed the lamp onto the bed and retreated against the farthest wall as a flash of brilliant fire exploded among the bedcovers. Flames devoured the rug, transformed plush furniture into shapeless mounds of conflagration.

Elrod, flush with a final sip of wine and eager for the evening's activities to begin, opened the door.

"Forgive my eagerness, dear girl, but I have waited a long—" Words died in his throat. He stared, transfixed in horror, eyes wide and jaw hanging slack. A rasping noise sounded deep in his throat. Sarah shielded her face from the flames and squirmed past the stunned figure in the doorway. Alerted by the motion, Elrod lunged for her and missed. He stumbled into the sitting room just as a swath of flames curled around the doorsill, exploring the walls of the outer room. Sarah collided with an end table and fell to her knees. The bell sash burst into flames as Elrod reached for it. Unable to summon help, the gambler retreated from the fire and turned on Sarah. She threw the wine bottle and then the glasses, as he closed in.

Sarah darted toward the door to the hall. The bedroom was a veritable furnace, and now the wallpaper of the sitting room blackened as flames spread over the dry surface. The length of her dress slowed her, allowing Elrod just time enough. He grabbed for an arm, tore a sleeve, his weight smashing Sarah off course. The door and freedom slipped past.

"You bitch," Elrod roared. The back of his hand caught her full in the face, knocking her off balance. He slapped her again; the rings on his fingers raised welts on her neck. She saw a stand of walking sticks centered in the billowing smoke. Elrod's strong hands grabbed her by the hair and lifted her up for more punishment. Her reach was almost . . . was . . . *God help me* . . . enough. Pale, slender fingers grasped a silver pommel. With a power born of fear, Sarah twisted loose. She tore a walking stick from the stand and swung it in a mighty arc to collide against Elrod's head. Too late she saw the glimmer of steel, thirty inches long, razor sharp. The cane had caught in the stand, allowing the blade to slip free. It ripped across the gambler's face. Blood spattered the wall. Blood welled between his fingers as he clawed at the wound. Then Elrod stretched to his full height, his arms suddenly flung wide revealing a hideous crimson furrow running from his scalp down across his left cheek to the jawline, leaving a gory crater where his left eye had been.

"AAAAAAAAAAAHHHHHHHHHH!" His scream rose to a shrill peak.

Still clutching the cane, Sarah grabbed for the door, found the latch, and fled the sound of his inhuman cry. She staggered, gasped for breath, and realizing the disaster she had instigated, she hammered with the silver hilt of the sword cane against the doors ranging the hall.

"Fire!" she shouted as she ran. "Fire!" to the sweat-streaked or dull or hostile faces that appeared behind partly opened doors. A potbellied, naked lout staggered out of a room and confronted Sarah. "What the hell are you doing?"

"Fire!" she shouted.

"Where?"

She slashed out with the sword cane. The slim sturdy blade shattered an oil lamp on a nearby table. Flames leaped up the wallpaper, turning printed flowers to flakes of ash.

"Here!" she said and ran toward the stairs, hammering on the doors as she went, yelling a warning to the denizens within. The man in the hall stared at the flames. Other doors opened and partly clad men and women hurried out of their rooms.

"Gawd damn," the man in the hall shouted. Women screamed. Their less than gallant consorts charged for the nearest escape routes. The first gunshot sounded as Sarah reached the stairway. A bloody towering figure of wrath emerged past the corner and leveled his gun at the first woman he saw, mistaking an unfortunate prostitute for the woman who had maimed him. Elrod killed the whore with a bullet through the skull and wounded a man who got in his way as he stumbled after Sarah. Then smoke obscured him. Sarah, along with several other men and women, broke into a headlong, panic-stricken flight down the stairs.

Music faded. Dancers and musicians turned their attention toward the stairway. Fire! The word roared among the patrons like an oncoming wave.

Fire. The most dread danger in the city. One scream became many. A knot of people at the double doors swelled as men and women fought to gain the safety of the street. Windows were broken out. The slow were trampled underfoot. The greedy fought over spilled change, grabbed what they could, and ran for the exits. Sarah caught a glimpse of a familiar face, and clinging to the wall, she worked her way to the stage. She had spied Eddie Paris scurrying to the rear of the proscenium, and following a hunch, Sarah scrambled after Elrod's henchman, up the steps, past the footlights. The hem of her dress ripped across a flat. The material tore. She left it behind on the snagging nail and darted upstage, beyond the backdrop of the Barbary Coast. Just as she suspected, a narrow passage offered an escape route to the back alley. Thankful the rest of the embroiled humanity beyond the orchestra pit had not thought of this exit or noticed Eddie Paris, she ran, following the corridor until it emptied through a stage door out into the night.

Eddie Paris stepped inside the barn. "Mose," he called. "Mose . . ." The idiot must have run off to watch the fire. He heard a child's muffled voice and traced it to its source, a dim narrow room at the rear of the stable. He opened the door, allowing the feeble light to spill across the frightened faces of Sean and Fiona McClinton. The fire might just spread to the barn. It might be best if they were brought to Elrod. Eddie reached in for the girl.

"You let my sister go," Sean yelled. Eddie Paris moved to block the entrance to the tack room and caught the struggling little girl who bawled in terror.

"Leave her be," Sean yelled. Escape was so close. He charged his sister's assailant. Eddie was too preoccupied with Fiona to protect himself. Sean kicked out, his foot whooshing up between Eddie's splayed legs, connecting with an audible smack. Eddie howled and dropped the girl. He sat down hard. Sean caught Fiona in his arms and leaped past the stricken ruffian. But not high enough or quick enough. Eddie grabbed him by the ankle.

"Run, Fiona," Sean shouted, setting her down. He kicked at the hand that would not let him go. Eddie groaned in a mixture of pain and rage, but he held on. The horses in the stalls whinnied in terror at the commotion.

"Run!" Sean ordered his sister once again. The little girl stood in the center of the stable, crying, calling to Sean. The boy fell. He clawed at the hard-packed earth and felt himself drawn toward Eddie . . .

Three things happened at once:
Eddie felt a razor-sharp point of steel prick his throat.
He released Sean.
And Fiona cried, "Mommy!"
Sarah managed to catch her daughter in an embrace, withstand Sean's exuberant assault, and keep the tip of the sword cane's naked blade at Eddie's throat.

"Ma, they said you were hurt, or I never would've opened the door, and I tried to fight them, but they said they would hurt Fiona, and . . ."

"Mommy, I wanna go home, I wanna go home . . ."

"Shh. My darlings, my darlings."

"I was going to bring them to you," Eddie said from ground level. Sarah put the children behind her. The clanging bells of fire wagons riddled the stillness.

"Sure. And pigs have wings," she said. Her hair had come undone and spilled down over her shoulders. Her face, stained with soot, radiated an aura of fury and reprisal. Eddie recognized the sword cane by its silver pommel and tried a new tactic.

"If Elrod finds out what you're about . . ."

"I'll cut out his other eye," Sarah said, her lips curled back in a predatory snarl, like a lioness defending her cubs. "Crawl to that post. The beam in the middle there."

Eddie gulped, his features a stark sickly gauze white. He looked over at the thick wooden post supporting the loft.

"What are you gonna do?" he managed to say.

"Kill you . . . if you don't crawl. Now!"

Eddie crawled.

"Stop."

He stopped, still on his hands and knees about a yard from the post.

"Stand."

Eddie stood.

"Bend over."

"Listen, Miss . . ." Eddie moaned in a tearful voice. He bent over. "Elrod tells me what to do. I just do . . ."

Sarah stabbed the honed steel point an inch deep in the man's buttock.

"YeeooWW!" Eddie shrieked, and on reflex he dived forward, headfirst into the wood post, then slumped unconscious onto his side. The children laughed to see their tormentor so foolishly disposed of, and as Sarah had hoped, it eased their terror.

"Hurry now," she said, gathering her son and daughter. She hugged and kissed them both and managed not to cry. "We have to hurry."

Fearing the fire might spread to the stable, Sarah quickly released all the horses, chasing them toward the rear doors that Sean had just opened. Sarah and the children followed the horses into a larger fenced area where a variety of carriages, coaches, and surreys belonging to the patrons of the Royale were kept. A number of livery hands were gathered at the far corner of the stableyard watching the firewagons gradually bring the blaze under control. Streams of water generated by steam pumps hosed down the neighboring buildings as well. Sarah wasn't choosy. She took the nearest carriage and led the brown mare to the yard gate.

"She taken the carriage. Mistuh Binckley's carriage. Hey!"

Sean lifted Fiona up into the seat and leaped beside her as Sarah flicked the whip hard across the mare's rump. The carriage lurched out of the yard and quickly gathered speed, vanishing in a cloud of alley dust and spattered debris.

27

"**M**ighty fine carriage," the police officer said. He stroked the mare's neck. "Good stout animal." He sauntered back to the boy and girl seated on the carriage seat. Fiona was asleep, using her brother's thigh for a pillow. "And what would the likes of a boy such as yourself be doing with a rich setup of this kind?"

Sean looked up at the dark doorway to the office building. His mind feverishly sorted through excuses.

"Uh, it ain't mine, sir."

"I can see that, me lad. Come now. Are you about some mischief?"

"Oh no sir. You see, it's my Ma . . ."

"You aren't expecting me to believe this is your Ma's rig?"

"No sir. We come by trolley. My Ma takes care of the building. Cleaning and the like. We come here 'cause we got no place to go until she gets paid." Sean tried his most sorrowful expression. "The rent's due, and the landlord won't let us in till he sees the money in our fist. Anyway sir, a fine gent come by while she's cleaning and said he left something inside. He asked me to watch his horse and carriage, there being no one else about to do it. Fiona got plumb tired and fell asleep."

"These are hard times. And hardest on the little ones," the policeman muttered. "But watching a carriage out here on the dark street is man's work. I've a good mind to tell this fellow—what's his name?" The officer had started toward the office building.

"Oh no sir, please sir. I *am* a man, at least in our family with Pa dead an' all. And the gent already paid me, and we need every cent. Oh please, mister . . ."

"Your Pa's dead?" The policeman shook his head and held up his hands. "Well, I reckon it's best left alone then. Ah, what black days these be." The officer tipped his hat. "And your Ma, I bet, works herself to the bone."

"Yessir. Practically night and day."

"She's a good woman. I'll warrant one of the best. Never forget, lad, a good mother is an angel. That's what she is. Mark my words . . . an angel as true as I stand here."

Sarah tried again with the sword blade, jimmying it between the sill and the edge of the door. Slowly, she increased the pressure. Sweat beaded her forehead and stung her eyes.

"C'mon," she whispered. "C'mon."

The blade snapped with a loud crack that seemed to reverberate the entire length of the hall. Her spirits sank, then surged anew as the door swung open. She wasted no time in scurrying inside the darkened room. She waited a moment, leaning against the door, her heart pounding in her chest, while her vision gradually accustomed itself to the inky darkness. Sarah took a tentative step, her arms outstretched, feeling her way. Gaining confidence, she hurried, tripped against an end table and caught a vase inches above the floor. She exhaled softly and placed the artifact on the couch. She inched her way to the opposite door without mishap and into the private office of Allan Cole. Risking light, she struck a match on the base of an oil lamp and touched the flame to the wick. *Please let it still be there. Please.* An amber glow bathed the desktop, delineating a pen and inkwell, a sheaf of papers, ledger, several issues of *Cole's Catalogue,* some brown paper packets. There were names printed on the front of each one: Carol Rosa, Peggy Weiss, Pamela Kania. Sarah gasped in recognition. Her name, with a heavy black line drawn through it, was on the next packet. She grabbed it and fumbled for a few seconds through its contents, finding train tickets, an envelope of currency, the daguerreotype of Joel Ryan. His slim, handsome countenance seemed to stare at her with a bemused expression as if to say, "I knew you'd be along sooner or later."

"We'll see about that, Mister Joel Ryan," Sarah muttered. "I may have a few surprises for you yet." And surprises for

Elrod Pierce as well. He was bound to come looking. Let him search the city for all eternity, because she wouldn't be here. She extinguished the lamp. Replacing the contents of the packet, she tucked it firmly beneath her arm and hurried from the office. Allan Cole would be furious of course, but she would try to make it up to him one day. The pieces of the broken sword cane fit nicely beneath the cushions of the couch. The quiet closing of the hall door put an end to her clandestine visit to *Cole's Catalogue*.

Two interminably long minutes later, she stepped out of the shadows of the building's vestibule and hurried across the sidewalk to the carriage.

"Thank heaven," Sean said. "I can't take too much more of this." Sarah grinned to see his old self returning. "We better hurry," the boy added.

"Why?"

"Because of him," Sean said, pointing to the police officer who was watching them with a mixture of curiosity and suspicion.

His mother was certainly behaving as if the carriage were hers and not some gent's, as Sean had described. She climbed aboard and took up the whip.

"Hold on, now, me fine Missus," the officer shouted, heavily retracing his steps. Sarah guided the mare into the empty street. The policeman's exhortations to "pull up" faded behind them.

"Now can we go home?" Sean asked, thoroughly puzzled by his mother's actions. Sarah shook her head no.

"When?" he asked in a faint voice.

"Never," she replied, guiding them into the mainstream of night traffic. "Never."

Pennsylvania Station was a vast gloomy place at midnight. From time to time someone moved, clinging to the anonymity of the shadows. Come morning and the benches and corridors would throng with passengers arriving and departing, and well-wishers greeting loved ones or bidding fond farewells.

Sarah led her family to the only ticket window that was

open. A balding, middle-aged official looked up, startled from his drowsy state by her presence.

"When does the Baltimore Flyer leave?" she asked.

"You're a tad early, ma'am."

"When does it leave?"

"Oh . . . in about eleven hours or so."

"Eleven hours!" Sarah glanced around, as if Elrod Pierce might appear at any second.

"Isn't there any way to hurry it up?"

"Sure, ma'am. I'll send a runner over to the engineer's house and get him out of bed so's he can make a special run down to Baltimore just for you." The man sighed. "Best you find yourself a room somewhere."

"We'll stay here."

"Don't seem proper," the man said, scratching at his nose. "Penn Station ain't what I'd call a fittin' bedroom for a 'lady.' " He used the term loosely, as if he were lending it and might want it back shortly. "But suit yourself."

"Thank you," Sarah said and, adjusting Fiona's weight in her arms, allowed Sean to lead her to a vacant row of benches out of the light. Eleven hours to wait, to wonder, to know he must be searching. Eleven hours.

Then ten.

"Mommy, I'm hungry," Fiona mewed, trying to find a comfortable spot on the hardwood bench.

"Sean will be back soon."

"But when?"

"Soon. And if he found anything to buy, he'll have food."

"Cake?"

"I don't know about cake. Here he comes, though."

Sean hurried past the huddled form of a vagrant on a nearby bench and crossed to his mother's side.

"I was beginning to worry," she said.

"I had to go outside a minute."

"On the street?"

"Yes," Sean said. Setting down his sack and digging into his coat pocket, he held out his hand. Nestled in the palm were half a dozen smooth round stones. "If I'd had these, dumb ol' Mister Pierce would never have got past the door."

He tugged his slingshot from his belt and placed one of the stones in the rawhide cup. A perfect fit.

"Well I do not expect the likes of him . . ." her voice faded. He had found their apartment. And more than likely was searching this very minute for her. Dispatch someone to her apartment, and when she did not show up, send his men out through the streets. The notion filled her with dread.

"What's this, Mommy?" Fiona said, rummaging in the sack. She held up a tin container.

"Peaches, stupid. It says it right in the front. I bought it from the man who stamped our tickets. Watch out. It's open."

Fiona tilted the can and spilled some juice on the floor. Sean rolled his eyes to heaven.

"Mommy, make him stop. I am not stupid. You are 'cause you didn't bring any cake."

"I bought everything he hadn't eaten," Sean answered, more to his mother than Fiona. "Even then I had to give him fifty cents."

"I wanted cake."

"You two settle down and eat. I think Sean did very well. Especially under the circumstances. So let's eat what we have and be thankful. And then rest. We have a long night ahead of us."

"I'll stand guard," Sean said, drawing himself up, swelling out his chest in manly fashion. Then he yawned, shedding his guise of adulthood, becoming a ten-year-old again.

"We'll take turns keeping watch."

"Even me?" Fiona asked excitedly. "I'll watch over us, Mommy."

"No. We'll let Sean."

"I want to be first." Fiona's lower lip puffed out.

"You can be first to sleep," Sarah explained. Fiona brightened. First, after all, was first.

Pain worked its way up her spine. By the time her shoulders cramped, Sarah was awake. She forced open her eyes and looked into the aged, wrinkled visage of an old woman hiding a hungry frame beneath a voluminous rag quilt dress. She smiled, revealing sickly pink toothless gums.

"Sweet young'uns," she said. Fiona stirred, repositioned her head on her mother's lap. Sean was stretched out on the bench opposite them, legs crossed, a forearm crooked across his face, slingshot tucked in his belt.

"Yes," Sarah agreed, looking with love over her sleeping family. The old woman gestured with a scrawny hand.

"Folks call me Ma Hubbard. Like in the nursery rhyme. Ol' Mother Hubbard went to the cupboard . . . Only I ain't got no cupboard. Nothin' but a push cart. I got me a keen eye, too. There be lots of things to see, if a body only look."

"I'm sure," Sarah replied and settled once more against the hardwood bench in an obvious gesture of one about to go to sleep. Ma Hubbard did not take the hint.

"Like tonight. I seen me a big fire," she said in a conspiratorial tone. "Yep. Big gambling hall and crib house— *woosh!*—up in flames. Now it's plumb nothing but black sticks and ashes."

"How interesting." Sarah began to sense there was more to Ma Hubbard than she had suspected.

"Was anyone killed?"

"Not the one you mean."

"You aren't making any sense. I'm sorry. I really do need to rest."

"Not Elrod Pierce, dear."

Sarah stiffened. She glanced around the station. The large oval clock displayed the hour. 4:12 A.M. A few people milled about, finding benches, arranging tickets, sorting luggage. Strangers one and all. And Elrod Pierce, thank heaven, was not among them.

"He ain't here," Ma Hubbard cackled.

"But he will be?" Sarah asked. "You work for him. You're one of his friends."

"No. Lawdie, no. You don't understand. I have eyes. I have ears. Mister Pierce sometimes pays for what I learn. There's others he treats the same. But only one Ma Hubbard. Only one." She gasped, took a breath, and continued. "Word has spread. Mister Pierce is very angry. Mister Pierce is looking for a woman, a pretty woman with hair like yours. A woman and two young'uns, boy and girl. They'll be runnin'. But Mister Pierce wants them. Bad."

"And you'll tell him?"

"Me?" The old woman cackled again. "You're safe, honey. No need to skedaddle. There's such a thing as pride. I ain't as hungry as I look. Wait here and catch your train. I won't be the cause of harm comin' to these children. Just say I warned you. Be on your guard. Mister Elrod Pierce never forgets a debt. Never. Don't trust a soul. Not a soul."

"Thanks for the warning."

"Least I could do," Ma Hubbard nodded and scuttled off.

Sarah watched the woman depart, then she leaned back against the armrest, trying not to think, trying not to worry.

They'd be gone. Soon. Free of Pierce. Free and safe.

She wanted desperately to believe that. She glanced over at her son. Sean was awake and had probably overheard Ma Hubbard's warning. Mother and son looked at one another, drawing an unspoken strength one from the other.

We'll be fine, Sarah thought, *safe. Very soon.*

Sean did not look convinced, but then neither did she.

Darkness ebbed. The shadows, too, gave way like a receding tide as morning sun spilled in through immense windows. And with the daylight, came the crowds—clamorous, congesting, jamming every available breathing space.

Yet there was safety in discomfort. A woman and two children could get lost in a crowd. And that was precisely what Sarah intended. Fiona clung to her skirt. Sean, more adventurous, circled the milling throng. And thus they passed the morning until at last a railroad attendant slid a white boarding card into the slot beside the words *Baltimore Flyer* on the huge scheduling board above the row of ticketing booths. Sarah cried in relief and gathering Fiona in her arms began searching the sea of faces for Sean. Instead, she found Elrod Pierce. Ma Hubbard was standing beside him at the entrance to the station. The old woman was pointing a gnarled finger right at . . .

Don't trust a soul.

The left side of Elrod's face was bandaged. He was turned toward her and though he was still too far away to distinguish his features, Sarah imagined the look of satisfaction.

He had her.

And even as the icy talons of fear and dismay clawed at her heart, from deep within Sarah's indomitable soul came the reply, "Not yet, Mister Elrod Pierce. Not yet."

"There she is. Still here. She waited just like I told you," Ma Hubbard exclaimed.

"I want her," Elrod said, his voice muted by the bandage covering the left half of his face. He stared at the woman who had half-blinded him and burned him out. He dropped a handful of coins in Ma Hubbard's outstretched hand and charged through the terminal, shoving aside anyone in his way. Travelers scattered as he thrust his way through the crowds, his attention centered on Sarah, who was standing with fists clenched by her daughter. Ignoring the throng of people around him in his outrage, he saw only Sarah.

And Sean, looking around a stone pillar, spotted Elrod. Standing on a crate, the boy watched as the gambler rudely pushed through the crowd. Sean spotted a particularly large man looming protectively over a diminutive and proper-looking young lady. Just the right sort. As Elrod closed on her, Sean fit a stone in his slingshot and, timing the shot, let fly. The stone sped to its mark, the young woman's side.

"Out of my way," Elrod commanded, prodding a porter with the tip of his cane, and noticing the size of the man ahead, he chose a course around him. To the gambler's surprise, a woman yelped as he passed. He had not touched her, yet she doubled over in pain.

Elrod couldn't be bothered. He was almost to his quarry. His pace quickened, and he grinned in triumph despite the agony involved.

"You leave me be, Elrod Pierce," Sarah hissed, placing herself in front of Fiona.

"You have much to answer for," Elrod said, reaching for her. Suddenly he was whirled around and a hulking, florid face snarled in his.

"You hit my wife. I ain't got much use for rude folks." Elrod struggled against the man's grip. Beyond the irate stranger, the woman Sean had aimed at was rubbing her side and pointing at Elrod.

"Let me alone, you insolent ass."

The large man had less use for a glib tongue. He knocked Elrod down. The gambler staggered to his feet. He yanked out a derringer. Sarah threw the empty can of peaches, and with pure luck she sent the short-barreled weapon spinning from the dazed gambler's grip.

"Obliged," the husband said to her.

"He hurt me. That's him," his wife yelled.

Elrod grappled with the brute, and the two men tumbled arm in arm over the back of a bench. A crowd of onlookers quickly formed a ring around them. Sarah grabbed a wailing Fiona in her arms.

She searched for and found her son. She pointed toward the tracks. They reached the boarding platform almost at the same instant.

"Hurry," she gasped, breaking into a run.

"I didn't mean to hurt her, really," Sean said.

"Who?"

"Forget it," he replied, thinking better of the idea. He looked back toward the commotion inside the station. Sarah grabbed him by the shoulder.

"Run," she ordered.

The three of them worked their way down the platform, hurrying past the passengers filing aboard the rearmost cars. All was a moving, shifting montage of steam and people and the smell of sweat and perfume and cigar smoke and grease. Toward the front of the train, the cars were less congested. Sarah brought her family up the steps and vanished into a car.

Sarah watched the figure in the swirling vapors slide by as the train pulled away. Indistinguishable in the steam, she knew precisely who he was. Despite the brawl that had allowed her to flee, Elrod Pierce had followed close behind.

"Do you see him?" Sean asked, his voice thick with apprehension.

"No," Sarah lied. She yanked down the shade. Sean sighed in relief.

"Mommy. Where are we going?" Fiona asked, looking up with wide innocent eyes.

"Far away," Sarah replied. "A place called Montana."

"Will Mister Pierce be there?"

"We aren't ever going to be bothered by Mister Pierce again. He's in the past."

"I'm glad," the little girl said with childish finality.

Sarah sensed their fellow passengers' disapproval of her torn and wrinkled dress. She tucked the hem under the seat and pretended to find special interest in the floor. But her patience wore thin. She changed tactics and proceeded to stare down each inquisitive person.

"What's a Mom-Tana?" Fiona asked.

"Montana," Sean exasperatedly corrected. "It's a territory."

The train had found its speed now. Heads bobbed in unison. Bodies, as one, rocked from side to side.

"I hate to admit it, but she has a point," Sean said. "What's in Montana?"

Sarah reached out and drew him over onto the bench beside her, making room for him on the aisle side. She hugged her children close, taking courage in their nearness. What *was* in Montana? What indeed?

"The future," said Sarah McClinton. "My own darlings . . . the future."

28

Captain Osage Bixby propped his bootheels on his desk, leaned back, and locked his fingers behind his neck. His gaze drifted over to the canvas on the wall, a riverscape of the wide Missouri. He never tired of studying the painting for the artist had successfully captured the Missouri's grandeur as it swept north into the wilderness. Here was a river whose headwaters nestled among snowy peaks of the High Lonesome, three thousand miles from where the *Lady Jane LaFarge* was moored at her St. Louis levee. Let other men retire to their easy chairs and cozy fires, not Osage Bixby. The captain was a rotund, wide-shouldered man of fifty with a full beard that hid his double chin. He had a round snub nose like a cherub's, the effect of which he sought to offset with a perpetually gruff demeanor. And he was becoming more temperamental with every passing day that found him still in St. Louis. He'd sooner face a hundred hidden snags than sit around with a ready boat unable to give the orders, "Fire the engine, full steam." He sighed, standing. "Waitings worse than sandbars." Bixby poured another drink and downed it in a single gulp. *Inaction's turning me into a lush*, he thought, as the liquor worked its rivulet of fire down his throat. Pacing was a nervous habit he had only recently acquired from watching other boats steam downriver, returning from their final trips of the summer. His shadow flitted across alcove and bed, over his desk with its maps and china lanterns, past his private dining table nestled in the corner. Porcelain and silver dinnerware awaited his pleasure, as if the cook hadn't got himself knifed in a waterfront brawl. Rich man's tableware for beans and bacon, Bixby thought sourly, and all because he had tarried this extra two weeks in port. He considered another drink but instead walked to the black

iron stove in the center of the room and helped himself to a
mug of coffee poured from the pot he always kept warming.
He managed a couple of swallows. Braced by the bitter brew
he pulled on his heavy blue coat. Though it was much too
hot for the garment, the brass buttons and military cut lent
him authority. He walked out of the cabin onto the boiler
deck and ambled past the doors of the other dark cabins.
They were crammed for the most part with merchandise, as
any prospective passenger had ridden to the gold fields on
the *Olympus*, the *Malta*, *Harry of the West*, and other boats
now moored for the winter at the St. Louis landing.

Bixby climbed the steps to the hurricane deck and stared
across its empty expanse toward the pilothouse. The palms
of his hands itched for the feel of the great wooden wheel,
the boat shuddering under full steam as he yelled to the chief
engineer, "Pile it on. More power, damn you. Steam up."
The hold was loaded; the main deck where the roustabouts
slept was crammed too with goods for the upriver settlements.

Bixby leaned on the railing and looked out over the Mississippi. The stars appeared to have fallen into the river and
twinkled on the surface of the water. The *Lady Jane* trembled
with the passing current and strained against the rope lash-
ings binding the steamboat to the posts of the levee.

"Eager to be off, girl?" he muttered. "So am I." But he
had given his word to Joel Ryan to delay departure as long
as possible. And no one could say Osage Bixby wasn't a
man of his word. He remembered the last time he had seen
and listened to Silvertip's excited plans, plans Bixby considered sheer folly.

"Send hard-earned money and railway tickets and such all
the way to New York, chance a year's profits on a woman
whose likeness you ripped from *Cole's Catalogue*? Man,
have you taken leave of your senses?"

"Maybe, but you'll wait for her, won't you, Osage?"

"Send all your money off like this. Sweeney, talk sense
to him."

"They say Cole's has a good reputation," Sweeney had
offered. Some help she was.

"Hell's bells, Joel. This McClinton woman probably don't

even look a thing like that there drawing. Probably round as a barn, mean as a mud dauber in a drought, with hair like a spread of roots from an upturned cottonwood. No doubt got a tongue sharp as a Cheyenne scalpin' knife."

"Just tell me if you'll wait."

"All right, dadburnit. All right. I'll wait. I'll give her every chance to show." Captain Osage Bixby chuckled deep in his chest remembering the way Joel Ryan's face had lit up with relief. "Fool man," Osage snorted, "Suppose a fellow owes it to himself to be a fool now and then."

Bixby turned from the rail and retraced his steps to his cabin. Once inside he tossed his hat onto the bench seat against the wall and headed for the brandy. He was draining the last of a snifter full when a knock sounded at his door. Displeased, Bixby yelled permission to enter. He was in no mood for visitors. Nick Green, his novice pilot and full-time mud clerk, whose duties included the procurement of cord-wood throughout the river trek, stepped into the room.

"Captain Bixby, sir?" The nineteen-year-old seemed excited and a bit bewildered.

"I know who I am, Green. What is it you want?"

"A woman, sir. And two little ones. She mentioned Mister Ryan by name, and she has some papers . . ."

"A woman, you say," Captain Bixby exclaimed. "Give her permission to come aboard." His spirits, so long on the wane, soared with relief. It had to be her. Had to be.

"I am already aboard," Sarah said, rounding the doorway and leading Sean and Fiona into the captain's cabin.

Bixby's eyes widened. Aside from the woman's obviously weary state, she was altogether remarkably handsome. Actually quite beautiful in her faded green dress.

"You show a poor sense of shipboard protocol, madam," the captain said, a frown wrinkling his brow. The mud clerk edged toward the door.

"Sorry, Captain Bixby. I figured she would stay put," Nick Green said.

"On the dock, to be stared at by the unwholesome-looking rabble you keep below? Don't be absurd," Sarah retorted.

"That'll be all, Nick." Bixby dismissed the hapless mud clerk with a wave of his hand. The captain fixed Sarah and her family in a steely glare. Sarah set down the carpetbag containing the few clothes she had purchased in Baltimore. Fiona disengaged herself from her mother's grasp and walked up to Bixby. She brushed a ringlet out of her face and looked past his girth to the stern humorless face. He returned her scrutiny. She pointed to his uniform.

"Are you a policeman?" she asked.

"I am a captain!"

"You don't have to shout. I'm just down here, under your tummy."

Bixby colored. "I am the captain of this steamboat," he said more civilly.

"Oh Mommy, look at the funny bed," Fiona shouted, running to the alcove that housed the captain's bed.

"Fiona." Sarah tried to stop her daughter, but the girl bounded onto the bed and stretched out.

"Just like a bunny's hidey nest. Who sleeps here?" Fiona yawned.

"I do," Bixby said.

"Oh you're too fat to fit in here," Fiona observed innocently, already losing ground to sleep.

"I manage," Bixby said sourly.

Sean winced at his sister's flirtation with disaster. "I hope he doesn't have a plank," the boy muttered to his mother. Osage Bixby turned on the boy; at least here was someone he could intimidate.

"On the contrary, boy. River this time of year ain't deep enough to drown a yearling. Out here we don't make you walk the plank, we just let you off upriver on your lonesome and leave you for the heathen Cheyenne or Blackfeet or Sioux. Ah, drownin's a sweet death compared to the skull-roastin' hair-liftin' excesses of them kind." Bixby chuckled low and horrible. In the silence that followed, Sean's gulp sounded as loud as a tolling funeral bell, and he backed toward his mother's skirt. Sarah put a protective arm around his shoulder.

"It seems your wit, sir, is as cruel as any of the savages you describe. Or does the famed 'code of the West' I've heard about also include frightening children with lies?"

"Your pardon, madam. Maybe I am a trifle out of sorts.

But then, I've risked much by waiting for you, risked life, limb, and fortune, I have."

"Captain Bixby, I have spent two weeks on a train. I have been ferried across the Mississippi at night in a leaking boat. My family and I have ridden through St. Louis on a freight wagon. I have done everything to hasten my arrival except sprout wings and fly." Sarah slumped into a bench seat by the door. "Now, I understand you have a room for us. A night's sleep, and I will be in better shape to decide what my next step is."

"Next step? We're full steam ahead come morning."

Sarah brushed back her long auburn curls and looked with dismay at the captain.

"You can't mean it? I need time—I mean, I'm not sure whether or not we are going with you."

"My instructions were to wait for you until you showed," Bixby said. "Well, you've showed. Your passage has been paid up to Sweeney's Landing in Montana. Whether or not you take advantage of the passage is of no concern to me. But come sunrise the *Lady Jane* will be underway. If you're aboard, so be it."

"But I have no place else to go. You must at least allow me . . ."

"I must do nothing except what I've a mind to. I'm captain of this steamboat," Bixby said. He turned on his heel. "And as for you, miss . . ." He saw that Fiona was no longer listening. She had pulled the bedsheet up to her chin and was sound asleep. Bixby sighed, watching the rise and fall of her little stomach and the pink round softness of her cheeks. Sarah crossed the room and started to gather the girl in her arms.

"Leave her be," Bixby said, the bluster leaving him. "I won't be using the cabin. I've much to do before morning."

"I don't want to put you out." Bixby stared at her. "Very well," she shrugged. "Thank you." The captain nodded in return.

"If you don't mind," Sarah continued, "there's room for me beside Fiona."

"I'll sleep here, too," Sean said, stretching out on the

hardwood bench and avoiding the captain's stern appraisal.

"Suit yourself," Captain Bixby said. He stalked from the room, closing the door behind him, then suddenly he reappeared. He stood in the doorway and glowered down at Sean who grew ghostly white beneath the captain's gaze.

"Up," Bixby said.

"Sir."

"Up! Are you deaf?!"

The boy jumped to his feet. Bixby retrieved his now-crumpled captain's hat from the seat where Sean had sat on it, crushing it to a shapeless lump. Bixby departed without saying another word. Outside he paused to stare at the broad, winding ribbon of water disappearing into the nothingness of night.

"Osage Bixby," he said to himself. "It's going to be a long trip."

A wild roar exploded beneath the pinewood deck, like a battering of howitzers firing in rapid succession without end. Sarah sat upright, startled awake by the sudden din. Fiona cried out and clung to her mother. Sarah at last recognized her surroundings. The window revealed the gray twilight of morning.

"Mommy, Mommy, I'm scared," Fiona protested. Sarah managed to clamber out of bed, patting the wrinkles out of the dress she had slept in. The cabin door was ajar, and Sean, absent. Sarah gasped and hurried across the room. The floor gave a shudder and lurch, knocking her off balance against the cold iron of the Franklin stove.

"Mommy, don't leave," Fiona wailed.

"Stay here," Sarah said. She shoved the door open and was relieved to see Sean standing just outside, leaning his elbows on the rail.

"You gave me quite a start, young man," Sarah shouted above the din. Voices drifted up from the maindeck. Men ran about in what appeared to be a state of panic, barely avoiding collisions, yelling at one another, seeing to tackle and line, hauling chain, and loading wood.

The deck shook, and Sarah's grip tightened on the rail.

My God, they were underway, leaving, and she hadn't even . . .

"Do you think we ought to do something?" Sean yelled. A forest of smokestacks began to slide by as the *Lady Jane LaFarge* pulled from dockside and passed the other boats moored in line at the levee. St. Louis with its storied offices and church steeples, its empty streets and neatly rowed brick houses drifted toward the stern, into a fine mist billowing above the paddle-wheel.

"Ma?" Sean tugged at his mother's arm and pointed to the railing on the hurricane deck above them, where Captain Bixby leaned on his elbows watching the city slide past. As she looked, he doffed his cap and stepped out of sight.

"Stay in the room with your sister," Sarah said to her son.

"Then we aren't gonna try and leave?" Sean asked.

"Of course not. How can we?" she replied, puzzled by the relief she felt that this morning's decision had been made for her. She leaned close to Sean and shouted above the din. "We're stuck aboard!"

"Ya-hoo!" Sean exclaimed.

Sarah looked at him in amazement. "You're happy? I thought you were afraid of Captain Bixby."

"Sure," Sean said. "But this . . ." He waved his hand to include the passing scene—the boat thrusting toward the main channel; the crew's helter-skelter activity; the billowing smoke and flaming sparks thrusting skyward from the smokestack, and the tremendous grinding, booming noise of the single horsepower steam engine that propelled the boat against the current. "This," Sean repeated, groping for words, "is *something!*" He trotted excitedly back to the cabin.

Sarah climbed the closest stairway to the hurricane deck and caught up to Captain Bixby at the bow of the ship. He had his hands folded behind his back. Ahead lay the sluggish brown waters of the Mississippi, an undulating invitation soon to be refused for the more treacherous channel of the mighty Missouri, leading west and then north to Montana. He noticed Sarah McClinton standing alongside him. She glanced over her shoulder at the pilothouse, a raised square structure with windows to every side.

"Who's steering?"

"Green. I'll take over as soon as we branch off to the Missouri." The captain reached inside his coat, withdrew a flask. He unscrewed the top that served as a tiny cup and poured Sarah a shot of bourbon.

"Truce?" he said, holding out the drink.

"Why?" Sarah asked, her suspicions aroused.

"Because we're underway. It's the law of the Missouri, dear lady. What's said in port is best forgotten on the river. I reckon I'm just not happy unless I'm fighting snags and sandbars. Friends?" Sarah stared at the thick-skinned hand holding the cup. Perhaps it was the light of day or the way Bixby's gruff demeanor hid a smile, but she suddenly felt hopeful. Sarah took the glass.

"Friends," she replied.

The steam whistle blared right on cue as if the *Lady Jane* herself approved.

These are the days of the river, when the world holds forth its promise and challenges the hardy to take it. These are the days of work and dream and the desperate gamble of a fragile craft, iron men, and steam. Chase the river and the wind, past creeks, and bends, and inlets whose names at last blend one into the other, past farms and farm children still struck by the clamorous beauty of riverboats, who gather to wave as the *Lady Jane* steams by, leaving in its wake more dreams, more visions, sowing seeds of a growing nation. For Sarah McClinton, America was a vaster place than she had ever imagined. She never tired of watching the landscape and wondering at the lives of people in such places, and did they wonder about her? First the minutes formed a pattern. Then the hours. Until the days of the river drifted by uncounted, taken one at a time and discarded for tomorrow and tomorrow and tomorrow. Cities became towns and towns mere settlements with names like Dauphin's Camp or Fort Illustrious or Beaver Tail or Cow Creek. Some were deserted and harbored only ghosts. Others looked so meager and uninviting that Sarah stayed aboard at such stops and refused to allow her children to disembark. She would watch from her cabin window the hard-bitten and dangerous lot who visited the *Lady Jane* to haggle for the goods Bixby had crammed on deck. Ax handles and rifles and vegetables and salt and gunpowder and whiskey. The visits never lasted long. With a rumble and roar the *Lady Jane* would steam upriver, her whistle giving a shrill farewell and proud stacks spewing banners of black smoke.

Weeks passed, and the days of the river were measured now in loneliness and quiet, vast empty spaces, in hills choked with pine trees rising in emerald contrast to the buffalo grass growing gold in the valleys; measured too in scudding clouds and the touch of autumn in the air, fresh as a first kiss, inebriating as wine.

At last, the spool of time unwound. The final thread fluttered free on the eighteenth of September at midmorning. Sarah was caught wholly unprepared. Perhaps Captain Bixby had planned it that way when he yelled down from the pilothouse, "Sweeney's Landing," and pointed to the shore ahead.

Sarah's heart fluttered to her throat.

The days of the river were ended.

September, 1878

29

Sarah McClinton had never heard such a commotion in her life, especially coming from so few people. The *Lady Jane*'s blaring call reverberated off the yellow bluffs upstream and down while the settlement of Sweeney's Landing greeted the arrival of the last riverboat of the season with a clamor that sounded more like an attack than welcome.

A dozen gunshooting, catcalling, quarreling, laughing men and women (a sparse sprinkling of the fairer sex to be sure) burst from the Three Vices saloon and raced on foot, horseback, and wagon down Main Street to the river's edge to watch Osage Bixby guide his mountain boat to the town's solitary dock. Osage wasn't at the wheel however, nor in the pilothouse. He stood at the rail on the hurricane deck alongside Sarah and the children while Nicholas Green maneuvered the craft to a standstill.

Sean watched with eyes wide, hardly blinking, as if fearful that a second's inattention might diminish what to him had become a grand and magnificent experience. Sarah looked out at the motley revelers, at the false-fronted buildings that seemed to stare with rain-faded façades at one another across the broad, wheel-rutted swath of churned earth called Main Street. The road began at the sturdily constructed dock and petered out about a hundred yards beyond the last false front, where hills of buffalo grass rose in graceful contours like the swells of an amber sea.

"Come November, they might be snowed in and won't see another mountain boat until spring thaw," Bixby said. "Makes 'em kind of raucous."

"I see," Sarah noted with misgiving as lines were thrown from the boat to the dock. When the *Lady Jane* was secured at bow and stern, the plank was lowered to the pier. A round-figured, rouge-cheeked belle of far too many balls attracted Sarah's and Bixby's attention.

"You-hoo," the woman shouted as the engine vented the last of its pressure, steam hissing like a plague of vipers. The woman stood in the bed of a buckboard and waved a scarlet silk handkerchief overhead, her bosom bouncing beneath the daring décolletage of her rumpled gown. Bixby turned crimson.

"Ahem," he said, noisily clearing his throat. "She's an old acquaintance," he added, a lame attempt at explanation.

"Osage Bixby, you rutting ol' goat, come to see your Kate have you?" the woman shouted tipsily. "I knew this would bring you home." The woman spun around and bending over, lifted her dress to reveal the pink loaves of her derriere. She wriggled her fanny, lost her balance, and fell over the lip of the buckboard into the waiting arms of a trapper, who promptly tossed the harlot over his shoulder and staggered back up the street toward a rickety-looking emporium where the false front was decorated with slapdash letters that read "KATE'S PLACE." Kate sang a bawdy tune that was lost in the ensuing laughter as the trapper carried her inside, presumably to bed.

Sarah looked down at her son who had watched the proceedings in open-mouthed astonishment.

"I think you had better help with our bags," she said.

"Oh, Ma," Sean protested.

"What is it?" Fiona said, straining to see.

"Nothing you'd understand," Sean replied with brotherly contempt.

"Mama," Fiona whined.

"I think you have 'understood' sufficiently for one morning." Sarah shooed him toward the stairs along with the little girl. More gunfire and the blaring off-key outburst of a bugle sounded from shore. Sean paused at the top of the stairs and looked toward the townsfolk and ranchhands and ladies of dubious reputation.

"Golly," he muttered in a voice tight with excitement, and then sensing his mother behind him, he reluctantly started down the stairway.

"If Joel isn't here, I'll have my men escort you to Sweeney's. She's a friend," Bixby said. Sarah looked at him, alarmed by the term "friend." "I mean a real friend. Sweeney has some rooms above her store. You'll be quite comfortable. And none of the riffraff will bother you there." Bixby held out his hand.

"I'll be in town a while," he went on. "Grasshoppering over that last stretch of bars tore up my winches. And there's some value in being the last boat out. There'll be men who've had their fill of hard winters, men with furs and gold too, anxious to spend their money amid the pleasures of city life or among family and friends. I can turn a pretty profit if I wait until the last minute and stay just ahead of the ice right on down to St. Louis. So maybe we'll have a chance to visit before I head out."

"I would like that," Sarah said, reluctant to release his handshake. She leaned forward and bussed his bewhiskered cheek. "Thank you, Osage."

"See here," Bixby said gruffly. "If the men should witness such familiarity . . ."

"I kissed the man, not the uniform," Sarah laughed. "Your authority is intact." She reassured him with a playful pat on the arm and then left him at the rail to follow her children down to the boiler deck below. The radiant smile on her face revealed none of her awful apprehensions.

Where was Joel Ryan? Could he be one of that rowdy lot ashore? Certainly not. She had memorized his picture and recalled in a second his fine, elegant features—dark, slight, sensitive, a gentleman of breeding. Just the type of father her children . . . *Sarah McClinton, what are you thinking? That I've not traveled three thousand miles to shake hands.* If Joel Ryan was anything like his picture, well then, she had been a widow long enough, it was time she became a woman again.

Sarah reached the passenger deck in time to see Sean and Fiona slowly backing out onto the boiler deck. Fiona was clinging to her brother's hand, and the boy looked pale with alarm. Sarah hurried protectively forward and brushed past her children to intercede between them and whatever had surprised them in Bixby's cabin. Stepping out of the harsh sunlight into the cool shadows of the cabin left her momen-

tarily disoriented and blinded. As her eyes adjusted to the
room's shaded interior, the man within moved forward to
her. Sarah gasped and retreated despite herself. He was big.
God in heaven, it seemed the low-ceilinged cabin strained to
hold him. His massive frame was clothed in buckskin, giving
him the appearance of a savage, an effect hardly tamed by
the beaded buckskin sheath and murderous bone-handled
knife belted at his waist. His chiseled features save for his
slightly crooked nose, were hidden behind a silver beard.
Hair, heavily-streaked with silver, hung to his shoulders. He
had a broad-brimmed felt hat in his rough-looking hands and
appraised her with ice blue eyes.

"Sarah," he said. His voice was deep and resonant, like
distant thunder. Sarah blanched. He knew her name. Sweet
hills of Eire, but how?

"Sarah McClinton," he repeated, looming over her.

"What do you want here? How do you know me?"

He reached for the bone-handled knife. Sarah felt a sudden surge of terror that turned to relief as he drew not the
knife but a worn and folded scrap of paper from his beaded
belt. He held it out to her. She summoned enough courage
to take the scrap from him and unfold it in her trembling
hands.

> *Sarah Joy McClinton*
> BORN: *March 27, 1851*
> *Widowed. Two children: boy, ten—girl, five.*
> *Auburn hair. Trim figure. Clean.*
> *Approximately five feet six. Green eyes . . .*

Sarah glanced up in amazement. This was a page from
Cole's Catalogue. She sighed, relief flooding through her.
But of course. She should have guessed.

"I beg your pardon, sir. You caught me unaware." She
turned to her children, who were still standing by the rail.
"It's all right, dears. This man is from Mister Ryan's ranch."
She looked back at him. "I must admit you gave me a fright."

"Your pardon, ma'am," the man said. "But . . ."

"Well, never mind. You certainly look capable of handling my few bags."

"Sarah . . ." The familiarity was uncalled for, and she started to reprimand him, but the expression on his face stilled her.

"I *am* . . . Joel Ryan," he said.

Sarah glanced about as if the words had come from someone else. Finally she turned toward him.

"What?"

"I am Joel Ryan."

"No," she corrected. She fumbled at her cloth purse and found the daguerreotype and held it up. "No, you are not."

"Ah—I can explain that," he said, blushing beneath his beard. The red was lost in the sun-burnished bronze of his cheeks.

"No," Sarah blurted out, already assailed by her own suspicions. She looked from the picture to the fierce individual across from her.

"I didn't have a picture of me," Joel said. "So I sent that, uh, one of my brother, Nate. Folks always said we, uh, favored one another." He tried for a winning grin but managed only an embarrassed and uncomfortable sort of grimace. "I figured it would be close enough not, uh, to matter. I figured you'd be different from your likeness too. And you are, by jingo, a whole sight prettier, if that's possible. I'll bet you gave Osage a start, especially after all the warnings he saddled me with. I'm sorry. I don't mean to make light. I guess this is a surprise for you."

Sarah's gaze kept alternating from the picture to the man in the room, from gentleman to barbarian, back and forth as if trying to transpose the image created from chemicals and paper onto that of flesh and blood. Could it be true? Had she come all this way to—to wed a—a wild Indian!

Then Sarah McClinton did the only thing she could do under the circumstances. She fainted into the arms of Joel Ryan.

30

Just enough of a drizzle had sprung up to make the afternoon unpleasant without being impassable.

"I don't see why we must wait." A boy of twelve confronted Joel sullenly on the porch of Sweeney's Store. The
boy did not like being in town longer than was necessary.
The people called his father squaw man and him . . . *breed*.

"I told you, Miss Sarah and her family will be staying for
a time at Morning Star."

"Who needs strangers?"

"We aren't leaving without them. Tell Caleb we'll come
for the team in the morning."

Cub Ryan kicked at the boardwalk. He glared stubbornly
at his father. Joel had to smile. Mourning Dove would have
been proud of her warrior son. The boy's coppery skin deepened and his eyes lost their gentleness; his fierce fighting
spirit, like his appearance, was more Cheyenne than white.

"Ta-naestse!" Joel exclaimed bad-temperedly. "Go on,
Little Bear. Do as I say." Where diplomacy and argument
had failed, a simple, abrupt directive in Cheyenne succeeded.
Cub Ryan leaped from the porch and stalked off through the
muddy furrows of the street in the general direction of
Caleb's Livery. Joel paused on the walk to gaze out at the
settlement, mentally tabulating its growth from the day
twelve years before when he had leaned upon his second
cord of wood to watch Bixby's riverboat fight the Yellowstone for a berth just offshore of Sweeney's.

Just a single-room store then, not much bigger than the
cabin on Otter Creek. Now the settlement at Sweeney's
Landing boasted a barber shop and livery stable, a faro house
and sporting parlor, an office for the territorial deputy marshal to use when he wasn't overseeing operations at the

Three Vices, a two-story hotel catering to prospectors heading up to the gold strikes, a lawyer's office sandwiched in between an assayer's shack, a smithy, and the three-room ward of Doc Thorndyke. The good doctor was seldom in one place for very long. Visiting the forts and homesteads in a four-hundred-mile area occupied his time. Shacks and cabins, all of humble origin formed a rough circle around the stores and shops in a haphazard semblance of civilization. Sweeney too had expanded her operations. Her broad-beamed, two-story trading post commanded the center of town and served not only as a store where anything could be purchased but also as a bank. She had invested in a ponderous cast-iron safe. Men who had made their fortunes and were on their way back east frequently entrusted most of their savings to Sweeney, leaving themselves with pocket money to guarantee a good time at the Three Vices. Two other shacks in town called themselves saloons, but if a man wanted to tickle his throat with fiery drink and afterwards enjoy the services of a prairie nymph, the Vices was the safest bet.

Sweeney lived above her store in one of the spacious rooms she had added on. The others were for friends or guests of some prestige who preferred not to triple up in bed over at the hotel.

"I couldn't help overhearing," Sweeney said from the doorway. In dungarees and plaid workshirt she looked more a dirt farmer than a successful merchant. "You ain't told that boy of yours the real reason for Miss McClinton comin' out here?"

"Why do I get the feeling you're about to butt in where it doesn't concern you?" said Joel.

"When you're this touchy," Sweeney said, hands on hips, "I know you been up to no good." Her squat frame retreated into the shadowy sanctuary of the store.

Joel followed her into the trading post past a mouth-watering world of newly delivered apples and peaches and tins of tea and barrels of salted pork and more barrels of pickles. "I'll tell Cub when the moment's right," he said curtly.

"Seems your moments are running mighty short. Remember a lit fuse only burns so long before it reaches powder, and then things have a way of arranging themselves."

"I'll tell him," Joel repeated.

Osage Bixby appeared at the top of the stairs. Sean and Fiona were close behind him.

"I promised my boat mates here a peppermint stick, one for each of them. I assume you can handle such an order, Miss Sweeney." Sweeney blushed at being called "miss."

"I suppose I can open the store for business just for a minute." She grinned, giving Joel one last probing look. The store was closed until Sweeney had inventoried the stock Bixby had brought. Sweeney fumbled over to a crystal candy jar and lifted the lid to allow the sharp sweet aroma of peppermint to escape. The children quickened their steps. While they were helping themselves to the candy, Bixby skirted them and walked directly to Joel.

"Sarah's upstairs and feeling better after emptying her stomach. Maybe it's all the traveling has her down."

"Maybe it's me," Joel said.

"Now that you bring it up—" Bixby scowled, about to offer his reprimand.

"Tell it to Sweeney," Joel said, heading for the stairs. As for Sarah, he had no plan on how to confront her. He just hoped she appreciated honesty. At least she believed him, that he was indeed Joel Ryan. It was a step, at least.

But in which direction?

Sarah stood at the window, her arms folded across her bosom. She had changed into a blue wool dress gathered close to her trim waist and flowing in heavy folds to the floor. She heard the knock at the door and called for the party to enter. She was not surprised to see that her visitor was Joel Ryan. Sarah took a seat near the window, leaning an arm on a mahogany end table, of which the japanned pedestal and round base crawled with carved monkeys and serpents in timeless conflict. The rest of the room was furnished with hand-carved furniture of bold, if blunt, design. A Hudson's Bay blanket covered the solid four-poster. The down mattress looked able to accommodate Sarah and her children with ease. Joel could see the yellow bluffs framed by the window, their brilliance dulled by the gentle rainfall.

The picture of Nate Ryan was propped against the coal-oil lamp on the table.

"We have a problem," Sarah said. "We have a problem, Mister Ryan." She sighed. When he drew near, she handed him the daguerreotype. Joel glanced down at his brother's face, remembering a rainy night thirteen years ago in Kentucky. It seemed a lifetime, a play of strangers, a drama of which the beginning and end no longer concerned him. He recognized none of the players, not even himself. He was Silvertip Ryan now. He had another life, a life called Morning Star.

"Miss ah . . . Sweeney told me you were a reasonable man."

"Sweeney is a wishful thinker," Joel said, sliding the picture inside his shirt.

"Oh, I see."

"No you don't, but you will. Stick with me, and you'll wind up wiser than a whole tree full of owls."

"I beg your pardon?"

"Never mind. Just something a friend said to me once."

Sarah was thoroughly perplexed. She glanced out the window. "I kept telling myself this was just the outskirts of town," she said. Raucous music drifted from the Three Vices Saloon. There were five horses tethered at the rail in front of the establishment, and she could see a man dressed in a black frock coat and ruffled silk shirt standing on the boardwalk in front of the doors.

"Ben Slade," Joel said by way of identification. "The government couldn't decide whether or not to run him out of the territory, so they compromised and made him a deputy marshal."

"Dear Lord," Sarah gasped. What indeed had she brought her family to?

"Look, Sarah."

"Mrs. McClinton, sir," she corrected.

"All right, Mrs. McClinton then. This isn't New York. I never promised you anything of the kind . . ."

"Promise? What promise! No . . ." She slowly regained her composure. "No. I will not lose my temper." She looked back at him. "What promise? Who are you to speak of such a thing? You-aren't-even-you," she stammered, unable to hold back the tears. "I mean . . . you're not . . . oh damn!" She buried her face in her hands. Joel started to reach for her. The door to the room swung open and Cub entered.

"You knock when entering!" Joel shouted. His son stared at him as if he were mad. The doors were always open at Morning Star.

"I saw Tod Jessup's horse in the stable. Slade said to tell you Tod's drinking pretty heavy." The boy straightened the red bandana that held back his black shoulder-length hair. The dark copper of his features grew flush with excitement.

"I'm not bothering Tod. I trust he won't bother me. Now wait for me downstairs. Mrs. McClinton and I are having a discussion," said Joel.

The half-breed youth looked sourly in Sarah's direction, then departed before his father had to ask him again.

"That was an Indian," Sarah said, alarmed. She'd read all about wild Indians in *Harper's Weekly* and felt she knew all there was to know. "I thought they were kept on reservations."

"He's my son," Joel replied. Sarah's eyes bored into him. "His mother was Cheyenne. I guess that's something else I forgot to mention when I wrote off to *Cole's Catalogue*. I didn't see it would matter being as you had children of your own and all."

"Is there anything else you might have forgotten to tell me?"

"No. I can't think of a thing."

"Good. I am doing very well, don't you agree?" Sarah said, standing. "I haven't even lost my temper. Now, if you will excuse me, I would like to be alone with my children. I'd like them to rest before supper. And frankly, I am tired as well."

"But oughtn't we to . . ."

Sarah crossed in front of Joel and walked to the door. She held it open for him. He would have protested, but he saw Sean and Fiona at the top of the stairs. He caught himself staring at the woman at the door. An auburn strand curled at her cheeks. He liked that. And the way she filled the dress in the right places. Fiona walked into the room, sucking on her peppermint stick, and continued right on up to Joel. She stood there, craning her neck as she looked up at him.

"How come your hair's so silver? Are you an old man?"

Joel smiled. "Not as old as you think."

"You carried my Mommy here."

"Yes I did."

"How come?"

"Because I . . . she couldn't walk."

"You scared her. You scared me, too. Know why? 'Cause you look like a big ol' grouchy bear."

Sean sidled into the room and, at an unspoken command from his mother, took Fiona by the hand to lead her out of Joel's path.

"You'll have to excuse my sister," Sean said, cowed by the man's size and appearance. "She's an idiot."

Fiona sensed she had been insulted and began to cry. Joel paused in the doorway to look down at Sarah. Their eyes met, and Sarah felt a disturbing sensation within. She closed the door and leaned against it. Fiona was still crying, and Sarah fixed her son in an angry stare.

"Sorry," he said. He shrugged and sat by the window. He smiled beatifically toward his baby sister but beneath his breath muttered, "The truth shall set us free."

31

Three Vices are the bane of man
When Christian Souls get out of hand
Three Vices to us Sinners be
Faith, Hope, and Charity.

Joel read the scroll-like sign in the foyer of Slade's out of habit. The three silhouettes in profile beneath the sign were skillfully rendered but bore no resemblance to the real Faith, Hope, and Charity. Faith and Charity were black-haired, brown-eyed señoritas hailing from Old Santa Fe. They spoke little English, relying on knowing smiles and flirtatious ways to cross the language barrier. Hope called herself an actress. She was a saucy blonde who at twenty-eight was on the verge of losing her figure to age and overwork. Still, she was a knowledgeable bedmate. Rumor had it she could spark the coil out of a lariat.

Romeo Jones, the emaciated-looking pianist Slade had hired off one of the riverboats, glanced up and nodded to Joel who waved back. Jones' gangly fingers never lost a beat. "The Rose of Alabam' " jangled merrily from the sounding board to tug at the hearts of all true Southern gentlemen. The saloon was crowded with roustabouts from the *Lady Jane* who were busily engaged in trying their luck at the gambling tables and polishing off bottle after bottle of rye whiskey. Faith, Hope, and Charity were nowhere to be seen. Joel glanced to the stairway leading to the upstairs bedrooms. More than one riverboatman would climb those stairs before morning. Joel recognized a few of the locals standing at the bar before carefully arranged crystal pyramids of tumblers and shot glasses. These men, latecomers to the territory, owned small homesteads in the area. They were jealous of the larger spreads and resented the likes of Frank Jessup and Joel Ryan, especially Joel because of his link with the Cheyenne whose depredations were recent history.

Above the boisterous conversation, the roulette wheel whirred on its axis, the metal ball danced upon the spinning chambers as the banker cried out to the men around him.

"Here it is, gents. Only roulette table this side of the Rockies. Come down, lads. On the red. On the black. Make your pile today. Why slave for a living? Step up gents. Fortune's awaitin'. Step up."

Joel watched the roustabouts drift toward the table but felt no calling in himself to lose what little money he had. He noticed Slade sitting in his usual place, at the table against the front window. Joel cut through patches of cigar smoke that clung to the motionless air like the slate-colored clouds outside hovering low over the rolling landscape. Joel Ryan attracted attention, his great size and silvery mane were hard to miss. One of the settlers at the bar jostled his friend, and both turned their unapproving stares at the man called Silvertip, but the roustabouts were merely curious in their appraisal. They did not know enough about the man to be hostile.

Ben Slade was sly, soft-spoken, and wiry as whipcord beneath his ruffled white shirt and black frock coat and trousers. A black string tie held his collar high about his throat to hide the ridged scar tissue circling his neck, the legacy of an attempted lynching. Rumor had it he had sided with the losing party in a West Texas range war, and from the looks of his rope-burned throat, he had almost paid the consequences. Slade's broad-brimmed, flat crown hat hid pale features, as expressionless and coolly detached as any gambler's. A black sash, from which the faded ivory grip of a Smith and Wesson revolver protruded, circled his waist. Slade had hidden his deputy's badge in his coat pocket. In Sweeney's Landing and the surrounding territory, he was the law only when the law was needed. He preferred folks just settle their minor differences themselves and allow him time to run his saloon. Because Slade had never lost a member of his family to the Indians (he had no family to lose, unless one counted his "royal relatives"—the kings and queens inhabiting his ever-handy deck of cards), he bore Joel no animosity. Now, he nodded and held out one of his cheroots. Joel waved it aside.

"How come you never offer me a drink?" Joel said, taking a seat opposite the gambler.

"Because I know you'll accept." Slade exhaled a ribbon of smoke through the slash of his smile. "How come you never do what I tell you?"

"How's that?" Joel asked, reaching over to snare the bottle on the table and fill a shot glass for himself. He tossed down the drink. It took a moment for the tremors to subside in his stomach.

"I nailed a rattlesnake head to the inside of the fermenting barrel. Gives it some character, don't you think?"

"Pour it outside and night won't fall," Joel muttered, staring out the window at the deepening dusk.

"Did Cub give you my message?"

"Sure. What's Tod riled about now?"

"He proposed to Hope."

Joel rolled his eyes and slowly shook his head. "What was her answer?"

"She told him it would be bad for business." Slade chuckled. "And then she took Bixby's mud clerk up to her room. I imagine that boy won't be able to mark a straight course for some time. Ah hell, I got to admit I was worried some. Tod will be a rich man some day. Hope's money is her own, just like the other girls. But she can't save near what Tod Jessup could bring her. I guess she figured ol' Frank would never let the marriage stand. I have to be concerned, though. If those girls all got themselves hitched, it would sure cut into my whiskey profits. Tod got loud and called her a slut, and I had to put on my badge and ask him to leave. Goes against my grain, wearing a badge on busy nights. Anyway, I saw him head off down the street toward Big Nose Kate's. Mean moods are welcome there. I'd steer clear of him, Ryan. He still hasn't forgotten you for dumping him in the horse trough last month."

"Maybe he'd better steer clear of me," Joel grumbled.

"Never known you to go looking for trouble."

"Slade, you don't know me at all."

"Maybe not. But I know this. Carl Friedkin, over there at the bar, came in this afternoon and told me he buried Lou Parrish. Cheyennes killed him, run his cattle off. Even butchered Lou's dog. They burned the cabin and barn."

"Carl saw the attack?"

"Hell no. He came along after, spied the smoke, and found poor old Lou. Carl brought in one of the arrows. It has the red feathers and all the blood markings like those damn Red Lances or whatever—"

"Red Shields," Joel said.

"Yeah. Like the Red Shield Cheyenne use."

"I still have my doubts. An arrow's no proof . . ." Joel said.

The last time he had seen Sacred Killer, months ago, the warrior had spoken of the waning days of the Morning Star People. They had refused deportation to reservations and were seeking a last haven among the mountains in the hopes of living their lives out in peace.

"It is to most folks," Slade replied. "But then, they don't have half-breed sons. They don't have friends among the Cheyenne. No, their friends are men like Lou Parrish, dead and scalped and six feet under."

"What the devil are you trying to say?" Joel snarled, his anger rising. He had botched the whole affair with Sarah McClinton and now this.

"All I'm saying," Slade replied evenly, "is that I've had four killings in the past month. And it looks like the Cheyenne have been pushed to the wall and have decided to go out with a bang. Four killings, and cattle and horses run off at the larger places, and yet Morning Star hasn't been hit. Folks are beginning to talk."

"Let them talk."

"Look, Ryan, the Cheyenne wouldn't be the first bunch of Indians to choose fighting over starving on the reservation. I'd do the same thing if I were in their moccasins. But I'm not. I know where my loyalties lie. The question is, do you?"

"If listening to your gab is the price of a drink, then the price is too high," Joel said.

Slade sighed. With a shake of his head, he folded his hands across his stomach and looked out the window.

"You're a stubborn, bad-tempered bastard, Mister Silver-tip. What happened? She failed to meet your expectations?"

"Huh?"

"The girl you carried up to Sweeney's. She looked a fair flower from here. When it comes to holding secrets, Sweeney is a sieve." Slade laughed. "You can't be on the prod 'cause of her looks; I could tell she was prettier than a royal flush even from the porch. Of course," Slade mused, stroking his thin moustache, "she might not be as tame as you'd like. You've been alone too long, compadre. A woman is better with a little of the wild left in her. It makes for an interesting life."

"She is a lady," Joel said. "What do you know of ladies?"

"I know that every lady is a whore, at times. And every whore is a lady. Salud." Slade lifted his shot glass, and downed the drink in a single swallow. Then he eased back in his chair and listened to the boisterous celebration of the roustabouts who knew that once Captain Bixby pointed the *Lady Jane* toward her St. Louis berth, there'd be nothing to cut the muck of a poor man's gullet but black coffee and river water. Drink up, my boys, Slade thought.

Joel stared out at the slow steady downpour. In the sullen light, the rain-spattered panes cast a writhing pattern upon his face. He thought of the past, of what Slade had told him, he thought of auburn hair and eyes like . . . emeralds.

"They say it rained like this at Appomattox," said Slade. It was an observation he had a habit of making on drizzly days.

"It did," muttered Joel, his answer of habit, as he stared out at the amber glow in the second-story window of Sweeney's Trading Post.

It took Joel a moment to realize the domain of Slade's private table had been invaded. He heard the gambler mutter, "Oh Lord," and turned in time to watch Tod Jessup approach.

"Tod, we're drinking by ourselves."

"You stay out of this, Slade," the youth said. He was a big-boned, callow lad with broad handsome features offset by mean little eyes that showed an inability to handle his liquor. His father, Frank Jessup, had been a colonel in the cavalry. Tod, like his father, though with none of Frank's credentials, expected to be obeyed. He leaned forward, bracing himself on the back of a chair.

"Squaw man," Tod said, steadying himself against a chair. Joel noticed the ranchers at the bar carefully watching from a safe distance. They hadn't drunk enough yet to join in Tod's fun.

"You heard what happened to Lou Parrish? Your murdering friends paid him a visit."

"Ease off, Tod. If not for your own, then your father's sake," Slade said.

"Leave my father out of it," Tod snarled. "What kind of deputy are you, siding with this squaw man and his red nigger son?"

Joel hooked the chair with his boots and yanked it from Tod's grasp. The youth crashed to the floor. The piano player quit playing. Conversation ceased. The roustabouts anxiously turned toward the first signs of trouble; they were men who relished a good fight. Tod crawled to his feet and drew his pistol out from under his rain slicker as several bystanders scattered out of harm's way. Tod grinned and staggered toward the table, pleased he had gotten the drop on Silvertip Ryan. He leaned close, his sour whiskey breath hot on Joel's cheek. Propping one hand on the table, Tod pressed the gun barrel against Joel's chest.

"Squaw man, you just made one hell of a mistake," he said.

"So did you." As Joel spoke, his right arm moved ever so slightly from underneath the table, lifting the razor-sharp blade of his bowie knife to Tod Jessup's crotch.

"Now put the gun away, Tod, or you'll be singing 'tweedle dum and tweedle dee' with the girls for the rest of your days."

Tod gulped, licked his suddenly dry mouth, and looked down at the heavy gleaming blade as the keen point began to dig with slow excruciating pressure into his testicles. He chanced an appealing glance in Slade's direction. The gambler pursed his lips and wagged his head in dismay. He poured a drink and slid the shot glass over to Tod's hand.

"Just a friendly drink, Tod. Take it and leave."

The youth stared at the knife and decided the exchange

was not to his liking. He holstered his revolver. Romeo, at
the piano, struck up a lively rendition of "Darlin' Clemen-
tine." Conversation resumed, disappointed in tone. Tod
whirled and stalked off across the crowded room to make a
slam-bang exit through the front doors, his shoulders
bunched against the laughter.

"Funny. Tod forgot his drink." Slade reached for the
glass. "I suppose he had more important things on his mind."

Joel returned his knife to its sheath.

"And under his belt," he added.

Sweeney put the finishing touches on her inventory. The rifles were neatly stacked in lethal rows, five to a rack. She
worked hard because from tomorrow stretching on to the
remainder of the month she would be open every day. Homesteaders and ranchers as well as the itinerant prospector and
drifter would eventually learn of the shipment of winter
goods and venture in while the weather permitted. Bixby had
also brought a mailbag crammed with magazines and news-
papers and letters for the various settlers in the area, letters
from friends and loved ones. As for the tabloids, it did not
matter that they were hopelessly dated. Folks would quickly
buy them up and carefully guard them throughout the long
months ahead. Here were pages to be read and reread by the
light of lamp and hearth, pages to bridge the loneliness of
winter's confinement.

Sarah, descending the stairs to the shop, saw Sweeney fit
the last of the Winchesters into the rifle rack and circle the
counter to manhandle a crate of .45 caliber bullets onto the
shelf. Sarah hurried across the room to lend her strength to
the task, and the two women lifted the crate to the countertop.

"Thank you, Sarah."

"Don't mention it. I wish I could do more to repay you
for supper. And giving us a room."

"Hospitality is freely offered. No payment necessary."
The storekeeper grinned. She tucked her brown hair underneath her floppy-brimmed hat.

"I feel strange just calling you Sweeney," said Sarah.

"I'm used to Sweeney. It's what my daddy called me. I'm

too old a pot to start over with a new handle."

Sarah pulled a ladder-back chair over into the center of the room near the black iron Franklin stove. Surrounded by shadowy mounds of merchandise, she closed her eyes and breathed in the sharp odors of freshly ground Arbuckle's Coffee, of tanned leather and gunpowder, tobacco and apples, a hint of cinnamon, nutmeg, thyme, and from some secret hiding place among all the necessities of frontier life, the sweet perfumes of scented soap—lilac, jasmine, and rosewater.

Night had come to the river community. Not stillness, however. A tinkling medley of music drifted from the Three Vices to clash in unharmonious discord with the tuneless renderings drifting up Main Street from Big Nose Kate's. Piano, fiddle, harmonica, and accordion pursued their conflicting melodies. The war between the orchestras, Sarah thought, enjoying despite herself the undisciplined racket that was such a far cry from Sunday afternoon concerts. A far cry indeed.

"Always a celebration when a boat comes in," Sweeney said, peering from the window at the mud-brown smear that was once Main Street. She turned away and followed the noise of the rumbling coffee pot to its source, the Franklin stove in the center of the room. She filled two cups and handed one to Sarah.

"Nothing like black coffee to cut the grease of my beans and hogjaw. Gives the corn dodgers something to float on, too."

"Supper was wonderful. I'm grateful."

Sweeney waved gratitude aside and took a seat on a covered corn meal barrel, then she suddenly stood, walked around behind the counter, and searched beneath bolts of fabric before finding what she was looking for, a handsome shawl woven of multicolored cloth, alternating woolen stripes of gold, green, purple, crimson, and blue.

"Here now," she said, handing it to Sarah. "Wrap this around your shoulders. Never understood a woman who didn't want to put enough meat on her bones to keep warm."

"It is very beautiful. Thank you. I think it's the sound of the rain that makes me feel so cold."

Sweeney sat again on the barrel while Sarah snuggled in the woven warmth of the shawl and edged closer to the stove.

"Your young'uns asleep?"

"Yes. I am afraid they were a little intimidated at supper. Fiona especially isn't usually so quiet."

"Can't blame them," Sweeney snorted, "What with Cub glaring at you all across the vittles. That boy sometimes can be more pure fire frustrating! Oh, I don't blame him really. His pa brought him to Morning Star when the boy was eight, and Joel raised him all on his lonesome. Been father and mother to him. Times change. Folks sort of gravitated to the area here and about. Before long we had us a town. Good people mostly, but a lot of wounds aren't healed yet. It was a shock for them both to come across folks like the Jessups and such who figure the only good Indian is a dead one and a breed's even worse. Cub's built a shell around his feelings. Nary a soul gets in 'less he lets them."

"It must have also been quite a surprise to learn he had a new mother. At least as far as his father intended."

"Haw! Silvertip didn't even tell him, the jughead."

"Oh, I see. Mister Ryan doesn't tell people much of anything, does he?"

"What did your young'uns say about having a man like Silvertip Ryan for a father?"

Sarah's expression immediately changed, became open and innocent. "I didn't . . . I mean I haven't brought the subject up yet."

Sweeney blew the steam from the cup and squinted at the woman by the stove.

"Seems you two got something in common after all. You're both a couple of jugheads."

Sarah blushed and frowned at what she considered an insult. It took a moment to realize she was really angry with herself. Sean and Fiona should have been told. At least something more than the flimsy excuse she had left them with, that Mister Ryan was a friend. She drained the contents of her cup, burning the roof of her mouth in the process. She filled a second cup and sat quietly in the chair and listened to the rain. Sweeney added a shot of whiskey to her own cup and held it out to Sarah who politely declined.

"Why do people call him Silvertip?" she asked.

"It's a name the Cheyenne gave him," Sweeney replied. "No telling what the story is behind it. There's always a story. The name fits him, though."

"If only the picture he sent me did," said Sarah.

"I admit he's cut from the craggy side of the mountain. But shave that beard, and he'll look a whole sight younger. Don't let the hair fool you. He's still a young man, mark my word. Oh, I warned him about the picture of his brother. I told him he wasn't playing by the rules, but I've had better luck talking to tree stumps."

Sarah sighed and glanced at the flames dancing in the belly of the stove, flickering molten tendrils like dreams of gold, so beautiful, but impossible to touch, much less keep.

"The funny thing," she said, "I'd lived with that picture for so many weeks—well, you may laugh, but I let myself love him. It made everything else sort of bearable."

"That wasn't love. Just an excuse to keep going. I've used the same trick on myself. It's something we ladies tend to do." Sweeney fished in her coat pocket and found the stub end of a slim black cigar. She walked over to the stove, picked a coal out with iron tongs, lit the cheroot, then dropped the coal back into the flames. Her blunt homely features grew pensive by firelight. "Love is . . . a pool that needs more than just a handsome reflection, Sarah. It's a spring—cleansed in the mountains of heaven, made pure by God's own soil. And love is a river that nourishes the parched heart and fills the barren soil. Pool and spring and flowing river, love has to be all three. And if it is to last through the world's dry days, it must have depth. Yes . . . it must have depth."

The woman tossed the last of the cheroot into the Franklin and, embarrassed by her discourse, started upstairs. Sarah watched her in silence, watched with growing affection this woman of coarseness and eloquence. Then she rose and started after Sweeney, but the storekeeper heard her and spun around on the stairs.

"No!"

"What?" Sarah said, taken aback.

"You stay here. You wait on your man."

"Sweeney. He's hardly my man, as you put it."

"You took his money—just about every cent. And used it to come out here. Now you two got to work out what happens next."

"Really!"

"You owe him a chance, Sarah. You know you do. And even if you decide to go back with Bixby, the captain told me he'd be tied up for a month. So you got yourself a month to wait, and you'll have to stay someplace."

"I assumed I could stay here."

"Sarah, you and your children are sweet'uns, and I've taken a shine to your company, but business is business. I ain't hiring nobody. And how do you figure to pay for a room? The hotel hasn't much to offer for a lady. There's rooms at the Three Vices, but you might not like the price you'd pay for them. The way I see it, you and Silvertip Ryan better work out something between you. For your sake and the little ones' upstairs. He'll be along. So wait up. The fire's hot, and there's plenty of coffee." Her spiel concluded, Sweeney of Sweeney's Landing continued on up the stairway to her bedroom, leaving Sarah with her thoughts.

Sarah waited. She drank coffee and concluded, *Once I get aboard the* Lady Jane, *I doubt Captain Bixby will put me off. I'll find work in St. Louis. I'll pay him back.* But how was she to live until then? Sweeney had backed her into a corner. Perhaps there was some of Joel Ryan's influence in the woman's actions. If such was the case, Mister Ryan was going to find out a thing or two about Sarah McClinton before this month was out. *So I owe him, do I? Well then, fair is fair, I'll accompany him to his ranch and stay a month. At least my darlings and I will have a roof over our heads. And at the end of the month I will insist we return to the landing and then take my leave.* She managed to suppress the guilt she felt at the idea of deceiving him. The past weeks had taught her one thing, her family's survival was in her hands. She could not afford the luxury of a conscience.

The door to the store opened and a gust of moist air sent a shiver up her spine as Joel entered; seeing Sarah by the stove, he gently closed the door behind him. His clothes were damp from the slow steady drizzle, and his boots were mud-spattered. He walked over to warm his hands at the stove.

"You missed supper," Sarah said, watching him for signs of drunkenness, but his eyes were cool and steady and able to meet her stare, not like Jaimie's eyes. Poor, weak, handsome Jaimie.

"I wasn't hungry. And I needed to think."

"I did too."

"Oh?"

"Are you surprised?"

"No. I just thought your mind was made up about, uh, about us."

"There is no 'us,' Mister Ryan. Not in the way I think you mean."

Joel held his felt hat over the stove hoping to dry it out. He searched his mind for arguments. Why was this so difficult? He felt awkward as a schoolboy at a church social.

"Look, Mrs. McClinton, no, Sarah—I paid your way out here, I can call you by your name, for pity's sake. I know I exaggerated the truth a bit and wasn't quite honest about the way—"

"I will go with you to the ranch," she said.

"—I got you out here, but it seems to me the least you can do is—huh?"

"My children and I will go with you to Morning Star."

"Go? GO!" He tossed his hat aside and scooped Sarah right out of the chair, caught her by the waist and lifted her high in the air. "You'll go, you say. By heaven, Sarah, that's wonderful. *Neheseha!* Say it again. Let me hear you."

"I'll go. I'll go," Sarah replied, breathless. "But please, put me down." She had never known anyone so strong. "Mister Ryan, please control yourself."

"My name is Joel." He laughed a full rich laugh as he quite literally swept her off her feet.

"Please, Joel," Sarah called out, alarmed and just a bit thrilled despite her misgivings and her ulterior motives. He lowered his arms, and when her feet touched floor, she stepped free of his embrace. "Really, Mist—" He started toward her again. "Joel," she quickly corrected. "Joel. I trust you will not expect too much from my decision."

"I always expect too much, Sarah. For me there is no other way to live," he said. His face drew close to hers, his lips drawn to hers. Sarah twisted aside and retreated toward the stairway. Joel wistfully allowed her escape and walked over to the farm equipment to retrieve his hat from a phalanx of rakes. He heard steps behind him and straightened as Sarah disappeared up the stairs.

"We leave tomorrow," he said.

"And the rain?" Her voice drifted down to him.

"Tomorrow," he repeated. Joel had sensed an especially ugly mood in town and did not want to press his luck. Lou Parrish's friends—friends, Joel reflected, now that he was dead—were doing a lot of talking and too much drinking. They could use his passing as an excuse to take it out on Cub. Whiskey courage and trouble walk hand in hand.

"Very well then. Good-night." Sarah was continuing up the stairs. Joel sauntered over to the stove and picked up the half-filled cup of coffee and watched her shadow skim past the bannister. A bedroom door opened and shut.

"Good-night," he answered softly. So close to her, a moment more to taste the wine of her kiss. He knew nothing about her and yet he knew everything. He knew his heart. He had recognized the emotions coursing through him the moment he first saw her in the cabin aboard the riverboat.

He had wanted a mother for his son. A mother to help his son grow to maturity in the world of the white man. Not for a moment had he ever expected the emotions that had died with Mourning Dove to be rekindled. He had loved one woman in his life, and she was dead and gone, so many years now. And yet, beneath the ashes of his heart, an ember burned, waiting.

How could there be another? How . . . forgive me, Hemené, for betraying you . . . could he feel this way again?

Her lips so close. To taste her. To hold her.

Joel Ryan brushed a hand through his silver mane and tried to come to terms with what had once seemed an impossible dream. He tried and failed and let it be. That was his way. Ryan's way.

32

The branches of the pines were wrapped in fleecy banners of mist. Otter Creek was a sober cold scar cutting a gray-speckled path through the high country.

And beyond, Morning Star.

Sarah watched in honest enchantment from the wagon seat while Cub Ryan guided the team after his father, over the last rise, allowing the gentle splendor of the ranch and valley to unfold.

"Mommy, what's happening?" Fiona asked from her makeshift seat among the wagon crates. Sean crawled to his knees and peered past his mother's shoulder.

"Golly," he muttered.

The forested slopes seemed ominous in the ashen landscape, a place of shadows drawing them into its mysteries.

"Stay here," Joel said from horseback, guiding his roan past the wagon and down the slope toward the ranch.

"Why are we waiting?"

"He always goes on alone," Cub said. "Whenever we return, he goes on ahead."

"Why?"

"It is my father's way," Cub retorted, exasperated by the woman's questions. Sarah decided against pursuing the matter any further. Joel Ryan was a curious man, and that's all there was to it.

Hemené. He screamed the name in his mind, standing on the precipice of his despair, he called the name, tried to summon back the life Henri Larocque had snuffed out in a moment of violence. The echo remained. The pain, eased by the years, returned at times, usually in the waning hours of a restless night, returned with haunting clarity, leaving Joel to suffer his loss, again and again.

The cabin was unchanged. A more practical man would have enlarged it for the basis of a a larger house. Joel had let things be, using the place for a bunkhouse until the last of his ranchhands had quit, hired away by Colonel Frank Jessup, Tod's father. Here was a man who not only offered better pay, but whose loyalty to the area's white settlers was, unlike Joel's, above suspicion. About fifty yards behind the cabin, Joel had laid the foundation for what was now the ranch house. A comfortable master bedroom, a living room with a kitchen at the back, and a partly completed study made up the bottom floor. Above the living room he had added a second story, a single spacious room with a balcony. This was Cub's room. It would serve as a common bedroom for all the children until he had time to divide the space into separate accommodations for Sean and Fiona. That Sarah might not stay never entered his mind. He placed his trust in fate and in the fact that Sarah had no way of returning to Sweeney's Landing without his help.

Returning.

Every return was the same, these few seconds when the past spilled into the present and left him hurt and needing reassurance. He trotted his roan gelding past the cabin, slowed to a walk in front of the house, and then headed for the barn. He listened; his senses reached out to discover intruders; his gaze swept the yard for tracks.

The Crow braves had come around the barn, even as the peg-legged man emerged from the cabin. Mourning Dove needed him, Joel knew, if only he could reach her. He always woke before he reached her in time.

One second your world is in order, the next, chaos. Utter confusion, and grief is all you can feel. Grief and rage.

The homesite showed no signs of having been visited. He rode to the center of the yard, clear of the buildings, and stood in his stirrups, raising one long arm to hold the Winchester rifle above his head, a signal for his son to bring on the wagon. Down the gentle slope, past stands of towering pines and clumps of chokecherry bushes, down to Otter Creek lined with its willows and cottonwoods, the wagon

raced across a smooth stretch of pasture merrily sporting a
pastel montage of purple and white flowers; here at last the
journey ended.

Sarah McClinton had come to Morning Star.

The dining room table Joel had laboriously hewn from the
remains of a lightning-blasted cottonwood was set with an
unmatched assortment of clay plates and platters, knives and
forks. Dinner consisted of a venison roast and boiled potatoes
harvested from the garden behind the house and snap beans
cooked with a slab of salt pork and an iron skillet of piping
hot cornbread to soak up the broth. He had prepared the meal
while Cub, with Sean's reluctant help, unloaded the wagon.
The two boys worked in silence, an unspoken state of war
existing between them as a result of Sean's misgivings and
Cub's open hostility. Sarah had marched Fiona upstairs to
inspect the living quarters and was pleasantly surprised at the
rustic but comfortable furnishings, a bunk bed, a single bed,
a table, and assorted chairs gathered around an open hearth.

The two families ate with little interchange. Cub on one
side, Sean and Fiona on the other, with Sarah and Joel at
either end.

"Nice to have a crowd around the table for a change,"
Joel said. The children continued to eat. Sarah was lost in
her own speculations. Other than the common room upstairs,
the only other bedroom was off the living room. Joel had
furnished it with an intricately carved dresser and a massive
bed with a downy mattress, covered with a heavy buffalo
robe. Calico curtains bordered the windows. An oil lamp was
aglow on a solid looking nightstand near the bed. A single
bed and none other in the house. Joel obviously intended her
to sleep there. And where did he intend to sleep?

"Yeah, nothing like a little dinner conversation," Joel said.
Sarah seemed to stare right through him. He glanced over at
Fiona whose smile was hidden behind cornbread crumbs and
bean broth.

"I like your house," she said. "Will we get to stay here
long?"

"As long as you want," Joel replied, catching Sarah's
alarmed expression, and ignoring it.

"I'm not afraid of you no more," the girl continued. "Can you guess why?"

"No," Joel said.

" 'Cause if you were bad, you would have cooked me and Sean in a big kettle and ate us up for supper, just like bad giants do."

"There's always dessert," Sean muttered, digging his elbows into his sister's side.

"Don't," Fiona protested. "Quit it." She struck her brother, who, in attempting to ward off the blow, accidentally struck her again and knocked over a cup of water in the process.

"Mommy," Fiona cried. "Sean's being mean."

"That will be enough," Joel said. Brother and sister grew quiet at his stern command.

"I will see to my children, thank you," Sarah said, bristling at the way he had usurped her authority. "I am their mother."

Joel started to reply but held back instead, sensing no good would come of this discussion. He shrugged and scooped a mammoth spoonful of snap beans into his mouth and chewed until his temper cooled; as long as he kept his mouth full he would not be able to retort. His silence put Sarah off her guard and left her somewhat flustered.

"The dinner table is certainly no place for such behavior. I think you owe Joel an apology," Sarah said.

"Sorry, sir." Sean stared at his plate.

"Me too. But Sean started it," Fiona said. She smiled beatifically at Joel.

Cub shoved his plate back and stood.

"I'm gonna go feed the horses," he said.

"It is customary to ask to be excused," Sarah interjected, suddenly realizing she had committed the same transgression she had accused Joel of. "But then," she added, looking at Joel, "you are his father."

Cub stared at Sarah as if she were a madwoman. "I'm going to feed the horses," he repeated, as if that were sufficient explanation.

"There are ladies present," Joel said. "Excusing oneself is the polite thing to do, son."

"Nahkohe," Cub said, amazed his father should side with

the white woman. "This is our house. Not theirs. I do not need her permission. I am Cub Ryan and I do as I please." He stalked from the room and slammed the door behind him. Joel stared down at his plate, at his half-finished dinner, aware he had lost his appetite.

Sarah heated water in a kettle and filled the wooden tub in the kitchen with hot soapy water. Fiona and then Sean took their baths while Joel built a fire in the hearth in their room; he soon had the upstairs delightfully warm and aglow with the dancing firelight.

Fiona found a surprise awaiting her when she came to bed. Joel had stitched a doll out of tanned buckskin, had used beads for the eyes, and snipped the mane of a colt to provide enough hair for the little girl to braid. Fiona squealed with delight and clutched the doll to her bosom, smothering it in an embrace that almost knocked the sawdust loose. Sarah noticed a pile of scraps that would provide a whole wardrobe of buckskin dresses.

"What's her name?" Fiona said, snuggling beneath sheets and Hudson's Bay blanket, the doll nestled beside her on the pillow. Joel knelt by the bed. His shadow draped across the girl like the shading wing of a bird.

"I think that's up to you. What will you call her?"

"Is she an Indian?"

"Maybe. But that doesn't matter."

"I don't know any Indian names."

"What would you like to call her?"

"Tiny."

"That's as good a name as any."

Fiona clutched the doll to her heart. She raised one arm to draw Joel close. He thought she wanted to whisper something in his ear, but when he leaned forward, she kissed him on the cheek just above his whiskers.

Sarah, sitting on the corner of the bed opposite Joel, hid a smile at the somewhat embarrassed expression that crossed his craggy good looks.

"Sleep tight," he said in a choked voice. Sean entered the room. He wore red flannel underwear and was wrapped in a towel. He hurried over near the fireplace and warmed his

backside. A chill had crept down off the mountains and stolen through the valley in subtle foreshadowings of the winter
to come. A branding iron rested on the mantle just within
reach of Sean's exploring hands. He took the iron down and
examined its curious design, a diamond, corner down with
four separate lines, one radiating from each side.

"The morning star," Joel said, drawing close. "Our brand.
It is also a Cheyenne marking."

"I saw it on your horse," Sean said.

"Horses, cattle, all wear my brand."

"Are you gonna brand us?" Fiona asked as her mother
leaned over to kiss her good-night.

"They don't brand people, silly," Sean said. He looked
back up at Joel with a suspicious "Do they?" expression in
his eyes.

"Just cattle and horses. That's how other people know
what belongs to me," Joel said. "There aren't many cattle or
horses right now, but Cub and I have had our hands full. A
man named Colonel Jessup hired away the few men I had
working for me. I imagine the colonel would like to have
the run of this whole valley clear on to Moon Woman Mountain."

"People have minds of their own," Sarah explained to her
daughter, although Joel had the impression the words were
for his benefit. "They don't wear brands and can do as they
please."

"Tiny, I won't brand you," Fiona said to her doll.

"I didn't see any horses *or* cattle," Sean said as Joel returned the branding iron to the mantle.

"The cattle are up on some grazing land across the creek.
On the other side of the hill. When word came through that
Bixby's riverboat was on the Yellowstone, I decided to head
on in to Sweeney's Landing. Couldn't be sure how long I'd
be away, so I turned loose the horses out of the stable. We
had it figured pretty close and only had to wait a few days."

"You just left everything? For someone to come along
and rob you of house and home?" Sarah asked.

"Not exactly," Joel said. Without elaborating further, he
started to leave the room. Sean hurried over to the bunk bed
and crawled beneath the blankets on the lower mattress. "I

can't say when Cub will be along, but if it's all the same to you, lad, take the upper bed. My son's a bit superstitious."

Sean shrugged and climbed up to the mattress and hunkered down beneath the blankets, his stocky frame making the wood supports creak.

"You see, the Cheyenne bury their dead in the air, on lodge pole racks. They give their departed to the sky instead of the earth," Joel explained.

Sean sat up and looked about, suddenly suspicious in his own right. Out in the dark woods, a mournful howl could be heard. A look of recognition came to Joel's face, and when he noticed Sarah studying him, he turned away.

"*O-kohome.* The coyote," he said. And then glancing at Sean, he added, "Maybe bunk beds was a bad idea. We'll saw the frame in half tomorrow. I'd better check on Cub." He nodded good-night again and left the room, the tread of his departure heavy on the stairs. Sean lay back upon the pillow and thought of Indian burial grounds. Fiona gave Tiny Doll a hug and kiss and closed her eyes. Sarah dimmed the oil lantern and added another log to the fire, working it to the back of the hearth and sending a shower of sparkling orange embers up the flue. She walked over to the bunk bed, looked up at her son, and felt a pang of remorse that she had given him, thus far, quite an unsettled life. Fiona was too young. As far as the girl was concerned, they might wind up at home any second, none the worse for wear. But Sean knew what was happening. That his natural father was dead. And for now, the three of them had no home. The riverboat days had momentarily replaced his misgivings with the excitement of the voyage. But here in the stillness of Morning Star—what had Bixby called it? The howling wilderness. Here his fears were slithering forth to overwhelm his youthful courage.

Sean sensed her concern and turned to look at his mother. He wiped his eyes on the sleeve of his long johns, sniffed and swallowed. "I'm not crying," he said manfully.

"I know," his mother gently replied. "You have certainly been a great help to me, Sean."

"Ma. Would we have come here if, uh, if Papa hadn't died?"

"Who knows? Probably not. But that would have been another life, and no one can really say. You miss your father, don't you?" Sarah had told them Jaimie's death was an accident and had never discussed the seamier aspects of his life or the true nature of his demise. The children had been exposed to his black moods from time to time. Once, in a drunken rage at the world, Jaimie had knocked Sean to the floor. Those were the last days, when poverty and liquor had changed Jaimie for the worst.

"Sometimes," Sean said. He glanced over at his sister who was already asleep. "Do you think the stories are true? I heard Miss Sweeney telling Captain Bixby. She said people are saying Mister Ryan and the Indians are killing people and everything."

"It isn't polite to eavesdrop."

"Ma?"

"Sweeney didn't believe it. And she knows Joel Ryan better than anyone practically. She certainly struck me as someone whose judgment we can take into account."

"I guess so," Sean replied. "Ma, are we home yet? I mean, is this where we stop?"

"I don't know," Sarah said, touching his cheek. "Now go to sleep." She left his bedside before her own composure dissolved into tearful self-pity. Sean was being so brave. Sarah was not about to let him see how tired and uncertain she felt. She kissed him and quietly made her way from the room and downstairs.

In the common living room, she began to take notice of the finer touches to the solid, heavy furniture. A score of diminutive rose buds had been worked into the table legs and laboriously polished into rich relief. A set of fine pewter candlesticks commanded either corner of the mantel above the living room fireplace. They had certainly taken some effort and expense to come by. A rifle rack dominated the space between the candlesticks. It had shocked her to find so many people in town wearing guns. Although she supposed it was necessary—Custer's massacre had been front-page news only two years ago in New York—the fact remained that Sarah felt no safer for their presence. Bear rugs kept the night chill from seeping through the wood floor. She noticed a stock of tabloids in the corner and blushed on further examination to discover they were issues of the *Police Gazette*, some several years old. From the look of the worn pages they had been read and reread at frequent intervals. In close and even sacrilegious proximity to the stack of gazettes rested a battered Bible, its leather cover creased and cracked with age. She gingerly opened the cover and on the brittle yellow page read the name "Priam" scrawled in wavering penmanship; the letters wandered like a lost caravan across the paper's fragile plain. A more controlled hand had written the dates "1800–b.—August 13, 1876–d. Rest well, na-vesene." She had no way of recognizing the Cheyenne word for "friend."

The door banged back against the wall behind her, and Sarah gasped and spun around only to find the door, left slightly ajar, had been victim to the gusting breeze. She returned the Bible to its scandalous pier, taking pains to obscure the cover illustration of "The Cat House Murders—Mad Madame's Massacre." She walked over and started to close the door and secure the bolt, but she paused in the middle of her effort as she glimpsed movement in the moonlight, tensing as she spied an Indian leading a horse up from the creekbed toward the house. She thought at first it was Cub, then she realized the newcomer was much too solidly built to be the twelve-year-old. Joel entered her line of vision from the side of the house and moved out to greet the stranger. The two were obviously friends. Sarah closed the door, glanced upward to where her children lay asleep. What did she really know of Joel Ryan? Maybe this clandestine visit was utterly innocent, but could she be certain? Once she had hinged her future on him. Now, if that wasn't foolish enough, Sarah McClinton had placed her very life in his hands. If anything should happen, who would know the difference? Or care? And yet, how could she suspect the motives of a man who had been so gentle with Fiona, whose broad strong hands had labored in the making of a doll for a little girl? She sighed and leaned against the door, thoroughly at a loss for what even to feel much less what to do. Sarah McClinton refused to act out of panic. *Wait, then remain watchful.* She moved quickly to the fireplace and lifted a revolver from a wooden shelf below the rifle and shotgun. It was a heavy ominous-looking weapon, a Dragoon Colt she was later to learn. Sarah checked the cylinder, saw it was loaded, and took it with her to the master bedroom. She stripped herself and donned a thick cotton nightshirt that hung to her ankles; after bracing a chair against the door, she climbed beneath the blankets in bed, tugging the buffalo robe up to her chest. She lay back upon the pillows and, reaching over, extinguished the oil lamp. A shaft of moonlight spilled between a gap in the wood shutters and drew a silvery blue slash from the window to the bed, the buffalo robe, and Sarah's slim pale hand resting on the gun's cold steel that glimmered in stark relief against the dark fur.

"Haa-he, Silvertip."

"It is good to see you, Rides The Horse."

"The whiteman-buffalo are beyond the hill. Saaa. Such work is unbefitting a warrior. How can you stand it, my friend?"

"The older I get, the more I find I can put up with." Joel chuckled. "It beats riding into the heart of a buffalo herd and getting trampled for a pound of meat."

"To follow the buffalo and make a kill, there was honor in it. Who can understand the ways of the white man?" Rides The Horse snorted in disgust. "It is time I rejoined my people."

"Friend, will you carry a message to my brother among the Red Shields?"

"Sacred Killer will always listen to the words of Nah-kohe."

"I must talk with Sacred Killer. It is important we meet. Have him send word to me the time and place, and I will come. Tell him we must meet soon."

"I will do as you ask," Rides The Horse said, his face crinkling in a grin. He brought his hand across his chest in salute and mounted his horse.

"And cut a cow or two out of the herd. I hear the hunting is poor in the high country this year."

"The hunting is bad," Rides The Horse agreed. "But one of the whiteman-buffalo will be plenty. There are not as many lodges now among the People. Many have gone to the reservations in the south. And many are dead. Too many." Rides The Horse turned his mount toward Otter Creek. "Farewell, Nahkohe Ryan."

Joel lifted his hand in salute and watched the brave splash across the moonlit creek before starting toward the house. A length of rawhide attached to the latch and dangling outside the door enabled Joel to free the bolt and enter the house. Stepping softly to the door of his bedroom, he tried the handle and gingerly eased pressure against the door panel. The door wouldn't budge. Sarah had contrived to lock him out of the room . . . his own bedroom. He sighed. *Well, Joel Ryan, what did you expect? Sarah to await you naked atop the buffalo robe? Her hot white flesh eager for your kisses?* It was a nice thought. In fact, if he continued, he might find his blood boiling in his veins. *Oh hell.* He left the house as stealthily as he had entered.

Cub Ryan was stretched out on a makeshift bed in the barn loft. He stirred and sat up as his father materialized—head and shoulders and long legs—through the opening in the floor. Joel dropped a horse blanket on the mounded straw, then he walked over to the loft doors, pushing them open to peer once more at the black and lifeless-looking house.

"Why have you brought this *ve-ho-a-e*, white woman, and her children to our house?" Cub asked, rolling on his side to face his father.

"It is my wish that she live here, with us. That we will be a family." No way of avoiding the issue, Joel reflected, bracing himself for the confrontation. "I hope to take her for my wife as soon as I can find us a circuit preacher."

"No!" Cub bolted upright. "I feared you would say such a thing. She is not my mother. She will never be. This woman is not Cheyenne."

"Son, the old ways are dying. Mrs. McClinton can teach you the new ways, help with your reading and ciphering and civilized ways. The world is changing. You have to change with it or be buried in its path. I tried many times to tell you about her; I wanted to, but instead I put it off, hoping to find an easier way. I am sorry for that."

"But she is not Cheyenne."

"Neither are you."

"My mother's blood . . ."

"Makes no difference. Listen to me, Cub. The Cheyenne are holed up in the mountains. All the tribes have gone south to the reservations. Only the Morning Star People remain, but one day they will be found. And then there will come a choice to be made, to die or to surrender and be sent south to the reservations. God knows, it is not what I wish. But I cannot save them. Only you, only my son. This is your land and will always be your land, and no one can ever steal it, unless you allow it. When I am gone, you will have to deal with the white man on your own. You must learn his ways as you did the ways of the Morning Star People."

"No. I would rather go with my uncle and fight alongside him. Better death than what you offer."

"It is always easy for the young to talk of death."

"I will listen no further." Cub turned away. "You have forgotten how my mother died, and who killed her."

Joel knelt alongside the boy and, grabbing him by the shoulder, savagely slammed him over, pinning him to the floor.

"I buried her! I washed her blood from my hands, and I gave her to the sky. Don't speak to me of forgetting. Don't you dare," he growled. Anger slowly seeped away, leached by the stillness, tempered by a slowly acquired wisdom. Joel sat in the hay, releasing his hold on his son. He had to give Cub time, allow him to get "alkalied" to the notion.

"You are my son. You will do as I say. Saaa! You speak of the old ways; all right then, a son obeys his father. Cub? Do you hear my words?"

"I hear," the boy said, tight-lipped, trying to be strong. "But no matter what you say, the white woman will never be my mother. My mother is dead. No matter what you say."

Hours later, Joel lay awake and listened to his son's easy breathing and the sounds of night, the owl's call and mournful cry of coyote and timber wolf. In his mind he saw Hemené, lying still, asleep. He reached out to touch her shoulder, to enfold her in his embrace. She woke at his touch and looked at him and held out her arms. Her face was soft, her smile, willing. But her eyes, her eyes were like twin emeralds flashing their lustrous green fire. The eyes of Sarah McClinton.

It was a curious fantasy.

Sarah cracked eggs into the skillet, and while the egg whites curled brown at the edges, she burned her fingers hauling another iron skillet of biscuits out of the stove. She carried the biscuits to the table and dumped them in a bowl and hurried back to the stove to salvage her frying eggs.

"Mommy, can I help?" Fiona asked, trying to keep abreast of her mother's harried pace. Sarah almost tripped over her daughter and looked around for something to occupy Fiona with while breakfast was being prepared. She looked in Sean's direction, thinking to put him in charge of amusing his sister, but the boy was intently studying his grammar lessons in the living room; only his sandy hair could be seen above his hardboard tablet. She had never known him to take his studying so seriously. Perhaps the mountain air was having a salutory effect on him after all.

"Mommy?"

"You can set the table, dear. I think Mister Ryan keeps the knives and forks in that cabinet." She pointed to a white-washed panel chest near the back door.

"Can Tiny eat with us?"

"I think so," Sarah said. "Yes, there ought to be plenty."

"Goody. Did you hear, Tiny?" Fiona said to her doll. "You can have breakfast with us." The little girl cradled the doll as she carried dishes and an assortment of silverware to the table. "Why doesn't Sean help?" Fiona said, noticing her brother slouched in one of the leather-backed easy chairs at the front of the house.

"Sean is reviewing his lessons for tonight. That's just as important," Sarah explained, ladling the eggs out of the sizzling grease and neatly stacking them on a round stoneware plate. She glanced out the kitchen window and saw a swarm of fat, round, charcoal-gray birds merrily circling and darting about in a flurry of activity, pausing only to scratch at the earth and from time to time come away with a plump insect. Soon the chickens she had loosed from their pen charged across the yard, flapping their russet wings and driving the comical birds from their feeding ground. The chickens milled around in a fair semblance of confusion. Chickens, she thought, always look either preoccupied or in a state of uncertainty and panic. Sarah recalled the streets of New York, smiling as she transposed her memories of the noisy crowded city streets to the hunt-and-peck activity of the hens. Animals and people were a good deal alike. Except it was easier to understand the motives of farm animals.

Secreted behind the hardboard writing tablet and his grammar book, Sean couldn't have cared less about the proper use of tenses, the appropriate arrangement of verbs and nouns. He was far more concerned with the misadventures of Stephen Allen Kerby II, the son of a Nob Hill philanthropist. Poor Kerby had fallen in love with a woman of the streets, only to become embroiled in a life of such degradation and godlessness as to "make a Saracen blush." At last the young scion met his doom at the hands of a drunken gambler "whose derringer held no respect for a man's station but dealt death in equal measure to all." A pencil sketch accompanied the tale, depicting the gambler firing his pocket pistol and the mortally wounded Stephen A. Kerby II reeling, one hand clutching his throat, the other held out to ward off a second bullet. Off to one side, a rather buxom woman clad in corset and dance tights, a lace bodice barely concealing the artistically rendered proportions of her bosom, recoiled in terror at the sight of violence. The caption beneath the lithograph read, "Seduction of the Innocent, The Wages of Sin."

Sean was so entranced by the wages of sin he failed to notice Joel until the tall man's shadow spread across the page.

"I bought those for the hands in the bunkhouse, but they upped and quit before I had a chance to bring them down."

Sean jumped and slammed his grammar book shut, concealing the *Police Gazette* between the covers of his school-work.

"It's a sight more interesting to read than 'Run, Tom, run.' " Joel winked, his voice low, a conspiratorial twinkle in his eye. Sean, embarrassed at first, smiled despite himself.

"Sarah, you are a woman of surprises," Joel continued, heading for the table, his stomach growling at the wonderful aroma of bacon, biscuits, and eggs.

"I fail to see how, Mister Ryan."

"I thought we had come to an understanding about names. Mine's Joel."

"Where's your son?"

"Saddling the horses. I thought I might show you the rest of Morning Star. Cub wasn't hungry, so I put him to work." Joel sat at the table. Fiona took the chair next to him, her doll in her lap.

"I have the distinct impression his appetite will suffer as long as I am staying here," Sarah remarked.

"Give him time. His stomach will talk some sense into him, wait and see. I appreciate the meal."

"My father was an O'Neill, and the O'Neills do not accept charity," Sarah replied. "If I am staying under your roof and taking over your room, then my children and I will work for our keep. It is the least we can do." Sarah sat down in her place, and Sean plopped himself down beside his sister. "I trust you did not suffer too much . . . in the . . . where did you sleep?"

"In the barn. Quite comfortable in the hay. Many a family started out that way."

Sarah's glance was almost as deadly as a dagger. Joel took a helping of biscuits, unable to meet her stare.

"Son, will you say grace for us?"

"Yes, Ma." Joel paused mid-bite in his biscuit, groaning inwardly. "Lord," Sean continued, "bless this food and the hands that prepared it and the folks that eat it. We give thee our abundant gratitude. Amen." Everyone echoed "Amen." Joel had to swallow to speak.

"Mister—uh, Joel. I admit I am unfamiliar with frontier etiquette," Sarah noted. "But I find it customary to close the door."

"Strategy," Joel explained good-naturedly, sopping egg yolk with his biscuit. "The smell of fresh-cooked bacon travels farther through an open door." Sarah frowned at first, wondering if he was having fun at her expense, then she understood when Cub appeared in the doorway, wrinkling his nose and looking at the group gathered at the table. The half-breed boy tried to remain unconcerned.

"Biscuits and bacon is his favorite meal next to buffalo hump," Joel explained softly.

Sarah hid a smile and instead admonished Sean for taking too liberal a helping of bacon; he had piled his plate full of rashers. Bacon was his favorite food, and he didn't care two flips about some old buffalo's hump. Sarah filled a plate, apportioning the bacon evenly between her son and Cub. She set the plate before the empty chair.

"Please close the door behind you, young man," Sarah said. Cub hesitated, then he stepped into the room and crossed to the table. He slid back his chair.

"There is soap and water in the basin in the sink," Sarah added. "You may work with horses. But you eat with people." Cub cast a smoldering look in her direction. Sarah remained undaunted. The boy looked in vain to his father for help.

"Mighty good breakfast, Sarah," Joel said. "Bacon's just the way I like it. And these biscuits all but melt in the mouth."

Cub stared at the steaming plate of food. Hunger warred with pride. Finally, he plodded toward the sink, like a condemned man, gallows-bound—except Cub Ryan's steps were leading not to the hangman's rope, but to civilization. At that moment, they seemed to him one and the same.

A day became two. Became ten. Mornings dawned clear and beautiful and passed into lovely afternoons. There were plenty of duties to occupy their time. The garden needed one final fall harvest before being plowed under. Sarah visited the root cellar and rearranged the drying vegetables to suit her fancy. She was pleasantly surprised that she had not lost her talent for canning preserves during her stint of city life. She and Fiona visited the blueberry and chokecherry bushes

growing wild in the turns and bends of Otter Creek, har-
vesting enough fruit to fill every spare jar with delicious
preserves. Against Sarah's wishes—or in spite of her concern, she could not decide which—Joel insisted on teaching
Sean to ride. It was hard for her to protest too vigorously
after seeing how her son's eyes lit up when Joel presented
the boy with an Appaloosa pony that Joel claimed came from
fine stock dating back to his first days in the area.

At last, the time came for Sean to help with the herd up
at Mission Meadow. The youth insisted his mother come
watch and grudgingly added that Fiona could come along
too. If she kept quiet and out of the way. And of course, the
little girl promised and crossed her heart.

Fiona thought chasing cows was the funniest sight ever; she
laughed and laughed at the curious antics of Cub and Joel
and her poor brother Sean, who barely managed to stay
astride his horse.

"Aren't they funny, Mommy?" the little girl said, astride
her mother's horse. Sarah had ridden plough horses on her
uncle's farm in Kilkenny and could hardly be called a novice,
but these spirited animals demanded constant attention. Even
Caboose, the slow-moving mare she and her daughter had
been assigned, now and then exercised a will of her own and
had to be fought back onto the trail. Sarah guessed immediately how the animal had come by its name—no matter
what the conditions, the mare always seemed to be last. Sarah
gasped as Sean's gelding began to buck. Thankfully the animal's exuberance subsided, leaving his rider still in the saddle. Sean turned a pasty white face toward his mother and
waved that everything was all right, a gesture that convinced
him as little as it convinced her. Cub chafed beneath the
girl's amusement and tried to ignore her; bringing the cattle
down from the meadow was serious business. His estimation
of these newcomers continued its dramatic decline.

Joel trotted his roan over to the audience of two. "The
boy's learning," he said, as he approached. A calf cut from
the rest of the herd, and Sean's horse moved on instinct to
head the wayward animal back into the mainstream.

"The horse is doing most of the work," Sarah replied.

"There's the most important part. Learning not to fight your horse if he knows what he's about." Joel stood in his stirrups and waved a hand to include the golden meadow and the green hills they had crossed in leaving the ranch house. "What do you think?"

Sarah read his thoughts and looked around her at the land lying lovely and as open and boundless as the dreams of men and women who challenged this wilderness. The sky, pale at the horizon, arced overhead, deepened in hue, becoming a dark sapphire blue stretching out to infinity.

"It's a big sky," she said. "And a high country."

"That it is," Joel chuckled. A breeze tugged at his silver mane, and he tilted his face to the sun, closing his eyes and letting the glare wash his face in golden warmth. He was like the land, Sarah thought, his features changing from merriment to introspection, intimidating and inviting in the same instant. Suddenly he was looking at her, and she averted her gaze, blushing despite herself that he had caught her in the act. Fiona was staring at them both, wondering why the grown-ups were being so quiet.

"Sarah," Joel said softly. Her heart was racing, and she did not know why, only that she hated feeling so confused within herself. Cub inadvertently saved her, calling to his father from across the meadow. Joel looked over his shoulder in the direction of his son and saw the riders cutting through his small herd and heading straight for him.

Sarah noticed Joel stiffen in recognition. She watched in curiosity as three horsemen approached. One took the lead, a broad-shouldered solid-looking individual in a dust-colored shirt, black vest, and Levi's. He wore a blue military hat and looked to be in his fifties. The two men behind him were nondescript cowpunchers who kept a low profile and rode for the brand, which meant they did as they were told. The lead man doffed his hat, removed the cigar from his mouth, and bowed in Sarah's direction. She nodded, accepting his courtesy.

"Howdy, ma'am. Frank Jessup at your service," the rider said. Sarah noted now that he was close how one of his eyes seemed to stare ahead almost without seeing her. She noticed the scar tissue then, a thin white line above his blind right

eye. "Indian wars," he explained, reading her thoughts. "Got
it chasing Sitting Bull back into Canada, right after the massacre of the Seventh. I planned to be a career man. Became
a rancher after the army mustered me out. No use for a one-
eyed colonel. But you aren't interested in me. By God, if I
wasn't happily married, I'd write to Cole's myself." He
slapped his thigh in a form of punctuation to what he considered a compliment.

"What brings you over on my land, Frank?"

"And a fair amount of land, too. A sight much for so few
cattle. What have you got, a hundred head?"

"There will be more."

"And who'll work them? The reasons your men quit before are the same reasons you won't find any willing to
work."

"Times change, Frank."

"No they don't," Jessup replied. "That's only an ugly rumor folks have been circulating. The older you get, the more
you realize nothing changes. Nothing changes at all."

"You rode over to preach to me, then?"

Jessup glanced over at Sarah and then down at Fiona. He
smiled kindly in her direction.

"You have a funny eye," the little girl giggled. Jessup's
smile remained, its piety severely diminished however. He
turned to Joel again.

"I suppose I should have expected hostility after the way
Tod behaved in town." He puffed at his cold cigar. "Muller,"
he said.

"Yes, Colonel," one of the drovers replied, edging forward to hand his boss a match. Jessup relit his cigar and
leaned forward on his saddle pommel. "I want to apologize
for my son. When I heard he had actually pulled a gun on
you last week, well, I was furious. He's a headstrong lad.
And has his own following among the hired hands. But
what's the point of being young if you can't scratch your
wild streak from time to time? That's what I always say.
Eh?"

Sarah looked from Joel to the colonel, aware of the uneasy
truce between the two men. "Anyway, I come to make
amends and let bygones be bygones and invite you and the

lady here over to my place this Friday. It isn't fitting, Miss Sarah—news travels fast—" he nodded to her, "that you arrive so pretty and all and are received without so much as a proper welcome. Mrs. Jessup loves a party. I trust you will do us the honor of your company, my dear. I feel obligated to demonstrate that even the frontier is not without a semblance of courtesy and celebration. And has its more civilized moments."

"A party sounds delightful. Thank you, Colonel Jessup," Sarah replied, ignoring Joel's warning glance. "I accept your invitation in the spirit in which it is offered."

"Good. Your children are welcome, of course. Then we shall see you Friday." Jessup donned his campaign hat and backed his Thoroughbred away from the couple. A wave of his hand and the two drovers wheeled their mounts and rode off in the direction they had come, holding their pace until Colonel Frank Jessup had pulled in front, out of the trailing cloud of dust in their wake.

"You needn't look at me like that," Sarah said, noticing Joel's displeasure. "Maybe you should make an effort to get along with people."

Joel started to reply when he heard Sean cry out and turned to see the youth sprawled on the ground. Joel trotted toward the boy.

"Oh my God," Sarah exclaimed and started after Joel. She was relieved to see Sean stagger to his feet. His Appaloosa pony stood motionless a few feet away, its tail switching back and forth, ears pricked forward. Sean dusted himself off and glared at Cub, who watched from a distance. "You did that on purpose," he shouted. "He cut in front of me and scared my horse," Sean added as his mother and Joel rode up.

"That Appaloosa's daddy made me eat dirt up to the day he died," Joel explained. "Oh, he likes to jump now and then, but he'll make you a fine mount."

"Or give him a broken neck. No thank you, Mister Silvertip Ryan," Sarah interrupted angrily. "Sean, you can ride with Fiona and me."

"I'll ride my own horse," Sean said, somewhat uncertainly. He walked over to the Appaloosa pony. The animal gazed warily at the youth. Sean gulped, then climbed up into the saddle, fully expecting the worst. To his amazement, for the first time in as long as he could remember it seemed, the worst didn't happen. Then he trotted the pony right past Cub, who glowered beneath his dark brows at Sarah's son. Sean rode back across the meadow, dust and bits of dry yellow grass rising in his wake.

"Sean is scared to death," Sarah said to Joel. "I hope you appreciate that."

"Yeah," Joel said, staring after the boy. "Fear's the price you pay."

"For what?" asked Sarah as she looked after her son. Sure and his hands trembled at the reins, but it seemed he sat as tall in the saddle as a ten-year-old could sit. Tall and . . . proud.

The Jessup ranch sprawled in rustic elegance at the end of Mission Valley, a broad level plain between two divides that backed into cliffs of iron-red scoria. Joel guided the wagon down the meandering lane leading to the main house, a low spacious structure surrounded by bunkhouses and a massive barn that an army pension could never have built. Frank Jessup had married well, taking the spinster daughter of a Philadelphia industrialist for his wife. Belva Afton Jessup had come with a generous dowry from a grateful father, a fact that more than made up for her lack of beauty.

The ranch house was of log and stone, surrounded by a low stone fence behind which a number of tables decorated with red-checkered cloths had been laden with platters of bread and roast beef, fresh vegetables from the root cellar, and golden-crust peach and apple cobblers for dessert. Barrels of beer had been tapped for the men, and bowls of spiced punch set out for the ladies and children. As the Ryan wagon pulled to a stop alongside more than a dozen other buckboards and carriages, the fiddlers and accordion players on a platform near the porch paused. Heads turned to study the new arrivals. Joel climbed down from the wagon, noting envy in the faces of the men close-by. The auburn-haired Irish beauty atop the wagon seat beamed a smile in their direction, and whatever imbibed animosity these ranchers harbored toward Silvertip Ryan was immediately replaced by a sudden and overwhelming desire to make Sarah's acquaintance. Joel helped Sarah down from the wagon seat and afterward Fiona. Sean climbed down off the back.

Joel watched the youth round the back of the wagon and pictured for a moment Cub, at Morning Star, refusing to attend the party. Granted, Sarah had done the accepting. But it did make sense that Jessup's party might serve to ease some of the tension between the homesteaders and ranchers in the area and Joel Ryan. He had decided it was worth a try and given his best at arguing the case with Cub. But Cub would not be swayed. Joel's son had endured too many slights to forgive and forget. Let Joel and the white woman sit down at Jessup's campfire, but not Cub Ryan. He was still at war. Eventually, Joel agreed to let him remain behind, knowing if there was any trouble at the ranch, Cub could take care of himself. And if Cub wanted to hide, he had the talents of a Cheyenne warrior and could be as elusive and impossible to track as a will-o'-the-wisp. *We have the country, the space, the breathing room, but do we have the time?* Joel reflected. Civilization was carving its inroads into the mountains, bringing inevitable change. And bringing a choice, to bend with the change or break.

"Glad you could make it," Frank Jessup exclaimed, leading his wife off the porch and through the families gathered in the front yard. The colonel turned toward the musicians on the porch and waved his hand. On command they eased into a rendition of "Green Grow the Lilacs." Wives hurried to snare their husbands away from their intense and none-too-innocent appraisal of Sarah McClinton. News of the arrival of the mail-order bride had spread like wildfire through the surrounding area. There was much speculation as to her looks, her background, and whether or not she would even consent to stay once she learned that Silvertip Ryan was a squaw man and had a breed boy. This was a scenario devoutly to be wished by the bachelors in the neighborhood. Several of them had attended Jessup's party for the purpose of seeing for themselves the new arrival and hoping to attract her interest and show she had more to choose from than an old grizzly and his half-breed whelp.

The wind tugged at Sarah's yellow bonnet as Joel escorted her toward Frank and Belva Afton Jessup. Belva was a plain, somewhat dumpy woman, who seemed forever in danger of losing her balance. Her hands were in constant motion, fussing with her brown hair, fidgeting with the lace on her cuffs, reaching out to touch and pat acquaintances and friends.

"Why, Sarah, my dear, may I discard formalities? You

must call me Belva. Welcome to the Bar Seven. You must be famished and in need of a cool drink. I insist you come right on inside and freshen up. And these are your children, what precious little ones." Sean narrowed his gaze; he never heard the word "precious" from grown-ups without growing suspicious. A rapid chain of explosions sounded from the back yard. Sarah winced, taken off guard.

"What's that, Mommy?" Fiona asked.

"Oh my, the other children have already found the fire-works," Belva answered.

"Fireworks?" Sean brightened.

"Yes, Colonel Jessup is just a child at heart. He likes having them around. But then, Thomas Jefferson was fond of fireworks, wasn't he? I wonder if that means anything." Belva tapped her finger against her chin, momentarily trying to make a connection. She shrugged, dropping the matter, unable to keep up with her own thoughts. Sean looked at his mother, his expression pleading.

"Very well. But be careful. And look after your sister," Sarah said. Sean grimaced. More fireworks exploded. He was missing all the excitement. Grabbing his sister by the hand, he disappeared past the corner of the house, his pace stiff in the confines of the one good suit of clothes Sarah had sewn for him during the riverboat leg of her journey west.

"I'm sure our men have new things to talk about," Belva said, taking Sarah through the open doorway.

Frank Jessup clapped Joel on the shoulder.

"Now that wasn't so hard, was it? Being neighborly might just become a way of life here and about."

"I've never had intentions otherwise, Colonel." Joel could see the man was visibly pleased at being addressed by his former title. Jessup stepped back a pace to study the big man clad in his buckskin trousers, loose cotton shirt, and beaded calf-length moccasins. "Is the barrel dry?"

"Just put the hammer to a new one," Jessup smiled, leading the way past the waltzing couples. A rancher Joel recognized, a Swede named Angstrom, stepped from the dancing area, his bride in arm.

"Nice party, Colonel Jessup. Me and the wife are grateful, for sure."

"Glad you could make it, Gus. My, you get lovelier every time I see you, Mrs. Angstrom."

The ruddy-cheeked woman blushed and gave a slight curtsy. Gus nodded to Joel.

"How are you, Gus?"

"Fair to middlin', Mister Ryan. Things all right out your way?" Gus had been the last of Joel's hired hands to quit. Joel suspected the Swede, a fair and honest man, had simply succumbed to the pressure of working for a man whom everyone knew was all but a brother to the blood-thirsty Cheyenne war chief, Sacred Killer.

"Making do, Gus. Sort of tight, to be truthful. Cub and I are managing the herd as well as we can. Had to sell off some stock to ease the load."

"Sorry to hear it."

Joel doffed his hat and bowed to Angstrom's wife. She retreated a step. "Pleased to meet you," he said. "Gus always said as soon as he had a place of his own he intended to raise a family."

"Olivia, this is Joel Ryan. He has a spread about the size of the colonel's here," Gus said.

"You're . . . excuse me. I pictured you—I mean from the descriptions I had heard . . . Well . . ."

"You pictured me with a bone in my nose and the blood of innocent Christians on my hands," Joel completed.

Olivia Angstrom's pretty features bunched with embarrassment. She was a simple, unassuming sort, and seemed a woman given to frankness. Joel laughed aloud and eased the tension. "I take the bone out for festive occasions." He shook her hand. "Gus is a good man. I wish you well, the both of you." Joel donned his hat and continued on over to the beer keg.

Jim Reasoner, Jessup's foreman, was standing alongside the keg, a roast beef sandwich in his left hand. Juice dribbled down his chin and threatened to stain the collar of his gray shirt; juice clung in greasy beads along his thick moustache and gave the unpleasant impression that someone had shot him in the mouth. Reasoner showed deference only to his boss. He stepped aside for no other man. His features were creased with worry lines. As an army sergeant, he had served many long hard days under Jessup and had departed with the colonel. The foreman had the reputation of being a seasoned Indian fighter, and he made no apologies that he had taken part in many a campaign against "the Hostiles." A band of woven Indian scalps taken in battle circled the brim of his hat.

Joel filled a glass with beer, blew the foam away, and met Reasoner's pensive watchful stare. "Afternoon, Jim," Joel said. Reasoner nodded to him and reached for another glass. He filled it and handed the beer to his boss.

"Thank you, Sergeant," the rancher said. He drank deep, slapped his stomach, and grinned. "God in heaven, but I love being top dog." He eyed Joel over the lip of the glass. "I take nothing away from you, now mark me. Nothing at all, Ryan. But you've got to admit you've seen better days. Hell, you got too much land for those few mossy horns you call a herd, and everyone here knows it." Jessup drained his glass. "But I admire your grit. So help me, I do." He noticed Joel scanning the crowd. "You looking for someone in particular?"

"Tod," Joel replied. "I like to know which way to face."

"I thought that was all settled. I apologized for his behavior."

"That's just it, Colonel. It was *his* behavior. Caution gets to be a way of life out here. At least a long life."

"I see," Jessup muttered. "Well, if it makes you feel any better, I sent him on up Mission Creek, to check on the herd. Actually it was his idea, so maybe he had no wish to see you, either. I wish you both could come to terms. He's a good boy. Just got a bit of the bark on him is all."

"Thorns, you mean," Joel said, finishing his beer.

"Damn it all, Ryan, you aren't the smoothest soul to back against either." Jessup ran a hand through his thinning hair, grimacing with displeasure as a couple of strands fell between his fingers.

Joel chuckled. "You got me there, Colonel." He had to give Sarah credit for accepting Jessup's invitation. Of course, it might never have been offered if it had not been for her

presence in the first place. Still, she had won him over to
her way of thinking. Maybe it was true, that sometimes it
took meeting people halfway. Already Mrs. Angstrom had
learned Silvertip Ryan didn't wear a bone in his nose. One
step in the right direction deserved another. He might even
ask Belva Afton Jessup for a dance. On second thought, a
man ought to know his limitations.

"May I have this dance, Mrs. McClinton?" Joel touched the
brim of his hat and half bowed to Belva Jessup. "It has been
a while, but I think I can manage the rudiments. If you will
pardon my intrusion . . ."

Sarah never thought she would feel so relieved to see
anyone in all her born days. Belva was a kind sweet woman,
but a talker. For the better part of an hour she had endured
a one-sided discussion of town gossip, of life in Philadelphia,
and how the West had so little to offer in the way of niceties.
Sarah managed to be born in Kilkenny, but she never attained
her childhood. Belva immediately launched into the curious
nature of being a mail-order bride and how pretty Sarah was
and how odd it seemed she could not find a husband in New
York. Sarah had no intention of regaling Belva with an account of Jaimie's suicide, much less the desperate circumstances that had precipitated her departure from New York.
Wagging tongues would love nothing better than to elaborate
on the circumstances of her children's kidnapping, depicting
how she submitted to the likes of Elrod Pierce. Lord only
knew what indecencies such gossip might conjure. Still,
Sarah had to fabricate some kind of story or risk being
damned by her clumsy inability to elaborate. She was mull-
ing over a choice between lies when Joel appeared in the
doorway, his powerful physique commanding their attention
as he asked her to join him.

"I can be quite agile when my toes are threatened," she
laughed. "You will excuse me for a moment, won't you,
Belva?"

"Why, uh, of course. But we must continue our talk afterwards. I simply must know all about you, my dear. I
should hate for us to be strangers."

Joel wrinkled his nose. The parlor smelled of incense,

almost obscuring the strong scent of cigar smoke. Frank Jessup's brand. The colonel had more than likely passed through the room and received a sound scolding from his wife afterwards. He walked with Sarah through the living room, a space as handsomely appointed as the rest of the house, demonstrating the wealth and position of the Jessups and especially Belva Afton. Furniture brought out from Philadelphia, handsome pieces, carved and cushioned, with thin round legs that didn't look quite adequate to support a man's weight, circled a table and bordered end tables and a bookshelf set against the wall. The coal-oil lamps boasted shades of rare and exquisite symmetry, finely blown glass delicately textured with Japanese dragons caught forever in the fluid motions of their prancing gait and curling seas, wind-tossed and reaching white frothy tips to a porcelain-colored sky. This was the proper home for a lady, a home he was unable to offer, Joel thought with some regret. But he had the land; he had Morning Star and a dream, his dream, waiting to be shared. Waiting and wanting, because of Sarah.

"What?" He blinked, his vision adjusting to the sunlight.

"I said you rescued me. From Mrs. Jessup. I am in your debt."

"She struck me as . . ."

"Sweet?"

"Precisely."

"And longwinded. And inquisitive."

"You have an acid tongue about you, Sarah."

"I think my sentiments are more of an honest observation," Sarah retorted. "And it seems you, sir, have a short memory. Or was your offer to dance merely another clever deception?"

The fiddle players had struck up a lilting melody, the tender strains of "Down in the Valley" drifted over the landscape. The gentle waltz provided just the excuse Joel needed to hold Sarah in his arms.

"Belva, what did you find out?" asked Agnes Turnbull.

"They're dancing. Look how he holds her," Deirdre Owens observed.

"No matter what she said," said Constance Seifert. "I'll

warrant they share the same bed, and them not even married."

"We were interrupted," Belva sighed. Her friends had entered, swift and silent after Sarah's departure from the room.
Belva's coterie had anxiously awaited the opportunity to find
out everything, just everything, Belva had learned.

"She's no better than a saloon girl if you ask me," Constance said. "Look at the two of them."

"I'd share the same bed and let the minister take his time,"
Deirdre giggled. "And you would too, Constance."

"How dare you?"

"Oh, Constance, calm down," Agnes said. "The veins in
your cheeks are showing." Constance Seifert's friends
laughed at her expense. Agnes, a portly woman of middle
age, similar to Frank Jessup's wife in appearance, plopped
herself down in the nearest chair. "Now, Belva, we want to
hear all you learned. Just who is Sarah McClinton? I'm dying
of curiosity. Imagine coming way out here to marry a man
she's never seen."

"If they even plan to marry," Constance added. Deirdre
hushed her.

"He is part savage," she continued.

"Yes, but which part?" Deirdre giggled.

Belva poured herself a sherry and, basking in the undi-
vided attention of her companions, retraced the path of her
conversation with Sarah. "She is a quiet sort. And really
didn't have much to say. I just about had to drag the few
words out of her . . ."

What Belva hadn't learned, she was about to invent.

Sarah wondered if people were watching her. Then she wondered why she no longer cared. Joel's arms were strong
around her, the feel of his body hard and powerful. His
movements were smooth and supple, like an animal's. She
liked the pressure of his hand on her back. She felt almost
weightless in his embrace, a curiously appealing sense of
powerlessness. No, Joel Ryan had clearly not been a man of
the wilderness all his life. But then, that had been obvious
in the fine and subtle touches in the house he had built. Oh,
it was not nearly the size of Jessup's and lacked a certain

sense of completeness. But then, Joel had admitted it wasn't complete. A dozen men had raised a roof over the colonel's head, while every plank, every log of Morning Star, and every stone of the chimney had been set in place by Joel. The home reflected the man. Solid, a bit rough, but Sarah had the feeling it would weather any storm.

"Where are you?" Joel said to her, as he kept in step with the music. "Your thoughts are far away."

"I was feeling guilty for turning you out of house and home." He and Cub had spent only one night in the barn. The next day Joel had replenished the woodpile by the cabin.

"The old place is comfortable enough. I spent many a month there. And with a fire in the hearth, it's comfortable. Of course, I would be happy to sleep elsewhere if you so wish. Beneath my own blankets perhaps." His eyes took on a falsely wicked gleam. Somehow his expression had trouble matching the look.

Sarah laughed aloud. The gleam faded.

"I never could do that well," he sighed. "You have to have the knack. Now my brother Nathan, Lord, but he could charm a snake out of its skin." His grin returned. It was a rare quality in a man to be able to laugh at himself.

"I'm glad," Sarah said. "It is nice to know someone who cannot wear a lie. My father had a saying, 'A truthful man dances with the leprechauns. A deceitful man dances alone.' "

"I think I would have liked your father," Joel said. She was close now, and what did it matter in public, his only concern was the aching he felt for her, the need to taste her kiss. His embrace tightened; her resistance ebbed, as if she wanted to yield, but not without a token resistance. Let her have her pride as long as he had his kiss.

Suddenly, Olivia Angstrom screamed. Her voice was a shrill, horror-filled cry. Flesh turned cold as ice. Another woman screamed. Then more. Outpourings of rage swept through the party and vanquished the happy atmosphere. More than one of the guests doubled over and vomited as sight and smell combined to overwhelm the weaker stomachs. The side of beef began to sizzle and burn without someone to turn it on the spit. The spout on the beer keg was left open, and the brown brew formed a spreading puddle of foam beneath the spigot.

At the first scream, Joel had grabbed for the gun he wasn't wearing, only to remember he had left it in the wagon, under the seat. Sarah paled and started to sag against him when she heard Fiona cry out, "Mommy!" She saw her daughter running to her across the front yard just ahead of Tod Jessup and his grisly parade.

Tod rounded the corner of the house at a brisk trot, then he slowed as he cut straight through the front yard. Men and women scrambled out of the way to let him pass, leading four horses with the mutilated remains of Jessup's men draped face down over the saddles. Tod reined his horse to a standstill, dropped the lead reins of the horse behind him. Then he turned his own mount and, spying Joel, walked the gelding to the man of Morning Star.

"Pope, Cal Luray, B.J., Shorty Adams," Tod said, his voice increasing in intensity and volume. "Count them, Ryan!"

"Oh my God," Belva wailed from the front door and hurried back inside. Frank Jessup strode down from the porch and along the train of his dead. These were *his* men, Jessup men. Their deaths and the manner in which they had died was an affront he could not allow to pass unpunished.

"When?" he said in a choked voice.

"Looks like this morning more than likely. They only just started to smell," Reasoner said. The foreman had appeared alongside his boss, and reaching out, he plucked one of the arrows from Pope's back. "Sacred Killer's bunch for certain, Colonel."

"Show it to Mister Silvertip Ryan," Tod ordered. "Let him see what those red niggers have done."

"Get Sean. Bring him to the wagon," Joel whispered, turning aside to Sarah. "Move!" She covered Fiona's face and led the girl away.

"What's happening, Mommy?"

"Shhh."

Joel faced the foreman, who held the arrow out for Joel's inspection.

"Red Shield markings. Just like the others. But then I

don't have to tell you," Reasoner said. "We both seen this work before but from different sides of the fence."

Joel looked at the arrow, refusing to believe even though the evidence was held out before him, its crimson markings showing through the dried blood. Reasoner dropped the arrow on the ground at Joel's feet. The man called Silvertip glanced about him. The faces of the homesteaders and ranchhands spoke eloquently of their silent accusation. He saw Sarah lead her two children to the wagon on the fringe of the yard.

"I think you had better leave," Frank Jessup said, his face red, the scar above his sightless right eye a fearful jagged streak of white. "I think you had better leave now." Joel started toward the wagon, but Reasoner was in his path. The foreman looked past Joel's shoulder, and on receiving some kind of signal from the colonel, he stepped aside.

"You can't let him just walk out of here," Tod said.

Joel walked. He tried not to seem in a hurry. Behind him, the flies began to gather, settling in droves on the corpses.

"He killed them. Just as sure as if he had been there with his red nigger brothers," Tod exclaimed. "Pa!"

"Mister Ryan is my guest," Frank said, fixing his son in place. "He came here as my guest, and he shall leave as my guest."

"But our men . . ."

"*My* men, Tod," Frank corrected. "Take them to the corral. We will have a proper burial at once."

Joel reached the wagon. A stone flew out of the crowd and struck him square between the shoulder blades. Sarah gasped, saw him wince and immediately hide the pain. He climbed up beside her.

"You can stay with us, Mrs. McClinton," Frank said. "We have plenty of room. Belva would be delighted for the company. And you might find it a more suitable atmosphere under the circumstances." He held out his hand to help her down.

"Thank you, Mister Jessup. Your offer is most kind." She made no move to leave. Joel caught the rein and called to the sturdy mares in their harness. Another stone glanced off the side of the buckboard.

"See here!" Jessup bellowed. He ranged the crowd with his fearsome gaze, unable to find the culprit and indicting all.

"I'm sorry about Pope and the others," Joel said.

"I am sorry too," Jessup replied. "I thought we had a start here. Something important, a kind of beginning. I was wrong. I don't intend to be wrong again." He swung away to join the gathering crowd. Without comment, Joel guided the wagon out onto the wheel-worn path leading to the ranch. He checked to make sure his rifle and revolver were beneath the seat.

"Are we going home?" Fiona asked.

"Yes, dear," Sarah said.

"Those men . . ." Sean seemed withered, his face blank and pale, bloodless in hue.

"Don't talk about it. Forget it," Sarah said.

"I'm trying," Sean replied earnestly.

They reached home by nightfall. Sarah lost no time in putting her children to bed after a brief supper of cold venison and day-old bread. Seated at the table with them, Cub had listened without a trace of emotion to the day's events, the horrible demise of four of Jessup's men. And Cub was the first to leave, muttering something about checking the horses in the barn. He had not touched a morsel of his dinner. Joel sensed the boy wanted to be alone and let him go. Then Sarah herded her son and daughter up the stairs while Joel cleared the table and turned the lights low. He sat in his big chair by the door and took the Bible from atop its stack of prurient news. He opened the book and stared at the pages for a long time, seeing in place of the holy text his own black thoughts. He heard footsteps on the stairs, and Sarah's voice made him bring his head up sharply, startled.

"I thought you were asleep," she said. She quickly regained her composure. "I doubt I'll close my eyes. I keep picturing . . . those poor men."

"Death is seldom pretty," Joel remarked, a hint of bitterness in his voice.

"When the police brought my husband to me," she said, calmly reflective, removed as she was from Jaimie's suicide by distance and time, "he wore a similar expression . . . surprised and terribly hurt that his day was done. But, of course, he had not been mutilated by Cheyenne savages."

"I have my doubts about that."

"You would. Am I cruel? I am speaking my mind is all. Joel, you must admit your past might be coloring your present judgment."

"That isn't what I mean. I know what state the Red Shields are in. Those men had been riddled with bullets. Shot with arrows. It is a matter of simple arithmetic. No Indian could afford to squander his ammunition in such a manner. It is too hard to come by. Those men weren't merely killed! They were made an example of."

"Can you be sure it wasn't your friends?"

"No. Not yet."

Sarah had misgivings as to what he meant. She glanced at the Bible in his hands, it was open to the Psalms.

"Who's Priam?"

Joel looked at her, puzzled, then realized she must have opened the Bible before.

"A friend. Just a good friend. He left the Bible for me. Said since I never took his advice, maybe I'd listen to a higher authority. Reckon I listened more than he knew." Joel closed the Bible, rubbing his hand across the worn leather binding. "He came here, sick with the fever, and no wish to slow up the others. Sacred Killer was on the run from General Crook's troopers. Priam stayed and the Cheyenne fell back into the mountains. The old man wasn't sick long."

Sarah caught his meaning. She found herself staring at him and decided she would be better off removed to her bedroom. She started back the way she had come.

"Sarah?"

"Yes." Turning, she saw how his eyes were like the cobalt reaches of the sky.

"I'm glad you came with me. When Jessup made his offer, I wasn't sure . . . well . . . what I am trying to . . ."

"Mister Silvertip Ryan, I am a woman of my word. Captain Bixby said the boat would not be ready for a month, and to that end I agreed to come here and tend your house. It was the least I could do as I am in your debt."

A fold of the blanket fell away revealing the bodice of her sleeping gown. She caught the material and clutched it close to her bosom.

"Good-night," she added, and blushing, closed the bedroom door. The latch within slid home with depressing finality. Joel returned the Bible to its place among the police gazettes.

"A debt," he muttered, mentally noting how Sarah was certainly a woman of fire.

Most certainly.

And keeping her at the center of his thoughts held at bay the myriad other worries. Who had killed the ranchhands? What course of action would Colonel Jessup choose now that war had been carried to him?

Joel cupped his hand and blew out the lamp.

He closed the front door and made his way down the gentle slope, passing the cabin set in its stillness and awash with dark memories. In the moonlight he saw Cub kneeling beside the sparkling waters of Otter Creek.

Joel spied the flames of Cub's cookfire and allowed the mouth-watering aroma of roasted rabbit to lead him to the youth's campfire. Cub said nothing, his attention riveted on his dinner. Joel cupped cold creekwater to his face and neck. Refreshed, he sat back on his haunches and watched his son. My God, he thought, twelve years, it seemed impossible. Cub lifted his catch from the fire and started to tear off a strip of meat, paused and offered the first portion to his father. Joel tore off a leg and handed the wooden spit back to the boy. Joel ate, making his satisfaction known, punctuating each swallow with a smack of the lips.

"Maybe I should have you do all the cooking," he grinned.

"I used to," Cub replied sourly. He devoured his portion of the meal. Joel let the matter drop without further comment. The subject of Sarah was a trap better avoided. But Cub would be a grown man someday and understand what needs had prompted Joel to bring Sarah and her family out to Morning Star. Joel finished eating, wiped his mouth on his sleeve, and stood.

"We Ryans have a sense about such things. It's right for

Sarah to be here. I feel it in my bones. And you do too. That's what has you treed."

The boy continued to eat, giving the impression he was totally ignoring his father.

"This is a matter a man must work out for himself. Know one thing, Cub, you are my son. And I love you." Joel tossed his bone scraps into the creek and started back up from the muddy bank. A wolf howled in the depths of the forest. Joel listened until he was certain the cry was indeed that of a wild animal. He resolved to keep his rifle close at hand, tonight and tomorrow and the next. If it wasn't Sacred Killer, still someone had killed Jessup's men. Who knew where the marauders might strike next?

Cub was glad for the solitude. His affection for his father was no less than Joel's love for him, yet he appreciated privacy. His mind and heart were troubled and had been since morning when Fiona found him in the barn and asked him if it were true he was staying alone at the ranch. He had been busy fetching a bait of grain to the horses in the stalls and had no time for little girls. He started to gruffly tell her so, but the gentle look on her face tamed him and tempered his reply.

"Yes," he had managed to say, in a tone that invited her to leave him alone.

"Won't you be lonely?"

"No."

"I'd be lonely. And scared."

"That's because you're a girl," Cub retorted.

Fiona ignored the slight with the casual disregard every child her age possessed. "I'll leave Tiny with you. She will look after you," she said, eyes bright with cleverness.

"I am not a child to play with toys," Cub answered to no avail. Fiona busily instructed her doll to mind Cub and do whatever Cub said and to behave and drink all her milk and keep Cub from feeling too sad because Cub was very nice even though he tried to act mean sometimes. Then Sarah had called, and Fiona turned to the half-breed youth.

"That's my Mommy. I have to go now."

"Take your—" Cub started to say, but the girl, with the

swiftness of a startled doe, was gone before the boy could finish. Cub had shrugged and gone about his chores, hesitating only once to listen to the wagon roll from the yard, axles creaking as Joel called out to the team of horses. Cub had felt an urge to run and join them, but he waited, and moments later the opportunity was lost.

The call of the wolf was answered by another, sounding faint and terribly forlorn in the darkness. Cub watched the rippling water of the creek, felt night close round him as the fire slowly exhausted itself. He mirrored then the man he would grow to be, a man caught between two worlds, at home in neither.

Obscured in darkness, safe within night's all-concealing womb, he reached inside his shirt for Fiona's doll, and looking down on it, he did a very strange thing for one whose mind and heart were so beleaguered.

He smiled.

Like a page of a book, the meadow told its story printed in blood. The churned earth about the blackened patch of yesterday's campfire told of death, terrible and swift. The yellow grass wore its garish red stain and trembled in the chill breeze. Joel dismounted. Calming the roan with a gentle pat on the neck, he glanced up to gauge the time of day. He had ridden out from Morning Star before dawn and wanted to be back by afternoon.

"Plenty of time," he said to himself and knelt beside the ashes of the camp. There was little to be made from the jumbled tracks. He studied the dirt, trying to form some kind of order out of the assault. There were boot tracks, but they belonged more than likely to Jessup's men, and a surfeit of moccasin tracks and those of unshod ponies as well, which only supported the claim that the attackers had been Indians. He poked the remains of the campfire with a twig, stirred something shiny out of the black earth. A button.

The last will and testament of a cowboy—a shirt button in the ashes of his camp. Precious little to leave behind. Joel tossed the memento aside and stood, letting the breeze wash his face with the cool breath of autumn. Why had he come? To prove to himself Sacred Killer's innocence? The chief of the Red Shields had shed his share of white man's blood. But that was the past. The battles of yesterday. Now the Cheyenne only wanted to be left alone, to live their lives out in the mountain sanctuaries that hid them. Joel began to circle the camp, increasing his radius from the campsite a few yards at a time. A hawk circled overhead. Clouds gathered behind Moon Woman Mountain to the west. The distant peak was capped with the gray bonnet of an isolated rain shower

that clung to the tree tops in a trail of vapors as ghostly as
the legend that gave the mountain its name.

Joel did not know what he was looking for until he found
it. A set of tracks. Two sets, really. A man had run barefoot
out into the meadow. And stopped. And from the look of the
blood-stamped ground, died. That was not the problem nor
what filled Joel with foreboding and a sense of fatedness, of
vengeful anticipation. And dread. An impression left by a
boot alternating with a curious round hole in the soft earth.
Bootprint and round hole. These were the tracks of a peg-
legged man.

*The man fleeing from the porch, the cabin stark and
empty, the feeling of panic like a knife in the gut, the sense
of loss, of unutterable pain, of her name repeated in his
mind. . . .*

It couldn't be, Joel stared at the tracks, at the footprints
trailing from violence to more violence. He lifted his eyes to
the hills, to the emerald hills and pearly clouds, to the clean
clear wondrous beauty of the wilderness that now seemed
sullied at the whisper of a name.

"Larocque."

Sean charged. Cub had size and speed on his side. Sean
missed, only to be clubbed by the half-breed's fist as he
rushed past. Sean howled, brought up sharp by the pain. He
took small comfort in the fact that Cub was nursing his sorely
bruised knuckles.

Sean rushed the older boy while he was preoccupied with
his aching fist and Sarah called for them both to stop. They
ignored her. Cub met the charge and threw Sean to the
ground and leaped on top of him, pinning his shoulders. Sean
bucked free. Both boys crawled to their knees and began to
flail at one another with their fists. They never heard the roan
charge through the garden furrows and were oblivious to the
man who towered over them until he yanked them apart.
Sean fell over on his backside. Cub staggered, then started
forward.

"Stop it. The both of you!" Joel snapped. His son was
brought up sharply at the command but continued to stare at
Sean, carrying on the contest in his look if not in practice.

Sarah ran up with tagalong Fiona not far behind.

"Don't," Joel said, turning on the woman before she had a chance to speak. He had ridden all the way from Mission Meadow hounded by his own dark misgivings and was in a sour mood from the ordeal. He appraised first the dirt-smudged and cut faces of the two boys; Sean's black eye, Cub's swollen lip. Behind them, and testimony to the youths' failure to cooperate, the split rail garden fence Joel had instructed them to mend lay in the same ruinous state as it had the afternoon of the McClintons' arrival at Morning Star. An inquisitive bear, from the paw prints, had decided to explore the garden and ripped his way through the blockade while Joel and Cub were at the settlement.

"He started it," Sean blurted out.

"You provoked me. It is your doing."

"He hit me."

"Hold it!" Joel demanded.

"He called me a stupid breed."

"I did not. I just said Fiona could read better than you," Sean retorted.

"Shut up! The both of you," Joel ordered, fixing one and then the other in his steely stare.

"Really, Joel," Sarah began. "I think I can—"

"You too!"

"Well I never," Sarah replied, exasperated at his behavior, but Joel had already turned his attention back to the boys who threatened any second to lunge at one another again. The only thing holding them at bay was the dominating presence of Joel Ryan. He intended to nip this in the bud, right now, for their sake. Maybe for their very survival.

"You see that stump yonder?" Joel said, pointing toward the yard behind the house. Both boys looked in the direction he indicated.

"Say, 'Yes sir!' " said Joel.

"Yes sir," answered Cub and Sean in ragged unison.

"Ever since I chopped down that pine, I've been meaning to clear the stump. Can't add on to the house with it right in the way. You boys are going to haul it out."

Cub glanced up in amazement. Sean paled. It was a good-sized stump.

"No food. Not a scrap until it's done," said Joel. "How you haul it out is your business. But haul it you will, no matter how long it takes."

"But—" Cub began. His father turned his back on him, grabbed Sarah by the arm, and hauled her toward the house, Fiona hurrying after them. Cub and Sean looked at one another and then at the massive old stump.

"Not a scrap of food," Cub mimicked sourly.

"It's going to be a long year," Sean moaned, his stomach already growling.

Joel brought a ladder-back chair out on the porch and, tilting it against the log wall, rested in the shade, balancing his gloomy speculations about the return of Larocque with the lighter task of listening to the boys grunt and groan as they strove with youthful muscles to wrest the stump from the hard ground. From time to time, Sarah appeared on the porch, her frowning expression speaking her disapproval. Once she said, "They're only boys."

"My order stands. There is a time a man bends to a woman's will. And time a woman accedes to the man's."

"Meaning I have no say in this," Sarah replied.

"Exactly."

Sarah spun and disappeared inside with a flounce of her skirt. It amused him to picture her fuming inside the house. He could hear Cub cry out, "Pull . . . pull!"

And Sean retort, "I am!"

He was, too.

Movement at the door. Sarah walked out onto the porch. She hung a round mirror from one of the pole supports and set a mug of lather and a bucket of water on the step. She held out a straight razor to him.

"I found this in the bedroom."

"It's mine," Joel said, scratching inadvertently at his silver-streaked beard.

"There is a time a man bends to a woman's will. This is one of those times," she said. "Not a scrap of peach cobbler shall you be getting, Mister Joel Ryan, until you come to the supper table looking like a proper and fitting gentleman instead of some wild man of the forest."

Sarah placed the razor in his hand and with a triumphant gleam in her eye returned to the house, leaving the door ajar to allow the mouth-watering aroma of a freshly baked peach cobbler to waft through the entranceway. Joel tried to ignore the wonderful smell. Who did she think she was, ordering him around? He ought to . . . Lord, it smelled good . . . ought to . . . peach cobbler. He ought to . . . shave.

Beneath the unruly silver mane, beneath the full beard, was a youthful man in his mid-thirties.

I'd forgotten I had a chin, Joel thought, running a hand over the lighter, smooth skin of his jaw. He sensed eyes on him and saw Cub and Sean staring from the side yard. They had just come out of the barn. There was a curious bulge in Cub's hip pocket. The boys had noticed Joel and stopped to watch. Sean and Cub looked much the worse for wear. Their shoulders sagged; their hands were blistered and raw from the afternoon's efforts. The sun was balanced on the tree tops to the west, promising no more than another hour of daylight. Shadows were on the march across Otter Creek.

"Peach cobbler for dessert, boys," Joel said with all good cheer. The boys cast sick glances at one another and hurried in step past the corner of the house. Sarah's pretty face materialized in the mirror. Joel turned to look at her.

"I dare say, it's quite an improvement, to be sure," Sarah said, caught off guard by his craggy but undeniably handsome features. The slightly askew slant of his nose was appealing in a way. Perhaps it was the suggestion of past pain that brought out a need to comfort him. She began to blush.

"I liked you better as a giant," Fiona observed, peeking past her mother's skirt.

"I haven't shrunk, I hope," Joel laughed. He touched his chin, gingerly patting the place where he had nicked himself. "I need to get the hang of shaving again." He caught Sarah's stare, meeting her gaze. She immediately glanced aside.

"I hope you're in a better mood then. I think the boys certainly have had their fill of labor."

The explosion rattled the shutters and knocked a loose shingle from the roof of the porch. Fiona cried out in alarm, and Sarah, off balance, fell into Joel's arms. He set her back on her feet and vaulted from the porch, hitting the ground at a dead run. An ominous gray brown cloud mushroomed upward from the rear of the house.

"Cub!" he shouted. "Sean!"

Sarah swept Fiona into her arms and hurried after Joel, too startled to utter a sound. Ears ringing from the detonation, Joel rounded the house, remembering the bulge in Cub's pocket. Dynamite! They must have taken dynamite from the storage room in the barn. Heart leaping to his throat, Joel cleared the dirt-covered back of the ranch house. Through the slow clearing haze of settling dust, he glimpsed the smoldering, blackened tree stump lying on its side, its roots like stubby tentacles jutting from the base.

"Cub! Sean!" Joel called, his throat constricted with fear for their safety.

"Oh my God," Sarah gasped, from behind, clutching Fiona to her for safety's sake. Suddenly, they heard laughter, a merry revelry sprung from two young throats. Tendrils of brown haze parted by the wind to reveal Cub and Sean, arms draped around each other's shoulders trying to hold one another up.

"Are we in time for dessert?" Cub asked. Sean pointed to the stump, and the boys, together, laughed and laughed. *Together*.

36

Like a tiger's eye burning in the cauldron of the night, firelight gleamed and beckoned Sarah as she walked down to the creek. Her restless thoughts kept her from sleep. It had been a day of remarkable change. She had watched Sean and Cub begin as antagonists. By sunset they were friends, their bond of mutual respect forged in the task of removing the stump. They had learned cooperation in the face of a common ordeal. Other changes she had noted in herself. Skills perfected during a childhood spent on her father's farm had surfaced anew these past weeks until it became as second nature to feed the chickens, gather eggs, and milk old Evelyn, the cow.

She kept the butter churn handy now and relished the first cool drink of buttermilk dipped right from the churn.

And then there was Joel. Not a day passed but she grew more accustomed to his fierce appearance. And she began to see the gentleness in him and a kind of wisdom that came from living without the ploys and petty subterfuges that the civilized world often demanded. She was attracted to him, yes. The clean lines of his face. The way his eyes seemed haunted with sadness and yet ever willing to dazzle her with their sudden merry frankness.

And so it came to pass that Sarah McClinton paused in her stroll to watch the cabin with its amber window gleaming against a dark façade. The firelight beckoned as it had on other nights when she wandered restless beneath the autumn moon. And as the day had been one of change, why not the night? She glanced at the ranch house, reassured the children were abed, and then answered the call of desire. It had been a long time. Too long, she thought and crossed soundlessly to the cabin.

• • •

Joel stared at his journal, tracing the hand-tooled buckskin binding with his fingertips. He wet his lips, dipped his pen in the inkwell at his side, and began to write.

It is the eleventh of October. Late evening. My son has deserted me, forsaken the pallet here in our cabin to sleep in his own bed, in his own room, with Fiona and Sean. I could not be happier, for the boys discovered something valuable today. Friendship. It is a lesson men must learn, or perish. Unfortunately, the satisfaction I feel must be weighed against this morning's disturbing discovery. Has Henri Larocque come back into my life? What harm, now, does he bring to plague me? And why has he returned now, after all these many years?

Joel sensed Sarah and looked up from his writing. A gust of wind stirred the pages of his journal, and his pen left a spreading black stain where the point had pressed against the page. The hem of her blanket wrap stirred in the passing wind.

"Am I disturbing you?"

"No," Joel said. He waved a hand toward one of the bunk beds. "Have a seat." He was stretched out on a buffalo robe near the hearth. The blaze highlighted the subtle textures of his bronzed flesh as he reached for his shirt. Sarah closed the door, walked across the room, and sat on the edge of a bunk bed. She smiled nervously and began to fidget with the corner of the blanket, picking at a loose thread while in her mind the woman marveled at her own conduct. Joel filled a cup with coffee and held it out to her. She accepted and took a tentative sip and scrunched her features.

"That's awful," she said.

"The grounds are a bit old," Joel agreed.

"You really ought to bury them and put them out of their misery."

Joel studied her a moment until she broke out in open laughter at his expression. Then he smiled.

"Suddenly you are as full of mischief as our two sons," he said.

"The dreadful little collaborators. I thank God they weren't hurt," Sarah said, changing the subject.

"I ought to have paddled their behinds," Joel added, as Sarah crawled down to warm her hands at the fire.

"At least Cub is under the roof. The two of them have their beds side by side," Sarah said. "They're talking about going hunting tomorrow. Sean has never hunted in his life, but Cub told him he would teach him to track. And Sean will help Cub with reading . . ." Her voice trailed away as her eyes met his.

"If you're cold, Sarah," Joel left his suggestion unspoken. Sarah blushed. Kneeling by the fire had been a ploy. Artifice had never been her strong suit. She averted her gaze and tried to stand.

"I better go," she said. But he caught her by the arm and pulled her back down to his hungry lips and impatient embrace.

"Stop," Sarah gasped. He held her close, forcing her down onto the robe. She did not resist.

"Say it as though you mean it, and I will," said Joel. Sarah looked at him and then answered with a kiss of fire.

In the silent passage of the night, lovers dare to touch and feel, to explore with tongue and lips and hand, the vulnerable flesh of their beloved. Hard bronze muscles tense, supple cream-colored flesh accepts his fierce strength, the heated climax and afterwards, passion's own humbling fulfillment. Love makes lust holy, enshrines the carnal need, the tender deed, two becoming one, two called together from horizons far, called together, made whole.

One is a sacred word in the language of the heart.

Joel stole softly from Sarah's side to watch from the window a star-flung panoply outlining in the dark distance a single dominating summit. Naked, Sarah took her place behind him. Their bodies radiated the warmth of their lovemaking. "You have been in the wilderness a long time," she said, more of an observation than a question.

"Long enough to know the lizards by their first names, except maybe the babies," Joel smiled.

"I think I know you. And then, a moment later, I don't."

"Do you know yourself so very well?"

"I thought I did. But now, I'm not certain."

"The land works its change. It happened to me too. And still does. I just let things take their own course and believe in the land. My past is the day before. My future is the morning," said Joel.

"Are things really so simple with you? Have you truly reduced all of life's frustration and hurt to that simple little formula?"

"No," Joel laughed softly. "But it sounds good. I try to live like that, though."

"Your wife was killed? I asked Sweeney and—well—I hope I wasn't prying too much."

Joel frowned a moment, as if an old wound had begun to ache. "She was murdered, here in this cabin by a man named Larocque." Sarah glanced around, stepped closer to him, not out of fear but a need to comfort him. "One day you think you have everything and then—nothing," he went on. "You stray too deep in the woods and can't find your way home. You ride too near the edge of a cliff, and it crumbles away. You duck to the left and stop the bullet that would have missed you if only you had jumped to the right."

"And sometimes," Sarah said, lost in her thoughts, "you simply give up because the world isn't quite what you expected, so you run and hide, you find a rope and sling it over a cross beam and tighten a noose about your neck and jump." She wiped moisture from the corner of her eye and rested her cheek against Joel's arm. "Funny, a man who doesn't have the courage to live can find the courage to die." She sniffed and sighed. "Look at us, trailing out our ghosts, like linen to be hung out to dry."

"There's a little of the washerwoman in each of us," Joel said, putting his arm around her. "I never thought I would be like this again, or feel like this."

Sarah placed her fingers on his lips. She did not want him to speak to her of love. She was not ready for endearments in the night. "Who was Moon Woman?" she asked, staring out at the mountain's dark silhouette.

"A woman of the Morning Star People. Her husband, Black Whirlwind, was a mighty warrior. While out hunting, he was set upon by a Pawnee war party intent on attacking Black Whirlwind's village. Rather than flee and risk leading the Pawnees to his village, Black Whirlwind chose to fight. He killed many Pawnee braves before being mortally wounded. His body was hacked to pieces and scattered over the mountainside. Moon Woman loved him deeply, and when she learned what had befallen him, she set out to roam the mountainside. A storm caught her as she was searching for the remains of her loved one. Moon Woman froze to death during the night. It's said her spirit roams the slopes and forest, still searching for Black Whirlwind, still trying to make him whole that she might give him a fitting and honorable burial. It is said her ghost can never rest until she has completed her task." He paused, "There are those who have seen her."

"Saints be praised," Sarah shuddered, stepping close. "I suppose to the primitive mind anything is possible."

"I have seen her," Joel added.

Sarah saw he was not jesting.

"Do you find it hard to believe, Sarah McClinton? Stranger things have happened," Joel said, taking her in his arms. "Tonight for instance. I never thought you would be here, like this, with me." Sarah started to reply, but he put his fingers to her lips, hushing her. Then he lifted her in his arms and carried her back to his bed of robes. She did not protest.

She lay beneath him, her eyes closed, giving herself to sensation as his lips explored the length of her excited flesh. She cupped her breasts, sighed deeply as his tongue found her stomach and circled her navel, as his teeth nipped a path down to the auburn ringlets of her sex. And when he loved her then, drinking the nectar of her, Sarah cried his name, and her body rippled with ecstasy. He would not allow the sea to calm but aroused one tempest after another until time itself became a single spinning storm, and when he sheathed himself at last, driving into her with a fury as uncontrollable as any act of nature, Sarah cried and clawed his shoulders and matched his passion with her own. At last, the world went crashing—like a mirror in the boundary of which lovers live and die and play out the sweet tormented skein of their lives—crashing, and his strength melted within her.

He whispered her name.

She held him.

Their shadows, made one, danced in flickering relief upon the wall until the fire died.

Sarah woke to an unearthly brilliance seeping through the partly shuttered window. She shivered; the room was as cold as the ashes in the hearth. The temperature had dropped with the arrival of a Canadian front, catching Otter Creek in its glory of golden fall foliage. Sarah crept from Joel's warm side and, wrapped in her blanket, she crossed to the window, tracking the brilliance to its source. The world wore a mantle of white flocking. Oak trees and pine, chokecherry bush and Russian thistle, blue stem and cattail, the buildings of Morning Star, the very earth itself as far as the eye could see was cloaked in fragile majesty, nature's wondrous and delicate creation, not rain or ice, not quite snow.

She turned to wake Joel and saw he was almost dressed.

"I saw it earlier. You were asleep. Yukon wind must have passed through. I doubt it will last the morning, the sun usually burns it off."

"I never saw anything like it," Sarah said.

"The bones of the rain," Joel said, buttoning his shirt. "There's a Cheyenne word, but that's what it means."

"So beautiful. As if we stepped into a fairy land."

"Sarah, the children will be up soon." Joel regretted the remark. She frowned, the enormity of her indiscretion coming home to roost in her Christian conscience. She stared out at the world—oh how exquisite in its magical trappings. And yet, how temporary. Like a dream that vanishes with the light of day, so too the bones of the rain.

"And what does morning hold for us?" Sarah asked, facing him now. "I came to you, I gave myself and took my pleasure as did you. I don't even know what I . . . feel toward you. Only that I acted like some animal in heat."

"Sarah, we are animals. But animals who can think and care and love," Joel said. He moved to take her in his arms. She stepped past him to gather her clothes. Suddenly her shoulders began to shudder. He heard a sob.

"Sarah . . ."

"Last night, you said, 'My future is tomorrow.' Maybe that's enough for you. But I need more."

His hands touched her naked shoulders.

"The first time I saw you . . . I knew. Like with Mourning Dove, I knew. Don't ask me how. But what happened last evening was good and right. You are trying so hard to pin down your emotions, you don't even have time to feel. You're like a . . . a store clerk, weighing everything. But the heart isn't apples and flour. Sarah, do you understand what I'm trying to say?"

"The children will be up soon," Sarah repeated his words. "Please, I should like to dress in privacy."

"I shouldn't see now what I saw last night?"

"Please," she pleaded, her eyes were red-rimmed and puffy. Joel sighed and slapped his thigh in exasperation.

"I have no regrets. I won't color what I feel with sin and damnation. I am what I am. And if you cannot accept the life I'm offering, then you'd best be certain you reach Osage Bixby in time to book passage to St. Louis. You asked what the morning holds for us." He opened the door and looked back at her. "I'll tell you. Breakfast!"

Joel spun on his heels, took two steps outside and came to an abrupt halt. Cub stood before him, looking past his father at Sarah, framed in the doorway and struggling into her dress.

Sarah managed to cover herself in a somewhat haphazard fashion. Silence, heavy as lead, lingered in the still air.

"I'll be needing to bring the cattle down from pasture. You want to come along?" asked Joel.

Cub made no reply but continued on down to Otter Creek, leaving his set of solitary tracks in the bones of the rain.

37

The sun, burning its molten gold trajectory past noon had long since melted the morning's frost when a rifle shot shattered the peaceful and pristine scene of cattle grazing in the upland meadow.

A shorthorn's compact, rust-colored frame shuddered on impact from the big .45 slug. The steer collapsed in the dust, its legs kicking out in a comic dance as the report of Tod Jessup's Winchester reverberated off the hills.

"You've had your fun," said Jim Reasoner, who was standing a few paces back from the son of his employer. A hundred and fifty yards away, the steer Tod had shot shuddered and died.

"Like hell," Tod snapped. "Ain't even begun." The youth flexed his arm and lifted the rifle to his shoulder.

"A man ought to celebrate his twentieth birthday with a bang, Pa always said. I'm just following his advice."

The Winchester cracked. Out in the meadow, another Morning Star steer, this time one of Joel's breed bulls, staggered and dropped. By this time the cattle were spooked. But with the echo of the rifle spilling back from a dozen hills, the stock could only mill in a circle, uncertain which way to run from danger.

"The colonel wouldn't approve of this," Reasoner said angrily. He had followed young Tod, suspecting the youth had mischief on his mind. The foreman reached for Tod who pulled free and leveled the rifle at Frank Jessup's right-hand man. Perspiration beaded Reasoner's forehead.

"Leave me alone or face the music," Tod snarled. Whiskey made him mean, and dangerous. "That no good squaw man's red brothers killed four of our men. You forgetting that?"

"No. But Ryan wasn't involved, boy. And if he was, it's for Slade to deal with him. It's business for the law."

"Slade's a gambler and whore runner." Tod lowered the rifle and returned his attention to the cattle, bawling in the meadow. A calf attracted his attention. "Ryan knew the attack was coming. Maybe he even planned it. I say the time has come to let him know the Bar Seven won't put up with any of his shenanigans. If Father's afraid to settle the score, I ain't." He spat a stream of tobacco on a nearby stump, and balancing his rifle in the crook of the tree he was using for cover, he sighted along the barrel, putting the gunsight a few inches above the calf.

"And I ain't a goddamn boy no more," Tod added.

Suddenly, the crook of the tree exploded in a shower of bark, and the Winchester was ripped from Tod's grasp by the slug glancing off his rifle barrel. He yelped and staggered away from the tree, his cheek numb where the rifle stock had caught him, his face bleeding from half-a-dozen superficial cuts.

Reasoner grabbed for his sidearm, but a voice challenged him from the depths of the forest, and his fingers loosened on the wooden grip of his Colt.

"I wouldn't, Jim. Unless you want to wind up like that bull of mine," Joel's voice rang out.

"Take him," Tod ordered through clenched teeth.

"Hell, I can't even see him. What are you saying?"

Tod dabbed at his bloody cheek and glanced forlornly at the rifle.

Hidden in the shadows, Joel glanced over at the meadow and his dead cattle. The steer he could butcher, but the bull was a staggering loss. Sarah's behavior this morning, Cub's silence, the tiring ride up from the ranch, and now this. Joel was angry. He could only guess why Tod had begun killing the cattle—as some form of retribution for the dead men of the Bar Seven. Tod had been aching for a confrontation with Joel; it was high time his wish came true.

"Saddle up, Jim," he yelled.

Down in the stand of post oak, Reasoner looked toward the woods in surprise. Tod started for his own mount.

"Not you, Jessup. You'll be along later. You and I have something to settle."

Tod looked at the gunbelt he had draped across his saddle pommel. If he could only reach the Colt. Reasoner read his thoughts.

"Don't be a fool. He's way out of range and probably would like nothing better than to dust the seat of your pants with a .45," Reasoner said, then shouted in the general direction of the voice, "He's been drinking, Ryan. I've come to bring him home to the colonel."

"I'll send him along directly. After we come to an understanding."

"The colonel won't like it," Reasoner said.

"That's too bad."

Reasoner shrugged and walked over to his horse. Tod paled.

"You aren't leaving?" he asked.

"This is between you and Silvertip. I warned you, but you wouldn't listen. Well listen now. Hit hard and dirty 'cause Ryan will be doing the same."

"Leave me your rifle?"

"And get you killed? Not hardly."

"I'll have your ass for this," Tod said. "I swear."

"Yeah you probably will." The foreman sighed. He glanced back at the forested slope. "You're buying yourself a whole peck of trouble, Ryan. You hear me?"

The land echoed back . . . hear me—hear me—hear me. Reasoner swore beneath his breath and rode out of the grove and across the meadow, scattering the cattle as he galloped over the yellow grass.

Tod waited. He stripped off his denim jacket and rolled up his sleeves.

"Come on, old man. Where the devil are you? Come on. You got a big mouth when you're hiding."

Nothing moved. Nothing stirred.

Tod might as well have been alone in the world. It dawned on him he had frightened Ryan off. Now wouldn't that be a hoot, to have made Mister Silvertip Ryan back down! Tod was alone and waiting on no one. That was it.

"Tod," a voice called from behind. The younger man

whirled about to face Joel as the man from Morning Star
emerged from concealment. Tod was visibly startled that Joel
had managed to approach without being discovered.

"You bastard," Tod hissed.

"An accident of birth for some," Joel replied. "But you,
boy, are self-taught." The absence of a beard might have
made Joel seem less forbidding were it not for the ice-blue
eyes, mercilessly cold, challenging, as unforgiving as the
howling wilderness itself. Tod shifted his weight, his hard
solid frame swaying from side to side like a bull preparing
to charge. Joel set his rifle aside and unbuttoned his sheep-
skin coat. As he pulled it down over his shoulders, Tod remembered Reasoner's advice, "Hit hard and dirty." The
younger man lowered his head and charged, his arms, like
tree limbs, ready to crush his opponent while Joel's arms
were imprisoned in the coat. Joel's beaded buckskin shirt
filled the younger man's vision. Just as Tod yelled in triumph
at having caught Silvertip off guard, Joel moved with a
quickness that seemed impossible for a man of his size. One
moment he was at the mercy of his attacker, and the next,
completely out of harm's way, darting aside with the quickness of a mountain cat. Tod shot past, tripped over Joel's
outstretched leg and slammed his skull against the slim trunk
of a post oak with enough force to bury himself in a momentary shower of golden leaves. Grunting, he sat on his
haunches and shook his head to clear his senses. He rolled
over on his back, a round hard lump protruding from his
swollen skull.

Joel pulled his coat on, knelt by Tod. He was unconscious
but none the worse for wear, except for the nasty bruise. Joel
made certain the young man's horse was securely tethered
and then started up the hill to his own mount. Tod was going
to have a nasty headache in a few hours, Joel thought to
himself, his anger dissipating. There was a certain satisfaction in seeing Tod stretched out unconscious. He'd have a
dandy headache for sure. And so would Colonel Jessup for
that matter—in the form of a bill for a full-grown cow and
the prize shorthorn breed bull Tod had wantonly destroyed.

A few minutes later Joel Ryan was preoccupied with
single-handedly driving the cattle down from their high

country grazing land to the smaller but adequate pasture around Otter Creek. He wanted them closer to home in case of an early snow. Once the hundred head got started in the same direction, the task became more manageable, but for a few hours Cub was sorely needed. Joel had no sooner rounded the steers and got them moving than the strays would break rank and scatter for the underbrush. Chasing them out into the open took its toll. Then the whole forward-moving process would have to be begun anew.

It was a time-consuming and demanding job requiring his complete attention. Joel assumed he was alone in the valley and paid no attention to where Tod was sprawled among the trees. Joel's efforts were riveted to the task at hand. He never noticed the glimmer of sunlight off a spyglass or the shad-owy shapes that stole from cover and headed for Tod Jes-sup's helpless form.

Still life in the wilderness: A man alone, riding a roan stal-lion. Cattle leave a trailing plume of dust, masking the green-gold majesty of the hills in a gritty haze at sunset.

> "Down in the valley
> my sweet lady lives,
> Sunrise and sunsets
> are all that she gives.
> And comfort a-plenty
> That sets my heart free,
> One Otter Creek lady
> is plenty for me.
>
> "So come on, you dogies,
> It's late in the day.
> Sing ti yi yee,
> Ti yi yi yay."

Joel tried for a second verse but gave up and decided to be satisfied with the first and a chorus. A calf bellowed for its ma, and Joel saw the steer head for the underbrush. He yanked on the reins and guided the roan behind the herd, holding his breath until he cleared the worst of the dust, then

he spurred his horse to a gallop and cut the stray off halfway
up the hillside. The animal tried to alter its course, came to
a skidding halt, bawled in terror, and started down the slope
at a brisk run with Joel's roan nipping at the steer's heels all
the way to the herd. The cattle at the rear hurried their pace,
alarmed at the horseman's brisk approach. The stray returned
to the fold; Joel eased to one side out of the dust, and the
roan settled into an easy gait, mindful as any good cowpony
of its charges. Suddenly, Joel saw the Appaloosa and its rider
emerge from the woods riding hell-bent across the meadow.
The cattle were visible on the sloping trail. The steers already
sensed good grazing in the meadow below and smelled the
clear cold water of Otter Creek as well as the springs dotting
their pasture. Joel had a premonition of emergency and grabbing his bedroll, loosed the blanket and gave a rebel yell.
The cattle, struck with terror at the blanket-waving, shrill-
voiced creature on the trail behind them, broke into a mad
dash for safety. Minutes later a hundred bawling, panic-
stricken steers spread out over the meadow, and those in
Joel's way scattered when he passed. Sean reined the Appaloosa alongside the roan.

"Mister Ryan," the boy blurted out. "The Indians—Indians got my Ma. I mean she's got them. I was hunting with
Cub, but I forgot my slingshot and headed home for it and
saw my Ma with the Indians. She told me to ride for help!"

Joel whipped the roan to a gallop. If these were the braves
who had killed Jessup's men, Sarah was in real danger. He
should never have left her alone. Never. If Larocque was
there . . . *Oh God! Not again. It can't happen again!*

The roan's hooves thundered on the earth. The animal
never slowed when it reached the forest. Joel held the horse
to a gallop, threading his way at top speed through stands of
white pine and aspen, keeping to the deer trails he had ridden
a thousand times from Otter Creek, ridden and worn into
paths he knew by heart, sensing every twist and turn and
hoping his memory would not fail him. A single lapse would
send him headlong to injury or death.

Then the forest grew less dense, gave way to a fringe of
post oaks and a gradual decline to the creekbed.

Water exploded in a shower of shimmering jewels,

drenching horse and rider. He reached the opposite bank. Was he too late? The barn was blocking his line of sight. *Hemené! Sarah!* he screamed in his mind. He slid his rifle from its scabbard and levered a fresh cartridge into the chamber.

The corral swept past and then the barn itself; the front yard and the tableau it contained brought Joel to a hasty stop, hauling on the reins to keep from colliding with the two braves who sat motionless upon their warpaint-decorated stallions in the waning light. Sarah stood at the top of the porch steps, a shotgun cradled in her arms, a breeze ruffling her long cotton shirt.

The braves turned as Joel approached. He had recognized their mounts and already knew the warriors' identities.

"Haa-he, White Frog. Haa-he, Sacred Killer, my brother," Joel called out. The braves, having been held at gunpoint by a woman for the better part of an hour did not look especially pleased. And Sarah looked equally perplexed at Joel's familiarity. She appeared to be trying to decide whether or not to lower the shotgun or swing the barrel to cover all three of the men.

"Sarah," Joel said. "Please don't shoot Cub's uncle." Sarah glanced from Joel to the stern-faced warrior he had nodded toward, and blushing with embarrassment, she lowered the muzzle of the shotgun.

"I didn't know," she said.

Sean, fearful he was too late for the excitement rode full tilt past the barn, managing to bring his skittish pony to an abrupt stop. The Appaloosa, with the sour disposition of his sire, bucked the boy out of the saddle. Sean landed on his seat in the dirt.

"Darn it, Patch," he shouted at the pony. The boy dusted his pants off and glared at the horse who glared right back. Sean watched in surprise as Joel led White Frog and Sacred Killer to the barn. Joel wanted the war ponies out of sight as quickly as possible. White Frog glanced at the boy, said something in Cheyenne to Sacred Killer who chuckled. *At my expense,* Sean thought, scowling. He walked somewhat stiffly to the house where his mother watched, concerned.

"I'm okay," he snapped, before she could caution him.

"Patch likes to run a lot more than he likes to stop is all. What happened, Mother?"

"Nothing," Sarah said. "They're friends." She watched the braves vanish into the barn, pausing to watch the sun disappear beyond the western hills.

"Friends of Joel," she added, wondering if that was good or bad.

Sarah hated surprises. Especially when they came to supper half naked, faces streaked with paint; especially when they came armed with war shields and cruel-looking lances and rifles.

Sarah ladled a portion of stew into each of the children's bowls, then she carried the cast-iron stewpot outside where the Indians, the children, and Joel squatted in a circle by a campfire.

"Your dinner is inside," Sarah said to Sean, Cub, and Fiona.

"Can't we eat out here, Mother?" Sean could not take his eyes off the first true Indians he had ever seen up close.

"No, you may not. We eat at tables in this family," Sarah said.

"Oh hell," Sean muttered.

"Sean McClinton!" Sarah exclaimed, fixing Joel rather than her son in a steely stare. Joel cleared his throat and took an intense interest in his coffee cup. There was only one way to make amends. He glanced at Cub.

"You too."

"What?"

"Go with the others. Sacred Killer and I must counsel together."

Cub scowled and refrained from meeting his father's gaze as he stood and walked to the house.

"Can you fly?" Fiona asked Sacred Killer, whose expression changed to one of mystification. "You wear feathers. How come, if you can't fly? Birds fly."

"Fiona . . . come," Sarah said.

"I been thinking. Would you like to have a new name? I don't like yours right now. I can give you a new one. Want me to? Yours is scary. I can think of one much friendlier."

Sacred Killer glanced from Joel to the girl. A faint smile touched the corners of his mouth.

"What name, little one?" he asked.

"Petey," Fiona said proudly. "Petey is much better."

Joel nearly choked on his coffee. Sacred Killer nodded most seriously.

"Pee-tee," he said. "It is a good name. Thank you for it, little one."

"You're welcome," Fiona replied, hurrying off after her brother.

"I shall put them to bed after supper," Sarah said, noticing Sacred Killer watching her. "Is something the matter?"

"You are pale like the clouds."

"Why thank you. That is a nice compliment," Sarah said.

"Clouds are blown away. A Cheyenne woman is like the earth." Sacred Killer scooped a handful of soil. "The earth lasts; a Cheyenne woman lasts. Clouds do not last."

"I see," Sarah said. "And what is the Cheyenne man who can be held prisoner by a cloud?"

Sacred Killer searched his friends' faces for help. None was offered.

"Good-night," said Sarah, and with a swirl of her dress she marched triumphantly into the house.

"This ve-ho-a-e has a tongue that cuts as sharply as a skinning knife," Sacred Killer observed.

"She has a will of her own. But you are wrong about her not lasting. I have a feeling Sarah McClinton is stronger than any of us," Joel said.

"She can cook," White Frog said, his mouth full of food.

"A little bird has whispered in my ear," Sacred Killer said, "and I am much troubled. Is this why you called me here? To show me the woman you have taken into your lodge."

"A little bird . . . saaa! A little bear I think," said Joel. "It is well you have met her. For what my son has told you is true. It is my wish that Sarah remain here with me."

"Cub has asked to return with me to his people in the mountains. It is his wish to carry a Red Shield into battle." Sacred Killer glanced toward the house. "Perhaps it is time he went with me."

"Over my dead body."

"A broken lance lies between us, Nahkohe. It can never be made whole. There must not be war between us."

"My son stays with me. Listen to my words, Sacred Killer, my brother."

Joel spoke then of his dream for Morning Star, his dream for his son. He told once more how important it was for Cub that the boy learn to live in the white man's world because the world of the Cheyenne was doomed, at least a great part of it.

Sacred Killer listened, the food before him untouched. He heard nothing that he already did not know in his heart to be true. And when Joel finished, Sacred Killer stood and walked out of the circle of light to stand alone in the growing darkness, alone and facing the lonely hills, the vastness of Moon Woman Mountain waiting in the approaching night. At last the war chief of the Red Shields returned to the campfire.

"There's truth in what you say, Nahkohe, but it is not a complete truth. There is more to be said. The old ways are not dead as long as one remembers. As long as Little Bear remembers. It is for this reason I would welcome him to our village in the mountains. He must be taught. However, I would not allow him to ride with us when we are driven to fight the long knives one more time."

"You couldn't stop him, by then, from going along," said Joel. "But I will keep him here, so the matter is closed."

Sacred Killer smiled. He recognized much of Mourning Dove in his sister's son, the same headstrong nature, the same stubbornness. If Little Bear Cub wished to join him, then nothing Joel said or did could stop the boy. He resolved to camp for a while near Moon Woman Mountain. Sacred Killer would whisper to the boy that if a certain Little Bear wished to join his uncle, he might look for that uncle on the east side of the mountain. Sacred Killer would watch the sunrise four times there before heading back into the Absarokas. Little Bear must make his choice.

But Silvertip had said the matter was closed.

"We shall see," Sacred Killer replied. Joel did not particularly like the tone of that. Suddenly, he decided against bringing up the subject of the murdered ranchhands. Having

seen the track of the peg-legged man, he had no doubt now
that Sacred Killer was innocent. However, the mere mention
of Henri Larocque would send the brother of Mourning Dove
scouring the countryside for the villain. Joel did not want to
risk having his blood brother encounter any of Jessup's men
who were primed to shoot on sight. No, the sooner Sacred
Killer returned to the Absarokas, the better. Joel intended to
search on his own.

He helped himself to the stew. And while he ate, he wondered what thoughts were at play behind Sacred Killer's expressionless face.

38

Night music. The rhythm of the wind in the branches of the pines. Coyotes howling in the mournful distance. Owls subtly underscoring in deep throaty notes the music of Otter Creek. Sarah listened for the fading cadence of departing horses. When Sacred Killer and White Frog had left, she rose from her bed, wrapping a blanket about her shoulders as she crossed into the living room. Sarah moved to the front door and stood on the edge of the porch and watched Joel emerge from the barn, a ghostly shape that moved soundlessly, floating to her out of the darkness, to stand illuminated in the glowing remains of the campfire.

"Your friends have left?"

"Yes. Conditions what they are."

"I did not mean to seem rude. Granted they gave me quite a start. They are—and aren't—what I expected . . . of wild Indians," Sarah stammered. "I hope it wasn't my fault . . ."

"No. It just isn't safe for them here." Joel began kicking dirt over the dying campfire. That struck him as funny in a sardonic sort of way. Ranchers and homesteaders lived in renewed fear that Sacred Killer had brought his Red Shields down out of the mountains to wage war against their incursions. The death of General Custer at the Little Big Horn had been the final victory in a war destined to be lost. The tribes of the Sioux and Cheyenne were scattered, driven into hiding in Canada or back into the lonely vastness of the mountains. Sacred Killer had fewer than twenty men to wage war against the entire United States Army, but the settlers were worried. And, in a fashion, rightly so. There was a danger present. Joel could not rid himself of his suspicions, the nagging fear that he was about to come face-to-face with his old adversary, Henri Larocque.

"Good-night," Sarah said. Her gentle voice filtered through his reverie.

"Good-night." He watched her vanish through the doorway, then he continued across the yard toward the cabin, seeing it in the moonlight silent and dark. He relived in an instant the death of his Cheyenne wife. He saw once more Larocque standing on the porch. The Frenchman turned and limped around the side of the cabin . . . *stop him stop him. Oh God. Hemené.*

Joel halted in his tracks. He sensed a presence behind him. The back of his neck prickled, the hairs rising.

He whirled around, fists clenched, ready to battle whatever had stolen up behind him.

Sarah gasped and retreated a step, alarmed by his sudden transformation. Joel recognized her. His look of astonishment matched her surprise.

"What are you doing?"

"I don't think I quite know," she said, catching her breath. "You looked about to kill me."

"I was."

His eyes glistened in the moonlight. Tears, she realized. He had been preoccupied with his private painful memories. It explained how she had been able to approach unnoticed until the last minute. She was close to him, close enough so that he could see the sweet fullness of her breasts. The filaments of her heather-soft hair stirred in the rustling breeze.

"What are you doing, Sarah?" He sighed, repeating the question. Despite the cool night, his flesh grew warm. The plaguing past loosed its grip on him. No pain now. Only her, Sarah. Only her. And what he wished from her. "Don't you know what I want to do right now, seeing you like this?"

"Yes," she said, trembling, unable to find a meaning in herself, or an explanation. But she knew what he was feeling. Perhaps it was enough for now. "Yes." Joel caught her, pulled her to his lips, and lost in the kiss, he lifted her in his arms and carried her back to the ranch house, to *his* room. To *his* bed.

Sarah woke when the bed shook. She opened her eyes. Joel was pulling on his trousers. He buttoned his buckskin work-shirt and tucked it into his pants.

"What is it?" she asked in a sleepy voice. He tried not to meet her gaze, but she sensed something was wrong.

"It's morning," he said. "Cub and the others will be awake soon."

"Joel . . ." Sarah knew there was something else.

Joel sat on the edge of the bed and reached out to take her hand.

"Sarah, I want you and the children . . . I'm taking you back to Sweeney's Landing."

Her hand slid from his grasp. "I see."

"No, you don't. There is something I have to do. You may be in danger here. I cannot leave you and Fiona and Sean alone for any length of time. Not here. But you'll be safe at Sweeney's Landing."

"You want me to go?"

"No. But you have to. There is a man named Larocque. A man with a peg leg. He murdered my first wife. And now, I think he has returned. But I can't be certain. I must be free to check out my suspicions. If they prove to be true, then you definitely are in danger."

"And you will be in danger too, then."

"Yes. But I can take care of myself."

"And I can take care of myself, Joel Ryan," said Sarah. "I have before, and I will again." She sat up in bed, the sheet fell away from her naked breasts. She caught the edge of the sheet and yanked it into place. "Joel . . . the riverboat will be there. I just know it. We could book passage back to St. Louis. Or anywhere that it would be safe."

"Morning Star is my home."

"A grave is the only home a dead man has," Sarah retorted. Her heart was torn with affection, maybe even love for this man of the wilderness. She could not help feeling a certain sense of betrayal, and it showed in her tone of voice. "You want me to share your life, but you don't want me to share its dangers."

"Not this danger. This is special," Joel said, standing. "I am not going to argue with you. I'm taking you to the settlement for your own good."

"You could have told me your plans last night," Sarah said, accusation sharp in her voice.

"I had other things on my mind," Joel said, and hat in hand he left the room.

The morning was damp and cold beneath a cover of gray clouds. Joel left a trail in the moist earth as he walked up the slope behind the house. His breath clouded the air, and he wondered if the sun would break through to drive the chill away and dry the land.

He reached the summit of the hill. Here he had placed Hemené's body on its scaffold. When he had returned a year later, not a trace of his efforts had remained. A fierce chinook could have blown the scaffold down, leaving the remains to be carried off by the wild creatures of the forest. Whatever the means, she had returned to the howling wilderness; she had returned home. Chipmunks scampered across a nearby granite ledge and paused to scold him for his intrusion. On the other side of the hill, a coyote studied him before padding off into the solace of the forest. Joel glanced down at the wooden plaque that bore the name "Priam" laboriously carved into its wooden surface.

"Well, Priam," Joel said, looking down at the Negro trapper's grave. "I'll be leaving again for a spell. Look after things." Joel reached inside his shirt and took the bronze cross from his pocket and strung it once more around his neck. "I shall search this countryside, and if Henri Larocque is about, I think I will return his cross to him." From imagination or something more supernatural, a sensation of caution and warning seemed to issue from the ground at Joel's feet. "Don't worry," Joel said. "I've learned a thing or two myself over the years." He smiled. "I'm wiser than a tree full of owls." Joel looked out over Morning Star. A formation of geese had appeared over Moon Woman Mountain, their cry a faint but moving evocation singing across the land. *Time for me to be going too*, Joel thought, and donning his hat he started down the hill.

The descent was trickier than climbing up. The grass was slick underfoot, and Joel had to dig his heels in the earth to keep from slipping. It took him a quarter of an hour to reach the yard. The back door opened with a bang, and Fiona trotted out, headed for the outhouse. She waved to Joel who returned her greeting. He didn't like the thought of her leaving. Or Sean. Or Sarah. Especially Sarah. But if Larocque had returned, what better way to strike at Joel than through his family? And then, there was Cub. He wanted the boy to remain with Sweeney. Joel didn't relish breaking the news. And there was the matter of Sarah in the cabin to explain. He didn't even know how to begin that. "Now or never," Joel muttered to himself, spying the youth at bath in the icy waters of Otter Creek. Joel shivered, regretting having left his coat in the bedroom. He stepped inside the cabin's spare, chilly interior. A fleece-lined denim coat hung from a wooden peg near the cold hearth. He grabbed the coat and, retracing his steps, darted through the open doorway. Cub had turned and was looking toward the cabin, his coppery features betraying his alarm. As Joel cleared the doorway, the boy shouted, "Pa!"

Something hard exploded against Joel's skull, and he dropped in his tracks and lay still, feeling the cold of the ground, cold as the black void into which he plummeted.

Voices. Memories. A woman. A child. A campfire. Faces and conversations jumbled together, sentences and fragments of sentences reverberating in the depths. Disembodied voices speaking. "Not this one . . . I love you . . . last forever . . . take care of myself . . . a grave is the only home a dead man has."

39

Joel kept his eyes shut and rode the waves of nausea that accompanied the jostling motion of the wagon bed. He assessed his situation as best he could. A cool compress helped ease his throbbing skull. His wrists were bound together with rope, but his legs were free. He was stretched out flat on his back. He heard Sarah speak, Sean reply, and later Fiona make a worried comment about the mean man who had hit Mister Ryan. He cracked one eye open, saw pine branches bob past. A wider glimpse revealed Cub on horseback riding directly to the left of the wagon.

Completely puzzled, Joel sat upright. The world creaked on its axis. He groaned and managed to keep his stomach from turning flip-flops.

"Pa," Cub shouted. Sean reined in the horses and braked the wagon to a halt. Joel managed to keep his balance as his son leaped onto the wagon bed. Knife in hand, the youth sliced at the bonds. Joel heard the sound of an approaching horse and a voice called out, "Hold it, boy, unless you want to be responsible for seeing your daddy laid out permanent."

Cub stared past his father. Joel turned, recognizing the voice, looking from Sarah's concerned expression to the deadly elegance of Ben Slade. Cub quit sawing at his father's bonds.

"He carried you to the door and told me I had half an hour to pack what I could," Sarah blurted out, still shocked by the morning's dramatic turn of events.

Joel stood and held out his hands as Slade rode up beside them.

"How's your head?" Slade said. Dust patched his black frock coat and trousers; his vest was stained with sweat. The pearl-handled Smith and Wesson gleamed where it jutted from his waist sash. A deputy's badge was pinned to the ruffled lace shirt.

"What the devil is going on?" Joel said, his senses clearing at last. "Cut me loose, Ben. Now."

"If I'd a known," Slade said, patting at his wrinkled, trailworn finery. "I would have dressed for the occasion." He looked at Joel. "You know why I came. You just didn't expect me so soon. Lucky for you. At least I'll bring you to town alive. Colonel Jessup would have had you dangling and dancing in the air by now."

"What are you saying?"

"I was at Jessup's yesterday evening, settling up for a mirror one of his boys shot out at the Three Vices when Reasoner rode in on a lame horse and told the colonel what Tod was up to. How you sent him packing and were going to read from the book to Tod. Jessup was mad as I've seen, and he had Reasoner saddle another gelding and take him to his son. I tagged along figuring to keep things from getting out of hand. Took us a hell of a while to find him at night. God in heaven, Joel, I know Tod was in the wrong, but you didn't have to kill him."

"Tod—dead?" Joel exclaimed. He could feel Sarah watching him, searching him to see if it was possibly true.

"Oh come on," Slade grumbled. "Man, you must have gone loco."

"He was alive when I left him, Ben. I swear."

"I don't know how. 'Cause if there was an unbroke bone on him, I didn't find it. What did you use, a tie iron?"

Joel felt the blood drain from his face. He slowly sat in the wagon. "I never laid a hand on him. Oh, I wanted to. But he made the first move and charged me. I tripped him, and he knocked himself out against a tree. I left him like that. I swear it."

"You expect me to believe somebody just came along and found him lying there and decided to beat him to death?"

Joel glanced at Slade, realization dawning.

"Not somebody," he said. "Larocque."

"Who?"

"Henri Larocque. The man who murdered Hemené. I can't prove it yet, but free me and I will."

"And why would this ... Larocque ... whoever-he-is want to kill Tod Jessup?"

"I don't know, but I plan on finding the answer as soon as I find Larocque. Cut me loose."

"Not hardly," Slade remarked. "I clubbed you so you wouldn't make me shoot it out. And I'm taking you to town. I'll ask around about this Larocque. But you're going to stay in jail. That's the law. And anyway, you'll be safer there. Jessup went crazy when we found Tod. He cursed Jim Reasoner and fired him on the spot. The colonel was going to take Tod home and then come after you. And not alone, either."

"Slade, cut me free!" Joel said. "I'm the only one who can find Larocque."

"Ma'am," the deputy marshal said, tipping his flat-brimmed hat. "You and the boy hold on and keep a whip to those horses. If Jessup finds us on the trail, I cannot answer for your husb—uh, for Joel's safety. We must reach Swee-ney's Landing, the sooner the better."

"Turn the wagon around, Sean," Joel said. "Come on, boy."

"Ma'am. Let's go," Slade ordered. "We don't have much time, and Jessup's men are sure to be on our trail by now."

"Sean, do as I say," Joel repeated. The youth looked over his shoulder at Joel, then to Slade, and then to his mother.

"Sarah?" Joel pleaded. Sarah could not meet his gaze. It was impossible that Joel had anything to do with Tod Jessup's death. But if nothing else, Joel's life was in danger. Jessup had so many men while Joel could count on no one to help him.

"Do as Mister Slade says," she told her son. Joel stared at her a long hard moment, then sagged back onto the wagon as it rolled forward. He was the picture of defeat.

"I'm sorry," Sarah said. "I'm trying to do what is best."

"I know. You take care of yourself," Joel snapped. "Bixby ought to be about ready to leave for St. Louis. This works out quite nicely for you, doesn't it?"

Stung by his words, Sarah turned back around as Slade

started up the trail winding through the pines. Maybe she had been wrong about Joel Ryan, about everything.

"Yes," she whispered and put her arms around Fiona and Sean.

40

Joel listened to the rain and pretended to sleep. Rain always used to relax him, calm him after a long hard day. He was always glad to see the thunderheads billow over Moon Woman Mountain and cloak the sunset in somber array. Crash, lightning. Roll, thunderous cascade. Come, rain. Come.

He listened to the rain, to the plodding drip drip drip where the ceiling in the jail had sprung a leak. Beneath the noise of the downpour, Joel heard Ben Slade's rattling snore sounding for all the world like the distant rumble of uprooted trees in the rushing flood.

The jail was a converted cabin near the banks of the Yellowstone. If Joel had stood and peered from his barred window, he would have spied the *Lady Jane* outlined against the violence of the storm. Osage Bixby was, in truth, preparing to race the winter back to St. Louis with a boat full of miners and trappers who had had their fill of the wilderness. Osage had offered to bring his crew of roustabouts and break Joel out of jail, but Joel refused to allow it. The last thing poor Bixby needed was trouble with the authorities. A riverboat captain was only as good as his unblemished reputation. Any day now the whistle would send its shrill cry echoing over the land, steam engine roaring, the paddle wheel churning in the water pulling the *Lady Jane* out to the middle of the river.

Sarah . . .

I was a fool, Joel thought to himself. *It's about time I quit following my instincts and grew up and learned to reason things out.* Sending for Sarah had seemed like such a right thing to do. And when he'd met her face-to-face, he had been so certain. Lord in heaven, had any man ever been so blessed but to find two women in this world to build a

life with, any man ever been so snakebit to love them both?
Joel stiffened, hearing footsteps sloshing outside his window.

"Hey you!" a voice shouted. Someone groaned. And the
voice called, "There he is." Footsteps running. "Damn breed
hit me with a rock."

Slade rolled off the cot in the adjoining jail cell. Joel
scrambled to the window in time to see Cub struggling in
the grasp of one of Jessup's men. Joel grabbed the bars, but
the iron and stone defied his strength.

"Slade, they've got my boy, blast your eyes; let me out
of here."

"Look for yourself," Slade retorted, peering out the window in his cell. Cub had kicked the ranchhand in the shin,
slipped from his grasp, and darted between two other men
who had arrived to help their friends. One of the ranchhands
leveled his rifle.

"Put it away," Slade shouted. The man slowly lowered his
weapon. The one who had been kicked limped toward the
back of the jail.

"The breed had a gun, Ben," the limping man said.
"Caught him slinking around back here. More than likely
trying to spring his pa."

"Just the same, we haven't taken to shooting down children," Slade said. "I can't do anything about Jessup's sta-
tioning you men in town in case the Cheyenne try to free
Ryan. But you boys go easy, Chance, or I swear you'll be
able to keep an eye on things from the inside of a cell."

"Yeah, yeah," the man named Chance said, hunkering
down in his slicker. "Come on," he called over his shoulder
to the men behind him. They disappeared in the downpour,
three weary figures in the early hours before morning. Joel
relaxed and eased back from the window. Slade grumbled in
satisfaction and perched on the edge of his cot. He ran his
fingers through his hair.

"I was having a terrific dream too. Hope and I were . . .
oh, what the hell. Blast Frank Jessup. He's got folks edgier
than a jackrabbit in a den of rattlers. For sure."

"He wants to be certain I get a fair trial and a fair hanging," Joel said.

"I don't like this any more than you do," Slade replied.

"Your sympathy is touching."

"Look, Ryan," Slade stood and leaned into the bars. "I am the representative of the law, like it or not. I'm doing my job, which for the moment is to keep you safe until we get a judge up here to hold a trial."

"Your job is to find Henri Larocque."

"I can't leave you here alone," Slade said. "Look, you should have brought Tod to me. If you had just done that instead of getting carried away and . . ." Slade's voice died out.

"Killing him?" Joel asked. "You think I'm guilty too. You really think so, Ben?"

Slade sighed and left the adjoining cell. He walked down the short hallway and vanished into the outer office. Frustrated at his own helplessness, Joel stretched out on the cot and listened to the storm. Rain always used to relax him.

The whore with the scarred face brushed aside her black hair and sat on the edge of the cot, her ravaged features in sad repose.

Years ago, a drunken trapper had carved his initials in her cheek in a fit of rage. She had left the man disemboweled and dying in a Virginia City alleyway. The whore, unable to find any other means of earning a living, had settled at Big Nose Kate's. She plied her trade among the miscreants and ruffians who frequented Kate's den. They were a rowdy lot, these men, and only as brave as the next drink. They seldom ventured into the more respectable sections of town lest they run afoul of Ben Slade.

Kid Bascomb had his reasons for visiting Kate. Here, he could keep an ear to the local gossip concerning Silvertip Ryan. As well, Jim Reasoner was in town. The foreman had yet to find employment and still chafed from the colonel's treatment of him.

"One dollar." The whore held out a glass jar for the gunman as he stood to hitch his pants and tuck in his faded checkered shirt. A knock sounded at the door and the knob turned. Bascomb reached for his low-slung Navy Colt, saw Cliff Thomas's face poke past the door. Thomas was an ex-teamster who had taken to a life of crime.

"I think he's about down to his last drink."

Bascomb nodded and dropped two bits in the whore's glass jar. "It was fun, honey, but not a dollar's worth," he said. The whore stared at the jar. With a man like Kid Bascomb she was happy to be paid at all. He was a lean, hollow-cheeked character with ten dead men to his credit who didn't care if he added a woman to his grisly account.

Bascomb stepped into the hall and caught a glimpse of Reasoner almost lost in the murky depths of the saloon. A roustabout brushed past Bascomb, muttered an apology, and staggered into the whore's back bedroom.

"Sonora, sweetheart, have I got a present for you," the man roared.

Kid Bascomb instructed Thomas to wait with the horses, and he sauntered over to Reasoner's whisky-stained table. Oil lamps burned in fitful attempts at illumination. A handful of men ringed a nearby table, their conversation muted, their attention centered on a game of five-card stud. Reasoner lifted his besotted gaze and focused briefly on Bascomb before sliding off toward the window and the rain-washed pre-dawn world. Kate's voice brayed across the room, and the two roustabouts she had just served at the bar laughed at her bawdy joke. She refilled their glasses, whispered something to the men. They wetted their lips and nodded.

Bascomb looked away.

"You remember me?" he asked Reasoner.

"Sure I know you, Kid," Reasoner said, squinting at the man across from him.

"Jessup fired me too," Bascomb said. "You told me to pack up and get. Of course, I hold no grudge against you. A man rides for the brand, he has to follow orders. Weren't your fault."

"None of it," Reasoner said, taking the bottle Bascomb placed on the table alongside the foreman's empty glass. "I served with the bastard many a bloody year. And pulled his butt out of the sand more than once. Sergeant Reasoner to the rescue. I got the saddle sores and he got the glory. But I didn't care. He took me with him, didn't he? Said the Bar Seven was as much mine as his. Promised me a share, he did. Colonel Jessup's as good as his word. Ha. No blasted good. Rot, I say. Let him rot."

"I'll drink to that," Bascomb grinned. "We're cut from the same cloth you and I."

Reasoner studied the gunman as if evaluating the truth of such a statement. But truth and illusion intermingled; in the drunken recesses of his brain, it was impossible to distinguish one from the other. He wiped the beads of liquor from his moustache, nodded, and filled his shot glass full to the brim. A tea-colored puddle spread outward from the bottom of the glass.

Bascomb grinned. Here was just the right kind of man. Dangerous and capable and full of hate. The boss could sure pick 'em.

"Come with me," Bascomb said. He grabbed the bottle and dangled it in front of Reasoner like bait.

Confused, Reasoner stood on reflex. He reached for the bottle and missed and stumbled after Bascomb who led the man down the hall to the back door. "Where you goin'?"

"Just out back a minute."

"Good idea. I'm about to pee in my pants," Reasoner mumbled. He followed Bascomb out behind the saloon and nearly slipped in the mud, kicking an empty bottle out of the way as he fumbled for his fly. Suddenly, Bascomb slammed him up against the building and slapped him across the face. Reasoner growled, shook his head, shoved Bascomb aside. A pistol appeared in the gunman's hand. Impressed at the quickness with which the gaunt killer handled his gun, Reasoner doubled his fists and calculated whether he wanted to risk getting shot.

"What is this?" he said.

"I just wanted to make certain you were sober."

Rain dripped from their hat brims, spattered their clothes, formed craters in the mud at their feet.

"I'm sober."

"Good." Bascomb smiled mirthlessly. "How would you like to meet a man who shares your feelings for Colonel Frank Jessup as well as Silvertip Ryan?" Bascomb heard Thomas approaching with the horses. "A man who has a plan to balance the ledger and make Jessup and Ryan pay in full."

It dawned on Kid Bascomb how Reasoner might well prove useful. The foreman undoubtedly knew the whereabouts of Jessup's safe. Perhaps the combination, too. "How would you like to come out of this with gold in your pockets and maybe your own spread? The man I'm talking about says he can make it happen. Well?"

Without a moment's hesitation, Reasoner said in a murderous tone, "I'd say take me to him."

Bascomb continued to smile.

Sweeney left a cup of coffee on the overturned barrel that sufficed as an end table in the front room of her store. Sarah, sitting between the barrel and the Franklin stove, took the cup and drank in silence. By the window, looking out at the rain, Osage Bixby rocked on his heels, his hands behind his back. He seemed less a bulwark of authority and more a confused and worried old man.

"I don't like leaving. I have no choice. The boat's ready. I can't chance dodging ice floes down to St. Louis. I have to leave."

"There's nothing you can do. You've said your good-byes." Sweeney handed him a cup of coffee. Bixby gulped down the steaming brew and set the cup on the countertop to his left. The shelves were not as full as they had been a month before, tangible evidence of the brisk business that had kept Sweeney jumping the last few weeks.

"I better see that Green has the crew rounded up and aboard. Blast Slade, anyway," Bixby said. He walked across the room to the front door. "Mrs. McClinton, have you decided whether or not you'll be coming with me?"

"No," Sarah answered, unable to meet Sweeney's accusing stare.

"When you hear the whistle blow, you'd better have made up your mind," Bixby replied. "Sweeney, I shall see you after thaw." He held out his hand and Sweeney shook it. Bixby sighed. "A nasty situation, this." The captain's remarks were lost when he closed the door. Sarah listened with regret to the captain's departure. Sweeney had been less than friendly toward Sarah since her return from Morning Star. The jailing of Silvertip Ryan had caused quite a commotion in the settlement. There were those who felt he deserved it—and those like Sweeney who knew the charges against him could only be so much hogwash.

"Mommy, I'm scared," Fiona called from the stairway. "Will you tell me a story?" Thunder bellowed in the distance, deepened in tone as it reached and rattled the windows. It was way too early for Fiona to be awake.

"Tell Sean to light a lamp."

"He's gone. He told me not to tell. He went out looking for Cub."

Sarah stood and walked to the stairway. "What?"

"He said he would pinch me if I told. But I'm scared up here by myself, and Tiny is too. You won't let him pinch me, will you?"

"No," Sarah said. "You go back to bed, and I'll be right up."

"And tell a story."

"We had a story last night. It's almost morning."

"I want a story."

"Okay," Sarah said, worried for her son. And for Cub, too.

"Okay," Fiona said and disappeared behind the railing. Sarah glanced around at Sweeney. "Did you see them sneak out?" Sweeney shook her head no. "May I use your slicker?"

"Suit yourself. Nasty weather for a morning stroll."

"You heard Fiona. Sean and Cub are outside. I better find them before they catch their deaths of cold."

"A little late to be worried about Cub, seeing as you helped bring his father in to jail."

"What was I supposed to do, grab a gun and shoot it out with Mister Slade? That seems to be the only solution anyone understands around here."

"I would have done whatever it took to save my man," Sweeney replied, her homely solid features bunched where she stood in the shadows behind the counter.

"You love him, don't you?" said Sarah.

"I've seen him in hard times. And good. We have been friends," Sweeney answered guardedly. "You'll be needing some boots."

A few minutes later, Sarah stepped out the front door and

closed it softly behind her so as not to alert Fiona. She eyed the mud with some misgiving and was grateful for the boots she had borrowed from Sweeney's storeroom.

Sarah cursed herself for not being alert enough to catch Sean. He must have slipped down the back stairs and out the back door. *Oh, I don't need this*, Sarah thought to herself. *Where to begin?* The settlement lay still and lifeless beneath its glaze of rain. She could barely distinguish the *Lady Jane* riding out the storm at the river's edge. Up from the sandy bank, the squat black outline of the jail loomed ominous in the downpour. *I would have done whatever it took to save my man.* Sarah had no reply to such a statement and self-reproach welled in her breast.

"Ma!" Sarah spun about as her son rode toward her through the drenching rain. "Ma!" The boy brought his horse to a halt in front of the general store. He wiped muddy water from his eyes. Sean had a puffy lip. "He's gone. I tried to stop him. He rode off all alone."

"Who? You're hurt."

"It's nothing. He didn't mean to hit me."

"Young man, calm down and get under the roof here." Sarah reached for the reins and missed.

"I'm trying to tell you," Sean gasped. "Cub is gone. He was crying, Ma. I've never seen him cry. He said he was going to find help for his Pa. Something about Moon Woman Mountain."

"When did he leave?"

"Just now. If I hurry, I can catch him. He doesn't even have a coat."

"I'll go after him," Sarah said. "You just go right on inside and get those wet clothes off and have Sweeney give you something warm to drink. Now do as I say."

"But—"

"Sean!"

"I can't. Cub's my friend. I've got to help him." The boy wheeled the Appaloosa and galloped through town.

"Sean!" She called to no avail. She turned and saw Sweeney standing in the doorway. The storekeeper read Sarah's mind.

"I'll tell Fiona her story," said Sweeney. Sarah lowered

her head, pulling the hood of the slicker forward to shield
her features. She stumbled, slipped in the mud, and regaining
her balance ran to the livery stable, forcing open the great
heavy doors. She stepped into the dim light.

"If that's you boys, I'll—" Caleb Walsh, the wizened ban-
dylegged owner of the stable stepped out of a nearby stall.
"S'cuse me, ma'am. Thought it was them damn . . . s'cuse
me again . . . them boys."

"I need a horse. We brought in several a few days ago."
Caleb wiped his specs on his overalls, then he fitted wire-
rimmed frames over his ears and squinted through the
glasses. "Why, you're Miss, uh, Mrs. Ryan or somethin'.
That gal ol' Silvertip sent for. My boy told me y'all brung
the horses in. I was fishin'. I can saddle the roan for ya. That
be all right? You know, terrible thing about Tod. Just between you and me, it couldn't a' happened to a meaner boy.
Once he . . ."

"The roan will be fine," Sarah said. The roan was Joel's
and was bred for speed and stamina. The boys had probably
taken the main road from town. Their tracks would be easy
to follow until the rain washed them away. The roan ought
to be able to catch them though.

"All right. All right. Everybody's in a hurry. Ryan's breed
didn't even take a saddle. I come out here and seen him
takin' off bareback. 'Course Injuns can ride bareback . . ."
Caleb lifted a saddle and carried it to the roan.

Sarah kept to the wheel-rutted path leading west out of town.
The tracks of the boys' horses were thankfully easy to discern for no one else had been fool enough to risk pneumonia
by riding out on such a stormy morning.

Her discomfort increased as the rain battered down, pelt-
ing her with icy drops, leaving her fingers chilled and
numbed where they gripped the reins.

Sarah lowered her head to the downpour and allowed her
mind to reach back for images of the past month, fragments
of memory to ease her present misery. Her remembrance
began and ended with the man called Silvertip, and she
smiled recalling the shock of meeting the real Joel Ryan. She
recalled her first glimpse of Otter Creek and Morning Star

ranch, the dying blossoms of the bitterroots, the heady fragrance of the pines, moonlight silver-soft and scattering the
creek with jewels. How strange to find the routine of life
becoming a pleasure, as she watched her children happy at
last and maturing in the shadow of the mountains.

Silvertip Ryan.

Joel.

A stranger at first and frightening for his size and fierce
appearance. A man of strength and tenderness and a tanta-
lizing blend of the gentle and the violent.

She pictured him against the big sky, and he fit. He had
been born to walk this land, and she had been right to give
herself to him. She had needed the fire of his strength. And
for a man of such raw, latent power, he had trembled like a
child in the aftermath of their lovemaking.

He had needed her, as well.

The sound of a gunshot drifted to her across the sodden
landscape, and she caught her breath, looked up, saw nothing
unusual, though her heart was beating rapidly. She shivered,
realizing how helpless she truly was. Not entirely helpless
though. She remembered a revolver and reaching back untied
the rawhide thongs of the saddlebag. Luckily Caleb had, out
of habit, saddled the roan with Joel's saddle, shortening the
stirrups for Sarah. And if good fortune might be imposed
upon once more . . .

Her fingers closed around the grip of the Navy Colt Joel
kept—"for emergencies," he liked to say. Sarah prayed this
was not too much of an emergency. She unwrapped the revolver, freeing it from its oilskin wrappings and rode on
through the rain.

Minutes passed, time reduced to an interminable crawl.
Then she heard the fast approach of a horse. As the sound
reached her through the lessening rain, she fought the rise of
panic. Out of the gloom, a horse and rider materialized, a
terrifying apparition that charged straight for her!

41

Colonel Frank Jessup stared at breakfast lying untouched on his plate. The biscuits were cold now, unappetizing with their buttered amber centers congealed and dotted with bacon grease. He shoved away from the table and stood, centering attention on himself by virtue of his very presence in the hotel dining room and by the aura of tragedy surrounding him. He stared at the curious faces turned to watch him. He did not speak, and eyes were soon downcast.

"You want something else, sir?" Ling Po, the Chinese cook said, warily approaching the colonel. Jessup seemed to look through the man and left without replying. The smell of coffee carried into the lobby with its mahogany clerk's desk and leather-backed chairs and framed chromolithographs depicting life on the St. Louis. He noted the frames needed dusting. He was a particular man who prided himself on his powers of observation. Buttoning his black frock coat about his stomach, he walked out onto the veranda. A ranch-hand slouching against the front post came to attention as his boss appeared.

"Everything all right, Chance?"

"The men are grabbing some shuteye. I'm keeping tabs on things," Jessup's new foreman replied. "Right as rain." He chuckled at his own wit. The colonel remained impassive, staring out at the muddy street. The rain had diminished in intensity; however, the temperature was dropping. His breath billowed on the air. The morning mirrored his mood. A shrill whistle reverberated over the landscape and turned his attention toward the Yellowstone. The dock was devoid of well-wishers. Everyone wanted to see Bixby arrive, but no one wanted to watch the departure of the last boat until spring thaw. The last link with civilization. The whistle sounded

again, and clouds of oily smoke gouted from the twin chim-
neys. Ropes were cast off. The paddle wheel slowly dipped
into the river, drawing the *Lady Jane* away from Sweeney's
Landing.

"Gonna be a long winter," Chance said. Jessup offered no
comment. His gaze had shifted to the jailhouse, his dark
thoughts brooding on the prisoner it housed—Silvertip Ryan,
the man Jessup intended personally to hang.

"Who the hell you think that is?" Chance muttered, and
Jessup diverted his attention to watch as a red-headed boy
on a lathered Appaloosa galloped headlong down Main
Street. Mud exploded where the flashing hooves struck.
Horse and rider thundered past and came to a skidding halt
before the jailhouse. The boy leaped down, fell in the mud,
and scrambled to his feet. He staggered to the door.

"The McClinton boy," Jessup said.

"What do you make of that?" Chance muttered. "Funny."

"Maybe you better alert the men." Jessup stepped down
from the porch and headed for the jail.

"You want my gun?" Chance called.

"Just wake the men," Jessup said, waving aside the ranch-
hand's offer. His boots caught in the mud. Mud sucked at
the gray wool of his pants cuff and slowed his progress. Icy
raindrops chilled him, but he pressed on toward the jail. He
wanted to know what was happening, especially if it concerned Ryan.

The call of the riverboat sounded again in a shrill blast
that rattled windows and doors and lost itself in the mournful
distance of the prairie.

Sean gulped a second cup of whisky-laced coffee and
glanced from Ben Slade, who sat with elbows propped on
his desk, to Joel Ryan standing in his cell, his fingers bloodless where he gripped the bars.

"Cub's horse pulled up lame. Caught a stone in its shoe
or something," Sean gasped. "I would have never caught him
otherwise." He choked a moment on the dregs in his cup.

"Go on, boy."

"I told him I'd go along. Didn't seem fair him being on
his own. And we are friends. So he said okay, but we needed

to work on his horse first, so we headed for that stand of boulders . . ." He looked at Joel. "The ones you said used to be an Indian campsite. We got there, and that's when those men jumped us. There were five, I think. And awful mean sounding, like as if we had interrupted their meeting or something, only I never meant to for sure. Then one of them, he was real scary, he recognized Cub and said to grab him. He went one way and me the other. I heard a shot and looked around and saw they had caught him. Cub's horse just couldn't run. I'm sorry, Joel. I didn't know what to do. I was scared. That one-legged man was too big and mean."

Joel stiffened. "Red hair and beard like fire," he muttered. "Sir?"

"He had red hair, a red beard. His right leg was gone."

"He had a peg leg. Like a pirate," Sean said. Tears began spilling down his cheeks. "I'm sorry."

Slade shifted uncomfortably in his chair. The hand of solitaire he'd been absorbed in held no interest for him now. First Joel's talk about a peg-leg man. Now Sean.

"It's him. I knew it," Joel said, rattling the barred door. "And he has my son! Slade, let me out."

"You've got to help my mother," Sean pleaded.

Slade's brows furrowed in puzzlement. "Sarah? What has she got to do with this?"

"I met her on the road. She had been following us. She told me to come here and that she would try and follow the men who took Cub."

"Damn!" Joel smacked his fist against the cell door. "Slade!"

"Just wait a minute," Slade said. "I'll call a posse—"

"Who will come? A few drunken trappers. Or Jessup's men; he'd soon as see me hang. That might make things easier for you, come to think of it. Maybe you ought to head out alone and leave me here for the colonel."

Slade brushed the cards from the desktop along with a wooden tray filled with wanted posters he had never bothered to appraise.

"I've had it up to here with you, Ryan," the gambler said, gesturing to his own throat.

"Then choke," Joel retorted.

"I didn't ask your boy to run off." Slade rose out of his chair, his pale features angry now as he tried to reach a decision.

"Excuse me, sir," Sean said. Slade glanced aside. The boy had moved and taken a revolver from a holster hung on a peg near the door. "Unlock Joel." The ten-year-old thumbed the hammer back. The barrel wavered as he fought to steady his hands. Slade snorted in disgust, walked around the desk. The boy followed him with his aim.

"I'll shoot," Sean warned in a trembling voice.

"Not unless you put your finger on the trigger," Slade observed. The boy checked his grip, and when his eyes lowered, Slade snatched the gun out of his grasp. Sean looked at his suddenly empty hands and then began to cry, stumbling forward into the gambler's surprised embrace.

"Don't let them kill my ma," the boy sobbed. "Please . . ."

Slade reached up uncertainly and then held the boy until the sobs that wracked his frame subsided enough for the youth to back away in embarrassment, rubbing his knuckles into his red-rimmed eyes.

"I did too have my finger on the trigger," he said defiantly.

"I know. It's always the cheap tricks that work." Slade turned from the boy and walked over to the cell. He stared at Joel and then sighed.

"Hold up your right hand."

Joel did.

"Do you solemnly swear to uphold the law, to abide . . . oh hell, this is ridiculous." Slade fit a large iron key into the lock, twisted twice. The lock clicked just as the front door opened and Frank Jessup entered the office. He held a derringer in his right fist.

"Just step in and join Ryan," Jessup said. "And you stay put," he added to Sean. "My men are on their way. Aiding and abetting a criminal, are we, Mister Slade? About to set Mister Ryan free?"

Joel stared at the unlocked door. Freedom so close. But in the narrow cell entrance, Jessup's derringer could be fired with deadly effect.

"Have it your way, Colonel." Slade shrugged. His hand was a blur of motion as he drew the Smith and Wesson from the sash of his waist. The revolver spat flame, its report deafening in the confines of the jailhouse. The derringer leaped from Jessup's grip. Blood welled from the gash along the back of the colonel's hand. He grunted in pain, wheeled about, and lunged toward the open doorway, but Sean kicked the door shut in his face. The rancher slammed into the door. A second later Slade had Jessup by the collar and had dragged him to the center of the room. Joel ran to the desk and slid open the top drawer. He selected a holster and Colt revolver, sheathed his knife, and retrieved his Winchester from the gun rack.

"Let me go. What kind of deputy marshal are you?" Jessup exclaimed.

"An 'ex' one," Slade growled. He tossed his badge on the desktop. "Anyway, the damn thing poked holes in my best suit."

"That shot alerted my men," said Jessup. "You'll never leave town alive."

"You better pray we do." Joel rounded the desk. He pulled out his Colt and placed the gun muzzle to the colonel's temple.

"Slade, open the door," Joel ordered. The gambler looked at Joel, seeing a facet in the man that Slade had never glimpsed before. Something primitive and deadly.

"I've been clubbed and jailed, and my son's been kidnapped by the man who murdered his mother. Sarah McClinton is out there, somewhere, all alone with Henri Larocque on the loose. No one on this earth is going to stop me from leaving this settlement—if I have to kill every one of your men, Colonel, and splatter your brains in the mud. Do you understand me?"

"Ye—Yes," Jessup stammered.

Slade opened the door as Joel, with Jessup in tow, stepped outside. Five of Jessup's men were ranged in a semicircle in the middle of the street. Rain glistened on their long coats, dripped from the muzzles of their rifles.

"Tell them to throw their guns in the street," Joel whispered. Chance and the others exchanged glances.

"Have it your way, you old bastard," Joel said softly, his voice traveling no further than the colonel's ear. Jessup felt the hand with the Colt tense. The gun's cylinder slowly turned.

"Throw your weapons down," Jessup shouted. "Do not try to stop these two men from leaving." The ranchhands balked a moment. The cylinder turned as Joel squeezed the trigger pressing the barrel into Jessup's skull.

"Throw down your weapons!" the colonel repeated. A moment of excruciating silence. Chance was the first. He dropped his rifle and then his sidearm into the mud. The other men followed suit. Behind Joel, Ben Slade muttered, "Thank God."

"Sean," Joel said. "Stay with Sweeney."

"But sir, I—"

"Do as I tell you, boy," Joel ordered. Sean wiped at his tear-red eyes. "I'll bring her back to you," Joel added. Sean nodded and hurried across the muddy street. Joel noticed Sweeney in the entrance of her store. She carried a shotgun and had obviously been about to back whatever play Joel chose to make. He waved. She returned the gesture and embracing Sean, brought the boy inside.

"Let's go," said the man called Silvertip.

Slade kept watch from the doorway of Caleb's stable. Jessup slumped dejectedly to one side. Joel and Caleb were saddling the horses. The ranchhands from the Bar Seven waited unarmed at a respectful distance under the porch of the Three Vices.

"He was spoiled. And rode a mean streak, there was no doubt. But he was my son. Tod was the first and only child. Belva just sits and stares out the window, stares at his marker. As God is my judge I'll hunt you down, the both of you. Hear that, Silvertip Ryan! I'll find you no matter how long it takes!"

Joel emerged from the rear of the stable, leading a horse. Caleb brought the others from their stalls. Mustangs all, these were animals used to the harsh land. "They're stayers," Caleb had said, summing up. Even Slade was surprised.

"Three?" he questioned.

"Don't worry, Colonel. You'll be able to find us. Because

we'll be right alongside. You're coming too. Chance and the others won't be so anxious to trail us."

Caleb handed the reins of one horse to Slade, the other to the colonel.

"If you break for it, I'll kill you," Joel added matter-of-factly. He mounted, drew his rifle, and levered a shell into the chamber. The action clicked ominously in the quiet of the stable.

Thunder rumbled overhead, a portent of violence to come. Jessup favored his wounded hand as he mounted. Joel brought the colonel once more into the storm. A dog barked in the distance. The boardwalks were lined with the settlement's inhabitants. They made for a curious audience as the three men galloped past the sullen stares of Jessup's hired hands and away from the settlement of Sweeney's Landing. Half a mile out, Joel veered south and west, taking the lead and riding straight into the heart of the tempest.

42

The years had not been kind to Henri Larocque. They showed not so much on his wind-chapped leathery features, but in the haunted wasteland of his eyes. Fleeing from the murder of Mourning Dove, he had returned to his native Canada. Henri Larocque, defrocked priest, wanted for the strangulation of a Calgary whore named Damsel Charbonneau, lighted in a nameless settlement on the banks of Grudge River and drank himself into a stupor at the nearest tavern hoping to drown in hard liquor the memory of Mourning Dove and the look on her face as she reached for her baby. Henri never felt the irons close around his wrist. A sergeant of the Northwest Mounted Police, a man with a long memory when it came to women-killers, brought a much disgruntled Henri Larocque to Calgary. Found guilty of his crimes after a brief but legal audience with the territorial magistrate, Larocque had been sentenced to prison for life. The magistrate could not bring himself to hang a priest, even a defrocked one. Larocque had a philosophy about prison. Escape. Pretending piety and reformation he eventually convinced his captors of his sincere desire to minister to his fellow inmates, his misguided flock as he called them. Years passed. He was appointed chaplain. More years passed. The prison built him a chapel. More years still. Henri Larocque was a changed man, said the guards. A true inspiration. A good man, a Christian man. Security eased. And one black and moonless night, Larocque crawled under the wall, crawled like a mole through the tunnel that began beneath the chapel floor and ended in the woods outside the prison walls.

Good man. Christian man. *Free* man, sayeth Henri Larocque. Free and ten years older. Hounded across the border

into Montana, Henri Larocque had pursued a life of petty
thievery ranging the gold camps from the Snake River to the
Wind. Fate and a morbid sense of curiosity had brought him
to Sweeney's Landing where he was surprised to learn that
Silvertip Ryan was still in the area. It was a cautious ride he
made one night to Otter Creek, and careful he was to leave
no trace of his passing. But from the moment he spied Joel
Ryan on his homestead, from that very instant, Larocque's
mind had begun plotting revenge. Joel had been the cause of
his misfortunes; Joel had shot off his leg. Larocque considered killing Ryan with a shot from ambush but disregarded
the notion as too simple and direct. He had gauged the hostility toward Ryan in the community of homesteaders and
ranchers and recognized that here was an opportunity for
profit. The Cheyenne had helped to massacre Custer. Ryan
was a friend to the Cheyenne. Race hatred smoldered like a
live coal waiting to burst into flames. And Henri Larocque
was a master when it came to fanning fires.

The dream always began in violence.

*A door opens. The woman enters. Larocque grabs for her,
pulls the woman to the center of the room. Only then does
he recognize Mourning Dove. She trips, falls to the dusty
floor, and almost loses her hold on the child. He had not
seen the infant until now. And now it is too late.*

*He orders her to be still, knowing she will not obey. She
will not let him kill her man. And that is why he has come.
The room smells of animal fat and the musty stale odor of
abandonment. Ryan is almost to the barn. See, his back is
turned. Precious little time yet. Hemené speaks.*

"Be still," Larocque grumbled aloud. Bascomb glanced
over at the sleeping man. Larocque shifted in his sleep. The
other men snored. Bascomb checked the breed boy. His eyes
were closed. The gunman was not fooled, but the boy was
bound hand and foot. Bascomb stared through the slitted
space in the ramshackle barn. The rain had stopped. But the
temperature continued to drop. It was dusk. And almost time
to wake the men.

*Larocque aims. Mourning Dove attacks. She has no
weapon, only herself. But she lunges for him, knocking the*

*Frenchman's gun hand down as he turns to fight her off. She
is no match for his great strength. He shoves her back. The
explosion jars them both. The fabric of her buckskin dress is
singed and blackened, and as she staggers and falls beside
her child, a crimson stain begins to blossom outward from
her mortal wound.*

*Larocque watches in horror the dying mother reaching
for her baby. The bloody hand outstretched. And in her hand,
the crucifix she had torn from around his throat. It dangles
and gleams, and he cannot take it back, and she keeps reaching for her child, wanting to hold him one last time.*

"No!" Larocque sat upright and bellowed. "No!" Men
rolled from their blankets, knives flashed, guns were drawn,
eyes in terror searching out the unseen attacker. They realized there was no one. They stared at Larocque's sweat-
streaked face, the wild-eyed expression he wore.

"Damnation," Reasoner said, speaking for them all. "You
scared the bejesus out of me."

Larocque stood, his massive girth looming in the dark.
The barn reeked of the stench of a dozen men confined in
its close quarters.

"We ride," the Frenchman said.

"The hell you say," a wiry, bowlegged lout named Vint
exclaimed. "Look, it's starting to snow. We ought to build a
fire and hole up." Sure enough, large fleecy flakes began
settling on the window.

"If the boy you let escape alerts the settlement, the posse
they send out won't 'hole up.' You can stay here if you wish.
And any man with you. But as for me, I am riding on to the
Jessup ranch. While so many of his men are in town it is
now or never. His gold is ripe for the taking. And we'll leave
enough signs that folks will think a whole nation of Cheyenne are on the warpath." Larocque gathered his blanket and
started for the door. Chill air blasted into the barn as he
shoved open the lean-to door and stepped outside. The men
looked to Kid Bascomb, tall and venomous-looking in his
own right.

"He may be crazy. But the way I see it, he's got folks in
these parts at each other's throats so they don't know what
to think next. He got Silvertip Ryan out of the way and

Colonel Jessup and Ben Slade, too. Looks to me like it's time to get rich. I ain't about to argue with that. I'll play it to the bust and then decide. Suit yourself, boys. Reasoner, bring the half-breed. Just in case we get dealt off the bottom, we might be able to do a bit of bargaining with him as an ace up our sleeve."

Reasoner nodded and lifted Cub by the scruff of his shirt. He untied the boy's legs and dragged the twelve-year-old toward the door. Cub did not resist.

"Hey, Reasoner," the man named Vint called out. "How much you reckon the colonel keeps in his safe?"

"He didn't believe in banks. He always liked to keep his money in sight. Said he slept better at night when he knew he could lay his hands on his worth any time he wanted to. All I know is that I drove many a herd up to the mining camps. And we always got paid in gold."

"Gold," Vint repeated, the word rolling off his tongue.

"Hell, what's a little snow?" another of the raiders muttered, already dabbing his face with war paint.

Approximately fifty yards from the ramshackle barn, Sarah McClinton lay curled beneath the remains of a broken-down wagon; the owner had never returned to claim the Conestoga. Barn, wagon, and stone foundation of a never-completed house were scattered in the night like signposts on the path to failed dreams. The roan snorted and raised its head to peer beyond the wreckage where Sarah had concealed herself, toward the barn where the door had just been swung open. Sarah, alerted by the horse's movement, watched as a peg-legged man and then the other raiders emerged from shelter. In their midst Sarah could make out a figure smaller than the rest in the wan light.

Cub! It had to be. The roan whinnied softly. Sarah glanced toward the horse in alarm. These men had proved themselves to be of desperate character, kidnapping Joel's son and attempting to kill Sean. Such men would have no compunction about murdering her as well. She crawled out from beneath the wagon and took the reins in one hand, calming the animal with soothing words and stroking its neck. The blanket and raincoat were inadequate protection from the elements. Although the rain had thankfully stopped and the wind had died, Sarah took small comfort as a silver-dollar-sized snowflake settled on the back of her hand. The roan stamped its hooves, its breath clouding the air. Sarah forced her shivering limbs into motion. She readjusted the extra saddle blanket around her head and shoulders, and then she pulled herself astride the stallion. Every movement was an effort. She shifted her dull stare from the departed bandits to the dim glow of their abandoned campfire, flickering fit-fully in the doorway. Sarah begrudged letting the kidnappers increase their lead on her, but her very survival was in ques-tion now. Her motions were leaden, and she was shivering uncontrollably. She needed to rest, needed to restore life to her limbs. Almost as if reading her thoughts, the roan altered its course and headed for the barn.

Like a supplicant to a pagan god, Sarah knelt by the coals and added chips of rotted wood and slivers of trampled straw and blew gently until they ignited. Gradually, she increased the size of the fire, tearing loose the shattered remains of a stall and crisscrossing the boards one atop the other over the flames. At last she had a blaze, and a banner of black smoke coruscated upward through a rent in the barn roof. She found a small sackful of oats in Joel's saddlebag and rewarded the roan with a paltry meal. A dusty strip of beef jerky served for her own supper. Sarah was hungry enough to relish each tough morsel. The warmth of the fire soothed her weary limbs and gave her renewed hope. She tried to perfect some sort of plan to rescue the boy but failed to see how she might prevail against such cutthroats. It seemed a far wiser course to remain at a distance, following the captors and leaving as much of a trail as she could for help from town to follow. However, if an opportunity presented itself, she was deter-mined to rescue Cub.

Gradually, life returned to her muscles; the warmth from the fire was simply heavenly, the most wonderful campfire in the whole world. Sarah stretched her arms, stood, and dangled the damp hem of her dress above the flames. When the radiant heat was warm enough, she stripped out of the frozen wool dress she had sewn for herself while at Morning

Star. Clad in an underblouse and pantalets, she crouched by the flames and spread the dress out to dry. She stared at the crackling flames.

By now the *Lady Jane* was steaming down the Yellowstone! She hadn't even thought of it till now. Did she regret not being aboard? She searched her conscience for remorse and came at last to the conclusion she had never intended to leave. *It's time to quit fooling yourself, Sarah my dear. Time to face the fact you like what happened between you and Joel Ryan,. and your only regret is that you waited so long. You may not know if you love him, but you want him. You want his strong arms around you. It doesn't mean you're a wanton, only that you have sense at last to understand what is right. What should be. You have sense to know when you're happy. So why not admit it?*

Sarah looked away from the flames, caught a glimpse at something gleaming silver in the straw. She started toward it, then froze as a horse whinnied outside. Joy that help from town had arrived, perhaps even Joel himself, died aborning as a small wiry figure slipped into the barn. The bowlegged man ambled forward, light playing on his features, a revolver gripped in his right hand.

"Well, well, well," he said, "look what I've gone and found. Come back looking for my lucky silver watch and, by jingo, struck it rich."

He noticed the roan. One horse meant the woman was alone; still he chanced a surreptitious glance about the barn's interior just to be on the safe side. He dusted the melting snow off his shoulders and unbuttoned his coat.

"My name's Vint, honey. I'm telling you 'cause I intend for us to get better acquainted. I think you understand." In an instant, Sarah assessed her predicament. Vint was obviously one of the bandits, obviously dangerous. And intent, as he so much as said, on having his way with her. Maybe she could give him more than he bargained for.

"Maybe you better tell me what exactly you're doing here," Vint said, drawing close. His eyes were slits set in a cruel expression.

"I got run out of Virginia City, dear heart," Sarah said in a thick brogue. "And it's east I've been heading. I am told there is a place up on the river where a lady like meself can find work. The Three Vices, I believe."

"Damn," Vince chuckled. "I knew you for a tart right off. The Three Vices it is, honey."

"And I'm thinkin' there's always room for a fourth vice," Sarah said with a wink and a lusty laugh. "Now won't you be helpin' a poor lass in distress and tell me how far I've to travel, for you see I'm lost. And if there's a spare bit of food you might have to share, well, I'd be happy to pay what you ask." Sarah cocked a hip to one side and thrust her breasts forward to bulge invitingly beneath her underblouse.

Vint holstered his gun, unfastened and dropped the gun-belt to one side. His coat and Levi's were as quickly shunted aside. His hungry eyes never left Sarah's voluptuous figure.

"Why don't you come over here by the fire and warm yourself, me darlin' boy? Or are you afraid of getting . . . burned?" Sarah purred. She knelt near the blaze, her left hand stealing toward one of the boards lying halfway in the flames. Vint, clad in a pair of ratty long johns, boots and hat, sauntered confidently toward the Irishwoman.

"The fellas are gonna kick themselves for leavin' when they did," Vint said aloud. "I might have to ride by my lonesome to Moon Woman Mountain, but it'll be worth it. I swear." As he reached for her, Sarah noticed once again a glint of silver on the straw-littered dirt floor.

"There's your watch." Sarah pointed to the shiny bit of metal. As Vint turned to see for himself, Sarah grabbed the board from the fire, and using its charred tip like a shovel, she flung a fiery load of live coals square into the bandit's face. Vint screamed and staggered backwards, clawing at his eyes.

"God damn bitch!" he bellowed. "Are you crazy?" Sarah ignored the Navy Colt lying atop her saddlebag. A gunshot might bring the bandit's friends. Vint staggered toward his own belongings, grabbed for his gunbelt, his fingers closing around the grip of his revolver. He jerked the weapon free. Sarah batted the gun out of his grasp. He howled as the flaming length of wood seared his knuckles. He lunged blindly for the woman, and in his fury he knocked her off her feet. Vint tripped over Sarah and flew past her to crash

through the weathered siding of another stall. Sarah heard a
muffled grunt, a savage intake of air. She crawled to her
knees and scrambled toward her belongings and the Navy
Colt. The outlaw was too powerful. She took the revolver in
both hands and thumbed the hammer back and pointed it at
the bandit as he staggered out of the stall. He stared at her
through a crimson mask of his own blood. He gingerly
touched the gash on his forehead, groaned, and, eyes glazing,
fell to his knees and rolled over onto his shoulder, unconscious.

Vint regained consciousness, groaning as life returned to his
securely bound arms and legs. He was still clad in his long
johns. He craned his head and caught a glimpse of Sarah's
conglomerate attire. She wore his trousers under her skirt,
his coat over her blouse, and the slicker over that. His hat
shaded her features. She was taking his horse, too.

"Hey," he said, wincing at the effort. Sarah noticed him.
"Hey, look, honey, maybe we got off on the, uh, wrong
foot." Her gaze was anything but cordial. He struggled to
free his wrists, but she had double-knotted the rawhide.

"I'll get you for this," he snarled.

"Not without a horse."

"You can't just leave me like this. I'll freeze to death."

Sarah nodded and draped a horse blanket over him. She
knelt and checked his hastily bandaged skull. The outlaw
would live, but he'd have a nasty headache for a while.

"As long as you lie still, you'll keep warm. The choice is
yours."

"Who are you?" Vint asked, his eyes narrowed. A white
hot lance of pain skewered his skull. She stood, pushed her
auburn hair back, and adjusted her new hat. She returned to
the roan and checked the lead rope that secured the bandit's
gelding. Sarah climbed into the saddle and looked out
through the open doorway at the darkness.

"Who are you!!" Vint's voice echoed over the rolling,
snow-covered landscape, returned to die in haunting repeti-
tion among the walls of the ramshackle barn. The tracks of
Larocque's raiders dotted the ivory expanse. *If he were my
man, . . . Sweeney* had said.

"Who are you?" Vint asked again, staring at Sarah as she at last turned to face the bandit. And when she answered, it was in a low, soft, dusky voice full of self-realization and purpose.

"Silvertip's woman."

43

Two hard cold days in the saddle brought Larocque and his men to the wooded slope of Moon Woman Mountain. There among the dense carpet of the forest the bandits halted at evening to camp and formulate the plan of attack on Jessup's Bar Seven. The early winter storm that had plagued them and slowed their progress had at last cleared. Over the frozen landscape a new presence crept—a chinook wind, ripping down the corridor of the Rockies, turned pristine fields of snow to unappealing slush, warming the ragged reaches of the peaks and leaving in its wake ghostly ribbons of mist that writhed and coiled in a danse macabre. After a fitful dinner of beans and coffee, the outlaws huddled close to the campfires for comfort and defense against the fears that haunted their conversation and kept them alert and watchful and increasingly restless.

"Sleep, hell," one of the bandits muttered in response to Bascomb's orders.

"Felker, you'll wish you *had* rested when you face another hard ride tomorrow."

"I've heard the stories. We all have," another man said. Other grizzled countenances nodded in accord. The man who had first spoken stood and thrust his round scruffy features forward, crowding the gunman.

"Moon Woman Mountain ain't no place to make a night camp," Felker said. "Now look here, Bascomb, you can't tell me you'd not rather be someplace else. I gotta say what I feel. These parts is ha'nted. I can feel it. We all can. It's like an ache that don't never go away." Several of the men grumbled in accord. They had wanted to press on even in the fog. No matter that poor visibility might lead them to disaster.

"I say let's break camp. I'd sooner risk busting a leg or

a knock on the head from a tree limb. A man can deal with
that. But he can't deal with no damn ghost."

"There's them that has seen her," Jim Reasoner, Jessup's
ex-foreman intoned. He had learned years ago to beware of
Indian myths. They were too often grounded in truth. "She's
searching for Black Whirlwind. Gathering up his butchered
remains, scattered on the mountain. The Moon Woman," his
voice grew fainter. "They say she walks at night." He
glanced over his shoulder and, despite himself, gulped as the
mist draped the trees in billowing gray shrouds.

"The only pain I feel is the one in my ass. And it's your
doing," Bascomb sneered at his companions. And yet even
he cocked an eye toward the tendrils of mist, apprehensive
about what might lay hidden in their phantasmal depths.

Larocque listened to his men grumble and complain and
promised himself that tomorrow, when he had his hands on
the money in Jessup's safe, he would take leave of their
company. He fished a twig from the campfire closest to him
and touched the glowing tip to the bowl of his pipe, looking
through the billowing smoke at the half-breed boy who
crouched on the other side of the flames. Larocque had the
unsettling feeling he was staring into the accusing eyes of
Mourning Dove, as if she were watching him from beyond
the grave, from the halls of the dead, watching him through
the eyes of a boy. Larocque shuddered inwardly and winced
as the leg that was no longer flesh and blood seemed to ache,
as if it were something more than wood tipped with iron.

"You never speak," Larocque said. "You just watch. And
wait. Perhaps you look for the moment when you can escape.
Maybe I should let you, eh? Leave you here for the Moon
Woman to find."

The boy looked about, alarm shaping his expression. He
returned his gaze to the Frenchman and Larocque laughed.
"Your father may be white, but you have redskin superstitions. Your father should have taught you better. I know your
father. Did you realize we are old friends, Monsieur Silvertip
and I? Old friends. Or maybe I should say acquaintances."
Larocque drew sharply, exhaled an acrid cloud of smoke,
and shifted his bulk. He stroked his shaggy red beard and
watched the tobacco smoke dissipate. Then he leaned for-

ward and growled deep in his throat. He growled and roared, and the men around the other campfire paused in their grumbling to stare in wonder at the Frenchman. Had he gone mad? Larocque began to laugh, great heaving laughs that shook his whole body, and then he leaned forward on his hands and knees.

As Henri Larocque crawled toward him, Cub backed away in alarm, retreating toward the main fire, his bound hands pawing at the ground as he inched along until he backed into Bascomb who pushed him aside. The boy hit on his shoulder and rolled over onto his back. Larocque stood over him, wide and terrible, his countenance filled with the wrath of some terrible demon, a face tinged with the madness of those who know they are damned.

"How was that?" Larocque laughed. "Like a bear. Your father is Nahkohe, the Silvertip. But does he growl as well as Henri Larocque? Mais oui. He clawed me. Clawed my leg away. But I have his whelp. I have you. And I shall have your father's life." Larocque stared at his men and back to the boy. "Your eyes never leave me. You hate me, no?"

"You killed my mother," Cub said, wiping a tear from his cheek. He was ashamed that the Frenchman had frightened him so badly.

"I killed your mother. I will kill your father. And then you. Why not? Should I let you live to hunt me down and exact your vengeance? Why not finish what I have begun? Can a man be twice damned?" Larocque looked at the men around him, and gradually he calmed. "When I am certain he has no value as our prisoner—perhaps at the Jessup ranch. Yes. Why not? Everyone will blame the Red Shields for the attack on Jessup's ranch. Why not have the nephew of Sacred Killer found among the dead? A boy, wearing the war paint of the Red Shields, riding to avenge his father's imprisonment." Larocque grinned, a grimace of pure evil. He looked at Bascomb and Reasoner, Felker and the other men. He chuckled. "There are ghosts. I know better than most. The trick is in keeping your perspective." Larocque snorted and returned to his own private campfire.

"I don't know about the rest of you, but I ain't gonna be quit of his company a moment too soon," said Felker. Several of the others nodded. Reasoner wagged his head and looked over at Bascomb.

"He always been that loco?"

"I couldn't account for always," the gunman said. "And just so long as he makes me a rich man, I don't care for spit." Bascomb spat on the ground. "Afore I crossed his trail, I had figured to rob ol' man Jessup myself. And I probably would have had a dozen riders chasing me clear down to Mexico for my trouble. Larocque was the man with the plan. And like I said before, I'm willing to play it to the bust." Bascomb looked at those men circling the main fire. "We'll spool our beds when the mist burns off come morning. Felker, you can take the first watch. And make sure you keep an easy trigger finger on your rifle. Vint won't take kindly to a bullet in the brisket if he manages to catch up to us tonight."

Bascomb walked over to his bedroll and stretched out beneath his blankets. Reasoner looked around at the shifting obscurity of the forest.

"Not a sound," the foreman muttered. "I never heard a forest so still."

"Like a tomb," a voice added from his left.

"Oh Jesus," the man named Felker groaned.

"Just you keep watch on the breed," Bascomb ordered from his bedding.

"I am," Felker said. He leaned over and grabbed the youth by his roped wrists and pulled the boy over to the other side of the campfire. "You just lie here, you little bastard. You bat an eye wrong, it will be the last grief you ever give. Savvy?"

Cub nodded, dejectedly. He had begun to suspect the hopelessness of his situation.

The rest of the men in the clearing crawled beneath blankets and slickers and tried to sleep, but they soon found themselves listening to the oppressive silence of the woods. Now and then the chinook wind howled, sending the mist like an onrush of lost souls streaming over the camp. The unseen moon transformed the shape of the billowing mist to bone-white wraiths.

Night had come at last to Moon Woman Mountain.

Sarah crouched beneath an overhanging ledge on the slope above the bandits' camp and listened to their conversation. Sound carried with stark clarity in the mountains, and despite the muffling effect of the mist, she was able to understand almost everything that was said. Larocque's mad outburst may have frightened her, but his threat had filled her with dread. She had to rescue Cub. Her mind was filled with doubts. She wasn't cut out for this. How much more comforting to leave now and try to make her way back to Sweeney's Landing. And abandon Cub? What if Larocque should lose all control and kill the boy outright before help could reach him? Such mental debate only made Sarah all the more tired. She had no intention of abandoning the boy, not now, not ever.

Sarah crawled out from beneath the ledge and, exercising every caution, gradually worked her way along the slope, passing as quiet as a ghost among the brooding pines, feeling her way as best she could, and trying to suppress a rising tide of panic. The fog was thicker than she had imagined. Sarah wasn't sure she could find her way back to the glade in which she had left the horses. The phantom mist lay heavy on the land as the earth gave up its chill to the laving breath of the chinook wind. *What have I done? How could anyone be so stupid? Don't panic. This isn't going to help Cub or you one bit. Think. Plan.* Of what use was a plan, she needed to find the horses! She veered from the path she was on and started downslope until she reached approximately the same level as the bandits' camp, somewhere to the west. Two hours earlier she had tethered the roan and Vint's horse to a sapling and proceeded on foot, hoping to locate the camp. But how incredibly foolish not to have marked the path, not to have taken an extra precaution to insure her ability to find her way back. She stopped. Listened. What was that? Wait. Something moved ahead. Listen. Silence . . . then a soft whinny. The roan. It had to be the roan. Just ahead, yes, yes, yes. Her pace quickened, she stumbled blindly forward, brushed too close to a pine whose branches loomed out of the blanketing mist to swipe at her face. She ducked, lost her balance, and slipped to a halt in the melting snow. The horses stood where she had left them. The outlaw's horse had pawed away the snow and was busily cropping the dry yellow grass at the base of the sapling. Sarah stared at the roan and breathed a sigh of relief that ended in a sudden surge of terror as a hand reached out from behind and clamped over her mouth. She twisted, dug her fingernails into the wrist. A voice whispered sharply in her ear, "Sarah! Not a sound! It's me."

Joel?

The hand slipped away, and she whirled around scarcely daring to believe . . . chiseled features, blue eyes, poor crooked nose, silver mane, Silvertip, a man . . . her man. She threw her arms around him and bruised his lips with the fury of her kiss. As abruptly, she ended the kiss; her eyes flashed with anger, her Irish temperament rising.

"How—when—oh, you nearly frightened me to death." Joel motioned for her to lower her voice. "Grabbing me like that, it's a fine thing!"

"I couldn't be certain it was you. Not in that get-up," said Joel. Sarah glanced down at the mixture of her own clothes and those she had stolen from Vint. She spied other movement and realized there were three other horses behind hers. The mist shifted and obscured them again. Two men materialized out of the shadows. She recognized Ben Slade and of all people, Frank Jessup. She looked questioningly at Joel.

"We found Vint in the barn. And he told us what had happened and just exactly what Larocque intended."

"I'm surprised the man helped you," Sarah said.

"Joel persuaded him," Slade added. Joel cleared his throat and glanced sharply at the gambler.

"We've just about ridden our horses to death to catch up," Jessup said. "I don't know how much more they have left in them."

"Did you see Cub?" Joel interrupted.

"He's all right," Sarah nodded. "But I wouldn't dare guess for how long. Larocque . . . I've never felt such menace from one individual. It's like he isn't . . . quite human. He threatened Cub."

"We've got to act now," Joel said. "Saddle up. We're
going in."

"Wait," Sarah said.

"I've waited too long for this," Joel snapped. "I want Larocque."

"Over your son's dead body?"

"She's right, Ryan," Jessup said.

"What the hell do you care?" Joel said angrily.

"My son is dead. Whatever else Tod was, I loved him.
That buys my way into this. My dues are paid in blood the
same as yours. Look, I have been wrong all the way. I didn't
know how wrong until that man, Vint, told me. I've been a
jackass, in town and on the trail, because I wouldn't listen
to anyone else. I figure one jackass in this group is enough."

Joel relaxed, breathed deeply, shook his head. "You got
a better plan, Colonel?" Jessup shrugged and shook his head
no as Joel shifted his gaze. "Gambler?"

"No," Slade sighed, hooking his thumbs in the sash at his
waist.

"So—" Joel said and started toward the horses.

"I do."

It was Sarah.

An hour of silence, an hour to think, to listen to the heart
beat, an hour for the mind to conjure nightmares out of the
misshapen shadows of trees and boulders where the vaporous
phantoms swirled and twisted.

*A man could learn to believe in ghosts on a night like
this,* the bandit named Felker thought to himself. Would
morning never come? Cry for the sun, cry for day to scour
the demon spirits from these hills. How many men had died
on this bloody ground? One for certain, the Cheyenne, Black
Whirlwind—cut to pieces and scattered over the land for his
woman to find. She walks by night. She walks . . .

He heard the moan, a low anguished appeal that stood his
hair on end and stilled the flow of blood in his veins. Was
he mad at last? No. Reasoner sat upright from his blankets.
The moan sounded again. Other men heard it, bodies shifted,
and men leaned on elbows or rose to look about in helpless
anger, searching among their own number for the prankster.

"Aaaaaaaahhhhhhhhhh . . ." A cry of pain, of anguish, of remorse. A woman's voice! Son of a bitch, that was a woman's voice.

"Do you hear that?" someone whispered uselessly. Even Larocque was standing now and staring at the shrouded woods.

"The wind," he muttered. "Only the wind."

A shape materialized out of the mist, a specter to haunt a man's sleep for years to come. A woman astride a dark horse. But what . . . who could possibly be out on a night like this, here in the middle of nowhere? She became more defined, horribly so, as she neared the camp.

"Hold it right there," Bascomb ordered in an unconvincing voice. "I said—"

"She can't hear you," Reasoner interrupted.

"God in heaven, she don't hear nobody!" Felker cried.

The woman was draped in blankets from head to foot, her hair was shimmering white and frizzed out in every direction like a mass of serpents sprouting from her skull. Her face was bleached white in the ghastly light, the face of a woman long dead, bloodless and bone-colored and utterly horrible to look upon. Her eyes were round black circles of evil. Her cry was terrible to hear, an outpouring of unearthly anguish.

The bandits nearest the intruder retreated and scattered. Cub, as frightened as the rest, backed into Felker. The bandit shoved him away.

"It's her. Heaven help us. The Moon Woman!"

"Can't be," Larocque said in a whisper. But it was. Who else but her? He stared, as awestruck as the rest.

"You idiots," Bascomb snarled and raised his revolver.

"No, you'll turn her agin' us," one of the men called out.

"Put the gun away," Reasoner ordered in a hushed voice, his own revolver pointed at Bascomb. "Let her pass. She'll leave us be."

The specter angled toward the camp, and men tripped over one another to keep out of her way. She looked neither to the left or right, and no man in his right mind would wish to attract the attention of a ghost.

"Christ almighty," Felker howled. The Moon Woman seemed to be headed straight for him. "Save yourself, boy!"

the outlaw shouted to Cub, who picked himself off the
ground and froze, watching in horror as the Moon Woman
approached. He waited, transfixed by the apparition. Yet
something caught his attention despite his terror, something
he tried to identify, something peculiar. He was unable to
run; fear had rooted him in place. The woman drew close.
The wind howled among the trees. Ribbons of hellish mist
swept over the clearing. Closer still. The Moon Woman and
the horse—the horse? That was it!

The roan! His father's horse. He could even see the Morning Star brand.

Cub glanced up at the face of the Moon Woman. Rec-
ognition flashed across his features in the same instant that
Sarah McClinton stretched out her hand and spoke his name.
"Nahkohe-ese!"

Several things happened at once. The boy clumsily
grabbed for her hand and swung up behind Sarah as the roan
bolted forward out of the clearing. Larocque, with the instinct
of a hunter who has just pried open the jaws of a trap and
seen the prey he had thought crippled leap away unharmed,
lunged for his rifle and roared for Bascomb to shoot. His
orders were drowned out by a wave of gunfire that came not
from his men but Joel, Slade, and Jessup, who charged on
horseback into the clearing. A wild rebel yell split the air as
Joel slashed through the camp, his revolver blazing a path.
His fury was contagious. Slade and Jessup loosed earsplitting
shrieks and emptied their guns at the bandits.

Men leaped aside; men crumbled beneath the flashing
hooves; others dived for their weapons as guns flashed fire
and smoke. For several seconds all was clamor and noise
and explosion. A horse bore down on Larocque. A bullet
notched his ear. The Frenchman howled and fired his Winchester at his attacker. Bascomb ran up, his revolvers trailing
gunsmoke. Behind Bascomb, the rest of the bandits who had
gone from blind terror to surprise to mind-numbing alarm
staggered back toward the scattered coals of the campfire.
The echoes of the brief gunfight rippled in the distance. Off
to the left, the horses whinnied and pulled in startled terror
at their tether lines. One of the outlaws rose groaning from

the ground, holding his head where the hooves of Slade's horse had slashed his scalp.

"See to the horses," Larocque bellowed, wiping the blood from the side of his head. Reasoner holstered his gun, and grabbing another man by the collar, he propelled him toward the horses. The foreman looked toward Larocque.

"I'd swear one of those riders was Colonel Jessup." He hurried off to check on their mounts. First a ghost, then Frank Jessup. What the hell?

"She's gone." Felker stumbled forward, holding his wounded right arm. "The ghost is gone. She captured the boy, Mister Larocque."

"You damn idiot," said Bascomb. Felker backed away. He wanted no confrontation with the gunman.

"I caught a glimpse of one of them," Bascomb said.

"Who?" Larocque asked.

"Silvertip Ryan."

Larocque chuckled. "Of course." He stared at the gradually reassembled camp. "Of course."

"You think it's funny? Ryan wasn't alone. The fat's in the fire. They know sure as hell we aren't a Red Shield war party. These hills are gonna get mighty hot for us. And soon," Bascomb said, his face livid as he reloaded his Colts.

"What the Sam Hill are we gonna do, you crazy bastard!"

Larocque ignored the outburst. His gaze was fixed on the forest. He wiped his ear and licked the blood from his hand and grinned a crimson smile that made even a hard case like Kid Bascomb shudder.

44

Joel took the lead and waved for those behind him to halt. Visibility was simply too poor, and he couldn't risk crippling a horse. He leaped down from the saddle and hurried to catch Cub as the boy climbed off the roan. Joel's knife flashed and the boy's bonds fell away, freeing him to embrace his father. The big man glanced up at Sarah.

"I won't ever forget," Joel said in a hushed voice. Then he laughed.

"You looks a sight."

Sarah blushed and ran her fingers through the tangle of her hair.

"It's amazing what a little clay and powdered limestone and charcoal will do," she said.

"They aren't following, as far as I can tell," Slade announced, joining them.

"Larocque's crafty. He knows we can't travel too far in this fog," Joel said. "He'll be along." He held his son at arm's length. "You all right?"

"Now I am," Cub replied, smiling bravely, his eyes moist. A deep and painful sigh escaped from Jessup. The colonel bowed forward over his saddle. Joel hurried to his side and in steadying the older man discovered the patch of blood on the back of the colonel's coat.

"I caught one," Jessup said through clenched teeth. "Belva would scold me and tell me I'm too old for such shenanigans, but by heaven, that was as pretty a charge as ever I saw." He winced. Joel felt for and found the ragged bullet hole in the material. "Waste of a good coat," Jessup added with a grimace. "You'll have to help me down."

"Maybe you better stay put," Joel said. "I'll lead your horse. The rest of us better walk. It's slow but safer going."

He removed his bandana and worked it up inside Jessup's coat in hopes of staunching the wound.

"You don't think they've had their fill of us?" Sarah asked hopefully.

Joel shook his head.

"God in heaven," Jessup groaned.

"Sorry," Joel said, gingerly adjusting the makeshift compress.

"Not your fault," Jessup said through clenched teeth. "Feels like my shoulder's broke." His face contorted as a wave of pain washed over him. "I guess I'm not as tough as I like to think."

"None of us is, Colonel. But you'll do to ride the trail with, sir," Joel said, his respect for the man increasing. They had all made mistakes. High time the slate was wiped clean. Jessup seemed to read his thoughts. He settled himself in the saddle. "I'm ready," he muttered.

"Son, you see to my horse," Joel said as he started forward, the reins from Jessup's horse securely in his grasp. Cub followed his father's instructions, though he paused when nearing Sarah who was busily scrubbing the powdered limestone from her face with a bandana she had soaked in the melting snow. She sensed his stare and looked up at him. He wore a confused expression, as if searching for the proper words to describe how he felt. He kicked at a clump of snow and pursed his lips and at last turned to follow his father. Slade walked up alongside Sarah and scratched at his stubbled jawline. His once elegant attire was trail-worn and patched with mud stains. It galled him to present such an unkempt appearance. He doffed his hat and coughed and indicated Joel's son.

"I believe he thanked you."

"In his own way," Sarah said. "I understood him perfectly well."

"He's a lucky boy," Slade commented. "And Ryan's a lucky man."

Sarah glanced over at the gambler, but he directed himself to watching the trail behind them. "After you, ma'am."

"You are gracious, sir," said Sarah. She stepped forward into the shifting patterns of mist.

• • •

Time became as meaningless as distance. Indistinguishable figures moving in a moonlit world of black and gray, a world of dimly recognized hollows and ravines.

Joel had hunted the slopes of Moon Woman Mountain hundreds of times over the years, but in its cloak of mist, the terrain shifted and defied his memory. He led the others forward, paused to get his bearings, reassured himself of their location. He kept his misgivings to himself. Larocque would undoubtedly pursue them. He was probably tracking them even now. Escape was out of the question. With the horses near exhaustion and Jessup barely able to stay in the saddle, Larocque's raiders would have no problem riding them down.

"Joel." Sarah's voice reached to him out of the gloom. He waited until she drew abreast of him.

"Colonel Jessup is in a bad way. We have to rest. His wound is still bleeding," she said, leaning forward, putting her hand on his arm. "He can't keep on like this."

The others pulled alongside now, leading their mounts except for the colonel. Cub had taken charge of Jessup's horse, allowing Joel to devote his attention to the mountain trail.

"Trouble?" Slade said. Joel shook his head no and pointed downslope.

"About fifty yards straight ahead you'll come to a spring or its runoff. Crazy Mule Spring. If you hit the runoff, just follow it uphill to its source. The spring itself is a depression in the ground. A fair-sized sink though, it ought to offer some protection and a clear field of fire."

"I know where it is," Cub said.

"Good boy. Can you lead them to it?"

"Yes, sir."

Joel clapped his son on the shoulder. "It's as good a place as any to make a stand."

"We won't die of thirst, Nahkohe," Cub grinned.

"Him lead us?" Slade asked. "What are you going to be doing?"

"Buying some time," Joel said. "And lessening the odds some if I can." He passed the reins to Sarah.

"My rifle's in the saddle boot. I'll travel faster without it."

"Joel," she hesitated, her tone worried. At last she gave way to impulse. And she didn't care a whit what anyone else might think. She leaned into Joel and kissed him on the lips. Joel held her in his arms and pressed her to him and drank in the sight, smell, and touch of her. Only grudgingly did she pull away. Joel turned to Cub and nodded.

"*Na-ase,* Little Bear."

"*Ne-sta-va-hóse-voomatse,*" the youth replied, a son cautioning his father to be careful.

"*E-peva-e.*" Joel glanced over at Slade. "I'll find you. And when I do, I might have company hard on my heels."

"I'll be careful where I point my gunsight." The gambler chuckled. "Just be sure you light a shuck back here."

"I don't aim to dally," Joel said.

Slade thumbed a card from his tattered vest. The Queen of Hearts. He tucked it inside Joel's buckskin shirt.

"She always brought me luck," Slade said. "Never failed yet."

"Thanks," said Joel. He looked at the colonel bowed low over his pommel, the pain-glazed slits of his eyes centered on the saddle horn. He was all but oblivious to any gesture of farewell. Joel turned and trotted back the way they had come.

"That's one hell of a man," Slade remarked. Sarah heard the gambler as she stared at the swirling vapors of night that had already swallowed Silvertip Ryan.

45

The world wore its mantle of obscurity. Morning approached. Above the jagged battlements to the east, the stars winked out one by one, as if reluctant to depart sweet heaven now that the clouds were blown away. Moon Woman Mountain in its ghostly majesty awaited the amber benediction of the sun.

By the time a golden tide of light spilled down the ridge and gave its Midas touch to the misted slopes, Henri Larocque led his men along the trail the fugitives had left him to follow. His keen eyes probed the gilded fog born of cool ground and warm air. It took little effort to find the trail, but caution slowed his progress. He did not intend to blunder into an ambush and ordered his men to space themselves to either side of him. Bathed in the richness of the risen sun, the forest had lost its macabre quality. The dawn's impressive display failed to elicit any appreciation from these hard riders. They were after a different gold, to be found in a safe at Frank Jessup's ranch. Their course of action was obvious: Ride the boy and his benefactors down, kill them, and head for the ranch. And, of course, leave evidence focusing blame on Sacred Killer's warriors.

What could be simpler?

Silence ruled the shrouded land, a quiet gradually disturbed by the tread of horses, the muttered epithets of saddle-weary men, the rustle and crack of trampled underbrush.

Henri Larocque kept his gelding to a slow, steady, unhurried pace. The Frenchman rode directly in the center of the trail Joel and the others had left. He followed more from instinct and lifted his eyes to the forest, searching the woods for any sign of trouble. Ryan would push his companions as far as stamina allowed. By now he was probably holed up somewhere ahead. Maybe even planning a surprise or two. Larocque was not a man who liked surprises. He preferred control. His carefully orchestrated plan for acquiring Jessup's wealth, as well as having his revenge on Silvertip Ryan, was dangerously close to going awry. This morning might well set the stage for success or failure. Come what may, Henri Larocque was ready. He rode through shimmering patches of mist. And his men rode with him.

One of them, Tug Collins, was riding alone on the far left of the desperadoes when he was distracted from his thoughts by a glimmer of something in the sunlight, a flash of metal, gold metal if his eyes weren't playing tricks on him. Collins was a boyish-faced vagabond of countless Texas border towns who had wandered north to the Rockies to try his luck at prospecting. Honest work proved much too arduous; panning for gold or grubbing a handful of nuggets out of a cliff at the risk of life and limb was not his style. A dangerous and greedy young man, Collins had fit easily into Larocque's gang of cutthroats.

A flash of sunfire. Damn. What on earth? He allowed his companions to pull ahead, his mind already filled with the prospect of discovering something of value. He pinpointed the reflection, a single golden eye blinking amid a tangle of fallen logs and blackberry bramble. He picked his way carefully through the rising mist. He heard voices, recognized Bascomb calling out to the others to tighten their ranks. They were too scattered, Bascomb was saying, tighten up.

"Yeah, yeah, yeah," muttered Collins, his attention rooted on the beckoning metal. He slid his rifle into the saddle boot and, gripping the pommel with his left hand, swung over to the right, his right leg bearing the brunt of his weight.

A gold double eagle lay balanced in the twining branches of the underbrush. Where it came from, who cared? Collins smiled, his eyes glittered as he stretched out to snare his discovery.

"Come here, easy money," he chuckled.

Too late he spied the bowie knife extending from a strong right arm and behind it, emerging from the mist, a merciless face framed by a silver mane. Collins opened his mouth in surprise, started to cry a warning, but the broad steel blade knocked the double eagle aside and buried itself in his throat. Collins collapsed like a rag doll. He dropped from horseback and slammed into Joel, who was reaching for the reins. The mare backstepped and leaped with startled grace down the trail toward the other horses. The reins flirted with Joel's outstretched fingers before being whisked away by the frightened animal.

Joel muttered a curse and emerged from hiding to give chase. He leaped over Collins's remains and ran with great leaping strides through the forest. The riderless mare would alert Larocque and the others.

Joel's eyes ranged the forest for another hiding place and a new point of attack. Alongside the trail, three tree trunks had managed to sprout from the earth in an unusual and crowded arrangement. They'd provide just enough cover. Joel wiped his knife blade in the moist earth, then he sheathed the weapon and headed for the trees.

"Collins! What the hell is going on?" Kid Bascomb shouted.

"It's him!" Larocque roared. "By heaven I would swear to it."

Collins's horse had given them all a start as it plunged through their midst.

"He could have fallen off," Reasoner offered as he brought his own gelding under control. Larocque wheeled his stallion around and waved for his men to follow him back up the trail. Bascomb, Reasoner, and the rest followed suit. Larocque wasted no time in retracing the stallion's route through the woods.

"Collins!" one of the men shouted. "Hey, Collins!" The riders once again fanned out, a feeling of uneasiness spreading through their ranks. Ghosts at night, then riders sweeping through camp with their guns blazing, now morning and Collins disappears—it was enough to give a man the willies for sure. In less than five minutes, Larocque had traced the mare's tracks to the blackberry thicket. His stallion shied at the smell of blood, but Larocque kept a tight rein and forced the animal to draw closer. Collins lay sprawled in death, wreathed by the sunlit vapors of dawn. Bascomb rode up beside the Frenchman and stared down at the corpse with its slashed throat and expression of surprise and almost comic disapproval.

"What the hell happened?" Bascomb asked, trying to clear the hoarseness from his throat.

"The grizzly has shown his claws," Larocque said, levering a cartridge into his rifle, his head craning around to search the woods.

"Silvertip," he added. And began to laugh.

"Silvertip!" he shouted, then.

The name reverberated through the forest. Joel waited while the bandits passed below him. One of them, cradling his wounded shoulder, brought up the rear. Joel silently willed the man to ride within range. The rider paused and seemed to debate whether to press on. His horse moved of his own volition, started toward the cluster of trees. Joel tensed, balanced himself on a branch.

Larocque, in the misty shadows ahead, shouted his name, again. The branch quivered beneath Joel's weight, a pine cone dropped, narrowly missing the rider, who glanced upward on reflex.

Joel leaped. His massive frame slammed into the wounded man. Larocque's call echoed in the dawn. Felker, the rider, screamed as Joel's knife glanced off his ribs. The horse, a sturdy little mustang, neighed and reared in terror. Joel tossed the outlaw from the horse. Figures plunged toward him out of the slanting sunlight. The stirrups were too short, but Joel gripped the mustang with his knees and brought the animal under control.

"He's killed Felker," someone shouted. "Over there. Get him."

A revolver cracked. Then another. A chunk of bark exploded from the pine tree nearest Joel. He sheathed his knife and, crouching low in the saddle, darted off among the trees. The outlaws took up the pursuit. Larocque and Bascomb were left to bring up the rear. The Frenchman shouted in vain for them to wait. Gunfire erupted in the dawn. Here was something tangible, a threat they could face, a man they could kill. And no one needed the likes of Henri Larocque to tell them how to kill.

• • •

The sun burned the last traces of mist from the mountains and bathed the valleys in its molten pureness until the land shimmered in amber and gold. Beneath the sapphire sky, remnants of snow clung to the lee side of ridges and checkered the forested slopes where the branches of pines fractured the sunlight and the chill of the recent storm lingered in pockets of perpetual twilight. Joel broke from the line of trees with his pursuers closing fast. The mustang was game, but it simply could not manage much of a gallop with its outsize rider clinging to his back.

Nearly a hundred yards of clear ground lay ahead. Joel could just make out the roan and the rest of the horses tethered at the spring. Sarah, Cub, Jessup, and the gambler were out of sight, hidden behind the natural cover afforded them by the depression. Joel never slowed his pace as he drew his Colt revolver and fired a single shot to alert his companions. He needn't have wasted the round, for a few moments later eight bandits burst from the cover of the trees charging hellfor-leather in his wake, the rapid fire from their guns rippling over the landscape.

Joel concentrated on staying alive. He holstered his gun and, crouching low in the saddle, drove his heels into the flanks of the mustang, urging the animal to its utmost effort. Only a hundred yards. Ninety. Seventy-five. Slugs tore at his sleeve, nipped at his buckskin pants, whispered fatal secrets as they cut past his ear and brushed his cheek.

Bascomb emerged from the woods, walking his horse out into the clear ground. He dismounted and drew his rifle from its boot; dropping to one knee, he sighted carefully along the barrel. He knew what needed to be done.

Fifty yards.

Bascomb fired. Joel felt the mustang stagger from the impact of the slug that ripped through the animal's lungs. Only the fact that Joel's feet weren't caught in the stirrups saved his life; the mustang pitched forward and sent him spinning head over heels. The horse lowered its head and tumbled forward as its front legs buckled. Joel rolled clear of the slashing hooves and crushing weight, gauged in a second his

chances of crossing the gently sloping ground and reaching
the relative safety of the spring. Bullets notched the ground
at his feet and decided for him. He leaped back toward the
dead mustang and curled himself against the twitching remains of the horse as the ground thundered to the wild charge
of Larocque's killers and bullet after bullet ploughed into the
carcass. Joel chanced a look toward the spring. Where the
devil was everybody?

Larocque! The death of Hemené, the return of her killer,
the kidnapping of Cub, and now Sarah—would she die too?
All because of one man. Anger welled in Joel like a fire
through his veins. Suddenly he was standing, this great huge
bear of a man, standing with his knife like a terrible steel
claw in one hand, a gun in the other. Defying the bullets that
ripped the air around him, defying these men to bring him
down if they dared, Joel charged the startled outlaws. He
roared his challenge. The revolver bucked in his fist, spat
flame. One of the bandits tumbled backward out of the saddle. The rest faltered, pulling up in alarm before this man
who seemed more like his namesake than human, more like
Lord Grizzly himself.

Silvertip.

The foreman, Jim Reasoner, was far too seasoned a cam-
paigner to be awed for long. He steadied his horse, not bothering to dismount. Here was an easy shot. He shouldered his
Winchester, determined to bring Joel down. He steadied his
aim, squeezed the trigger, and heard the crack of a rifle—
not his own—then the report of several rifles as blossoms of
gunsmoke sprouted from the rim of Crazy Mule Spring. Panic spread through the bandits as gunfire poured into them,
dropping more of their number as they fought to bring their
startled horses under control. Joel was surprised at the volume of gunfire exploding from the spring, but he could not
spare a glance. The bandit he had shot, a bearded lout with
bandoleros crisscrossing his chest rose from the ground, a
patch of blood spreading across his stomach. He yelled his
challenge and leveled his guns. Joel fired, and the man flew
backward on his haunches leaving an empty boot upright in
the churned earth. Suddenly, the high-pitched war cry of the
Red Shields rent the air, and Joel glanced around in amaze-

ment as Sacred Killer and White Frog, along with Ben Slade, galloped up out of the spring.

The two Cheyenne braves wore the garish red paint of their warrior clan, but instead of lances, they brandished rifles painted blood red like their war shields. Reasoner's bullet tore a crescent of flesh out of Joel's left arm and knocked him to the ground. The foreman chambered another round. Joel fired and missed. Reasoner aimed, then he changed targets as Sacred Killer split the air with a wild war whoop. Joel squeezed off a second shot, and Reasoner doubled over and fired into the ground before sliding from the saddle. Sacred Killer swept past and shot the wounded man. The force of the bullet slammed Reasoner into the dirt. He did not move again.

Joel stood as the gunfire increased in intensity. He saw Sacred Killer jerk around in surprise, blood spurting from him. The warrior dropped his rifle to clutch his shattered shoulder with his good hand. The outlaw who had shot him rode in to finish off the chief at point-blank range. Joel raised his Colt, steadied, squeezed the trigger. The hammer struck an empty cylinder. Suddenly, a fountain of crimson jetted from the outlaw's chest as Ben Slade cut between the combatants and emptied his gun into the man. White Frog scattered the remainder of the gang, as he charged into the melee with his rifle spitting fire and death. When the rifle clicked empty, he used his razor-sharp tomahawk, splitting skulls and ripping flesh in a killing frenzy as impossible to contain as an avalanche. And Joel was with him, the bowie knife red to the hilt like the paw of a grizzly fresh from the kill. Stab and slash and twist the blade free.

"Larocque!" he shouted. Not among the dead. Not among the living. Where?

A horse galloped out of the fray, trailing a gunman who splashed the yellow grass with blood as he was dragged, bouncing, over the rocky terrain. A quarter of a mile later his back was in tatters, and he had quit screaming, though the horse continued to run.

The fight was over as quickly as it had begun. There had been the violent clamor of guns. Now came the equally unsettling aftermath of stillness. White Frog held three outlaws at gunpoint, the savage look on his face inviting them to continue the fight. Sacred Killer walked his horse back toward Joel. Slade, alongside the war chief, stabbed a thumb in the Indian's direction. "The cavalry," the gambler chuckled.

"Haa-he, Nahkohe," said Sacred Killer, gingerly cradling his arm. "Last night we heard the guns speak on the mountains. We found Little Bear and the others before *ese-he*, the sun, showed itself above the hills. We thought you might wish our help." Sacred Killer grinned, then his expression grew serious beneath the veneer of war paint. "Little Bear told me of the white woman's courage." The chief of the Red Shields winced with pain. "I have wronged her with my thoughts." Joel looked back toward the spring and saw Sarah standing with Cub on the lip of the depression. Sarah in her ragged garments and unkempt hair had never looked lovelier to him.

Bascomb had retreated to the forest the minute he saw the Cheyenne braves charge from Crazy Mule Spring. He watched as one after another of Larocque's men were shot out of the saddle, each death a nail in the coffin of Bascomb's hopes and dreams. He checked the area to either side and wondered just where the hell Larocque had gone. The Frenchman had to have witnessed the destruction of his company of killers.

"Larocque," Bascomb shouted. "What do you think of your plans now? I should have known better, you crazy bastard!" He turned and, still on foot, led his horse up the forested slope, searching the ground for the tracks left by the departed Frenchman.

"He played us all for a bunch of blasted idiots," Bascomb muttered aloud. *Idiots. I should never have listened*, he thought. *I should have known better than to trust in his schemes*. He searched the surrounding woods and could find no sign of Henri Larocque. But he had to be somewhere. And not too far off. Bascomb began to widen his circle, his eyes searching the spongy earth with its carpet of pine needles and snow-patched shadows. Bascomb stopped in his tracks and listened. No sound of birds fluttering among the branches, no squirrels searching out their fall harvest among barricades of dead wood. Not even the sound of distant gunfire. Only an ominous quiet, as if the forest was holding its breath. As if the mountain itself awaited the day's final disaster. Bascomb tucked the flaps of his duster back behind his twin holsters. Cocked rifle in one hand and reins in the other, he paused. His gaunt features set, he gazed malevolently at the surrounding forest. *Nobody makes a fool out of me*, he thought to himself. *Nobody. A day will come, and I'll teach Mister Henri Larocque a thing or two.*

He heard the peculiar whir of an arrow and tried to dodge it, loosing the reins of his horse, leaping, trying to turn. The shaft struck him between the shoulder blades. The pain took his breath away. He lost his grip on the Winchester. It skidded across the ground. But not his Colt revolvers that leaped into his hands almost with a will of their own. He stumbled toward an outcropping of stone, the nearest cover. If he could only reach . . .

Movement! Bascomb whirled and brought his guns to bear and blasted a flicker of sunlight. There! He fired and shattered a branch that had trembled in a passing breeze.

"Show yourself, you yellow son of a bitch!" Bascomb shouted in a cracked voice. He spun and fired three times and chased a fawn from concealment. As the frightened animal scampered out of sight, an arrow passed completely through Bascomb's throat and thwacked into the trunk of a nearby pine tree. Bascomb coughed blood and tried to scream. He stumbled toward the rocks. Another arrow sank to its scarlet feathers in his stomach, the quivering length skewered him like an insect on a collector's pallet. He tripped and fell. The ground rose up to slap him. The gunman writhed in agony as the weight of his body drove the flint-pointed shafts deeper into his vitals.

The twin Colts lay a few feet away. Kid Bascomb didn't remember losing them. He reached out, gagged, and, dying, heard someone laugh.

The noon sun stared down at the freshly dug graves and the dark and bloody ground, on the three remaining outlaws

bound hand and foot on horseback, on the travois that carried
Frank Jessup, too weak to ride but strong enough to complain
that no one had given him a gun in the fight. Joel had kept
apart from the preparations, watching White Frog bind up
Sacred Killer's wound. The war chief of the Red Shields
glanced at Joel from time to time, his face betraying a mixture of frustration and pain. He had read Joel's thoughts. He
knew that Larocque was not among the dead, that the mur-
derer of his sister, Joel's wife, was still on the loose. When
the warrior could move, he walked unsteadily over to Joel.
Cub was sitting near his father. Sarah came up from the
spring, carrying a canteen freshly filled with icy water. She
handed the canteen to Joel. When he reached for it, his fingers touched her right hand and lingered a moment. Cub
watched the subtle display of affection. He did not seem to
mind. Joel looked over at Sacred Killer heading toward them.
Then he turned to his son.

"Little Bear, my son, it is time you made a man's decision. I give you your freedom; if you wish it, return to your
mother's people or remain at Morning Star with"—a sidelong look at Sarah—"with us. The choice is yours to make."

The youth watched his uncle approach. He stared at his
father and Sarah, then glanced over his shoulder at Moon
Woman Mountain where only a day ago he had been a captive. He drew close and, reaching out, entwined his fingers
in Sarah's left hand. It was answer aplenty. Tears came to
Sarah's eyes, and she embraced the half-breed boy, hugging
him close as any mother would her son.

Sacred Killer stopped before them, his stern features softened. He seemed to understand what had transpired. "It is
good," he said. He looked at Joel. "You are going?"

Joel cast a worried glance in Sarah's direction. He had
yet to reveal his intentions to her. "You are going," Sacred
Killer continued, this time more a statement of understanding
than a question. The chief of the Red Shields took a knife
from the beaded belt at his waist and pressed the blade
against the bloodstained bandages binding his wounded
shoulder. The blade came away moist and crimson at the tip.
Sacred Killer passed the knife to Joel.

"A part of me will ride with you, Nahkohe. It is all I can do now."

Joel removed his own knife from its sheath and exchanged it with the Cheyenne brave's.

"It is a long day's ride to Jessup's ranch," Joel said. "Will you be all right?"

"It will be a strange thing, to enter Jessup's lodge in peace."

"You saved his life. All our lives," Joel said.

"Yet I leave the most difficult task for you, Nahkohe. Be watchful, my brother." Sacred Killer looked toward Cub. "Little Bear, help your uncle to his horse."

The youth appeared puzzled a moment. Then he realized the Cheyenne warrior was providing a few seconds of privacy for Joel and Sarah. Relinquishing his hold on the Irishwoman, Cub came to Sacred Killer's aid and accompanied the wounded chief back to the camp.

Joel sighed and faced Sarah, alone with her at last.

"I was going to tell you, as soon as I figured out how." The wind played between them, brushing them with the breath of the blessed land and carrying the scent of the pines. It smelled of sweat and earth and growing and dying. There were words in the wind. Sarah had heard them, lying asleep upon the land, lying at twilight and watching the stars unfold in glory, lying alone in her bed at Morning Star, and lying not alone but in the fury, in the trembling climax and sweet peace of Joel's arms.

She had listened and understood; she had found him in the wind, in the forest; she had found him in the land. He was Joel Ryan. And he was Nahkohe—Silvertip. He was the wilderness: its savagery, tenderness, ugliness and beauty, the mirror to all its moods, every storm, every moment of peace.

And now he must be its justice.

"When I heard Henri Larocque had escaped, I knew you would follow," said Sarah. "So I filled your canteen." She touched his stubbled cheek. "You will do what must be done. You could no more behave any differently than the sun could rise in the west." Sarah kissed him, resisting the thought that this might be the last time. "I'll be waiting," she whispered.

Joel noticed Cub standing somewhat aloof from the others; he knew his father was leaving. He knew why. The pride on his face was worth dying for, thought Joel Ryan, as was the love in Sarah's eyes.

46

The hills had eyes. Joel rode beneath their blank staring faces and pretended not to notice that they watched. Days passed. His flesh wound stiffened and formed a crust. By the time he forded the Big Horn River and entered the Crow Reservation, his arm was nearly healed. The trail he followed crisscrossed over rippling terrain, veering east, south, west, and south again, gradually angling into Crow territory. Joel remembered that in the past, Larocque could count on a friend or two among the Crow nation. Joel had none.

The sun, looking like a blood clot in the sky, did not move—at least not when Joel paused to stare at it. But every time he looked away, it inched toward the western hills, dipping downward to the distant pink cliffs. It colored the endless caravan of clouds overhead, clouds that plodded out of the north, shaping and reshaping themselves into bears and dragons and faceless sheiks whose airy mounts were the advance guard of winter.

Joel shivered, soaked from the river crossing. He guided the roan to a promising campsite. Wood was scarce except along the meandering riverbank where cottonwood, box elder, willow, and scrub oak resplendent in their autumnal foliage grew in thick profusion. Beyond the river, the treeless, convoluted landscape stretched for mile after bitter mile, terrain that had hidden more than two thousand Cheyenne and Sioux warriors while Custer led his Seventh Cavalry to its doom. Joel discovered enough deadwood to last him the night, and before an hour passed, he was warming himself before a cheerful, if lonely, blaze. He did not listen for battlefield ghosts; being victim to his own haunting, he needed no other.

Joel slept. Or thought he did. And yet he opened his eyes,

feeling the presence of his visitor. Two yellow orbs glimmering like medieval pools in the darkness. The pad of feet
and faint rustle of fur as the coyote stalked through the underbrush and emerged out of the jade darkness to rest on its
haunches by the campfire. A howling in the forest. Joel
looked away, then back at his visitor. The coyote was gone,
and in its place was a hunchbacked, wizened man dressed in
furs. Joel could hear the old man's bones creak beneath the
leathery trappings of flesh.

It was Maomé—Ice. And he was dead. Or so the legends
said.

"Nahkohe." His voice was like the rising of the wind.
Drums sounded faint in the distance. A drum or a heartbeat.
Perhaps Joel's heart.

"Haa-he, old teacher," Joel replied. "It is said you walk
the forests of the dead."

"A man chooses which forest he will walk," the medicine
man said with customary indifference. "Is it not so?"

"Still full of questions, coyote-man," Joel said.

"Answers if you would listen."

"Am I mad at last that I converse with the dead?"

"You have said it, not I." The medicine man shrugged.

"If I am mad, so be it," Joel replied. "Tell me, old friend
for I am weary of this chase. Yet I cannot rest until the one
called Larocque pays for his crimes."

"Revenge is a knife without a handle. It cuts him that
holds it as well."

"You always knew my thoughts, old father. Then know
them now. Mourning Dove was taken from me. And I wept.
But now another has come into my life, her name is Sarah.
She has eased the pain within me."

"And still you hunt this man?"

"Not for revenge. As men leave footprints on the earth,
so wherever he walks, Larocque leaves tracks of pain and
violence. It is time the world was rid of him and rid of the
misery he causes."

"So you will do the will of the Great Spirit," said Maomé.

"I do what must be done. Tell me if I am wrong."

Was it the wind or did the old man sigh once more? Joel
heard him say, "Perhaps you are both doomed. This I cannot

tell." Maomé wagged his head and stroked his wrinkled war map of a face with his knobby fingers. Still squatting he drew a circle in the dirt.

"You remember the teachings of the People?"

"That life is a circle, that our childhood mirrors all our childhoods, the sun rises, sets, we face the east again," Joel muttered. "But how does this help me?"

"The circle ends where it began. It ends where it began. It ends where it began."

Joel awoke. The circle! Of course! It explained why La-rocque had suddenly quit trying to lose him. As if the Frenchman too had reached a decision. Now Joel knew where Larocque was heading. He looked toward the Pryor Mountains, invisible in the distance, seeing them in his mind, though. At last he turned and stretched back out on his blanket, mentally thanking the figment of his dreams who had ridden on wings of sleep to his aid. Joel reached over to stoke the campfire and froze. The hair stood on the back of his neck as he stared at the circle drawn in the dirt between him and the fire.

The wind stirred the leaves in the branches overhead and made the trees sound as if they were laughing. Or at least it was the custom of the Morning Star People to think so, Joel remembered. And a smile replaced his fear. He placed his hand upon the circle.

"So be it, old teacher, my friend." He lay back upon his blankets and was soon asleep.

In the distance, he heard the cry of a coyote . . .

47

It was exactly as Joel remembered. He waited in the emerald twilight of the forest and studied the cave and the meadow surrounding it. Two days of hard riding had brought him to the Pryor Mountains and the end of the circle. Here Mourning Dove had hidden with him. Sweet distant memory of her, worried for him, ready to fight at his side. Dead now. She should have been allowed a life. But the fates deemed otherwise. And now, was he the deadly hand of that same fate or about to be its victim?

"Time to find out," Joel said, fingering the bronze crucifix at his throat. "Larocque! Henri Larocque!"

How still the forest. How quiet the normally lively wilderness. The sun-washed world stretched clear and beautiful and brisk with the breath of winter. It never occurred to Joel that the cave was empty. Ice, the medicine man, would not lie. Not even in death. There. Something moved at the mouth of the cave. A faint glimmer. Shadows materialized into substance, into a man.

Henri Larocque stepped from the cave. He shielded his eyes against the glare. He was as massive and formidable as Joel remembered. The Frenchman carried a rifle and used no crutch. He had no doubt mastered his iron-tipped leg long ago.

"I knew you would come, mon ami," Larocque called out. "You are not the youth I matched wits with long ago. When I could not lose you, I decided to try the opposite. To lead you, my friend, to this place. You recognize it, yes. It is here I offered you my friendship. It is here you spit in the face of Henri Larocque. It is here you took my leg, eh? And it is here you will lose your life."

Joel levered a shell into the chamber of his Winchester.

The air smelled cold, redolent with the perfume of the pines, the cleansing fragrance of the wilderness.

"Well, what do you have to say for yourself?" Larocque shouted.

"It is a good day to die!" Joel's cry reverberated among the hills. He drove his booted heels into the roan's flanks. As the horse lunged forward, Joel loosed a shout. Gunsmoke blossomed from Larocque's rifle. Joel could not hear the report, only the drumming hooves beneath him, only the rapid fire explosion from his Winchester as he charged the mouth of the cave. Vision blurred. Fire streaked across his cheek and left a bloody welt in its wake. The Winchester repeater bucked against his shoulder. Larocque seemed to stagger. A horse bolted from the mouth of the cave, almost colliding with the roan. Joel veered to miss the plunging beast and slid from the saddle as his horse and Larocque's raced away. For a moment Larocque was visible in the dim recesses of the cave. Joel fired his rifle. Larocque screamed as the slugs knocked him backward into the dark, tearing his chest and abdomen with terrible accuracy. Joel emptied the Winchester, dragged his revolver free, and stood panting, his Colt aimed at the spot where Larocque had been standing.

Echoes of gunfire pealed in the distance like thunder in the hills. Larocque was nowhere in sight, but the stone entranceway was smeared with blood. Joel wiped at his cheek. The sleeve of his shirt came away glistening red. The whole side of his face felt on fire. He waited. And breathed. Just breathed. His hearing gradually returned. Then he took a step toward the cave, drawing close to the forbidding gloom of the cave's interior. He rested his empty rifle against the wall and thumbed the hammer on his Colt. Sweat trickled down his jaw—red sweat from his bullet-gashed cheek. He entered the twilight, the dank gray world of the immense outer chamber.

Memory did not fail him. It seemed only yesterday he had explored the chamber to the icy slope at its rear, and looked down into the forbidding pit with the skeletal remains protruding from its icy floor. Only yesterday he had returned to Mourning Dove's side and held her close and tasted her kiss. His toe nudged something in the dark and brought him back from foolish reverie, and he knelt in the dim charcoal-colored light and found the rifle Larocque had dropped. The weapon rested at the base of a stalagmite jutting from the floor as jagged and ominous as the ceiling of stalactites overhead. Like the jaws of a trap . . .

Don't reach for the rifle, came the inner warning—much too late, for he had already crouched forward. Larocque charged past the pillar behind which he had concealed himself. Joel glimpsed the threat out of the corner of his eye and twisted to one side as Larocque's wooden leg shot out. The brutal kick missed Joel's skull but glanced off his right hand, knocking the Colt across the chamber. The iron tip struck sparks off the stalagmite. Larocque whirled and caught Joel in the side. The younger man slipped and fell backward, rolled to his feet. The peg leg slashed upward and slammed its iron tip against Joel's chest. Larocque roared in triumph as Joel staggered back into the gloom. He tried to clear his senses and heard Larocque chuckle aloud.

"You see, mon ami, you did me a favor when you took my leg. The one I have now is much better. Oui? Better for me. Not you."

Joel gasped in agony. A rib was broken. Maybe two. He wanted to vomit.

"The leg is most effective. You should have seen Tod Jessup when I finished with him," the Frenchman added.

Larocque drew close. Joel leaped forward. For a moment the two men grappled. Joel pummeled the Frenchman's face with a series of short jabs while Larocque tried to pin his arms. The Frenchman's chest was sticky and moist with blood. He was wounded but far from dead. The peg leg hammered Joel's knee, crippling him long enough for Larocque to stagger back and kick out, knocking Joel's legs out from under him. Larocque retreated. Joel started to push himself off the ground in agony and fell back. He rode a carousel of nausea and pain that gradually subsided in time for him to see Larocque as a patch of darkness against a greater darkness. Lumbering forward, the Frenchman held a massive, smooth chunk of limestone, lifting it high overhead as he advanced.

"As you said," Larocque gasped, "it is a good day to die."

Joel's fingers closed around the hilt of the knife Sacred Killer
had given him. The blade slid free. Biting his lip against the
pain of exertion, Joel threw the knife at the terrible silhouette
that seemed to fill the cave. Larocque howled. The rock
slipped from his grasp and bounced off his shoulder, shattering a stalagmite as it hit the cave floor. Larocque stumbled
backward, his boots losing their purchase on the icy incline.
He screamed and slipped out of sight, rolling and skidding
toward the mouth of the pit. At the last moment, his outstretched hand closed around a tooth-shaped deposit rising
from the slope. Larocque screamed, and defying the agony
of his shattered shoulder, he managed to hang on until he
could wedge his peg leg into a depression just below the lip
of the pit. Something had recently fallen in, for the stench
of rotting meat assailed his senses. Larocque could not discover the source of the fetid aroma, nor could he see the
lattice-work of bones rising cruel from the surface of the
frozen pool. He did not need to.

"Ryan!"

Joel lay on his back and closed his eyes and listened to
his name reverberate in the depths of the earth.

"Ryan. Help me."

Joel sighed.

"Ryan . . . help. I cannot hold on much longer. I thought
you would be hung for the death of Tod Jessup. But it is
you who have killed me. Let me die in the sun. Not here.
Oh God, I'm slipping. Help me."

"Go to hell."

"Let me die in the sun. We have fought each other too
long. We are brothers, you and I. You must help me. We are
brothers in hate, brothers just the same. I'm slipping. Ryan
. . . It was not me. But God. God made us enemies. Now it
is ended. Let me die in the sun."

"God," Joel softly repeated. "What do you know of God?"
And yet, after all the years of hatred, in the final moment he
could not bring himself to lie in darkness and do nothing.
No man deserved to die such a horrible death. He rolled over
onto his stomach and began to crawl. The stone floor became
icy beneath him and began to slope downward. He rested for
a moment.

"Ryan!" Larocque shouted. Joel gave a start. The man was quite close-by.

"I'm coming, for Christ's sake. Be quiet."

"Be careful, the floor is slick. Don't try to walk."

"I'm crawling. I hurt too damn much to walk, thanks to you."

"Got you, did I?" Larocque chuckled. "Ohhh . . . I'm gut-shot. And the knife, hit me in the face. Lucky I ducked. Damn near cut my nose off anyway. My leg wasn't enough for you. Did I tell you? How the bullet wound turned green? Gangrene. I rode until I was certain it was infected. And then I cut it off. I cut my own goddamn leg off! I stuck the stump in a fire and burned the tip black. Oh, I screamed, yes indeed. I passed out. Blue Jacket and his Crows found me, bless his drunken soul. Kept me alive, to live to fight again . . . eh? Where are you?"

Joel started forward. Common sense told him to stay clear of Larocque and still he crawled. Because he was Joel Ryan and not Henri Larocque, and even after all these years of hatred, he could not bring himself to leave another man to die in blackness.

"Larocque?"

"Here. You are close. My strength is failing. Hurry. Hurry."

Joel followed the sound of the voice, and reaching out, he touched the Frenchman's outstretched hand where it gripped the limestone deposit. He crawled past the arm and tried to get hold of the dying man's belt. Larocque suddenly lurched to one side. His massive hand caught Joel by the throat in an iron stranglehold. Larocque roared in triumph.

"Caught!" he laughed; he threw back his head, his voice shrill and high-pitched and utterly devoid of sanity. "Let us dance together in the dark." He chortled gleefully as he began to choke the life out of Joel.

As the madman's weight bore Joel toward the brink of the pit, he managed to snare the same toothlike outcropping the Frenchman had been holding onto. Joel started to lose consciousness as Larocque increased his crushing pressure. The man called Silvertip maintained a one-handed grip on the stone while he battered and gouged Larocque with the other. But the Frenchman was beyond feeling any pain. All he needed to do was to hold on and drag Joel with him as they fell to their deaths. Joel's leg brushed against the peg leg where the iron tip was braced in its stone notch. Summoning every last bit of strength, Joel kicked out—once, twice, a third time. The wooden leg snapped with a loud sharp pop.

Deprived of its support, Larocque's own bulk ripped loose his stranglehold, and he dropped backwards. Joel felt a sudden release of pressure. Something raked his numb throat. The chain!

For a single second Larocque seemed to hang suspended in space—in his hand, the crucifix he had torn from around Joel's neck. Then Henri Larocque plummeted out of sight. Joel held on and listened to the shriek that ended as the mad Frenchman impaled himself on the bones below.

The silence seemed an eternity. It was broken by the most horrible sound Joel had ever heard. It was his name, spoken in a whisper, by Henri Larocque.

"Ryan . . ."

Joel waited, trembling despite himself, *Dear God in heaven*.

"Ry . . . an . . . I never . . . meant . . . tooooooo . . . toooooo . . . kill . . . herrrr. . . ." The whisper rattled, rasped something unintelligible, coughed.

And then there was nothing but stillness in the pit, in the cave, in all the hills.

Epilogue

"**M**orning Star," Joel said as he paused on the ridge above Otter Creek. He watched the smoke rising from the chimney coil in lazy tendrils toward the winter sky. He spied a figure walking from the barn to the house and recognized Sean by his build and the color of his hair. The boy stopped and looked directly at the ragged rider on the slope, then he took off lickety split for the cabin. He disappeared inside and a moment later emerged with his sister and Cub. All three of the children flanked Sarah who stood waiting on the porch. There had been a frost during the night, and all the world wore a mantle of flocking, a veneer of frost it had sported once before on the morning when Joel and Sarah had first loved.

"It's him," Cub said, craning his neck. "Isn't it?" His hand entwined itself with Sarah's. "Isn't it?"

"Yes," said Sarah. Though a tear spilled out of the corner of her voice was strong.

"I knew he was all right. All along, didn't I, Mommy?" Fiona said, tugging on her mother's apron.

"Silly. Just how did you know?" Sean retorted, hiding his relief behind a façade of brotherly disregard.

"Tiny told me so," Fiona proudly proclaimed, holding up her doll. Sean rolled his eyes and looked away.

Sarah smiled. And tried to contain the wild throbbing of her heart. "Silvertip," she said softly.

"Sarah," Joel whispered from the hillside. The roan pawed at the earth.

Home . . . Once a place just to spend the night. And now, a place to spend a life.

Behind lay the past, buried at last in the black depths of the Pryor Mountains. Ahead the future waited in the land, in the children growing strong, waited in the arms of his Otter Creek woman, in the love of Sarah.

Waiting.

Joel Ryan started down the hill, riding sure and swift through the bones of the rain.

HE LEFT HOME A BOY.
RETURNED A MAN.
AND RODE OUT AGAIN A RENEGADE ...

TEXAS ANTHEM

KERRY NEWCOMB

AT THE BONNET RANCH, they thought Johnny Anthem had died on the Mexican border. But then Anthem came home, escaped from the living hell of a Mexican prison, and returned to find the woman he loved married to the man who betrayed him. For Johnny Anthem, the time had come to face his betrayer, to stand up to the powerful rancher who had raised him as his own son, and to fight for the only love of his life.

"Kerry Newcomb is one of those writers who lets you know from his very first lines that you're in for a ride. And he keeps his promise ... Newcomb knows what he is doing, and does it enviably well."
—Cameron Judd, author of *Confederate Gold*

AVAILABLE WHEREVER BOOKS ARE SOLD FROM
ST. MARTIN'S PAPERBACKS

TA 12/00

"An entertaining tale of high adventure
and low villains." —*Booklist*

RED RIPPER

❖ KERRY NEWCOMB ❖

NEW ORLEANS, SEPTEMBER 1829. Brothers William
and Samuel Wallace board a ship for Mexico with
bold visions of wealth and adventure in a new land.
But when a vicious storm lands the two on the shores
of Mexico, clinging for dear life, a brutal band of
freebooters attack the brothers, murdering Samuel in
front of William's very eyes. Now William has sworn
to avenge his brother's death. This haunting quest will
take Wallace to the mist-laden bayous of Texas,
where he will become embroiled in the fight for its
independence and earn himself the name that strikes
fear in the hearts of his enemies . . . The Red Ripper.

"A compelling mix of passion, revenge, and a
gallant people's quest for freedom."
—John J. Gobbell, bestselling
author of *The Last Lieutenant*

"[An] action-filled plot, [with] broad-brush sagebrush scenes and the romance of the Texas
Republic." —*Publishers Weekly*

AVAILABLE WHEREVER BOOKS ARE SOLD FROM
ST. MARTIN'S PAPERBACKS

RR 12/00